The SECRETS

of

BLOOD *and* BONE

The SECRETS of BLOOD and BONE

A NOVEL

Rebecca Alexander

UNCORRECTED PROOF

B\D\W\Y
BROADWAY BOOKS
NEW YORK

Copyright © 2014 by Rebecca Alexander

All rights reserved.

Published in the United States by Broadway Books, an imprint of the Crown Publishing Group, a division of Penguin Random House LLC, New York.

www.crownpublishing.com

BROADWAY BOOKS and its logo, B \ D \ W \ Y, are trademarks of Penguin Random House LLC.

Originally published in hardcover in the United Kingdom by Del Rey, an imprint of Ebury Publishing, a member of the Random House Group, London, in 2014.

Library of Congress Cataloging-in-Publication Data is available upon request

ISBN 978-0-8041-4070-6
eBook ISBN 978-0-8041-4071-3

Printed in the United States of America

Book design by Lauren Dong
Cover design by
Cover photographs by

10 9 8 7 6 5 4 3 2 1

First U.S. Edition

To the people who shaped my storytelling:

my brothers, Guy and Simon, and my sister, Sarah

Chapter 1

*The garden has forgotten what it waits for and guards
against; it waits and guards anyway. It twitches out a
few lime nettle shoots and uncoils brambles to search for
unwary rabbits.*

*Paths wind between shrubs and trees, some unknown
to modern science. A lone rhododendron has been chased
into the shadow of the wall, harried by native plants, its
branches defending itself against attacks by blackthorns
and a spiteful dog rose.*

*And everywhere the elder trees, children of the great
elder mother, who sits in the middle of the walled acre.
She is defended by her progeny, and sheds fat, berried
tears for the loss of the witch.*

THE STENCH OF CHARRED FLESH HUNG OVER THE COT-
tage. Jackdaw Hammond had forced the door, swollen
with damp, to enter Ellen's house. She couldn't walk
much farther than the bottom of the stairs because there were
piles of rubbish stacked almost to the ceiling.

"This is the worst house in the world." Fourteen-year-old

Sadie took two steps into the hall and stopped. "We can't live here."

Barricades of newspapers were still damp from the soaking by the fire brigade. Some mounds leaned against the wall, others had toppled over. The hall had one door straight ahead and one on each side, with stairs barely passable up the middle, rubbish heaped onto each tread. Jack pushed on the left-hand door but could hardly get it open halfway. Peering in, she realized it was tightly packed with boxes, packing cases and more papers.

"Ugh. It stinks." Sadie seemed reluctant to risk her new trainers on the slimy floor. She covered her mouth while she gagged. "We can't live here, it's horrible."

Jack almost agreed with her as her nose gradually distinguished the stench of putrefying flesh from scorched wood, charred meat and moldy rubbish. She pushed against the right-hand door, which swung open easily.

It was a well-proportioned room. Light gleamed in slivers across bare walls, sneaking in between the boards over the windows. It had high ceilings, a square bay in the front, and was empty of furniture. The walls were barely smoke damaged below about a meter high where the blackening really started, building up to a dense sooty layer across the top of the room. It hung in greasy droplets from the ceiling, and even Jack was nauseated at the reek of seared flesh. An oval on the floor had burned down into the boards, breaching a couple of joists in the middle.

A scream from Sadie made her dart back into the hall.

"There are rats in there!" The girl pointed at the other door, open a few inches. She wrapped her arms around herself, and shuddered. "I'm going to sit in the car. And I am *not* living here. My mum would go mad if she knew what this place is like." She stalked toward the front door.

"It will be better once it's cleaned up." Jack looked around the hall, seeing the old electrical fittings and cracks in the plaster, the bare wooden laths visible in places. "You won't recognize it, once it's been . . ." She realized Sadie had already gone, and added ". . . bulldozed" under her breath. She tucked her fair hair into her collar in case it touched anything.

Trying to stop her coat from brushing the rubbish, she squeezed down the passageway and pushed at the door at the back of the hall. It was swollen shut and Jack pushed harder until it creaked, then gave way.

The room was different in style, with two deep-set windows glazed with small panes of cracked glass and a door barely six feet high. The ceiling was only a few inches higher. One side wall was mostly taken up with a wide fireplace, with a pile of rusty pans sitting on what looked like a Victorian range. Under the window ran a work surface, swollen open with the damp, the layers peeling back like a wet paperback. In the middle of it sat a ceramic sink, a white deposit of limescale sitting under a dripping tap. Beside the central door an old enamel electric cooker squatted, covered with opened tins, some topped with mold or half filled with greasy water.

Standing back, she could see the reason for the lack of light. Plastered against each surviving pane were wet leaves. Broken glass had allowed the ingress of ivy branches, which had spread across the walls, almost reaching the inner door frame. Brambles thicker than her thumb carpeted the tiled floor, squeezed under the old door as if searching for something. Mushrooms sprouted along the damp edge of the window frame and seeds were germinating on the threshold to the garden.

Jack stepped over the brambles, avoiding piles of rubbish, and found bolts on the door at top and bottom. They were rusted almost solid and she hit them with one of the heavy pots from the range. In a shower of rust, she managed to get the bolts moving, working them up and down before trying to drag them back. The top one wasn't too bad, but she was sweating by the time she forced the bottom one. The door sprang inward as soon as it was released, and opening it farther she realized why.

A wall of green was pushing against the door, climbers toppling onto the threshold, shrubs leaning against the wood. Branches of an elder tree must have been bent against the handle as leaves had been torn off when she opened the door. Squinting along the outside wall, brambles reaching for her hair, Jack could see the greenery had grown up the building almost to the roof, and embedded itself into the lime render. It was completely impassable. Jack had to put her whole weight against the door to get it shut enough to ram the top bolt home.

The smell in the room was getting worse: mold certainly, and the smoke from the fire, but under it all was the stink of decomposition. Jack nudged the brambles on the floor away from what seemed to be the source of the stench.

It was a pile of oily slime, recognizable as previously a cat from the fineness of the brown and black hair. A white skull was emerging from a mass of maggots and the slick of fur, the canines stretched apart in a defiant last snarl. In the middle of the forehead was a round cavity, which looked exactly like a bullet hole.

Walnut Grove, the bed and breakfast, had been organized by Maggie, Jack's foster mother. The twin-bedded room had stripped floorboards and a large shower room. The landlord looked curiously at Sadie's white skin and lips and offered the teenager a hot chocolate to warm her up. Jack had been looking after Sadie for a few months now, and was always surprised at how friendly and open she was with strangers. Not today, though. She folded herself onto one of the beds, and even let Jack undo her trainers.

When the landlady brought up the chocolate and a mug of tea for Jack, she looked at the collapsed teenager with concern.

"Is she all right?"

"She's been ill. She's in remission now, but she's very tired and we had a seven-hour drive up."

"And you're going to do up Bee Cottage. Now, there's a job. Old Ellen went a bit senile at the end: it's a mess. Such a tragic way to go, though. Call me if you need anything." She paused at the door, looking down at the huddled girl before she left. "Poor little thing."

Jack opened her rucksack and rummaged for a bottle of colloidal silver solution and an artist's paintbrush. The ceiling was a bit high to reach without a chair, but the floor was a perfect surface to paint on. Jack started by pulling the beds away from the wall, and drew a complete circle enclosing both. She put a compass down to determine north, and began drawing the symbols in the almost invisible ink. By the time she had finished the second circle, within the first, Sadie was stirring, a little color in her lips.

She sat up and reached for the hot chocolate, wrapping the quilt over her legs. "Thank God for the circles. That's better. What is that stuff? Invisible ink?"

"Felix suggested it," Jack said. The professor had theorized that, as well as being more discreet, silver would be more effective than ink at creating the sixteenth-century magic circles that helped "borrowed timers" survive. The sorcery that had caught both Jack and Sadie and suspended them on the edge of death relied on sixty-six sigils, inscribed in protective circles. Jack had them tattooed onto her skin, Sadie's were drawn on every few days. "I didn't think the landlady would be keen on permanent markers all over her nice floorboards."

Sadie sipped the chocolate, sighing. "I was getting so cold."

Jack lifted her bag onto the bed. "You're able to survive out of the circle better than I did at first. Here, put a jumper on."

Sadie put her drink down and buried herself in a knitted jacket. "Talking about Felix . . ."

"We aren't." Jack unloaded the contents of her bag into several drawers. "That's all over."

Sadie cupped the warm drink again, catching Jack's gaze for a second. She sipped the froth off the top. "Mm. They have a telly here. I bet they even have broadband and satellite."

Jack handed her the remote, and for a few minutes the girl seemed occupied with swapping channels.

"So, what do we do about the cottage?" Sadie looked up, swamped by the jacket, looking more like twelve than nearly fifteen, she had lost so much weight.

"Maggie's the new owner, legally, and she's made me her agent. Ellen was her mother's younger sister, I think. I have to organize getting the place cleaned up and habitable so we can decide whether to sell it or live in it. We're booked in here for a week, but it may take a lot longer." She started sorting through Sadie's clothes from another bag. "We don't have to do all the work ourselves. We can get people in to help."

"I know that." Sadie turned the television off. "I was just wondering how Ellen died? I mean, was she dead when the house caught fire?"

"I don't know. I think so." Jack sat on the other bed and looked at the girl. "We have a lot to do at the cottage, but we'll have time to do other things as well. I know it was too dangerous to let you go out in Devon in case someone recognized you, but you should be OK here. I thought we'd get you to a hairdresser. All the pictures in the press have you with black hair, and you look different now it's growing out."

"Maybe get some new clothes?" The girl had added a note of pleading. "It's my birthday in a few weeks."

"I know, your mum told me." Jack kicked off her boots and stretched back on the pillows. "We have to get the house habitable because she's coming up to visit in the summer. Angie's been telling friends she's going on a retreat to grieve for you."

"Only, I'm not actually dead." Sadie dragged a music player from her rucksack. "Well, I won't be if you pass me some of that herbal stuff."

Jack passed over a bottle of the decoction they both used to maintain their energy. "I'll go back tomorrow and start clearing the worst of the debris from the kitchen. The smell, by the way, was from a dead cat."

"That's horrible." Sadie screwed up her face as she measured out a few tablespoons into a glass and swigged it back. "I thought it was—you know, Ellen's body."

Jack wondered how frank she could be with Sadie but the girl was bright and, so far, had survived the nightmare of being hunted by a sadistic predator. Not to mention two brushes with death. "Well, that was probably part of it." Jack looked at Sadie, whose eyes promptly narrowed. "The smell of burning, anyway."

"What's bothering you?" Sadie put her head on one side, staring at Jack through long lashes. She was a pretty girl, with a heart-shaped face and vivid blue eyes. She was very thin after months of illness.

"The cat, I thought—it had a hole in its head. Perfectly round."

Sadie stared into the dregs of the drink. "Like a bullet hole? Who would shoot a cat?"

"I don't know. Maggie said Ellen used to do what I do, supply things for magic, but in recent years she only had one customer."

Sadie put the glass down and picked up the remote again. "Well, we need to find out if Ellen was shot before she was incinerated, then. Or burned alive." Sadie shuddered.

Jack nodded. "I thought I would go to the inquest next month. She was old; I'm sure she died before the fire." She didn't sound convincing even in her own ears.

Before Sadie switched the television back on she paused, bit her lip and looked toward Jack. The expression on her face was troubled, as if she weren't sure how Jack would react.

"The garden's overgrown," the girl said. "Ten feet high overgrown."

"Completely. It's worse at the back, right up to the roof in places. It's even growing into the house."

Sadie studied the back of her hand; the skin on her fingers was loose and dry. "I thought—you're going to laugh at me."

"Try me."

"I thought the garden was—sort of whispering. I can't explain it. Not words, just—" She looked toward the window and scowled. "I know it sounds mad. But it seemed like it was watching us."

Before Jack said anything, she remembered the feeling of the garden pressing back against the door. "I felt a bit the same." The presence wasn't oppressive, just enormous, as if she were being scrutinized by an elephant, or a whale.

"I think we ought to be careful, that's all." Sadie switched the television on and Jack retrieved the bottle of herbal medicine for herself.

Sadie's energy recharged inside the circles; she slept well and bounced out of bed the next day, ready to go back to the house.

"I thought you hated the cottage?" grumbled Jack, who was slow to wake up these days.

"You're such a grump." Sadie, dressed in pale blue pajamas decorated with penguins, beat her into the bathroom. "You said we could go shopping after we've made lists in the house."

Jack laid her head back on the pillow and looked at the ceiling. The top circle of sigils was almost invisible, painted by Jack standing on a wobbly chair. Her body, which she had ignored for most of her thirty-one years, ached. Her breasts were uncomfortable, and when she felt them they seemed bigger. She ran her hands over her hips, feeling the slight padding that had developed over the last few months with the resurgence of her appetite. She was losing her childish figure.

Sadie was showering, the splashing sound drifting into the room as Jack closed her eyes . . .

"Jack." She woke to see Sadie frowning down at her, her head nudged to one side. "You're going to miss breakfast. And you look funny."

Jack pushed herself up to sitting. "Funny how?"

"I don't know. Different."

Looking in the mirror in the bathroom, Jack could only see sleep-creased skin and bleary eyes. Sadness washed through her, bringing the sting of tears. She was missing Felix, his warm presence around the house, the way he always smiled when she met his gaze. Evenings at his house had followed the same pattern, Sadie playing computer games or backgammon with Felix, winning mythical thousands, laughing and teasing him while Jack dug through her research. She remembered Felix cooking, taking every pinch of salt or sprig of herbs seriously. The unspoken relationship had buzzed softly between them.

Tears ran down her cheeks and she started to cry, soft sobs. She ran the tap, as she drowned in something like grief.

When she came out, she was sure Sadie had heard her because the teenager didn't pester her, just led the way down to breakfast.

The dining room was old-fashioned, but the food was excellent. Jack helped herself to more toast, after porridge and bacon and eggs. Sadie nibbled a little toast, having eaten most of her porridge.

Sadie waved her hand down her own frame. "I've lost loads and you're getting fatter." She half smiled. "It suits you. But you need some new clothes."

"Borrowed timers are always skinny." Jack thought back

to the moment when she had augmented her life-preserving magic with a mouthful of fresh blood. It had infused her with energy, enough to last three months. For a moment, the craving for Felix's warm arm, the cut skin against her tongue, the slow pulsing of salt into her mouth, overwhelmed her.

"So, shopping." Sadie, at least, could keep her focus. Her eyes narrowed as she stared at Jack, but she didn't say anything.

"*After* we look at the house and get some lists written." Jack's throat was dry and she slaked it with a slurp of tea. "And find a good rubbish clearance firm."

Chapter 2

Venice, in this twenty-eighth year of her Grace the Queen Elizabeth's reign, rises out the lagoon like a fairy town. But once one sets foot to it, it is revealed as the antechamber to hell in its stench, its debauchery, its treachery, and its battle with the sea. All delivered in a smiling mask.

—EDWARD KELLEY, private letter to Lord Dannick
dated 15 May 1586, held in Dannick family archive
(facsimile held by British Library dated 1975)

MY FIRST VIEW OF VENICE, OF THIS MARVEL OF MAN'S mastery over the sea, was of a line of buildings topped by a risen dome gilded by the sun. My boatman, who talked continuously despite my lack of comprehension, gabbled and pointed.

"San Marco!" he shouted, pointing at the dome. The great cathedral of St. Mark's, famous all over Europe. The buildings beside it seemed to float upon a sea of fog, tall mansions squeezed together. The lagoon was calm and the man turned as if onto an invisible path, then looked across at another island and turned again. He babbled something that sounded like Italian, but left me with little understanding. Shoals, I feared, on which we might ground.

I clutched my bags more closely around me, and he glanced

again at them, his tongue touching his lips. I lifted my head and looked away while my fingers crawled along my belt to my dagger. I am counted a good judge of character, and was certain that while the man would not hesitate to rob a lesser man, he would back down in a fight.

As he wove patterns in the water behind us, whirls and bubbles that trailed away, we were diverted along the waterfront. My stomach, never at ease at sea, lurched in my belly. The buildings, some giant complex of palaces and churches, led to a row of great houses, bright with color and extravagantly glazed, mirroring the light back upon the water. It was a marvelous sight.

My boatman, now concentrating on his work and heaving upon the single large oar, pulled his craft about into a narrow lane. It was almost a road of water, shaded by the walls of wooden and stone houses above us. The sounds of hand carts, clogs, traders, boatmen and whores assaulted us. He pointed ahead to an area filled with pontoons and, as the port came into view, all manner of ships. I marveled at a great galleon as we slipped into its lee, a few sailors watching from its deck, casting down scornful comments upon us. My boatman pointed his thumb at me and spat into the water. The men above laughed, but we left them behind as he brought his boat into an area of pontoons lined with vessels three and four deep. He tied up alongside one.

"*Arsenale*," he said, holding out his brown hand, much callused. I gave the man some coins, and when he whined for more shook my head sternly, for the ambassador in Prague had visited Venice many times and warned me the boatmen were robbers. When his face turned angry, I added one more *scudo*, and he was happy. I grasped my largest bag, swung it over my shoulder, and indicated that he should carry the other. I stepped onto the seat to disembark.

The whole city stank like death, and eyes followed me with

every move. I trod with care from one flatboat to another to reach the quayside and grasp one of the wooden piers that supported it. I swayed more upon the dock than I had on the sea. I leaned over the black water and spat bile. My oarsman, hopping nimbly, threw my belongings toward me. I barely caught them before they spilled into the lagoon. I sat down upon a mooring block and opened my bags to check the contents. I carried my most important possessions upon my person, but any educated man knew the value of books. Lord Robert Dannick, my patron, had entrusted me with the most secret mission, and promised enough funds to complete my experiments back in the house in Prague. In addition, my friend Amyas Ratcliffe had charged me with a mission to answer a question we had both concerned ourselves with: the very nature of our animus, our base human form and its spiritual frailties.

The first I knew of a companion was a pair of long-toed, polished boots of an oxblood color. I glanced up then stood, for the fellow who wore the boots was clearly of some importance, attended as he was by two servants. He was a little round man, wearing such bright colors and clashing garments that I might have thought him in motley, like a fool.

"Signor." I made my best bow. My Italian was rudimentary at best but my Venetian was worse, so I attempted a greeting in Latin. "I am honored to meet you, sir."

The man squinted into the sun, then looked me over in a fashion which in England would be most rude.

"Ah!" he exclaimed in Latin. He had a high-pitched, musical voice. "You are German?"

I stepped back, a little nervous at his waving and loud voice. At least a dozen fellows stopped working on boats or nets to watch us.

I bowed again, with a flourish of my cloak I had learned in Prague. "Sir. My name is Edward Kelley, late from England, and I am come here on business."

"It is more correct to address me as Excellency, Signor Kelley." His Latin was heavily accented, his tongue stretching the vowels and rolling the "r"s. He smiled again, showing a row of blackened teeth. "I am sent to welcome you to our city-state and learn your business."

It seemed strange to be quizzed by the man, but I thought perhaps it was part of the habits of this city. No doubt this was some custom official, as he wore upon his breast a heavy gold chain and some sort of emblem.

"I am here on the business of Lord Dannick of England, to visit a nobleman of Venice to discuss some important research, your Excellency." One of his servants hefted my bags onto his broad back and the other lifted a cudgel. I opened my mouth to protest, but shut it again. Trust me to keep close watch upon my baggage.

"And, no doubt, you have papers and letters of introduction, signor?" The man started walking ahead of me, a fat, bouncy fellow, in his red shoes.

I fumbled within my pocket where lay my purse. "I do, of course, but I—" The man was getting ahead of me so I pushed past the servants to catch up. "Your Excellency, whom do I have the honor of addressing?"

"I?" The man grinned over his shoulder at me. "Why, Master Kelley, I am no one."

I felt a blow upon my head, and my senses were lost as my face hit the planks of the quayside.

Chapter 3

PRESENT DAY: BEE COTTAGE, LAKE DISTRICT

Apple and plum trees tease children with fruit, hanging just out of reach over the garden wall, as if tempting them to try their footing between the shamble of stones. They always fall. Once, many seasons ago, a child died when the slab of limestone on top of the wall slid after his tumbling body and crushed his skull. Now the fruit goes unpicked, prey only to the wasps and the boldest of the rooks that grow fat and unmolested around the house. They nest between the chimneys, and hide behind its shattered windows.

THE IDEA OF CLEARING THE OLD HOUSE WAS OVERWHELMing. Jack prioritized cleaning up the dead cat, slimier and stinkier after another day, and unbolted the back door again for air. It sprang inward, if possible with more force than before, ivy pressing its green gloss into the room as if searching for something.

"There really are rats!" shouted Sadie. She was wearing Jack's old riding boots against the dirt and was rummaging in the packed dining room at the front of the house. "There's shit everywhere—" There was more swearing, which Jack ignored, followed by a squeaking sound. "I got the window open."

Jack carried the bagged cat to the open front door. Sadie was leaning out of the window, probably trying to get some fresh air. Jack dumped the package into an available bin and closed the lid on it. "How much stuff is in there?"

Sadie looked back. "I'm kneeling on it, it's all over the whole room. Mostly just papers, though, and a few boxes of old tins. But . . ." She disappeared, then waved a metal item out of the window. "I found a sword!"

Jack went indoors and fought her way past the damp papers to the dining room. Sadie met her holding the rusted thing. Calling it a sword seemed fanciful until Jack made out the cross guard. "OK, it is a sword. Probably some ornamental thing."

"The newspapers go back to the nineties. Twenty years. That must be when she started to go mad."

Jack smiled, and leaned in to estimate the amount of clutter in the room. There were sagging cardboard boxes filled with china, glass and empty tins. "That's a whole Dumpster full, just there by the window. It's a miracle the floor's held."

"There's one place where the floor is rotted right through. I think that's where the rats get in." Sadie dropped the sword and brushed past her into the hall. "Let's try upstairs."

Jack made a note about the floor, and followed Sadie up the creaking, uncarpeted steps. There were four rooms off the landing, all closed up, and several piles of boxes in front of two of them. Sadie tried the nearest door, to the room over the kitchen, but it was stuck. It took all of Jack's strength to force the door open.

The room was like something from Miss Havisham's house. It looked hundreds of years old, but Jack recognized a plastic radio and an aluminum walking frame from the modern era. The bed was Victorian brass, and the room had a huge mahogany chest of drawers in one corner and a marble-topped table under the window. Everything was covered with dust and stank of mildew. But that wasn't what caught Jack's eye after a second—when it moved.

It was a rook, cowering but defiant, its gray beak switching direction as it looked first from one eye, then the other. Before Jack could say anything, it launched itself at them, forcing them to duck, and flapped over their heads toward the doorway, cawing loudly.

"How did it get in?" shouted Sadie, over the screeching.

Jack pointed at the window, where a corner of the glass of the bottom sash was missing. As her eyes adjusted to the low light—the rest of the window was covered with leaves, like the downstairs room—she could see the mess over every surface. She went back onto the landing. The bird was now walking with its rolling gait toward the back of the house. Jack chased after it down the landing. Just when Jack thought she would have to catch it, it opened its wings and glided over her head and down the stairs. She could hear its squawks diminishing as it flew out of the open front door.

Sadie pulled at the bedclothes and wrinkled her nose. "This room isn't too bad. If we strip it right out and start again, obviously."

"I'm going to clean up the furniture," Jack said. She ran her eyes over the piles of papers on the table. "These look like bills. Legal papers, vet invoices, utilities."

"Maybe the cat was ill."

"Maybe." Jack peeled one disintegrating sheet from the next. Everything was wet. "This is a letter from Blackwell and Whist, the solicitors who managed Ellen's will. They wrote to Maggie telling her she was the sole heir." She squinted at the blurred characters.

Sadie had wandered off, and after some banging managed to squeak another door open.

"There's a bathroom," she shouted back. The sound of running water was reassuring. "And a sink."

"It's a good thing we haven't had a cold snap," Jack said. "There's enough water in the house already." One paper caught her eye. The heading had a drawing of a castle on it. The ink had run but she could make out some of the words. "Breach of contract" jumped out at her.

Sadie banged the new door shut, and after a few moments emerged again to the sound of rushing water and clanking pipes. "The toilet flushes."

"So I hear." Jack followed the sound of Sadie's voice onto the landing.

"There's a tank up on the wall, it's so old-fashioned." Sadie fumbled in her pocket for a bottle of decoction, and took a sip. "It's weird, I don't feel too bad here. I've even got some energy. What's in here?"

Sadie wrenched open a door at the front of the house, then stumbled back, hands over her face in a maelstrom of feathers and screeches. A dozen birds flew at her. She screamed, staggering toward Jack. The two cowered in the doorway of the back bedroom as the birds flapped around the hallway before one led the others down the stairs. Jack, her arms around the teenager, could feel her shaking.

"It's OK," she said, as she let go. "Just birds. Rooks."

"They took me by surprise. My mum made me sit up and watch this old film, once. These crows went mad and killed people." Sadie shrugged Jack off and brushed herself down. She gingerly pushed the new door open farther. "I can't forget what happened before . . ."

Jack remembered Sadie's experience of seeing an air elemental rip through a rookery, dismembering the birds and nearly killing the girl. "Well, these seem healthy, anyway, but we don't want a rookery in the house." She leaned into the bedroom.

The birds had found a way in through the missing pane of a whole sash, bringing in thousands of sticks and covering the lot with excrement.

Jack checked the nests but none had eggs in them yet. "Maybe Ellen liked them being here. They would make a fuss if anyone broke in, like guard dogs."

Water had eroded and darkened the floorboards by the window, underneath a hole in the ceiling that gave access to the loft. A few holes between the slates allowed daylight in. From the middle of the room, piled high with more rubbish, there was a fantastic view through the shattered window over the nearest field. The light purpled what Jack guessed was heather, over a whole hillside.

A man's voice made her jump.

"Hello! Is anyone there?"

His words echoed up the hall and stairs. Jack struggled through the mountains of paper to look down the stairs. The man, in his late forties or early fifties she judged, was smiling up at her. "Ah. The lady of the house, I presume? Mrs. Slee?" He was wearing a suit, incongruous against all the rubbish.

"No. I'm acting on her behalf." Jack negotiated the piles of rubbish on each step with care, and took the offered hand. Strong fingers, warm. Close up, he could be older than she first guessed. "I'm Jack Hammond." Sadie was keeping out of sight upstairs, yet he cocked his head as if he heard something.

"I'm Henry Dannick. And your companion?"

She ignored the question and released the hand. The hairs on the back of her neck were prickling. She looked past him to a long, expensive car and a uniformed driver. "I'm just here to decide how to clear and empty the house."

"I was hoping to speak to Mrs. Slee but if you are close to her perhaps you can help me."

"OK." Jack stepped away from him, feeling some unnamed alarm but also the pull of the man. He was very charming. He spread out his hands, palms up, as if to say "I'm harmless."

"My family and Ellen Ratcliffe's have had a long association. But recently—"

"What's the problem, Mr. Dannick?"

"Actually, it's Sir Henry. Ellen worked for my family for many years." He looked around the hallway and his lips twisted. "I had no idea she had got into such a mess. She was always eccentric, of course."

"Worked for you, how?" As far as she knew Ellen supplied items for magic, much as Jack did.

"The garden—I know it's hard to see it now, but it used to be full of rare herbs. Ellen was my family's herbalist. We were hoping to come to a similar arrangement with Mrs. Slee, we know she is an—herbalist—as well."

"I understand." *Herbalist, or a witch, like Maggie?* She motioned toward the door. "Perhaps we could talk outside? The smell in here is rather strong." The charred meat stink was starting to nauseate her again.

"Of course." He stepped outside, careful not to touch the door frame with his sleeves. "It really is disgusting in there. We were so sorry to hear what had happened."

"What item in particular did you need?"

"It's an herb. I'm afraid I only know its colloquial name, black hair-root. At least, that's what they call it in this area." There was no trace of a northern accent in his voice, which suggested some upper-class education. He waited as if he expected Jack to understand the reference to the herb.

"Hair-root. You're going to have to give me more than that. A picture, maybe?"

"Ellen makes it into a tincture for us. She said it was rare, and this was the only place it grew in any quantity to her knowledge." He looked down at her, and she got the impression he was trying to read her, too. "This is a very important herbal medicine for us. Ellen must have made notes somewhere."

"We haven't found any personal papers yet. A lot of stuff was ruined by the fire brigade."

"She also had Thomazine's papers; they may describe the herb. They are written on vellum, and so would be more resistant to water, perhaps. I assume she kept them safe—they are very valuable."

"Thomazine?" Jack could hear the shuffling of Sadie's soles at the top of the stairs.

He didn't seem to notice. "Thomazine Ratcliffe was the first herbalist to my family, more than four hundred years ago. Ellen inherited her papers."

"I'll look out for them."

She stepped forward into the doorway, making him step back. He glanced up at the window again, as if he knew Sadie was up there somewhere. He felt in his pocket, and brought out a card.

"My number is on there. If you find the herb—or Thomazine's notes—please call. The matter is urgent."

She took it, the embossed card snowy white against her grubby fingers. "I'll let you know." The card had a small picture of the castle on it, the same one she had seen on the ruined legal papers.

"Let me give you more of an incentive. My family would pay good money for the herb in the correct formulation. The last payment we made was for four thousand pounds. Given the urgency, I would be prepared to give you the same for the tincture, and a further twenty thousand for Thomazine's notes. You can reach me at the castle, the number is on the card."

Jack was astonished. "Well, that sounds very generous."

"A member of my family is very ill: the need is great." He crooked a finger to the driver, who opened the back door of the shining car for him. "If you need a good builder, as I suggest you do, John Cartwright in Hawkshead is very good. If you mention my name, he might be able to come a bit quicker."

"Thank you. I don't know anyone in the area yet."

"And as we are going to be neighbors, perhaps you and your . . . friend might like to visit the castle sometime? Knowle Castle is our family seat."

"Thank you. I'd like to see it."

He stepped into the car, and the driver shut the door. The window slid down with the faintest of whines. "I mean it. Do come and meet Callum. Then you'll understand the urgency. He doesn't have much time left."

Chapter 4

Venice is a place much beset by rogues and thieves, as I had the misfortune to find. While their victims are foreigners the authorities are amused, and turn their back upon the honest traveller. Your father must be ever vigilant to avoid such varlets and villains.

—EDWARD KELLEY, personal letter to his daughter
Elizabeth Jane Weston dated 16 March 1586, in the
Czech collection, British Library

I AWOKE IN AN ALLEY MUCH FREQUENTED, I FELT, BY CATS and rats. My heavy jacket was gone, my boots also, which I much lamented when my head stopped banging like a drum. My luggage was stolen with my letters and notes and their leather case and all of my books: all were gone. I had retained within my small garments some little money in gold, a sketch of some importance to my mission, my letter of introduction from Lord Dannick, and my wits. These were not the least of my assets, so I put my stockinged foot to the cobbles and looked around me.

The alley ran between two great houses, one end leading onto a narrow street, and the other upon a great canal. It seemed evening was drawing in, for the sky was a deep blue and I saw a few stars. A yellow glow upon the canal alerted me to the torches burning at the front of the houses, for the Venetians, as I have heard, account the waterside the grander entrance. Here, a jetty led from a great portico, which was in the classic style. Within the columns was a pair of doors, one opened, light spilling onto steps that ran into the water. I saw upon the waterway boats floating each way, many much decorated. I hid in the shadow of a column then crept toward the door. Peering in, I saw a great hall lit by lamps and a servant balanced upon a ladder, setting a taper to yet more branches of candles.

The next moment, I was buffeted between the shoulders with a great blow, and staggered into the house. I turned in a second, reaching for my dagger—alas, also missing. The man looked me over, then laughed with a great bellow and spoke to me in rapid words that I could not comprehend.

"Forgive me, sir, I am at a disadvantage." I gave him some respect, as he was dressed in black velvets and long boots encased his thick calves. I repeated the words in German, then in Latin. Finally, his smile widened.

"Who are you, that enters my house undressed, yet speaks Latin like a priest?"

He was a big man with a deep chest and black beard, much of mine own age and coloring. That is, he had deeply tanned skin and dark eyes.

"I am Sir Edward Kelley, come lately from England on an important mission." I titled myself for I have often found this means I am treated with the respect I deserve. "I was beaten and robbed and my belongings and clothing were stolen. I awoke outside your house."

"English?" He stroked his beard, which was thick and sleek, and close cropped over a strong jaw.

"I would be grateful for your help, sir, for I find myself the victim of villains." I touched a hand to the tender lump on the back of my head.

"Help you?" He grinned again, looking me up and down.

"It's treason to give haven to a foreigner without a witness from the council. It is treason even to speak to one."

"Then, are you not at risk of being accused?" I asked, a little sharply perhaps, because the cold was creeping up my ankles from the icy touch of the tiled floor.

"I, little man, am not easily accused. Now tell me, what is your real reason for being in Venice and, more important, why were you left at *my* door?" He took pity upon my shivering and called out in his own tongue to the servant. "Come with me, *Master* Kelley."

I followed him up the cold stairs to a landing, much ornamented with a marble balustrade and decorated with many carved and painted doors, each a work of art. He turned the handle of one, and I followed him onto—God be praised—a carpet. Another servant appeared and listened to a command from his master.

I spoke. "I would be grateful to know your name, sir."

He did not answer me, but poured two cups of wine, and handed me one. The glass was extraordinary, a beaker with decoration in the style of a family crest upon it. The wine, by contrast, was raw and acid. It was warming, and I looked up to see him staring at me.

A sound from beyond the door heralded the entrance of other men in conversation. When I stood back, ashamed of my attire, one entered dressed in the robes of a priest of high degree.

"Ah, Your Highness. Look at the gift the lagoon has brought me." My bearded host bowed to me with a flourish. "I, my little friend, am known as Franco, Count Marinello. I am known to be the friend of several English visitors, which may explain your thief's choice of benefactors. This is His Highness Prince Malipiero, the cardinal of the church of San Nicolò."

The older man, his bald head nodding on a thin neck, looked

at me like a hawk eyes a mouse, his curved nose sniffing in my direction. He said something in a low voice and Marinello laughed. "Indeed, we should at least clean him up! Go with my manservant, Bartolomeo, Master Kelley. Then you can tell us your story."

I was taken to a chamber much decorated with pictures upon the walls and embroidered chairs, and a carved bed that could sleep a whole family. I was presented with a bowl of warm water and some soft soap, much as we use for washing clothes in England but better perfumed. The servant, who spoke no Latin nor Italian as far as I could divine, gave me fresh hose that were a little too long and wide for my taste. He then handed me a shirt to replace my own, now sadly stained by contact with the alley, and a suit of clothes as he himself was wearing. I excused myself to a narrow garderobe, to transfer my precious papers, and hastily dressed in the clean underclothes. When I returned to the chamber I had finally stopped shivering, and slid my feet into borrowed shoes for the servant to lace. Then I was beckoned to the door, and into a further room that I had not yet entered.

It was a dining chamber, and the candlelight gilded every plate and glass. The napery was snowy white over the table, and draped almost to the floor. One end had many dishes of food, and the smells filled my mouth with water.

"Ah, our young friend." Even though Lord Marinello could not be much older than myself, I bowed and allowed myself to be seated in a chair, my shoulder draped with a napkin, and to be served some fish, browned and curling in a plate of sauce. Lord Marinello lifted a tiny trident, much as we use their greater cousins to carve meat, and to my astonishment used it to spear a fish and take it to his mouth. Since I wished to be a good guest, I attempted the same. The food, some sort of pilchard, was delicious.

The cardinal, who sat opposite me, ate sparingly of bread

and a few fish. He cleared his mouth with a mouthful of wine from another decorated glass beaker and looked at me.

"You were robbed, you say?" said His Eminence, his Latin much accented.

"By a fat fellow and his servant."

Marinello leaned forward. "Describe him."

I struggled to explain the extraordinary fellow. Clean-shaven, certainly, older than myself but no graybeard, round in stature but agile on small feet, and he wore red shoes with high heels. His doublet, I recalled, was red and yellow and much slashed and decorated. He wore hose gathered at the knee with many ribbons.

Marinello nodded to the cardinal. "Bezio."

"He has my papers and books." I was indignant. "My money, everything."

"And he left you at my door, instead of rolling you into the canal."

I looked at him, but his beard concealed his expression well. The cardinal choked a laugh, and muttered something in, I supposed, Venetian. The bigger man laughed back before turning to me.

"Bezio knows that the greatest value of stolen goods is to the original owner." He shrugged. "I would expect him to offer them back to you—at the right price."

I choked on my wine. The impudence of it! I rolled Marinello's words around my mind. "So, why would he choose your house, my lord? Is it that I am English?"

"That is what I was wondering, little man." He waved servants away, and the great carved doors shut with a clunk. "Speak sooth, my man, and gently. I do not want to be overheard. What was your purpose in coming to Venice?"

"I am a seeker of knowledge, a scientist. I was hoping to confer with other scholars upon the subject of a medical nature." Half-truths are always preferable to outright lies.

He drank the last of his wine and spoke to the cardinal in words I could not catch. The cardinal seemed to raise himself from half sleep to stare at me with malice in his gaze. I heard him hiss the word *Inquisizione*, a word to put the hairs up on my neck. The lord laughed at him, waving away such a suggestion.

"Master Kelley. I shall offer you hospitality, for where else shall you go, penniless and a foreigner? But you may have to be questioned by the council, and must come up with better lies than the ones you offer me."

"My Lord Marinello," I stammered. "I have a commission from a powerful and wealthy English family. They gave me gold and letters of introduction. In truth, I seek the answer to a medical question."

"Then you must make your introductions." He poured more wine from a decanter, which sparkled with gold wires embedded within the rose-colored glass. "But first, I think we must negotiate with Bezio for your belongings."

Chapter 5

Felix looked around the office of Gina Larabie, professor of cultural anthropology. Lining the walls were glass cases of bondage equipment, instruments of torture and a variety of leather masks.

"Sexual behavior is your area of research?"

"Currently." She carried a cup of coffee over to him, and set it on the desk. "I have funding for exploring sexual fetishes that carry specific risks to participants. Including the sharing of blood."

He looked at the objects, some based on medieval torture. Some had a function that he couldn't even guess at. "It's a fascinating area." He looked at her over the cup. "I found your name in a database of researchers into vampirism. Then I realized you also had an interest in John Dee and Edward Kelley."

She smiled. "Vampires are big at the moment. The sexual-fetish vampires get mixed up with the energy-exchange vampires and the blood drinkers. But Dee was the real deal, a sorcerer. As you describe in your books, they looked at the magical properties of imbibing blood."

"Dee was believed to be very powerful, at the time, but Kelley went on to become more influential in the field of magic." He looked around the room again. It was much bigger than his own office, and much neater, journals arranged by title and date, books under the window in precise rows. Some had lurid titles like *Vampires Today!* and *Blood: The Ultimate High.* "Dee wrote about the border between life and death. He certainly had an interest in blood's magical properties. Is vampirism very prevalent as a phenomenon?" He watched her as she sipped her coffee.

"Not huge." She looked up, and smiled, her dark eyes narrowing. "There are maybe ten or twelve thousand energy vampires in the US, we think. Maybe the same number of fetishists, but it's hard to get numbers. Most don't actually drink blood, except symbolically."

"But some do?"

She chose her words carefully. "Some believe they are dependent on blood to sustain themselves. There is a subculture of blood givers, donors, which is another of my areas of interest. In some ways it is the ultimate submission, to literally become food as a way of entering another person." She shrugged. "The line between fetish- and belief-based behavior is a blurred one, in some cases."

"It's the possible side effects of drinking blood that interest me."

"Side effects? Other than the obvious infection risks?" She stretched back in her chair.

He was aware of a wave of attraction to the woman, her skin a creamy brown, dark hair sleeked over her shoulders, and her curvy figure. She couldn't be more different to Jack: cultured, mature, educated. Jack was . . . in the past. She had rejected him completely, and he was a free agent.

He nodded. "I'm specifically interested in people who believe blood improves their health."

"We have interviewed a few individuals who believe that blood is the only thing that makes them feel they have energy." She smoothed her hair. "They believe it can heal terminal illnesses, even restrict the aging process."

"I was hoping that, through your research, you might know someone who would be willing to discuss it with me."

"Ah." She smiled, wider this time, her teeth perfectly white and straight. "But these are the most private people I know. They would not want to be written or even talked about. And my studies were completely confidential."

"My interest is on behalf of someone who has taken blood, and there is some evidence that she is biologically dependent on it."

"I'm not sure that is even medically possible, though some do believe it—" She opened a drawer in her desk, and took out a pen and pad. "What are her symptoms?"

"She suffered from extreme weakness and coldness. When she was admitted to the hospital they diagnosed her with hypothermia, but she said she had lived with those symptoms for years." He remembered her teeth clamped upon his forearm, sucking hungrily at the cut. He touched the wound, which in three months hadn't completely healed. "With even a small amount of blood her basal temperature returned to near normal, she had more energy, more color." He stood, and walked in front of the exhibits. It was a struggle to put his fears into words. "She belongs to a European tradition which believes that people can avoid death with the use of sorcery."

"That sounds like the mythology of medieval revenants, the stories that gave rise to the first legends of vampires." Her voice was soft, sympathetic. "Many of my modern-day 'vampires' talk about those traditions, and they follow research into vampire burials and folklore. They even fund it."

"My own involvement is through the necromantic work of Dee and Kelley." The picture of Jack, vulnerable after her battle with a sadistic serial killer, flew into his mind. "My friend describes her condition as 'living on borrowed time.' Dee and Kelley described similar cases in the 1580s in Eastern Europe."

The chair creaked as Gina stood and stepped closer to him.

A wave of her scent hit him, and he turned. She was close to his own height, and the fabric of her dress draped over her curves. He turned back to the instruments of torture.

"I'm intrigued," she said. "I've always had an interest in Kelley. He was more adventurous in his experiments." She leaned one hip on the edge of the desk beside him. "Here, the belief about the creation of revenants through blood rituals is called 'ascension.'"

"Do you know anyone who understands this belief system?"

"I do—but to understand the taking of blood, its effects, you need to meet people who actually do it," she said. "You need to immerse yourself in that culture, because they are very secretive."

"I thought it was a well-known subculture? There are a million references on the Internet, anyway."

"Sure, on the surface. But you need to disentangle the mainly sexually motivated members and role players from the others, the energy vampires. There are subgroups even within those communities: sanguinarians and spiritual vampires, for example."

Felix suddenly felt very tired. Watching Jack step away from him over the last few months had been exhausting. "Sanguinarians being involved in blood taking?"

"Either symbolically or literally, but they are reluctant to talk about it. Some interpretations of the Bible suggest that any blood rituals are dangerous and against God's ordinances. My contacts have to avoid exposure to religious groups." She smiled wryly. "In some states, American culture is getting less inclusive, more conservative."

"It would help to interview someone who has knowledge of drinking blood." He shrugged. "It sounds crazy when I say it like that."

She smiled and opened one of the glass doors to a display case. "There is one person who might be interested in an exchange of knowledge. He may not want to meet you on your own." She pulled out an oval object, dotted with metal studs. "He'll talk to me, though. If you come along, and don't act so— British—he might get you into one of the clubs." She handed him the piece.

"What is it?" It was beautifully made, the plastic as cool and hard as ivory and the size of a large mango. She mimed unscrewing it, and he found that there was a fine line dividing it across the middle. As he started to loosen it one end opened like a flower. He stopped turning, recognizing it from Inquisition diagrams. "It's—it's a choke pear. A torture device."

"They used to call them 'pears of anguish.' Now, it's an extreme form of sex play."

He closed the thing and handed it back to her. "Extreme? I would have thought dangerous."

"Pain, carefully controlled, can also be pleasurable. The individual, couple or group explore these tools as far as they are able, in a moment of complete trust and intimacy." She shrugged. "Sensation is sensation, pleasure and pain are very close. Danger can be . . . arousing."

"Have you—" He managed to avoid finishing the sentence.

She smiled and put the object back in the case. "My method of research is immersive participation."

He stared at her, slightly shocked, slightly aroused.

Her smile widened. "So I gain the trust of people who *do* use such objects, and I interview them."

His face must have given away his reaction, because she laughed out loud. "You really are *very* English, aren't you? I thought with a name like *Gee-shar*, you would be a little more— French."

"The Guichards emigrated to England in the nineteenth century. My father worked in the civil service, terribly old school and extra English."

"And your mother?"

"His one divergence from the mainstream. Her name was Amélie Verdier, she was a teacher from the Ivory Coast, *République de Côte d'Ivoire*." He slipped easily into the French. "They met when he was working for the diplomatic service. Her grandmother was Mandé."

"So you are part African?" She smiled.

"I spent some of my childhood traveling around West Africa. I still consult there."

She laid her slim hand next to his, comparing her darker tone with his tanned skin. "But your beautiful green eyes, they came from your father?"

He nodded, feeling a faint blush at the compliment, but gestured at the cases lining the wall to change the subject. "This is all fascinating. These blood-drinking clubs, are they difficult to attend?"

She smiled. "Most are very exclusive, and I doubt you would want to attempt the membership—test." She smiled to herself, as if at some private joke. "No, I think you need to meet Julian Prudhomme."

"Who is?"

She was disturbingly close, almost touching his arm as she turned back to the exhibits. "He's someone I've been working with who happens to belong to one of these clubs. I could introduce you."

"Thank you." He stepped away from her scent and her warmth, and pulled his collar away from his throat.

She followed him, laying a hand on his forearm for a moment. "You have to loosen up, Felix. You're in New Orleans now."

He smiled, feeling awkward and too hot in the spring weather drifting in the open window. "I might need a few days to acclimatize. It was a lot cooler in England."

"And you'll like Julian," she continued. "He's sexy and funny, and smart. He knows all about blood and its occult properties."

"You said you were working with him?"

"We share an interest in healing rituals."

Felix looked across the campus from the high window, at students sitting in groups on the grass. "Is he a researcher too?"

"Much better. He's a *babalorisha*, a priest of the local Santería tradition. A sorcerer."

Chapter 6

Riches are on display even where utter poverty exists.
Venice is all stolen wealth, promises and lies. But I have
found also great spirits among the imposture, strong
men whose characters write Venice's history with their
adventures.

—EDWARD KELLEY, 1586, Venice

I WAS BEDDED WITHIN A SUMPTUOUS CHAMBER, WITH A
mattress set up for myself in a room overlooking the canal.
I awoke when a soft-footed servant made up a fire, bade me
good morning in his own language, and returned with breakfast. Good bread, still fresh, that must have been baked overnight, served with dried meats full of spices. I broke my fast
and dressed myself in my borrowed clothes. I opened the door
to find another servant awaiting me, who led me to the large
chamber from the evening before. Here Marinello sat in conversation with the cardinal, who inclined his head toward me,
and then I saw a third man seated. It was the fat little man who
had so cruelly used me on my arrival—I was shocked to see him
drinking from one of the lustrous glasses, and casting a sly eye
over me.

"Sirrah!" I exclaimed, forgetting for a moment that none but
I spoke English. I turned to the ponderous wording of Latin. "I
respectfully ask for the return of my belongings, immediately."

The man cocked an eyebrow at Marinello.

"That is all arranged, Master Kelley," said my lord. "A simple transfer of coins in exchange for these."

He held in his hand the books I had chosen to risk upon this journey: one essential to my task, the others filled with my notes and jottings, and my leather satchels of clothes and other belongings.

"I thank you, of course, my lord," I said, while bowing deep. "But that man is a thief, and a ruffian."

My lord waved at the fat man, who rose instantly while grinning with his blackened teeth. "He certainly is. Bezio mistook your purpose, Master Kelley. He had no idea you were a man of such learning and knowledge."

Bezio babbled a little in his own tongue to Marinello, then addressed me in fair Latin.

"No man, great or humble," the rogue said, "travels without a servant, unless he be a villain or a spy." He spread his hands before me, as if offering me some truth. "I am a loyal Venetian. I must defend our vulnerable state."

I stretched out a hand for my books, but Marinello did not give them to me, opening one instead. It was a stained and much annotated version of the *Demonica* by Bacon, and within it were diverse papers and diagrams I had made in Dee's great inquiry upon the nature of death. My face heated under my beard.

"You are indeed much traveled," Marinello said, turning another page. "London, Marseilles, Prague, Vienna, Krakow. Your patron is the Holy Roman Emperor, Rudolf?"

"Indeed." I puffed my chest out a little at that. "Perhaps I shall speak with his ambassador while I am here."

"You could try," said Marinello, but he smiled slyly, "though he is likely to hand you to the Inquisition as a heretic Protestant."

I swallowed the lump that congealed in my throat. I looked at the cardinal, and he was openly smirking. "I thought Venice was secular."

"Venice, my dear Kelley, is whatever a rich man wants to make of it. Poor men . . ." He shrugged. "For poor men, Venice is a harsh mistress. And at the moment you don't even own the clothes you stand in."

I turned to Bezio. "But my money, my letters, my notebooks—"

He shrugged. "Money? I found no gold."

My chest tightened at the loss of my purse, with as many as forty golden crowns. "My papers, then."

The fat rogue sighed, and reached into some inner pocket. He handed me the leather packet and I opened it, thumbing through the documents. My introductions and promissory notes all seemed present. Bezio looked to Marinello, who nodded, and held out his own hand to me.

"I think," said the suddenly stern lord, "that I had better inspect these, Master Kelley. It would not do to pass letters that could be seen as treasonable."

"I merely have letters of introduction that say I am the agent of Lord Robert Dannick of England." I gave them into his outstretched hand.

Marinello pointed a finger at the door and Bezio bowed deeply to him, less so to me, and kissed the hand of the cardinal, who seemed half asleep. He drew the door shut—almost. Marinello stood, walked over and put his boot against it to close it properly, then beckoned to me to follow him to the window.

He opened first one letter, then another. "Lord Dannick, hm? A great landowner in your country, no doubt?"

"Indeed." I pointed at one passage. "I was his son's tutor at Cambridge, and on his travels abroad I acted as his guide."

"Better we speak in German, do you not think?" he murmured to me. "Since Latin is known to all learned men, and English is—impossible." I was glad now of the notes that I had written in that "impossible" language. He finally handed over the packet and the papers.

"Certainly," I replied in German, better since I have resided in Bohemia. I tucked my precious papers away, and placed the leather case within my bag.

"I have been approached by someone who wishes to meet you." He stepped over to the fire, resting a boot that stretched above his knee on the fender. He dressed more like a seafaring pirate than a noble of Venice, in a black leather baldric ornamented with silver studs. A leather frog rested upon his hip, ready to take I thought a giant sword or cutlass. He smiled at me. "Before you rose this morning, discreet inquiries had been made of my servants, and, more directly, to the cardinal. A guest of the doge, working through intermediaries, seeks an audience." He reached up to the fireplace and took down a letter with a great black seal upon it, sagging open.

I had convinced myself of my incognito, but clearly I was mistaken. "Who is this person?"

"I don't know, but they are apparently interested in some work you did in Poland or Hungary or some such place, with the learned Dr. Dee." I flinched, and looked over at the cardinal. Despite his chin, dropped onto his thin chest, I was not convinced of the priest's deafness nor sleep.

I lowered my voice. "That work we have pledged never to discuss with others. We were led astray by forces of evil that even now we do not understand."

Marinello nodded slowly. "Well, it is a large purse for you, and for me, if you consent to a single meeting. You are here as an agent of your master, Lord Dannick, not Dr. Dee. What you choose to divulge is your business, not theirs."

"I am an agent of Lord Robert, yes. But I also wish to speak to several scholars of Venice, to help me with my own work."

Marinello's smile disappeared into a frown as if the sun had gone in. "What is the nature of this work, Master Kelley? And speak the truth, for I may be a great help to you, or a hindrance."

I glanced at the cardinal, and lowered my voice. "I am upon a quest, to divine the secrets of alchemy."

"Alchemy? Sorcery, more like. Perhaps I should hand you to the Inquisition myself."

"It is a legitimate area for research," I said, hastily, "entirely done to glory in God and his works. We divine the nature of the universe He created."

"And make ourselves rich along the way?" He stroked his thick beard. "Is that God's purpose, also, or Man's?"

I was silent, unwilling to enter into the spiritual arguments as Dee might have done. Anyway, I was confident of breaching the mystery of gold's purity by myself. My actual purpose, on behalf of my sponsor, was more important.

Marinello leaned close, looking deeply into my eyes, and held the letter out to me. I took it, but his fingers still grasped the other end. "My little friend, you need to know what dangers face you in Venice. This is a closed state, a place of suspicions and stories. Your arrival has already sparked rumors and questions."

I stood still, clutching my end of the heavy, folded paper, waiting for him to release his. I took some offense—I am of middle height, indeed, and slight, but I am no "little man," nor am I unable to judge a man's purpose myself.

Marinello released it with a sudden laugh. "Let me say then, Edward Kelley, that in Venice you need a friend. I will be that friend, and even fill your sadly empty purse with coins, if you will meet this one person, and answer his questions. How say you?"

"Just questions?"

"And you need not breach that confidence that you hold dear. All I ask is that I be allowed to join you and listen, and if needs be protect you."

I opened the letter, which was worded in the most cordial terms.

"My Lord Marinello, if it will please Your Lordship, a person of high scholarship seeks an introduction to a learned and famous gentleman presently enjoying your patronage. This gentleman being one Edward Kelley, well known to his beloved majesty King Istvan Báthory, and being of assistance to him in Transylvania. My master permits me to offer a reward to Master Kelley and to yourself, upon a single meeting and conversation at your convenience."

It was signed with some scribble. With some difficulty I unraveled it as a László Bánki, secretary.

"Very well," I said, looking up at Marinello. "I will serve you and this guest of the doge in any way that I can, within my conscience."

He smiled, and reached inside his jacket for a small bag, which clinked musically. He tossed the money to me. "You will need a few coins for your stay."

I thanked him, even as I regretted the loss of the heavy purse I had carried all the way from England.

"I would like to see something of your city," I said, thinking of the alchemists who might be willing to see me.

"Remember, in Venice you will be considered a spy if you do anything in private beyond eat, drink or fornicate," he warned. "Speak to a Venetian in private and they can be impeached. I will arrange a public meeting for your admirer, and we will both be rewarded."

I bowed in real gratitude, for my heart had been heavy and my purse empty. "Thank you, my Lord Marinello."

He smiled at me. "You have saved me from tedium, my little man, and none is more deadly to a sea captain than boredom."

Chapter 7

FELIX HEARD HIS PHONE DING AS HE REACHED HIS HOTEL room. It had been a long day guest lecturing in one of Gina's classes. Sadie had left another message on his mobile phone and the pictures she had attached made him smile. Despite being in a coma for several weeks only a few months ago, Sadie had bounced back. She also had accepted him into her unusual new family instantly, slotting him in somewhere between surrogate father and co-conspirator. He checked his watch, and dialed the number.

"Hello, Sadie." There seemed to be a lot of noise going on in the background.

"Felix! Hang on, I have to turn the telly down . . ." The sound reduced. "That's better. Jack's in the shower, she's been helping hack all the plaster off the front-room walls. It's soaked in grease and smoke, you know, from the old lady. She was burned."

"Oh." A moment's discomfort at the reality of Sadie's involvement in restoring the house shot through him. "Are you all right with that?"

"It stinks, that's all." She scuffled and he could hear her sigh. "It's nicer up here, though, than in Devon. I've been out in the car loads of times, and I've had my hair dyed bright red. It looks really cool. And Jack let me choose some new clothes for my birthday."

"Oh. Good." Anything that made her look different from the abducted Sadie Williams, tragic victim of a fire in Devon, had to be a good idea.

"Everyone thinks I have cancer, which is kind of weird, but they're really nice. We went shopping for furniture, too. Jack wanted this old secondhand stuff, but I did get her to buy a few new bits too. You'll have to come up and see it when it's done."

"I will." He wondered whether Jack would want that, but he felt responsible for Sadie. "There's a package in the post for your birthday, I don't know when it will get there."

"Thank you." She sounded like she was smiling. "And my mum's coming up to stay soon, only we have to pretend she's my auntie."

"You sound like you've adapted really well." He was surprised that Sadie wasn't missing her mother more, but after the coma Sadie seemed to have accepted the strange conditions of living on borrowed time.

"Jack makes me eat all this organic stuff because I can't handle chemicals, but she's found this amazing shop in Ambleside, it has fantastic organic ice cream. The landlady at the B&B, she makes me an organic breakfast, and we're staying for another couple of weeks. She even got Jack chatting."

Felix couldn't imagine Jack making small talk. "How is she?"

"Good. Strong, since—you know. A bit sad, though."

"Sad?"

"Just in the evenings. She looks down. When we're at the house she's busy, and we have a bit of a laugh, and the builders joke with us. One of them is," she dropped her voice, "really flirty with her, which is even funnier. She goes red when he talks to her. But then she gets sad."

He felt a pang of something, but refused to consider whether it was jealousy.

Sadie carried on chattering. "What about you? Are you still in America?"

"I'm in New Orleans. It's warm here, really nice."

"So, what exactly are you doing?"

He opened his mouth, and closed it again. "Uh, I'm hoping to meet with some people who know something about borrowed time."

"You're looking into the blood-drinking thing, aren't you?" He couldn't get much past Sadie: she was sharply observant. "To help Jack? Because I know you're worried about what happened when she did—though that is completely gross."

"I'm looking into it." He opened the wardrobe and wondered what to wear to a blood-drinking fetish club. "Only I don't really understand why normal people would drink human blood."

"There's lots of kinky vampire groups on the Internet." Sadie rustled something, then her voice was a bit distorted. "*Very* strange." She sounded as if she were eating something.

"Well, I have to get ready to meet some kinky vampire people, and I have no idea what to wear. What are you crunching?"

Indistinctly, she muttered, "Organic sherbet lemon." Then, more clearly, "Wear one of your old-man suits. That will keep you safe." She started laughing. "Isn't it a bit late to go out?"

"There's a six-hour time difference, it's only four o'clock here, tea time." He pulled out his most formal suit and laid it on the bed. "I'll just dress smart. Look after yourself, Sadie, and keep an eye on Jack for me."

"I will. And I'll look forward to my parcel. Be careful at this place, with all the weirdo vampire women. Bye, Felix."

He rang off. He guessed wearing a suit might be better than being too informal, and at least he would look professional. Even in April, the city was warm and a little humid but starting to cool down as the light faded.

He sat down at the laptop. E-mails from work could mostly wait, a few needed acknowledgments. He typed in "Julian Prudhomme" and did a search. There was a lot of information.

Prudhomme was well known as a priest of a blended religion Felix was familiar with called Santería. When Africans were abducted into slavery they brought their own beliefs, which they adapted into the Christian beliefs of the Caribbean. Gods and goddesses were renamed as saints, rituals subtly adapted or carried out in secret, the core African beliefs hidden in the new religion of Santería. With the selling of slaves between the Caribbean and America, the new beliefs spread.

Felix was familiar with the similar development of "voodoo" from the West African tradition of *vodun*, the animistic religion he had encountered in Nigeria. New Orleans was filled with references to it, including at least one voodoo museum.

He ordered a sandwich from room service and started looking on the Internet for associations between Santería and drinking blood. There was a connection made between the sacrifice of live animals in rituals, and possible breaches of laws in various states. But nowhere could he find any mention of drinking blood, although one or two mysterious cases of unexplained murders did make a possible link to Santería. He finished his tea looking out over the town as the light started to fall.

The hotel on St. Louis Street in the French quarter was the largest in the road. The other buildings were largely Creole and French colonial town houses, huddled against each other in bright shades, festooned with balconies and contrasting shutters. Lights twinkled in windows, music rose and fell like ocean waves from the street below, blending everything from brassy jazz to classical.

He stepped into the shower and thought about his reaction to Gina Larabie. She had made an impact on him every time they met, and working together had produced a lot of opportunities to talk. Gina had made it clear she wanted more.

He stood in the hot water speculating for the thousandth time about where he stood with Jack. Turning the temperature down for a moment, he let the cooler water run down his body.

This was a chance to understand what might happen to Jack, who had been forced to drink blood to save Sadie. He could remember the look on her face—energized, exultant, ready for anything. The last time he had seen her, some weeks ago, she had still been buzzing with life, very different from the faded, cold woman he had first encountered.

She had also pushed him away, and made it clear that any relationship that may have started was now over.

The hotel desk clerk gave him a look that suggested approval. Body language, one of his areas of interest, had its uses. She called him a cab to the address Gina had written down, and immediately he felt a measure of interest from the young woman.

"It's only a few minutes away," she said, her voice lower and softer than seconds ago.

"Oh. Good." The look she was giving him was definitely speculative now. "I'm an anthropologist. I'm studying aspects of social behavior."

She smiled. "Well, there'll be plenty to study there."

It was a relief to step into the taxi. The driver, an elderly black man in a red scarf, sounded surprised. "You wanna go there? Hell, why?"

Felix repeated his story, and the man turned on the meter and pulled out amid a chorus of horns.

Gina was waiting in the lobby of what looked like a discreet hotel: a long wooden bar, a couple of well-dressed attendants, and a pair of mahogany doors furnished in brass. She turned to face him, wearing a gray silky dress with a low back that showed off her long neck.

"Gina. You look lovely." He was glad now he had worn a suit.

"Felix! Come and get a drink." She led the way through the doors and onto a staircase stretching down to a basement level.

A second pair of doors opened into a bar area, the walls covered with wooden paneling. Music murmured in the background, contemporary but not too loud, and it took a few moments to appreciate the clientele.

Many were very young, some dressed in dark colors with stark black and white makeup. Some wore exotic outfits, from corsets that cinched tiny waists—a few of them male—to heels that looked like they were designed to hurt. The clothes appeared expensive, the behavior was subtly sexual but not aggressively so.

"How did you find this place?" He smiled, and she leaned on the bar. It emphasized her cleavage.

"I came here for my initial research, but no one would help me. Until I met Julian." She ordered a cocktail, and Felix chose a mineral water.

"Why did he help?"

"I don't know—maybe he found me attractive." She sipped her drink with her eyes closed. "Mm." She looked back at Felix. "Maybe he was curious himself. He likes to explore."

"I looked this Julian up. He seems like a mysterious character." He shrugged. "I'm still a bit unclear how he can help me with my questions about blood."

She put the glass down and her manner changed, became more like a lecturer, he thought. "Julian knows about the living dead—what we might describe as 'revenants'—through the Santería tradition. Well, he knows the legends, anyway."

"But he's never met one?"

She nodded. "He's met people who were trying to *become* revenants."

Felix sipped the water. "Why would anyone do that? To live a short life of constant weakness sounds counterproductive."

She shrugged. "Counterproductive? With regular donations of blood they don't age, they are rumored to be essentially immortal." She sipped a little of her drink, watching the other people at the bar. "For someone who is terminally ill, for example, it must be an attractive prospect."

A girl slipped past, skeletally thin and with a black dog collar around her neck attached to a chain held by another equally thin girl. Felix's attention was distracted for a moment.

"Julian?" He turned back to Gina to see a man, dressed in a suit but without a tie, standing beside her at the bar. "Professor Guichard, Julian Prudhomme."

Felix took a good look at him. He was taller than Felix's six feet, and much heavier, although he wasn't fat. His skin was so dark that in the low light his features were difficult to make out, except for his eyes, vivid and roaming over Felix's face and body. He held out a large hand, two fingers ornamented with gold rings.

"Felix," he said, his voice deep. Felix could see people turning to watch them. "Call me Julian." His voice had a Caribbean lilt.

"It's nice to meet you," Felix murmured, feeling the brief pressure of the man's hand.

"I hear you are a researcher into magic?" The man nodded to the bartender and a drink was placed on the bar.

"I am interested in magical belief systems, yes."

The man sipped his drink, and as he turned to the light Felix could see fine lines around the man's eyes that suggested he was older than he at first appeared. "I understand you are a leading expert on John Dee."

It was a statement rather than a question, but Felix answered anyway. "I would say I've been more interested recently in the work of his associate, Edward Kelley."

"But you are open-minded about whether magic is possible?" Julian sipped his drink, turning his intense gaze upon Felix again.

Feeling his color rise, Felix replied, "I have had some experiences that I cannot explain, both in Europe and in Africa." He didn't want to elaborate. "I understand you are a practitioner of Santería?"

"I am a priest of that tradition, certainly." He nodded to the bartender, who brought over what looked like another sparkling water. "My family has that responsibility within our community. I understand your interest is in this," he waved his hand around at the room, "blood ritual?"

"Is there a tradition of using blood in rituals in Santería?" Felix said.

The man waited for a long moment, apparently considering his answer. "There is a tradition of sacrifice, certainly, and animal blood is commonly used. But the use of human blood is different." Felix noticed he hadn't answered the question. Julian continued in his deep, measured voice. "But your Western traditions of magic value blood highly. There are many references to it."

"I was interested in the beliefs of sanguinarians."

Julian glanced at Gina then back at Felix, his gaze intense. "What, especially, are you interested in?"

"I am concerned about the effects of drinking blood on people who are drawn to ingesting it, or feel addicted to the experience. I want to find out how they feel after drinking blood, and whether there are any side effects."

"I see." Julian stared at Felix, making him feel a little uncomfortable.

He looked back, relaxing the muscles of his face, trying to appear calm.

Finally, Julian smiled. "Then I think I can help you. Let me explain aspects of the modern vampire phenomenon. For example, look at the man on the sofa."

Felix looked around the room. As his eyes adjusted to the light levels he could see more of the dark wood furniture and the comfortable leather sofas. One man sat between two youths, both whispering to him and stroking his body. Neither boy looked eighteen and the overt sexuality was disturbing.

"My friend over there calls himself an energy vampire," Julian said. "He is generous to his lovers in exchange for a little of their youthful vitality. No harm done to any party."

"And nothing to do with blood?"

"No. As far as I know. The exchange, he claims, is of sexual and spiritual energy. Now, the lady in the purple over there—"

Felix looked toward the corner of the room. A large woman, perhaps in her thirties, was talking to a younger man, running long painted nails over his neck and chest.

Julian continued. "She will take blood as part of a sexual ritual. I have had the good fortune to be one of her lovers—and the blood seemed completely part of the ecstasy of a night in her bed. Well worth a few drops I could spare. The sensation of submission—" He paused, smiling. "Is very alluring. I could introduce you."

"No, thank you." The woman stared at him as if she had heard Julian's suggestion, and he flushed with embarrassment. He sipped the rest of the water to cool down. "But she is a blood fetishist?"

"I would call her more of a role-player. You are sure you don't want an introduction?"

"No!" Felix smiled. "I mean, I wouldn't want to waste her time."

Gina laughed. "So, you were hoping to talk to people who take blood, but wouldn't go so far as to sleep with them?" She laid a hand on his briefly when he blushed a little. "Forgive us. You're very easy to tease."

Felix turned away from the intense study, looking around the room. People were standing in couples and groups, all watching the taller man. "I suppose I am. No offense, but I was hoping to just interview someone who had drunk human blood for magical purposes," he said, his voice coming out drier than he had intended.

After a long moment, Julian spoke again. "You understand, there is a lot of prurient curiosity, not to mention journalists and dilettantes. There are very few discreet establishments where people are able to follow their desires in complete privacy." The way he lingered on the word "desires" involuntarily drew Felix's eyes to Gina. Her attention was locked onto the speaker. "There must be no judgments, simply acceptance."

"I understand." Felix finished his drink.

"Then let's go to a real 'vampire' club." The big man snapped his fingers and threw several banknotes on the bar. Felix let Gina take his arm and steer him toward the door.

"Where are we going now?" he murmured to her as they stepped onto the street.

"I don't know. Just give in to it, Felix, relax."

That was the problem. There was something in the air, some crackling energy emanating from the big man that stood every hair on Felix's body on end. His instincts were dragging him back from the black limo that reflected the lights from the street. He overcame them and slid onto the seat beside Gina, opposite the man.

The man smiled suddenly, his teeth flashing in the low light. "You look nervous."

Felix smiled. "I think I am, a little."

"Let me give you a little background." Julian settled back into the leather seat. "The taking of blood has two very different purposes, two subcultures. In one, the woman you saw today, the main focus is on the erotic charge of sharing blood. That is the lovely Mariella's preference."

Felix smiled, feeling his stomach squirm. "That is something I find strange." Cars sounded their horns around the limo. The car slowed down into a queue of traffic.

Julian leaned forward a little, as if studying Felix. "But not altogether alien? Have you been a participant?"

The scar on his forearm, where Jack had sucked blood from his skin, seemed to itch and he had to suppress an impulse to scratch it. "Not in an erotic situation, no." He took a deep breath. "I was a donor, in a belief-based ritual to do with energy, with vitality."

"Interesting. Describe the sensation."

"Painful." Felix smiled in the dark, but the man waited for more. "It was a moment of high tension, I suppose, and it was very intimate. It was as if the world had stopped and it was just Jack and me for a moment. But it was a situation of life and death at the time."

Gina slid her hand onto his for a second, in the dark. It was strangely comforting.

"And it had some effect on this Jack?" Julian's voice was deep.

"It seemed to energize her. Gina may have mentioned, my friend believes she is a revenant, although she would call herself a 'borrowed timer.' She exists by using sorcery from Dee's research in Eastern Europe."

"And this doesn't use blood?"

"No. Just herbs and symbols."

"The use of blood in magic, as I'm sure you know, is an ancient one," Julian said. "Many cultures have believed that partaking increases strength or other qualities." The cacophony of horns outside the limo had become almost deafening, and the car had come to a complete stop. Julian sighed. "Ah, a little local color."

Gina leaned toward the window. "Looks like police lights ahead."

Julian spoke to the driver. "Thank you, Auguste. We'll walk from here."

The driver slid out of the front seat and opened the back

door. Felix found himself jostled by a crowd of people as he left the car, then reached a hand in to help Gina. People on the wide sidewalk were good-natured, but packed together, craning their necks to look over the drama ahead. It looked like an accident, but all Felix could see were two men shouting at each other and a lot of flashing lights.

Felix, Gina clutching his arm, followed Julian, for whom a path seemed to have been magically created. He turned into a side road, barely more than an alley, and they followed it toward a quieter street entrance.

"This is a shortcut. I grew up in this neighborhood," Julian said, a quick flash of a smile in the darkness. "Here." Along the quiet lane was a black door, solid, locked. Felix turned to see a couple of young men lounging in the alley entrance, hands in their pockets. Gina squeezed his arm.

Julian spoke into his phone. "Leonard? It's Julian—we're at the side door."

The door swung inward, and the watchers disappeared back into the shadows.

The atmosphere of the club enfolded Felix the moment he stepped inside. The street sounds disappeared, the noise of shoes were muffled in a thick carpet. Even the walls seemed padded. His eyes slowly adjusted to the soft lighting.

The room, and the one beyond, appeared to be filled with sofas, the black walls decorated with branches of candles and huge mirrors. People, male and female, lounged in pairs and trios on the seats, all wearing vivid black and white masks. Some were elaborate, with plumes of feathers or cat ears. Others were plain, just covering the eyes.

When Felix turned back to his companions, he found them adjusting masks as well.

"None for you, I'm afraid," Gina said, from under one covered in feathers like an owl, dotted with shiny stones that picked up the low light and flashed. "Members only. This way everyone knows you are an outsider and no one will inadvertently reveal their identity."

It was reminiscent of Venice, the Carnevale parties. One of his students had written her thesis on the symbolism of masks in modern Venetian culture. Her photographs, stunning enough to publish separately, were filled with the blank faces and the freedom it brought to the wearers. There was another similarity. The club members looked like lovers, groups of people who knew each other intimately, exchanging caresses that Felix wouldn't expect to be shared in public. He felt exposed, especially as many of them were looking at him and appeared to be discussing him.

Gina's eyes gleamed behind the mask. "Come on, Felix, no one's going to bite you." She laughed. "Not unless you want them to, anyway."

"Yes. Sit where you can observe the company." Julian's voice had a definite mocking quality now. His mask was black, a stylized human face with echoes of a skull.

The curved walls and mirrors maximized exposure, and before very long, the patrons' attention had reverted to their previous activities. Gina sat beside him, her thigh pressed against his in a skirt that divided as she sat, revealing her long legs almost completely, which he hadn't noticed before.

"Julian explained this place to me," she murmured into his ear. "This is the social room, where people meet their friends or dally with strangers."

"Dally. What a great word," he said, looking around the room trying not to be distracted by the warm silkiness against his leg. "There are other rooms?"

Julian took a glass from a tray held out by a young man, who was almost naked apart from red silk shorts and a bow tie. Felix declined a drink or one of the pills arranged in a pattern around the glasses.

"This club is mostly interested in sexual freedoms," Julian said, "although others come here for spiritual reasons."

"Spiritual?"

"Many of them believe blood is a gift of energy. Drinking blood, for them, is a sacred act, a gift of life from one being to another." He smiled at Gina. "Others consider blood the ultimate sexual and emotional submission."

Gina's eyes gleamed behind the mask as she sipped her drink. "I have met blood takers who believe the ingesting of blood is essential for their health," she said. "The ultimate antidote to death."

Felix glanced around at the others in the room, who seemed to be kissing and touching each other with a freedom perhaps enhanced by the masks. "Doesn't that sound more like a psychological dependence? It was described to me as an addiction, the sufferer feels that they need rather than want the drug."

"It is somewhat like a drug." Gina leaned closer. "Before I met Julian I thought it was just a fetish, and a dangerous one at that. But then—I tried it."

"You did? Is that what you meant by immersive research?"

"And you tried it too, with this woman, the revenant." She touched his knee briefly. "No judgments, remember? We are just here to help you understand." Her smile broadened. "And have a little fun teasing the shy Englishman, of course."

He smiled, but it felt like a grimace. "So, explain to me: what has this to do with what you call revenants?"

Julian stretched back in his seat as a woman came over to him, placed a card in his open hand, and sauntered away, swaying like a tree in a storm. "Some of the patrons of this club hope to become immortal by becoming revenants in the European tradition."

Felix's understanding of borrowed time was that only people close to death, those who were destined to die without supernatural intervention, could become borrowed timers. "I don't understand."

"In the tradition of *our* revenants, willing subjects, offer themselves to the 'blood ritual' over months or even years as donors." Julian looked at the card and smiled. "Eventually they require a ritual we call 'ascension,' then a regular treatment of traditional remedies, and, of course, libations of blood from willing volunteers."

"Our tradition is different." Felix wondered how much he should share with the man.

"We must compare notes." Julian nodded to a passing couple. "This woman, this friend of yours—"

"Was close to death in childhood. She was saved by someone who knew the sorcery of Dee and Kelley. She uses symbols which seem to strengthen her, and herbs to keep her healthy."

Julian turned back to Felix and stared at him. "What kind of symbols?" His interest was intense, almost sexually speculative, and Felix felt even more uncomfortable.

"It was based on a European tradition." He took a deep breath. "I am deciphering private journals that Kelley kept in his travel through Europe. He was involved in treating a woman who was born to someone who was a revenant herself, and Dee tried to find a way to prevent her death. These are the symbols borrowed timers still use."

"But no blood?" The man stood. "Interesting. Come with me, Felix. Let me introduce you to a supplicant who is being transformed—she hopes—by the blood ritual."

Gina turned to talk to another woman, and Felix rose and followed Julian into the adjoining room, and to an alcove. Here a raised platform was occupied by a woman who appeared to be in her thirties, lying on a heap of cushions. Another woman, perhaps only in her teens or early twenties, was kissing her, murmuring to her. A man, half-naked and clearly aroused, was bent over her wrist, his mouth pressed to her skin.

"Aurélie," Julian said softly. "May we speak with you?"

The woman turned to them. Her skin was chalky white, her body too thin, bones visible where her scanty clothing was disordered. "Julian, darling." Her voice was breathy and soft. "Do you come to share?"

"Not today. I have brought a friend, whose interest is in ascension."

The gaze swiveled onto Felix. "I am tired. Perhaps another day." She tensed, and made a little mew of pain. The man suckling at her wrist lifted his face and licked his lips. The torn flesh was vivid against her pale skin, slowly oozing drops of blood. The young man bent his head again, this time to caress the woman, trailing kisses up the inside of her elbow.

"I think his knowledge of the immortals is unique. He seeks only to understand." Julian looked around, then reached for a dressing. "You have given enough, today, perhaps too much. You cannot hurry ascension, Aurélie; it is dangerous."

"So people are progressively weakened through giving blood?" Felix was interested in spite of himself. "At what point would you intervene with the ritual?"

The woman stared at him, and then at Julian, but after a long moment she answered, "When the spirits advise us."

"Spirits?"

Julian finished dressing the superficial wound. "As people grow weaker the spirits gather around. They make it clear when death is close. Then the blood ritual begins."

"These spirits—"

"Angels," the young woman murmured.

Julian turned to Felix. "I would rather describe them as *orishas*, spirits or aspects of gods. They gather, they whisper. Sometimes they speak through chosen oracles."

"And what are the benefits for the—ascended?"

The woman weakly struggled to sit, her female companion helping to lift her up the cushions. "The ascended are our superiors. To be chosen to become one is to become an immortal walking among mortals."

Julian added, "The body is healed, and continues without aging."

"And you have been chosen?" Felix spoke gently, as the woman seemed stiffly hostile.

"I hope to be." She lifted her injured arm and stared at it.

"And if you are not? Chosen?"

She looked back at Felix, blue eyes shining in sunken sockets. "Then I will die."

Chapter 8

FELIX STRETCHED OUT IN THE KING-SIZED BED BEFORE HE remembered the details of the evening before. The soft breathing beside him made him aware of the recollection of the hours of drinking on nothing more substantial than a sandwich, and the effect of the sensual atmosphere in the club. More than anything, he was conscious of the proximity of Gina.

The last time he had had sex it had been with his wife, Marianne, nearly a year before. A moment of tenderness so ordinary and spontaneous that he had barely remembered it, not knowing it was the last time. Jack had made it plain that she didn't want a relationship, so why did he feel unfaithful?

"Mm, Felix." Gina ran one hand down his back, and it felt good. "Good morning."

"Ah." He rolled over to see her leaning on one elbow, smiling. "Good morning."

Her grin broadened. "I'm guessing you don't have a lot of spontaneous sex?"

He managed a smile. "Not for a long time. I've only just got divorced. Was it obvious?"

"Not last night." She lay back down on the pillow. "God, I don't want to get up. But I have to teach a seminar."

His hand reached out, almost involuntarily, and touched her shoulder. Her skin was perfectly smooth, stretched over long limbs. He shrugged off the lingering guilt. "Anything I would be interested in?"

"Not really. But later I was going to take you to a *bembé*, at Julian's house." She slipped out of bed, and stood beside it. "I've never been to one before, it's a huge privilege to be invited. It's a ritual of dancing and chanting, to invite an *orisha* into a willing participant."

"I think I've been to similar events in Africa." He looked at her as she stood, unselfconsciously naked, lifting a corner of a curtain to look outside. She was as relaxed as if they had been lovers for years. He pushed the memory of Jack away.

"Come on."

"Come on?" He was only puzzled for a moment as she grinned at him.

"If I'm going to miss breakfast *and* be late for my seminar, I want to clean my teeth first."

Felix had had an interesting morning in the university library, reading more of Gina's research. He was grateful that she didn't seem to share some of the more extreme fetishes she researched. He was self-conscious just reading the journals in the crowded library, and jumped when she tapped him on the shoulder.

They shared a taxi to Prudhomme's house. Julian lived in Faubourg Marigny, a neighborhood adjacent to the French Quarter, and slightly less busy. The building, a Greek revival mansion, had a large garden to one side and railings along the front. The door was opened by a man Felix recognized as Auguste, the chauffeur from the night before.

"Please follow me."

Gina slipped her hand into Felix's, her fingers trembling against his. "What's wrong?"

"Nothing. I'm excited," she said, but something about her

expression suggested there was more to it. "I've always wanted to attend one of Julian's *bembés*."

"Tell me more."

"It's a ceremony where people open themselves up to the spirits. It's a state of ecstasy, a kind of spiritual intoxication." She took a deep breath. "It's supposed to have healing qualities."

Before he could pursue that thought, Auguste threw open double doors which led into a room the whole width of the house. The space was probably over forty feet wide and more than half that deep. Four pairs of French doors led outside but they were shuttered, slivers of light spattering the polished wood floor.

"Wait here, please," Auguste said in a soft voice, and he disappeared back through the doors.

Felix looked out of one of the shutters' narrow slits, onto the garden. It was rambling, enclosed by a wall and a number of trees and shrubs. The room was stuffy and he wished he could open the doors. "This *bembé* sounds like some of the rituals in Benin I attended. In fact, a lot of Western African countries have festivals where various manifestations of God are invited into willing volunteers."

"Exactly." Julian's deep voice took Felix by surprise. "Those traditions traveled to Cuba and other Caribbean islands with the enslaved Africans. The roots are in Yoruba, the indigenous belief system." Felix turned to see Julian walking toward them dressed in a long, colorful robe, his head and feet bare.

Felix shook the other man's hand. "I studied similar rituals in Togo and Benin back in the nineties."

Julian laughed. "That's why I invited you." He bowed slightly as he took Gina's hand, then shook Felix's with both hands. "This is similar. My friends, my congregation, as it were, will be here shortly. I just wanted the chance to speak privately with you first."

"Thank you. This is very kind of you." Felix looked around the room, half in shadow from the drawn curtains covering most of a wall of windows. Auguste carried in a large box, which sounded like it had something scuffling inside it.

"I hope you aren't squeamish," Julian said. "Sometimes the ritual demands an animal sacrifice. We are as humane as possible, of course."

"How do the authorities view sacrifice?" Felix said, feeling Gina grip his arm more tightly.

"Provided the animals are dispatched without cruelty, no more than if we killed it to eat it. This ritual is focused on healing the sick, an interest I know Gina shares."

The doors opened again and three people entered, also dressed in colorful clothes. One was an elderly white woman, leaning on a stick, another was a rather tired-looking black youth, and a woman who appeared to be his mother. More followed, a mixture of ethnicities and ages. Julian gathered them around him, speaking to them quietly, shaking hands.

Felix turned to Gina. "If this is anything like the rituals I have observed it's going to get loud." He pointed at the drums being carried by two of the men, large cylindrical objects painted with symbols. He smiled at one of the men, and walked over. "These are great, what are they?"

"They are called *bembé*, like the ritual," one man answered. He put his hand protectively around the drum.

"Do you play them?"

"The *orisha* plays them through me."

Before Felix could ask any more questions, Julian called for the group to gather. Felix rejoined Gina at the edge of the room. "I know an *orisha* is a spirit that mediates between mortals and God. These rituals, in Africa anyway, call upon the spirit to inhabit a person, who will then relay messages and work the spells. What Julian described as an 'oracle,' a vessel for the *orisha*."

"I'm getting goose bumps." She sounded uneasy.

He smiled at her. "Last night you took me to a fetish club. You think that didn't make me nervous?"

She smiled back, but then the drumming started. At first it was just a heartbeat, resonating around the room, *ju-jum, ju-jum*, slowly echoing. The circle of people swayed to its rhythm, and the room seemed to fill with a dense quiet that was only pierced by the deep sound of the *bembé*.

The second one joined in, the drummer bringing his whole body into each beat. The group began to chant, not English as he'd expected, but fragments of another language. He recognized the odd ritual phrase which sounded like a Bantu dialect. It seemed to be pleading with someone to join them.

An older woman started singing, a wail of entreaty, and she danced into the center of the circle, stamping with emphasis. Others clapped in counterpoint to the drums, the swaying becoming dancing. Felix clapped along, letting the energy of the music that was building pull him in.

"I'm scared." Gina clutched his arm, pulling it down to stop him clapping.

"This is just the welcome. You get this at any religious service, even Christianity. Music, shared purpose, chanted words, they all create a certain kind of resonance in the brain." He gripped her hand, trying to reassure her, but she was shaking.

"I don't like it. We have to go."

He was torn. Julian seemed the most likely person to help with his research into the blood rituals, and he didn't want to offend him. He pulled Gina, unresisting, into his arms. "It's fine. It's just dancing."

She seemed to relax a little, so he turned back to the circle.

Julian threw back his head and called to the *orishas* to join them. His voice boomed out again and again. The music was wilder now, creating a trancelike state in some of the dancers.

An older woman, tall and gaunt, swayed over to the animal

box, her feet stamping in rhythm with the drums. She reached in and dragged out a flapping black chicken. Still dancing, she held it up by one wing and the neck and showed it to the group. It fought, attempting to crow, flapping its free wing in distress. She started to whirl, as if showing off the wretched animal. It was passed overhead to another dancer, then a third, its struggles more desperate as it was almost thrown from one to another. Finally, Julian snatched it from another man, and held it firmly in both hands, its wings pressed onto its body, only its open beak and staring eyes registering its distress. He put it under one arm and drew a silver knife. With a theatrical sweep he sliced the bird's head straight off. Blood spurted over the waiting crowd, as if they waited to be anointed with it.

A shriek was followed by a man falling to the ground, his back arched, his whole body vibrating as if in an epileptic fit. Gina buried her face against Felix's shoulder; he could feel her shaking. More shrieks, more wild dancing, as a young woman tore at her clothes, then whirled around in the space, her bare feet padding on the polished wood. Stamping feet, the drums and the rhythmic grunting and wailing set up a vibration inside Felix, who remembered the joyful beat of local weddings and funerals at his grandmother's house in Yamoussoukro in the Côte d'Ivoire. Gina clung to him, but he hardly noticed her until one of her nails grazed his chest through his shirt.

She started to pant as if she were running up stairs, and when she looked at Felix her eyes were huge, wide open in what looked like terror. She mouthed something, maybe his name, before she fell back so abruptly he barely caught her, falling to one knee with her slumped in his arms. She twitched, before starting to shake, as he had seen the others do. He became aware that people were starting to stamp toward them, forming a loose circle, the chanting more focused now. She convulsed, and he laid her gently on the ground. When she screamed aloud the noise seemed to pierce his head, and he stood, stepping back one pace. He looked at Julian, scarcely recognizing the man, his whole face contorted, eyes rolled back, his arms rigid and trembling in front of him. He seemed to be summoning something, and, in a moment, Felix felt something change in the room. Objectively he couldn't identify it, but the atmosphere in the room seemed to get hotter, and the air vibrated with the sound of the drums. He couldn't help raising his hands to his ears to protect them.

Gina writhed on the floor as he had seen the others do, tearing at her clothes, until her shirt was ripped. Her tongue was stretched out of her mouth, her eyes staring, her hands claws that tore at her skin, livid scratches appearing on her chest and arms. Finally, she screeched, and slumped back, eyes closed.

He stepped forward, worried, but two men grabbed his arms and held him. He waited, and watched. The room fell silent, even the drums stopping.

She was breathing, her chest rising and falling in an exaggerated way. When her eyes snapped open it was a shock, and he realized there was a low growling coming from her throat, squirming itself into words, as if she no longer had an idea how to speak.

Julian started a new chant. "Elegba," he called, his voice ringing around the room. The drums sounded, once, twice. "Elegba, speak to us!" A low hum of others' voices chanting joined in. Felix recognized the name of the *orisha*, Elegba, from his reading, Èṣù, in the original Yoruba, the trickster. Gina closed her eyes and moaned as if in agony, and this time Felix shook off the hands restraining him and dropped to one knee beside her.

"Do not touch her!" boomed Julian. A note of urgency in his voice made Felix pull his hand back.

Gina opened her eyes and stared straight at him. She seemed conscious of him, or at least some part of her did, because her mouth stretched into a grimace, and the grinding words started again. Finally, he began to recognize some elements of what she was trying to say.

"Death—fast—deathfast—touches her. Touches her—with death." She moaned, not in pain, but in some sensual frenzy, her body writhing. "He lives—within." Her words came faster, less intelligible. "Stop him—stop him!"

She screamed, as if in terror, and the crowd around him shouted in some reply, the drums beating faster now, the dancers swaying, whirling, stamping closer and closer. When she looked at him again, it was with terrified eyes and this time he reached to touch her, to comfort. A shock hit him as if he'd been electrocuted and ran through his body as it was jerked back. He hit the floor hard, bright flashes before his eyes as his head smacked against the wooden floor. He rolled over, his muscles slow to respond, landing on all fours, staring at Gina. She was white-faced, her eyes still staring, as if she were dead.

It took Julian some time to persuade Felix not to call 911 as he assured him Gina's state was normal. It was one of the crowd, a doctor, who finally persuaded him to leave her for a few minutes. A cautious hand to her neck, not followed by a shock, assured him that her pulse was strong, and within a minute her eyes closed and she lapsed into a sleeplike state. Julian helped him lift her onto a rapidly supplied couch, and the other celebrants formed a circle at the other end of the room and started singing. Julian stood with him, watching Gina.

"That was surprising," he said, looking at Felix intently. "Tell me, what did you feel when Elegba traveled through you?"

"Is that what you think happened?" Felix knelt beside her. "Gina?"

Julian spoke to someone and after a few moments Auguste appeared with a glass of what Felix hoped was water.

"Felix?" Her voice was weak.

"You're back." He smiled, a warm wave of relief spreading through him. "I was really worried for a second."

"What happened? I remember the drumming and dancing—did I join in?"

"No, but you did start talking."

"Anything interesting?" Gina put her hand to her temple, and winced. "My head hurts."

Julian's voice was soothing. "You were blessed by a visitation by an *orisha*, Elegba. He seemed to have a message for us, or perhaps for our professor."

"But I wasn't part of—" Gina rubbed her forehead for a moment. "I think I need to go home. Felix?"

Julian began shaking his head. "She has been blessed; she should stay and recover."

"Thank you, Julian, for a very interesting session, but I think I'll take Gina home now." Felix injected as much authority as he could into his voice, and gripped Gina's hand, helping her to stand. "Are you OK?"

"At least let Auguste drop you home," suggested the older man, but Gina waved the suggestion away.

"I'm fine, I'm really all right. I just need to get rid of this headache." She pulled on Felix's hand, as if she couldn't bear to stay any longer.

They escaped into the spring day, clouds scudding overhead, the street quiet after the cacophony of singing and drums. She leaned heavily on Felix's arm.

"What do you want me to do?" He was beginning to get concerned, now he could see how pale her lips were in the light.

"Get a cab." She smiled at him, her lips quivering. "I really am fine. What the hell happened?"

"I think Julian would say you were possessed by an *orisha*, a spirit connection to the divine, to give us a message."

"That sounds like a lot more fun than what happened." She tried again to pull the torn shirt together.

"Here." He slipped off his jacket and she pulled it on.

"I'm sorry—he said there was a message?"

"Never mind that now." His waving attracted the attention of a cabdriver, who pulled up smartly next to the curb. "Do you want me to come with you? I'm not sure you ought to be alone."

"I'll be fine. Thank you, Felix. I'll phone you after I've had a rest. I'm just tired." A little mischief creased the corners of her eyes. "I didn't get much sleep last night, you know."

He stepped back and waved as the door shut and the driver pulled away. He started walking in the direction of the French Quarter, well signposted for tourists. Without his jacket the sunshine was misleading, there was still a little nip in the air. A message for him? He tried to recall what she had mumbled.

Deathfast? And who was the "he" she had shouted, something about something that lives within? And death, did it refer to the strange half-life Jack lived in? He stopped at a crossing, waiting for the lights to change. The message could be coincidence, even Julian made no attempt to interpret it as a message for his group. The focus was on Felix, and he felt uneasy at the few words. "Touches her in death?" He realized as he crossed the road that he had thought little about Gina, who had been knocked out, and all about Jack, who hadn't even been present.

Chapter 9

The garden watches. It feels the pressure of life in the house, sees the taking away of the witch's possessions, the scrubbing and scouring.

It watches the bats streaming out of the eaves, thin and hungry after the dark months, looking for moths and midges. Lights glow from the back of the house and the garden leans in to look. Two of them: one a witch, one—maybe not. The garden shifts its roots as the ground shrivels under the dry spell, and bursts a few buds into leaves. A pigeon perches in one of the plum trees, cooing nervously, and takes off after no birds reply. Wise. The bones of the previous thieves litter the garden like porcelain shards, bleached by the sun and scattered by burying beetles. The ivy protects its berries.

TWO WEEKS LATER, ONCE THE RUBBISH REMOVAL FIRM had emptied the old house and taken away Dumpster after Dumpster of refuse, Jack could inspect the whole property. The top floor had two large front bedrooms, both basically dry except for areas in front of broken windows, and a smaller back room next to a large bathroom. The chipped, claw-footed bath presided over the room with an old toilet in the corner. It had a cistern near the ceiling, which worked, as Sadie had testified. Everything was filthy. The sink was green with algae, and the drain half blocked. The bathroom was a good place to start cleaning. With the glazier replacing window glass at the front of the property, she set to with tools and detergents, scouring off years of grime. Finally, she cut the stinking vinyl flooring into bits, and carried it down to the new Dumpster.

Sadie met her on the way back into the hall, holding a book. She had been curled up in a folding chair, reading in the sunshine coming through the new glass in the dining room and, Jack suspected, occasionally flirting with the good-looking builders.

The glazier met her on the landing, sipping from the top of a flask.

"I can repair the front room window today, but the frames need stripping and repainting. The back windows are much worse, and I can't get to them without scaffolding. They're in a terrible mess, and I'm not sure the frames are salvageable." Jack looked through the open bathroom door to the glass, so covered with leaves they made it feel as if it were underwater, infused with green light.

"Don't worry, I'll call you when the garden's cleared. Can you board up the back windows where the birds are getting in, anyway?"

"Of course. I can do that from inside."

Banging from a downstairs room suggested the decorators were taking down the lounge ceiling, which had been ruined by the smoke.

"I need to empty the kitchen first," she said, "and get all the units out. You could come back then to do the window frames when we have cleared the garden."

She smiled at him and went downstairs to see how the dining room was coming on.

At least the stink of charred flesh from the adjacent room

had been reduced, with windows and doors propped open, and wallpaper coming off ready for skimming with new plaster and paint. A company had removed all the internal doors for stripping, and then returned them. Jack rather liked the stripped pine and planned to wax them all. Maggie had given her a recipe for the polish, with its scents of natural turpentine and beeswax, which were melting together on an electric ring in the kitchen. Jack went to prod the lump of wax and stir it. She added half a tiny bottle of lavender oil and a few drops of geranium, as Maggie had prescribed, and the warm scents immediately lifted her mood. She turned off the heat as the last of the solids molded into a teardrop on the bottom of the pan, and left it to dissolve.

"Hey!" The shout from one of the builders outside made her look up. "There's a lady here, says she wants someone called Maggie."

"I'm coming." She walked down the hall. An old woman with bright orange hair and scarlet lips, whose age Jack couldn't begin to guess, was standing at the doorway, leaning on a stick. Her eyes looked pink, as if she'd been crying.

"You aren't Magpie."

"Magpie? Oh, Maggie. No, I'm sorry. I'm Jack Hammond, Maggie's foster daughter."

The woman's eyes, almost lost in webs of wrinkles and drooping lids, brightened as she stared at Jack. "You?" she said, looking her up and down. "You are Jackdaw?"

"I am, Mrs.—?"

"I am Maisie Talbot. I was Ellen's friend. She mentioned you, and, of course, I knew Magpie from when she was a child. I was hoping to see her."

"She'll be here next week."

"Then she will miss the inquest tomorrow." The old woman seemed to lean heavily on her stick. "But you'll be there?"

"Certainly." Jack couldn't even offer her a chair, as most of Ellen's had gone in the Dumpsters with everything else and the rest were being repaired along with the bedroom furniture. "Are you going?"

"Of course. I was the last person to see her alive. In fact, I was on my way to see her when it happened." She nodded to the living-room doorway. "I came in, pushed the door open. It was a terrible sight to see my friend, dead—and like that. Burned up."

Jack looked at her feet for a moment, as the old woman dabbed at her eyes with a tissue. "I'm so sorry."

"Just tell Magpie to come and see me, when she gets here. I have to go, I've left my taxi driver waiting—" Her face twisted with an expression that looked like something between pain and rage.

Jack watched her struggle with her cane across to the taxi. "It was a terrible accident," she said.

The woman's voice was suddenly strident. "Accident?" She swung around, holding on to the car door, and pointed a trembling finger at Jack. "It was no accident. Ellen Ratcliffe was murdered."

Chapter 10

The great city of Venetia or Venice is a masterpiece of engineering. It sits upon a multitude of islands, made from Illyrian alder trees thrust into the soft mud of the lagoon and filled with sand and silt. Upon this soft matter are all the houses and churches erected, some as great as such buildings seen in London. Over all, the towering grandeur of St. Mark's with its stolen treasures.

—HENRY WOTTON, *Upon the State of Venetia*, 1589

M Y NEW HOST COULD NOT HAVE BEEN MORE GENIAL. Although a son of a noble house, Marinello had been sailing with his father, a sea trader, since he was a young boy. He took me around the city on one of his narrow open boats called a *pupparin*, showing me the wonders of the architecture and the people.

The waterways fell into deep shadows between the palazzos, gaudy in their brightly painted windows and walls. Everywhere bridges, walkways and boats filled every available space on the canals, which, according to Marinello, were created by the ancestors of modern Venice.

We shivered in the shade then basked in the spring sun as the boatman criss-crossed the city. The air was not fresh, having a scent of fish and ordure, but Marinello laughed at my wrinkled nose. "I have seen the waters clogged with everything from dead horses to whole trees," he said. "Then a spring tide and whoosh!" He waved his arm over the side of the boat. "It is gone, and the sea returns."

"But what of potable water to drink?" I said, looking at the tightly woven houses.

"Aquifers, under the city. Each large house and some court-yards have one. Water is precious currency in Venice. In long summers, people suffer." He stretched back on the cushions behind him. "Not me. My ships trade mostly between Easter and winter, bringing everything from spices and silk to meats and wine. I sail with them in the dry season."

Music drifted out of the back of a tall building, the sweet thrum of a harp perhaps and some sort of viol, followed by the voice of a young man. "Your people are always singing," I observed, seeing a group of children stop playing to crowd under the window and listen.

"Yes, we sing." He turned his head toward me. "You English are more . . . how would you say, *dour*?"

I smiled. "We are a serious people, yes, but we love our theater, our poetry, our music, also. And dancing." It seemed a long time since I had been there, yet it was scarcely two months. It had been my first visit in several years, and it had been pleasant to think and speak English again.

"Tell me of your great houses, your lords," he said, smiling and waving at two women laughing on one of the bridges. They blew him kisses as we passed underneath them.

I thought back to Knowle Castle, the great seat of the Dannicks. "My patron, Lord Robert Dannick, his castle is a great house indeed." I embellished a little here, for, in truth, the place is a gray fortress. "His great hall can have several hundred dancers and revelers. He has hosted hunting parties for the queen herself."

"Is she a great beauty, as you English claim?"

I moderated my more loyal answer in favor of a modicum of truth. "She is a handsome lady, my lord, for her age, which is over fifty years. Slender still, with a fine figure and brilliant eyes." I had seen her twice, once in Dee's employ and once in Dannick's. She looked like a hawk, her eyes darting everywhere as if looking to pounce. No beauty, but a queen in every inch.

"And your mission here, Master Kelley? For I know you are a scholar of the new science of nature." Although he lay back on the cushions and played with a pomander, sometimes lifting it to his face to overcome the stink of the water, I was sure he was listening carefully.

"I have an interest in meeting a count of Padua and Venice, my lord," I said. "A Lord Contarini, who I was advised shall be able to advance my studies in alchemy. I have information for his lordship, and am willing to share my own knowledge."

He looked at me, and sat forward in his seat. "Contarini? I know of him, of course, but we move in different circles."

"I bear letters from Lord Robert Dannick. They seek information about a cure for one of his sons who is mortally sick."

Marinello dangled the pomander from a ribbon, swinging it back and forth. "Some medicine? The Contarinis are not doctors. Perhaps you should consult one of our physicians."

I thought swiftly, for it is foolish to advance knowledge too quickly, or to the wrong ears. "Perhaps I shall. And you, my lord? You must have visited many distant lands, and seen many strange things."

"Some." He grinned at me, his face lightening. "I have certainly met some strange people. But you were telling me about the Dannicks."

Since Marinello's tastes ran to adventuring, I told him of Lord Robert's battles in Ireland on behalf of the queen. He soon tired of this, and diverted the conversation back to me.

"Tell me, what riches lie in alchemy?"

I took a deep breath, and outlined some of what I had myself seen and experienced. He showed a keen interest and some knowledge of science.

"So," he said, swinging the pomander. "You need funds for these experiments to buy base metals such as silver and mercury, as well as rare minerals?"

Hope burned briefly in my breast. "Indeed, for I have known an alchemist transmute such a volume of silver into gold that his fortunes were made for generations. He was my master, one Seabourne, and shared many of his secrets with me."

He smiled at me. "But not the secret of unlimited wealth."

"I need but some sponsorship—"

"Sad for both of us then, that I barely have one ducat to rub against another."

"But, my lord?" I was astonished, as such wealth seemed to exist within his palazzo and upon his person.

"Last winter we lost three ships, two of them filled with pepper and silk. That is the nature of seafaring for profit, Master Kelley, it is a gamble. I throw the dice, and there! My family fortunes are gone."

"I am sorry, my lord." I was, and not just for myself, for he was a likable companion.

"And this year I shall win it all back, no doubt." He shrugged. "I would not have it different. My mistress is lending me gold so I can repair a couple of old ships to carry goods to Constantinople and Candia. I also have warehoused goods under guard in Alexandria."

I recognized Marinello's palazzo in the distance as our oarsman rowed against the current along the Canalasso, the great canal. "So, this one meeting with the guest of the doge will relieve both our financial embarrassments?" I said.

"That is true." He grinned at me. "For a generous price, the work of a few minutes. It seems that neither of us can refuse."

"And when I can do so," I said, in a gush of enthusiasm I shortly regretted, "I shall pay back the money you have already spent to succor me. For I hope to earn a good bonus visiting Count Contarini, from my Lord Dannick." Easy offered, thought I, since I shall be far away in England when I am paid.

He reached out for a tall pole beside his house to halt the boat, and the oarsman secured ropes. Marinello sprang onto the pier, then reached a hand to steady me, less used to the waves.

"I commend your courage, little man," he said, but with only half a smile. "Watch yourself with the Contarinis and their kind, my friend. They are a pack of wolves."

Chapter 11

The badgers stir beneath the ground in the sett they have won through generations of territorial battles, cave-ins and upheavals. They scratch themselves awake. The garden tolerates them: they do more good than harm, rooting out slugs and snails, digging out superfluous nests of rats, and they keep the rabbits down.

Bees stir in the hives, stretching crackling wing joints, tending the new eggs. The workers are old, needing more honey than the hive can spare, so they work until they die. The hive buzzes and wonders where the witch is. A few launch themselves into the cool air in the middle of the day, but there is little nectar and the cold dulls their muscles until they drop under the hive. It doesn't matter. There are thousands more.

JACK WAS EARLY FOR ELLEN'S INQUEST, AND WATCHED THE local people enter in ones and twos. High windows filled the paneled room with light, which painted shapes on the north wall of the court. There were several reporters and as the evidence unfolded she realized why.

The coroner called the pathologist to the stand. "Dr. Chen,

you have performed a postmortem on the body of Miss Ellen Jennifer Ratcliffe, I understand?"

"I have. I have also asked another pathologist, Dr. Edward Lemmon, to perform a second examination. This is a very unusual case."

"Is Dr. Lemmon in attendance?"

"Since we concurred, broadly, on cause of death and the manner in which the body presented, I have his report here for the court. Dr. Lemmon would be willing to attend if necessary, on a separate date, but he is unable to be here today."

"Well, let's hope we don't need to question him, then." The coroner, a spare man in his fifties or sixties, smiled thinly around the court. No one laughed. "Carry on, Dr. Chen."

"The body was that of a poorly nourished elderly woman, consistent with an age of seventy-nine years old. She had evidence of type two diabetes, and her blood sugar was raised at postmortem."

"What evidence was this, doctor?"

"She had a condition called acanthosis nigricans, extensive abnormal skin pigmentation. And her feet had ulcers with some areas of ischemia. Poorly controlled diabetes is a cause of circulation problems and enervation of the extremities. On examination, other complications of diabetes were recorded, including some sight impairment." She scanned her notes. "Blood tests, of course, confirmed it."

"And what conclusion did you reach about the cause of Miss Ratcliffe's death?" The room, previously a little restless with the odd murmur, became quieter.

"I found indications of heart failure. But . . ." She paused, looking uncomfortable. "Dr. Lemmon and I concurred that the fire may have started before death occurred." She looked around the room. "Miss Ratcliffe was found close to the fireplace, and there was evidence that a coal fire had been lit there recently. It is possible that an ember caught her clothing alight, and that Miss Ratcliffe died as a result of pain, or shock."

"I see." The coroner frowned at people starting a buzz of whispers. "You say this is likely?"

"No, I said it's possible. The body was . . . I have never seen a case like it. This phenomenon is rare even in the literature."

"Can you explain?" The coroner leaned forward. Jack noticed the woman next to her was scribbling furiously in what looked like makeshift shorthand.

"It is possible for the human body to burn very slowly, over a considerable period of time. The clothing acts as a wick, and the slowly melting body fat is drawn up and burned above the body like a candle. We were unable to find evidence of the initial flame or ember, however."

The coroner's face was a picture of dismay. "I hope you aren't suggesting some sort of paranormal manifestation?"

The doctor winced. "Unfortunately, even scholarly journals have called this form of burning spontaneous human combustion. But there's nothing paranormal or spontaneous about it. The body was hosed down by the fire brigade—it's perfectly possible that evidence of an ember was simply washed away."

The fire officer's evidence was about dousing the smoldering floor and clearing the hoarded rubbish in the living room so it didn't catch. Looking around the courtroom, Jack caught the eye of Maisie Talbot, sitting bolt upright, staring straight back at her. Jack looked away, but when she glanced back, there was the stare.

Maisie looked even smaller in the court. Jack suspected her feet didn't reach the ground from the chair she was perched in. Her hair was dyed red, a white blaze down the center parting where her hair was growing back. Her face fell into stacks of wrinkles around her mouth and radiated from each eye. She sat with her back straight, in a black-and-white herringbone jacket, and a large brooch set with some sparkling stones on the lapel.

"Mrs. Maisie Talbot." When the name was called, the woman finally broke eye contact and slipped out of her chair. She walked with as much dignity as someone barely four and half feet tall could manage. She sat in the witness seat, her feet swinging a little, like a child's.

The coroner smiled at her. "You went to see the deceased on the evening of the fire?"

"I certainly did. I took a taxi from my home, and went to Bee Cottage to see Ellen Ratcliffe. I arrived at ten minutes past seven, by my watch. We—that is, the taxi driver and I—saw the glow of the flames through the sooty window." Her voice was gruff.

"Indeed. And the driver called the fire brigade, is that so?"

"I instructed him to do so, while I attempted to rescue my friend." A flutter of surprise wandered around the room, and the witness turned and stared at Jack, addressing her next words to her. "The front door was unlocked."

"Did you enter the house?" The coroner glanced at Jack too, so intense was the old woman's stare.

"I did. It was unlocked, which was out of character for Ellen. I pushed open the door, calling my friend's name loudly." She turned back to the coroner for a moment. "I looked inside the living room and when I saw . . . when I saw that life was extinct, I returned to the garden to await the emergency services." She looked back at Jack, her voice shaking. "I have never seen anything more shocking in my life. My friend, killed and burning like a pile of rubbish. Killed."

The word rattled and echoed around the silent court.

"Yes, yes, thank you, Mrs. Talbot."

"I have never known her to leave her front door unlocked. Indeed, if Ellen had one weakness, it was a paranoia that the house would be broken into."

"Yes. Thank you for your testimony. We will consider all the facts, of course." The coroner's voice was firm. "Please return to your seat."

The little figure slid down onto the floor and walked, not back to her chair, but through the courtroom and out of the double doors at the back. Her patent leather shoes clacked on the wooden floor. The assembly waited until the doors had swung back before they started talking again.

The rest of the inquest was straightforward, and the verdict of accidental death was recorded. Jack was already pushing the doors open when she heard the word, and she looked around for the old woman. She found her outside, smoking a cigarette under a NO SMOKING sign, defiantly blowing the blue haze against an office window.

"Mrs. Talbot?"

"You came." Her face twisted up into a grimace. "They didn't listen. In thirty years, I have never known Ellen to leave the front door unlocked. It wasn't just unlocked, you know, the door had been forced open. The police didn't believe me."

"Why didn't you say so?"

The old woman scowled at her. "I told the police. They shuffled me off like I was demented. They said the frame was too old and rotten to prove the house was broken into."

Jack leaned against the wall and brushed away a tendril of smoke. "Who would want to hurt Ellen?"

The old woman snorted, and stood on tiptoe to stub the cigarette out on the sign. "Health nazis all of them," she muttered. "I'm eighty-four, and a pack a day and a few nips of sherry will keep me going. Ellen, young woman, knew things," she said, looking at Jack with the intense stare. "Things that were threatening her. And Magpie's coming?"

"Maggie, yes."

"I knew her when she was just a girl visiting Ellen on her school holidays. I never liked her much," she added. "Full of modern, New Age tripe. Smart girl, though."

"You said Ellen would never have left the door unlocked.

But she knew you were coming, didn't she? Maybe she left it open for you."

"You haven't been at the cottage long, have you? Even if Ellen did, the door would have locked itself, or stuck. The place is like a prison, it protects itself." She started walking down the road, rolling with a crab gait on legs that looked bowed. "Come on, I need to show you something. I hoped Magpie would come, but you'll have to do."

Maisie's house wasn't far away, but the old woman paused for breath a few times, spat orange phlegm onto the pavement and started off again. Her home was a tiny Victorian end of terrace, the only one in the row with the original windows, the frames painted a garish green and peeling into the wind. Jack looked up the stone walls, hardly an inch of which was free of ivy, lichens or moss. It made a vertical garden to make up for the tiny concrete forecourt in front of the house. Ellen unlocked the door and Jack followed her inside. The house looked about twelve feet across and the door led straight into a living room.

Inside the house every surface was covered with ornaments. Books and china sat on shelves, each in its own place, and the whole lot was embedded in a layer of dust and ash. The room reeked of tobacco smoke and the walls had a brown glaze, enhanced by the light feeling its way around heavy curtains, half drawn, and the nicotine-yellow window.

Cats were plumped like cushions on an upright sofa and two armchairs. A pair of tabbies and one black cat, which stared with luminous eyes for a moment before slinking off, and a fat ginger took up most of the sofa. Maisie led the way through to a back room, a sort of kitchen, equally cluttered.

"Sit down," she said, pulling out an old chair that looked full of woodworm.

"Thank you." Jack sat carefully on the chair, but apart from a few creaks, it held her weight.

Maisie took Jack's chin in one hard, knobbly hand. The fingertips dug into her face before she could object, as if they were reaching for jaw and cheekbone. Maisie leaned down, her tobacco scent adding to what smelled like lavender and mothballs. The old woman stared into one of her eyes, then the other. When she let go, Jack's teeth were clenched.

"You're not a witch." The old woman turned away and reached for a battered, blackened kettle, and put it on the hob of a cooker as old as the one in Ellen's kitchen. She lit the burner with a trembling match, the gas lighting with a whoosh. "You aren't a witch. But you're not . . ." She turned her gaze back to Jack. "I don't know what you are."

"I'm Jackdaw Hammond. Maggie is my foster mother." Jack looked around the kitchen. "She brought me up." The room was square, lined with stained and torn floral wallpaper. In the middle was a faded table with a Formica top, wobbling on spindly legs and surrounded by three mismatched chairs. The underlying smell was sharp and caught in Jack's throat—cat urine, stale food, and drying herbs. Along the ceiling was a rail, hung with bunches of dried stems, some dusty and brown, some still green.

"Jack for short?" The old woman poured water, clinked cups. "I don't have any sugar."

"That's fine—no, black is fine, too." The milk seemed to have separated, but Maisie still poured some into her own cup. Jack hoped the hot water would kill anything living in it.

"So. Ellen was murdered, you believe that?" She sat on another of the old chairs, peering over the rim of her cup at Jack, her head on one side like a bird.

"Who would murder an old lady?"

Maisie waved her free hand. "That I already know. What I need to do is prove it."

Jack looked into the brown brew. She could see rings of previous use lining the mug, and put it back on the table. "You may have your suspicions, but all the evidence points to an accidental death. She was . . . a bit eccentric, a bit strange at the end by everyone's account. She wasn't looking after herself very well."

"Of course she wasn't." Maisie slurped her hot tea, with every appearance of enjoyment. "She was under siege from the Dannicks."

Jack stood up, looking around at the kitchen. The garden, which she could see through a steamed-up side window, looked almost as overgrown as Bee Cottage's. "Do you mean Henry Dannick?"

"They're big landowners around here. They say they were descended from Vikings. They own the land around the cottage. They have married into the Ratcliffes over the years and I know Ellen had Dannick cousins."

"Henry Dannick came to the house." She looked down at the old woman, meeting her dark eyes. "He wanted a herbal tincture that Ellen used to make for his family."

Ellen snorted. "Describe him."

"I don't know. Fifties. Tall, heavy but not fat. Good-looking, strong jaw, blue eyes, dark hair." She shrugged. "He was very persuasive, told me a child is really sick. Ellen used to make a hair-root tincture for him, apparently, and he wants us to supply it instead."

"Tincture, he said, did he?"

"I don't understand."

Maisie finished her tea and folded her arms across her slight chest. Her hands were large for her body, the fingers gnarled as tree roots. "Sir Henry Dannick, the man you met, is eight or ten years younger than me."

"What? No—"

"And the grandson you spoke about? He's seventeen or eighteen by now." Maisie cackled at the expression on Jack's face.

"I don't understand." The man Jack had met seemed too young to have a grandson of that age. She leaned on the plastic table for a moment, then realized how sticky it was and moved back. Perhaps Maisie's potion worked like Maggie's did, as part of a spell. "What's this tincture for, anyway?"

"Ah. There's a story." Maisie lit another cigarette, and made herself comfortable on her chair. "It started with Thomazine Ratcliffe back in the fifteen hundreds. She was the first woman to live at Bee Cottage: her husband built it. But she didn't have any children, and she kept bees and grew herbs for the locals. Then one day, according to legend, one of the Dannick sons rode past and saw her working in the garden. The walls were just enough to keep the animals in, then. He raped her, and she got pregnant. The story goes, she didn't tell her husband but named the child 'Amyas,' beloved." She dragged a deep breath through the cigarette and puffed blue smoke across the room. "But every day, tending the garden, she found stones, and placed them on the wall, building them higher. Legend has it that her precious trees dug them up for her, to keep the Dannicks out."

"So this Amyas—"

"Got sick. He grew weak as he got older. Like the Dannick boy, Callum, some muscular dystrophy thing. The Dannick boys sometimes get it, especially the golden-haired ones, the ones they call the 'Dannick Lions.'"

Jack leaned back, making the chair squeak more fiercely. "And this Thomazine found a cure for her son?"

"The Dannicks had a cure, of sorts, but it made them mad. Thomazine was learning herbal medicine from her mother, Margery. They made up this potion to save the boy. In the end, the Dannicks acknowledged Amyas as one of theirs and some-how, with the treatment and being brought up alongside the Dannicks, he got better. There's even a picture of him up at the castle."

"So, Thomazine had to deal with her rapist?" Jack looked around the kitchen, now her eyes had adjusted to the gloom.

"To save her child? Of course she did." Maisie stubbed out

her cigarette and struggled to her feet. "Get my walker, will you? I'm a bit stiff."

Jack saw a frame by the back door, and put it in front of Maisie. "This Callum has the same disease?"

"And the Dannicks need the potion to finish their ritual."

Jack stepped back as Maisie gripped the handle and started to shuffle forward. "So this is a magical cure?"

Maisie cackled a laugh. "Yes, why would they get Ellen to make it, otherwise? That's not all, though." She pushed the walker forward in increments toward the back door, which streamed with condensation like the windows.

Beyond the kitchen was a single-glazed lean-to, housing an old twin tub washing machine, a rusty chest freezer and the door to the garden. On the top of the freezer was a cage about the same size, partly covered with a floral curtain. As Maisie shuffled over the floor, a rustling like dry leaves alerted Jack to the living creature inside. With a flourish that made the unseen bird flap, Maisie whipped off the cloth. She revealed a large bundle of black feathers, sheened with violet and green on the wings. The bird turned its head to glare at them, hunched in the inadequate enclosure. The beak seemed too heavy for its sleek head, one brown eye closely observing Jack. The feathers were tattered, and new shafts were sprouting along the length of one shoulder.

"It's a raven." Jack was enchanted. She had lived in the shadow of a rookery most of her life, and she and Maggie had rescued corvids—members of the crow family—but she had never seen a raven up close.

"It's just a young one; Ellen was bringing it on. I took it for her when she started worrying about the Dannicks. I should have taken the cat, too, but I thought my tabbies would fight with him."

"She knew something was going to happen?"

The old woman held out a bowl of cat biscuits that had been

soaking in water, by the look of it. "Here, you can feed him. He's tried to tear my fingers off a few times already. If you don't take him, I think I'll have to get the RSPCA to come in."

"No, I'll take him."

The old woman leaned on her walker, her face suddenly sad. "She said she got the order for the potion back, I don't know, before Christmas. I don't know what that meant, exactly, but she took the money. You'll have to ask the solicitor; he's got all the details. But she was terrified."

Jack took the bowl, and the bird cocked its head with interest, but his eyes were set on her face. Suddenly, she became aware how vulnerable she was. "Come on, my lovely boy." She reached for the door but his beak was there first, stabbing through the bars, clunking off the metal dish. "Wow, you're quick aren't you?"

On impulse, she took a softened biscuit and, over a startled objection from Maisie, held out her hand slowly—slowly—and the bird tapped forward with his beak, taking the food and just brushing her fingers. The second biscuit went the same way, and with the third he just pecked her hand a bit harder, as if he was warning her off. She put the bowl in the cage while he was distracted swallowing his food.

"I'll take him as soon as the builders have gone. He needs to get out of that cage, anyway. It's miles too small, his tail feathers are broken."

Maisie snorted. "She used to give him the run of the house. Mind you, it's a mystery to me how you can tell if it's a boy or a girl."

"Body language. He's one of last year's babies." Jack blew softly through the bars of the cage, and the bird lifted the tiny feathers on its forehead. "Look, he's flirting with me." She turned to Maisie. "Tell me what you know about Ellen and the Dannicks. What happened when they ordered this potion?"

"I don't know." Maisie stepped back into the warmth of the

kitchen, rubbing her arms. "But I can tell you they killed her for something in that garden. She knew—we knew—about the wild hunt."

"Hunt?"

"There's been rumors for generations that the Dannicks hunt poachers to their death. Ellen believed it was somehow part of the healing ritual, linked to the potion."

"Say I believe you." She'd heard stranger things as a dealer in magic-related items. With a last look at the bird, Jack shut the door to the lean-to. "Have you any idea what this hair-root is or how to make the potion?"

"Hair-root is an herb, but I don't remember seeing it. But there are details in Thomazine's book."

"Which we can't find."

Jack watched a smile crease Maisie's face into even more wrinkles. "It's there. She put it somewhere safe."

"We went through the whole house, and threw almost everything into Dumpsters. We kept a few bits of furniture to clean up, but there weren't any old books."

"You have to know where to look." She hunched up her shoulders.

"And you know?"

"When Magpie comes. I'll show her where the book is, but not before."

"I can't see the need for all this secrecy."

Maisie started the slow turn back toward the living room. "Ellen died defending that book."

"So you say, but . . ." Jack steadied the old woman by the elbow as she struggled with a step. Maisie coughed a few times, then got her balance.

"Which, means, young Jackdaw, that the Dannicks were prepared to kill for it."

Chapter 12

It is said that nowhere do diamonds and gold gleam so brightly as against the lagoons and canals of Venice. The Mediterranean moon looks down on us players, and Venice is the stage. All is show, but underneath, all is corrupt like flowers on a corpse.

—EDWARD KELLEY, 1586, Venice

L ORD MARINELLO ARRANGED FOR ME TO BE TRANSPORTED to the house of Count Contarini at dusk. The count, I had learned from Marinello, was a powerful and feared member of the ruling council. Not the government as such but a far more sinister conclave that had the power of summary judgment and execution upon the people of Venice. I was to travel openly and be observed at all times lest I plot treason. In my borrowed velvets I looked like an English lord, which imposture I planned to maintain. Certainly, had Dee and I returned to England, such honors would likely have followed.

The trip was short and by water. I was handed from one of the narrow boats by a servant, who carried my bag of books. When we entered the beautiful hall, the walls were painted with scenes of nymphs and satyrs. The floor was of polished stones laid in great patterns. I was taken by a different servant up a flight of steps that meandered gently to the upper floor. I protested the loss of my books, but was swept along into a salon much like Lord Marinello's, if more richly caparisoned. My eyes took in the golden candle holders and gilded plates, portraits with heavy frames dripping with gold leaf over carved fruit. I could see nothing like the ancient carving I had hoped to see; indeed it was my reason for traveling to Venice.

There were six or seven black-suited men standing about the room like guards. The chairs, and there were many, were covered with velvet in a midnight blue. The single nobleman who sat upon one was equally well dressed. Scarlet robes draped his form, and his heavy-lidded eyes regarded me. Brown eyes, I divined, to match brown hair untouched by time, although something in his face made me think him older. If one man may describe another as such, he was a man of dark beauty such as one sees in paintings or frescos all over Venice.

"Lord Kelley. Welcome." He spoke in English, and inclined his head. As I gave him an English bow, I noticed the servant enter, with my books and papers unpacked in his hand. I decided it was politic to hold my words.

"It is a great honor, your lordship," I replied in Latin. This seemed the best way to address this great man.

"You have a letter for me, I hear?"

I rose from my bow, and stepped toward the count. As I did so, two of the men around him, whom I had hardly noticed, stepped forward. "I—"

The seated man waved a languid hand much adorned with rings, and the guards stepped back. I reached the servant holding my books and took them, rummaging through them to the missive Lord Dannick had written. The fellow then retrieved my books.

"Here is the letter of introduction written by my patron, my lord." I held it out to him, but another of the black-clad men took it. For the first time, I glanced at this man's face, and saw he was an African, as dark-skinned as one of the queen's pages. Embroideries across his coat marked him as the more senior of the men. He opened the letter, scanned it quickly, and spoke to the count in the liquid notes of the Venetian tongue.

Throughout, the count stared at me, his head inclined toward his servant. Finally, he waved the man away.

"Enrico tells me that your interest here is as a natural scientist, Master Kelley."

I bowed.

"I have heard of your work with Dee in Prague and Vienna." His quick eyes stared at me, perhaps to gauge my response. "Your work with King Istvan, in Krakow, also. Magical work."

I waited, knowing what the letter said, but being unsure as to its entire meaning.

"You lodge with Marinello, I hear?"

"Indeed, your Excellency." I was still unsure as to the correct honorific. "My lord."

"Lord Contarini will suffice, Master Kelley." He flashed a smile at me, baring long white teeth through the dark beard. "I have a great interest in your 'natural science' myself. We must compare treatises on the subject."

Now I knew he would take me seriously. He wanted to see my books, like any scholar.

"I have some in Latin, my lord," I suggested, "but some are in base German or English. I would be happy to translate anything you have a special interest in. The alchemical text is in Latin, by Sendivogius, recently acquired in Poland. It is in the bundle your man is holding."

"I read German but poorly, and English not at all." But his long teeth smiled in a way that belied his words. "But I would be grateful to see this—Sendivogius, you say?"

"A young man of promise," I said, knowing King Istvan's patronage had embraced him, thus enhancing my own reputation. "And one who might visit Venice, with the right sponsor."

He indicated that I should sit upon one of the chairs, and

waved away most of the servants. Enrico stayed close, holding my books even as my fingers itched to take them.

"I shall arrange an invitation." He pressed the fingers of one hand into the palm of the other, watching me. "The carving your patron wishes you to see is very ancient and precious to my family."

I smiled and nodded. "My sponsor is a rich and clever man. He simply wishes a sketch so he can compare it to his own artifacts."

"But perhaps he would wish to publish it." He pressed his palms together in a position of prayer. "This is the emblem of my family, Master Kelley, the symbol of our name and prosperity. It is not to become the property of the world."

I stood and bowed, my hands clasped together. This, at least, was part of the plan. "I understand completely. Then, if it is possible, may I simply report privately to Lord Dannick? We have been fortunate to discover a second Roman carving of great magical significance, and my Lord Dannick wishes to discern the differences between them, if any."

"A second plaque was rumored, but believed ground into rubble by soldiers." His look was still and piercing, but I saw some interest nevertheless.

"An evil report." I bowed more deeply. "My Lord Dannick divined your interest and sent me with a likeness of his own stone carving as a gesture of goodwill and scholarliness. He asks only that I compare his stone to yours, by actually viewing it."

He exchanged glances with his manservant Enrico, who appeared to be following our conversation easily. "Such a drawing—is it in your papers?"

"A drawing of such importance would never be trusted to be carried around when it might be lost." I did not add that I had carried it into Venice within my underclothes for fear of just such an event, nor that it was almost the only thing Bezio had not divested me of.

He lifted a hand to half cover a smile, and I knew that he had heard the manner of my welcome into Venice.

"Please sit," he said, "and take wine with me. I feel we shall become friends. After all, we are both interested in the most ancient of magics, of my Roman ancestors." He waved a white hand at his servant. "Put those books down, Enrico, and get us good wine."

Enrico placed my books upon a small table, much carved and inlaid with mother of pearl in the pattern of a snarling animal's head. He served my wine first, bowing as if to a prince.

The count drank his blood-red wine from a glass as beautiful and ornamented as my own, swirling lines of bubbles within the glass, tinted red toward the base such as I have never seen before.

"What is Lord Dannick's understanding of the carving?" he asked.

I took a deep breath. "Lord Dannick's family is blessed with great health and strength, my lord, save one weakness. Some of its sons are born with a crippling 'falling disease' that weakens them unto death before they reach manhood. The family believes that the tablet describes an ancient cure for this ailment."

"Interesting." He stroked his beard, his eyes on my face until I lowered my own.

"Then Lord Dannick's son took himself a local woman named Thomazine Ratcliffe, and got her with child. This boy developed the family sickness, and Thomazine and her mother, who are renowned healers, found a cure for him. The boy, Amyas, thrived and now acts as steward for the Dannicks." I did not mention that Lord Dannick's son had forced himself upon the woman, who was a witch and the daughter of witches, or that he had suffered an accident that had crippled him when he returned to her land.

"Using the ritual from the English tablet?" Contarini looked at Enrico. "And is the boy as the other Dannicks?"

"Nay, my lord. The Dannicks are a fierce, warrior race, reckless and dangerous. Gentle Amyas is much loved upon the estate, even by his father and grandfather. The Dannicks wonder if the stone holds some mystery that they have misread."

"Perhaps they have. I shall think on it, Master Kelley." He smiled at me, his head a little tilted, as if trying to divine my thoughts. "I am invited to a private meeting of fellow students of the occult. The only way I can meet with others who share our interest is to do so in secret. Do you understand?"

I nodded, sipping the wine. My glance strayed to Enrico, still as a statue, his face the color of old oak and his fingers hovering over my books. "What is your interest in natural science, my lord?"

"Ah. I would be foolish to answer, even with my loyal Enrico here. Every wall in Venice, every boat and church has ears. And even rumors can be reported to the council."

I frowned, putting the heady wine back on the table with great care. "My understanding was that you are an esteemed member of this council?"

"I am. Therefore none is more suspected. Our mutual friend, your host, is already under suspicion."

"I see." Though, in honesty, I did not understand.

"Will you attend this meeting with me?"

"I should be honored, Lord Contarini." I was filled with excitement at gaining access so easily into the inner circle of sorcerers I had heard whispers of as far away as Prague, Vienna and London. "My lord, may I ask your advice?"

He smiled, and waved for Enrico to refill my goblet.

I continued. "Lord Marinello asks that I meet an acquaintance of his. He has an interest in an experiment Dee and I attempted last year."

"Indeed?" He feigned disinterest but I could see he knew

something of our sorcery. "He will not dare visit you at Marinello's. Anyone who did so could be impeached."

I was confused. "Then how may I meet this gentleman?"

"I too have heard the rumors. This guest of the doge himself has offered many *scudi* for the pleasure of a private introduction." He waved his glass at me. "And many more for the person who arranges such an introduction. Do not be fooled by Marinello's glitter, he is close to bankruptcy."

"Surely not." I dissembled, but Contarini just shrugged.

"He is an adventurer, an amusing scoundrel. Let him make the introduction; it will give him a few more months before he has to sell some more land. Or a few more *scudi* to gamble away."

"I would be honored to be able to pay back my benefactor, my lord."

"Have you heard, Master Kelley, about the Carnevale that starts within a few days?"

Lord Dannick had explained this to me, a little. It is a season of events where the people, nobles and commoners alike, make merry behind masks and costumes. "I understand that society takes a holiday."

"Then tell him to bring you to the ball held at the house of Isabella Grimani, my mistress, two nights hence." He waved a hand and Enrico gave him a square of card on which he inscribed a message in a flowing hand. He gave it to me—a card of invitation to a dance at a grand house. "I will make the introduction possible under the guise of the entertainment."

I reached for my books and, after the slightest resistance, tugged them from Enrico's hands. "Thank you, my lord." I tucked the card within a book.

"I look forward to seeing you in company with others who share our interests."

I bowed, and watched Enrico open the door for me. He smiled at me, his even teeth very white against his dark skin, and I found I liked the fellow. I nodded my thanks, and he bowed in response.

I had but to step outside to be bundled by Marinello's servants into the waiting boat. Clearly my sea captain really did not trust Count Contarini, who seemed a pleasant and educated fellow that I was glad to set among my friends. Wolves indeed.

Chapter 13

The garden stretches against the house, defending itself and its occupants. The soil flexes under the weight of the life it carries, millions of beings as small as pollen or as large as trees. Everywhere, the strands of death-seeking fungi wind, weaving a story. An elder tree withers, too old to regenerate. The threads reach into the wood, eating it from the inside. Water pools from a broken gutter, filaments of fungus sipping from the dampness. Under the corpse the juices run rich as wine, full of organics that taste like life, and sporing, and growth.

JACK AND SADIE HAD MOVED INTO THE NEWLY PLASTERED cottage, but the garden was as oppressive as ever. Jack unlocked the back door, which creaked open under the weight of foliage pressing against it. If anything, there seemed to be more branches reaching into the doorway, as if stretching in for Jack. She tucked her gloves into her jacket sleeves, took a deep breath, and started hacking with the loppers. After a few minutes she was hot, the kitchen floor was obstructed by a heap of branches and leaves, and she had barely made a dent in the mountain of green. She piled the cuttings into a heavy-duty bag, flattening it further with one booted foot, before turning back to the task. She couldn't see where she had been cutting; the hedge seemed to have re-formed. Cursing the low light, she forced herself against the leaves, reaching through layers of brambles so she could reach the thickest branches with the loppers. There—a bramble stem almost as wide as her wrist, which gave way after a couple of hacks. Then, just out of reach, another trunk with maybe a dozen branches arcing off it straight toward the kitchen. She stood on tiptoes to reach farther into the hedge of thorns. It was only when she tried to pull back that she realized she was caught somewhere.

She lifted her arm away from one bramble, only to find it was held above on a bigger one. Pulling back just seemed to lock them into the weave of her coat. She managed to glance at her body, to see stems wound around her jeans, over her shoulders, and when she looked up, one was dangerously close to her face. She couldn't move as much as a hand. She panicked, trying to move, her breath coming hard, but the spines dug in deeper, through her jacket, catching in her skin. When she tried to lift a knee a dozen thorns reached into her leg, pain shooting through her. She stopped struggling.

A chorus of rooks started up from the trees at the back of land. They sounded as if they were laughing at her with their raucous calls. Maybe in revenge for being evicted from the house—she tried not to think of them coming to investigate while she literally couldn't move.

"Sadie!" she called, trying to catch her breath. "Sadie!" Nothing. The girl was probably listening to music with her headphones on.

Twenty minutes later Jack had cramp in both shoulders from holding her arms above the thorns prickling her skin. The light was going fast, and without the work she had cooled down. She could feel something trickling down her thigh, and suspected it was blood.

"Sadie!" she bellowed for the hundredth time, trying not to

struggle again out of sheer frustration. Nothing. Finally, a ringing from the newly installed doorbell.

At last, movement. Jack could hear the girl's light footsteps cross the landing above, and down the stairs.

"Sadie!" This time it came out hoarse, but the girl didn't divert her steps to the back of the house, but went toward the front door.

"Maggie!" Sadie's shout was full of warmth and welcome.

Jack's breath caught in her throat in something that felt like a sob. She leaned forward a few inches, jerking her head up as a thorn stabbed into her cheekbone, but the movement ensnared more branches in her hair.

"Help!" she managed and, finally, footsteps hurried down the hallway.

"Jack!" Maggie's voice sounded like it was just a little amused. "Oh, you idiot, you can't just hack at a witch's garden! I told you to wait for me."

Her hands reached over to detach the bramble from Jack's face. She seemed to almost stroke the leaves and the barbs popped out of Jack's cheekbone, where they were snagged.

"I just wanted to get to the back windows—" Jack mumbled in protest, but Maggie was talking to Sadie.

"Here, put these gloves on. Just unhook them very gently. I'll ask for permission to prune them back a bit."

"Permission?" Jack's temper bubbled to the surface with a few angry tears. "A machete and a flamethrower might be more—" Her voice faded. It felt as if the bands were tightening, the thorns in her leg digging deeper. "OK, OK, I'm sorry!" She tried to find some calm center that might reassure the plants, even when the logical part of her mind scoffed at the thought. She was never very good at this back-to-nature stuff.

"Jack, shut up." Maggie's voice had a note of alarm that made Jack stand still, and close her eyes. "Let us do it. That's right,

Sadie, you've really got the knack. Think of the plants as just trying to look after each other—"

While they worked, Jack could feel a tear track down one cheek and then the plant prickling her face shifted, almost as if it were exploring the salty liquid.

"Right," Maggie said, with some authority. "I'm going to prune these big branches back carefully, then they should let you go."

"That's what I was doing!" Jack mumbled, trying to stand still even as the edge of a leaf explored her chin and something pricked her eyelid. "It's going for my eyes—"

"Shut up, Jack. Stand completely still and think nice, planty thoughts. Think of hot sunshine, imagine your feet in water."

A few snipping sounds, close to Jack's ear, then the brushing of leaves and Maggie murmuring something in Latin. The barbs just caught in Jack's eyelid were somehow released. Sadie reached down and popped out, one by one, a long strand of thorns that felt like they were deeply embedded in Jack's thigh.

Sadie was talking to the brambles. "Poor plants, just minding your own business, just growing, here you go—"

"Ow. Ow." Jack tried to stay still but the pain was intense and, worse, there was an intense itching.

"Look. Look at your arm." Maggie was serious.

Jack opened her eyes and turned her head a fraction, very carefully.

Her right arm was completely encased in greenery, maybe forty or fifty branches whipped and woven around her wrist and forearm. "What—?"

"Think of the garden as a sentient colony of interrelated beings, not a wall of inanimate objects," Maggie said. "This is a witch's garden, so it's more reactive than most, but all gardens do this to some extent."

"But at Rook Cottage I just weeded and planted—"

"You were trying to cultivate, you were conserving the

trees, pruning out diseased wood. You weren't trying to destroy it." Maggie stood by Jack's side, pressed against her, and stroked away brambles and ivy stems. "You never did get this green witchcraft stuff, did you, just the fighting spells."

It was true, Jack's limited manipulation of magic was confined to protection and aggression, which had proved very helpful on occasions. "Was the garden always like this?"

Maggie untangled a particularly prickly stem. "I remember when my grandmother had the cottage, it was always a bit wild, but no, it was lovely. A little orchard, a lot of vegetables, the bees of course. And the elder trees."

"Maisie Talbot said—did I tell you I met her? She told me a bit about Ellen."

Sadie leaned in the other side now Jack's flanks were clear, murmuring something that sounded a lot like "nice bramble."

"Maisie? I'm surprised she's still alive." Maggie's voice had a drop of acid in it. "She and Ellen were good friends."

"She said she knows where Thomazine's papers are. I suppose you know all about them?"

Maggie's hands stilled for a long moment. "The book's still here?"

Jack's left arm sagged when the last bramble holding it up was removed and a cramp stabbed through her shoulder muscles. "Oh, thank God," she said, turning away to allow Maggie to work on her right arm. "She won't tell me, only you. Why?"

"If there was one reason to break into this house it was to get the book. Thomazine's journal. I've only seen it a few times but—there you are." She undid Jack's coat. "Just slide out of your jacket."

"Ow. Ow." Jack's jeans were studded with dozens of curved hooks that Sadie had detached from the stems that had trapped her. Spots of blood oozed through the cotton when she pulled them out.

Maggie looked over her glasses to remove another thorn from Jack's neck. "Stand still," she fussed. "There."

Jack felt along her forearms. "Ouch. It was trying to kill me."

Maggie tutted, untangling more branches from Jack's hair, tugging a little. "Thomazine, the first witch here, planted that garden. Everyone who has lived here since came from her line, and her tradition. The garden is used to a more collaborative approach than having a machete taken to it."

Jack turned to the door, filled with a solid wall of greenery once again, a few cut branches oozing sap onto the kitchen floor. "How am I supposed to shut this?"

"Like this." Maggie walked to the brambles, ran her hands softly over the leaves, tucking a few stray ones out of the way, and pushed the door shut. It still took all of Jack's strength to press it firmly enough to shoot one of the bolts.

Jack licked a drop of blood off the back of her hand. "How are we ever going to get out there, then?"

Maggie picked up the kettle and filled it from the tap. "It responds to the right approach." Sadie had scrubbed the sink and tap—under protest—but it was still encrusted with limescale. "I hope a new sink and tap are on the list."

"The kitchen units are in the spare room, waiting to be made up and put in." Jack held out her hands in the light of the single bulb. "I think I'm allergic to brambles. These scratches are swelling up."

Sadie perched on the single remaining kitchen chair. The table had been salvageable, but most of the chairs had been riddled with woodworm and covered in bird shit. "This Sir Henry something, he came here and offered thousands for the book," the girl said. "And some potion. Tell her, Jack."

Jack turned around, brushing off stray leaves. "Dannick, his name was."

Maggie opened her mouth as if she were going to say something, then closed it again. "I know Ellen used to make a potion for the family. I don't know exactly what was in it."

"Well, they are desperate for it." Jack took the cup of tea Maggie was offering. "Thank you. I thought I was going to be stuck there for hours."

"Why didn't you call me?" Sadie looked up at her, as inquisitive as a bird.

"I did. Repeatedly." Jack sipped the tea. "Look, we should get back to the B&B. I could do with a shower and about three hundred plasters."

Maggie sighed. "I was hoping I could stay here."

The room, lined with damp plaster on each wall, looked even less hospitable to Jack. "Why?"

"We need to start connecting with the house so we can get out in the garden."

Sadie hugged her knees, curled up on the chair. "We could. It might be fun, you know, now the rubbish is all gone."

"I thought you said this was a terrible house?" Jack could see the appeal of staying, and at least she could rescue the bird sooner. "We'll see. There are plenty of rooms at the guesthouse in the meantime. And there's a lovely restaurant around the corner, if you don't mind square plates and fancy sauces."

Maggie laughed, steering Jack into the hall. "Let's have a look at what else you've done, then."

Apart from the still wrecked living room, plaster hacked away and ceiling removed, the house was feeling fresh and clear. The dining room was cleaned up, the floor repaired, and newly stripped and primed window frames were ready for painting. The fireplace had been cleared and the chimney swept, ready for the woodburner which stood shrouded in plastic to one side.

Maggie placed a hand on the wall, and stood, as if listening. "We could keep this as the living room, it's the same size as the other one. The stove is nice."

"It's drafty." Jack looked down at the gaps between the scrubbed floorboards.

"Well, we'll pick up a carpet remnant and cover the boards. And putting the burner in will seal off the chimney. That should help, and we'll get some coal and logs in. What do you think, Sadie?"

The teenager, looking tired and pale again, leaned against the door frame. "We need to do the symbols in here. Jack did them upstairs in the front bedroom so I could sit up there, but I think I need some downstairs too."

Jack turned to Maggie. "I didn't want to upset the builders. I think I'll do them in the silver ink Felix gave me."

"When are they back? The plasterers?"

Jack wrapped her arms around herself. "Monday. I thought I could make a start on the garden while they weren't here, so we could work on the back of the house."

"And look for the book. You're sure you haven't thrown it out by accident?"

"I'm sure." Jack turned her head to look over her shoulder.

Maggie sighed. "Well, we'll come back tomorrow and see what we can do. Come on, Sadie, drink up and we'll go back to this B&B. Hopefully, once we've moved into the cottage, you can have Ches with you. Charley will bring him up, so you'll have some company."

Even the thought of Ches filled Jack with a longing for home, for the big wolf-dog. Jack could hear Maggie and Sadie chattering as she rinsed the mugs in the sink and started turning off lights. Dusk had darkened the rooms, filling the corners with shadows, yet the house felt less creepy, more welcoming than it had. As if she had been tested, and had passed in some way.

She walked out of the front door, barring the door with the new lock, and looked up at the blank windows. It felt as if something—maybe the house itself—was looking back.

Chapter 14

Within the Roman world were sects so dark and magical they were feared as monsters or demigods. That they survive today I have no doubt. Wielding such magic and ruthlessness, they perpetuate and grow, their devilish ways penetrating even unto the ruling houses and chapels of this land.

—EDWARD KELLEY, 1586, Venice

I WAS FORCED INTO A STRANGE IMPOSTURE WHEN I AT-tended the meeting of sorcerers. A man much as my own build wore clothes akin to mine own under a scarlet robe, and donned a mask. He then, with great ceremony, was taken onto a boat to be borne to some public ball or party, where no doubt he would despoil my reputation. I was clad safely in black like a servant, and carried by a hired boat to the conference with some of Count Contarini's associates at the house of his mistress.

I was handed a mask before I left the palazzo, a cunning face in silver foil attached to a bar which I was told to hold with my teeth. Thus would I be unable to speak, reveal my Englishness or my identity. The waterside doors were wide open, servants run-ning hither and thither with cloaks and torches, and we—Lord Marinello and I—were led in a slow-moving caravan of people in bright robes and masks. Many, like myself, did not speak, and it was left to those who did to fill the halls with chatter.

I was at liberty to stare at the Venetians at play. Many wore elaborate animal masks. A tall woman had one glittering with stones, like a peacock feather. Another was formed into the snarling face of a wolf. Suns and moons abounded, as well as many mouthless blank stares, like the mask I gripped between my own teeth. Men wore elaborate and padded cods within embroidered britches. The women were taller than the men in their raised soles, their feet contorted until they were almost on tiptoe. One lady, seeing my interest, placed one hand under the front panel of her dress. She slid it aside to reveal undergarments laced with stitched patterns and so fine her skin showed pink beneath. I turned away, grateful for the mask which covered the blushes of an Englishman.

It was a surprise then when a young boy came to my side and tugged upon my sleeve. He babbled something and gestured as if to follow him. I looked for Marinello, but he had already been absorbed by the crowd.

I stepped into the throng, but people allowed me to squeeze between them after the boy. He pulled me through a gap in the revelers and along a darker corridor, which I judged the servants' access. Then to a door, the light spilling through the crack 'twixt it and the frame, and the murmur of men's voices.

I pushed upon the door, and was confronted by a table, each tall chair with a man seated, each one in black clothing, each masked but the host. Contarini. He stood, and bowed to me, letting me bow before him in return.

"I am Count Contarini, fellow scientist," he said, in Latin. "It is my great pleasure to meet you, Master Kelley, late of Bohemia and England." His eyes flashed a warning, as I bowed again, wondering, what shall I say? Clearly he wished to pretend we were unacquainted. I took my mask off.

"My Lord Contarini," I said, after bowing so deeply I almost rubbed my nose on my knees. "I am thankful for the chance to meet with you. This is a great honor."

"Let me introduce you." Some let their masks fall, and I bent my head as each name was intoned. I recognized the cardinal, who scowled at me as before and grunted some greeting. Contarini sat in a throne-like seat at the middle of the table, and I bowed again. A servant carried over another chair, and I was encouraged to sit. The boy, darting about the room, set a goblet before me. I dared not drink, wondering at the purpose of the group.

Contarini smiled at me. "You must be wondering what house this is."

"Indeed, my lord." I allowed the wine to wet my upper lip, mimicked swallowing, and wiped my hand across my lips with every appearance of enjoyment. The boy scuttled up to me, and knelt, presenting me with a snowy napkin. I dabbed my lips with it.

"This is the house of my mistress, Isabella. Since she holds a ball for Carnevale, she allows me to meet with my learned friends in a private chamber."

I looked around the apartment we were seated in with some amazement. The room, though certainly smaller than those in Marinello's home, was painted with forest scenes and the furniture was all gilded. He smiled, the candlelight gleaming off his teeth.

"A lovely home." I was astonished that a whore should live so richly.

He laughed at my confusion. "Here women need not be confined by marriage, but play their own games. Isabella is of the *cortigiana onesta*, she is a free woman. I am one of her court. I am privileged to sit at her feet occasionally when she is in the mood for my games."

Several of the men smiled. One man's face was still masked but he looked at me through the holes of a mask of a resplendent sun, all gilded and glittering as if it were scattered with shards of glass. His gaze was intense upon me.

Contarini raised his goblet. "To our scientific endeavors, my friends!"

All but the masked man drank, and a buzz of murmured conversation spread around the room.

"Tell me, Master Kelley of England," one man said, grinning at me. "How do you fare with the great quest?"

I knew this meant transmutation, the very essence of alchemy, and wondered if they knew how close to success I really was. "I have some theories, of course—"

"We all have theories!" The man leaned back in his chair, and spoke more generally. "But we hear you have succeeded in changing mercury to some degree."

This trick I had done in Prague, being the dissolving by alchemical means of gold dust within mercury, then using "black element" to force the gold to bubble to the surface as if being created. Indeed, the process is but a step away from the creative transformation, and I believe I make more gold than I dissolve, but the gain is so slight it is difficult to measure.

"I am beginning to make progress," I said, cautiously, "in the area of purification."

A general conversation arose, largely conducted in Latin but also in their own language. "Tell us of your experiments with silver," one man, I forget his name, called out.

"I have, with my colleague Dr. Dee, transmuted twelve grains of silver into gold. This was observed by the royal astronomer of the court of His Imperial Majesty Emperor Rudolph."

More exclamations and some disbelief. Questions about our technique, which I politely lied about.

Then, a black-haired man much of my own age, leaned forward. "What of your help from the dark forces, Master Kelley? There are rumors about a man named Seabourne. Did he raise a demon to do his bidding?"

"Our investigations were without such assistance," I said. I took a draft of the sour wine, since no one seemed hostile. "Such interventions would be too dangerous." I shuddered inside at the abomination Seabourne had roused, a creature of hell itself.

"But not impossible." The words came from the masked man, and the others fell into silence, watching him. The voice, muffled somewhat by the mask, was familiar.

He wrapped a hand gloved in velvet about his goblet.

"I do not deal with demons, my lord," I said with dignity. "Such is the devil's work."

"Hard words from a man who jousted with the Báthorys, and lived to tell his story."

Then I knew that voice, and shrank back in my chair.

"Under duress of certain death," I stammered, "we did assist His Majesty King Istvan in preserving the life of an innocent woman." I could feel sweat prickle the skin of my brow and shoulders.

The man stood. He was tall and strongly built, wearing a robe which fell to his feet. He carried a sword as befitted a knight of the Holy Roman Empire, and his black hair was but lightly touched with gray over the mask.

"That woman is not saved, Master Kelley. She is in the thrall of a demon, a creature of death and darkness. You have created a repository to contain a monster."

He removed his mask with a flourish. In the light of the candles I saw him clearly, his glittering dark eyes, his crucifix on his breast.

It was Reichsritter Johann Konrad von Schönborn, of the

Holy Inquisition. I leaned back into my chair, my words strangled in my throat.

He turned to the company, extending his hands toward me in something of a flourish. "See, here is your sorcerer, my lords. He has created, with demonic forces, a fiend that feasts on children. Not just Transylvanian children, but now the babies of Venice and all Europe." He rested his hand upon the hilt of his sword.

A ripple of murmurs crept about the room as men whispered. He waited for the noise to stop while he stared at me, not with hostility but with the authority of the church, the empire and the yard of steel at his side. I swallowed my fears and stood also, gripping the table edge for support.

"Father Konrad," I said, and was pleased my voice came out as I had intended, strong but respectful. "If I can be of any assistance undoing the magics I was coerced into, tell me, and I am at your service."

He allowed a smile to touch his lips. "For the right price? Venality is your greatest sin, my son. That you will do aught for money—"

"Not anything, I assure you," I said, stung at the charge. My moral code, if uniquely my own, has its limits. "I wish with all my heart to undo that which we were compelled to do."

"You raised a demon, however unwillingly. Better you were dead—for God cannot forgive you such a sin."

There it was, the very thought that woke me in a sweat some nights, the fear that reached into my very sleep. "Then let me help put it right!" I exclaimed, much agitated. "Let me find a way to repent and put nature back."

He touched his crucifix, and it drew my eyes. "Come back to the church," he said, in heavily accented English. "Repent, confess, be forgiven."

My eyes stung with tears, for part of my conscience cried

out for confession, yet I had been converted Protestant these twenty years. "Let me repair what I have done. Let me make amends."

Finally, he nodded and spoke in Latin, that all might hear. "Let your alchemical experiments continue with great fortune, my lords. But do not dabble in raising demons, for there lies damnation, and all the torments of hell."

Chapter 15

The carcass lies beside an elder tree, putrefying. The garden reaches up and onto it, fingers the juices that ooze from orifices, punctures the loosening skin and suckles at the nectars within. Beetles swarm upon it, biting at the soft entrances, the eyes, the nostrils, the easy tunnel to the brain. The crows have cleared the way. They have feasted on the meat, and the beetles and maggots boil over the bones.

The garden rustles, and waits. Spring makes it restless, the trees throbbing with sap, flowers bursting into the light with each morning. It is a good time to replace the witch.

JACK WAS GROUTING THE NEWLY TILED KITCHEN WALL when she heard a knock at the door. Before she could react, Sadie had bounced down the stairs with a scream of "Charley!" and the next moment, Jack was hit with a hundred pounds of canine muscle and bone. She crashed into the new kitchen units, laughing at Ches's efforts to whine, bark and lick her face all at the same time. His tail was wagging so hard he couldn't keep his balance on two legs and dropped onto his haunches. She knelt down to hug him, to press her face into the soft pelt on his head. In one surge, all the pain of missing him caught up with her. Was it her imagination, or were there more white hairs around his gray muzzle?

"Six weeks—you'd have thought it was a year at least." Maggie reached out her arms to hug Charley, and squeezed her tight.

"I'm never babysitting Ches ever again," Charley managed, muffled by her mother's embrace. "He was a nightmare in the car and it's about a million miles."

Then it was Jack's turn for a hug from her foster sister, dressed as eclectically as ever in tie-dyed dungarees and a head scarf.

"But you're here now," said Jack. "And we've moved in. What do you think of the kitchen?"

Apart from one run of units containing the new sink and cooker, the room was bare boards, plaster and newly tiled walls. Jack had managed to trim back the brambles and ivy enough to patch the old windows, but the soft wooden frames had already allowed a few green fingers back in.

Charley ran her hand over the work surface. "The kitchen is great. It's big, isn't it? It was probably the whole downstairs of the cottage."

"Bill, the plasterer, said he thought this part was the original Tudor building." Jack rubbed Ches's head. "I am so pleased to see you both."

Maggie's lips twisted into a half smile. "It was built in the fifteen-fifties by Thomazine Ratcliffe and her husband, Henry. She was the first herbalist here, and a beekeeper." She brushed her fingers over a tiny leaf of ivy, sneaking in past the door frame. "That's her garden."

"What do you mean, her garden? She's been dead for hundreds of years." Charley sat down on one of the "new" second-hand kitchen chairs, and stroked Ches. "Oh, *now* you like me, vile mutt."

Maggie turned to face her and waved at the window, so plastered with leaves they looked almost black. "The story goes, Thomazine was married for ten years, but didn't have a baby. One day, a rich young man was riding by and he saw Thomazine in her garden, picking herbs, and he raped her. That produced a child, Amyas. The father is supposed to have tried to steal the child. But she built her garden to protect them from future attacks, and he was crushed by the wall collapsing on him."

The dog pattered to the front room. Jack opened a tin of cookies, baked by Maggie to christen the new oven. "And you think it still is protecting the cottage? Hundreds of years later?"

Sadie was squealing in the new living room, no doubt being squashed by the dog on one of the recently delivered sofas.

Charley took a cookie, and stretched back in the kitchen chair.

"Well, *you* didn't get very far," said Maggie. She looked at Charley. "Jack took a pair of loppers to the garden and it fought back."

Charley grinned. "I'm guessing, by the cuts on her face, that the garden won."

"It was a witch's garden," Maggie repeated. "Through the generations, even though Amyas fathered a very prosperous family and ended up in a manor house with many acres, the cottage was always left to the member of the family most able to live in it."

Jack brushed a sponge over the tiles, rubbing off excess grout. "So, the family was rich?"

"Amyas was, fathered by the eldest son of Lord Dannick, Lord Robert. He treated him well, paid for his education and settled a large estate on him." Maggie reached for a cookie for herself.

"We had a Dannick come here looking for an herb, Charley. Hang on—" Jack rummaged in a biscuit tin they were using for paperwork. "Here. Knowle Castle, Sir Henry Dannick."

Charley studied the card. "Do you remember what herb he was looking for?"

"Turn it over, I wrote the name on the back. There, black hair-root. Do you know it?"

Charley frowned. "I could ask around, but not off the top of my head."

"We haven't heard of it before." Maggie filled a bowl with water and put it down for the dog. "We haven't been able to find a Latin name, or a picture. Which is odd, given that I've been an herbalist for forty years."

"He said it was rare," Jack said. "He gave me the impression only Ellen knew where to find it. He said it was important to his grandson." She half smiled. "He didn't look old enough to have a grandson, to be honest, but Maisie says he's older than he looks. Maisie's a friend of Ellen's," she explained to Charley.

Charley looked around. "And you didn't find any old books, documents, that sort of thing?"

"Apparently this Thomazine kept a journal and it's somewhere in the property, but we can't find it. We haven't gone up in the loft yet, and the builder said there might be a small void under this floor." She stamped on the floorboards. "Maybe there's a cellar." She recalled the old woman. "Maisie said she knows where Thomazine hid the book. Or maybe she would recognize this hair-root in the garden somewhere. We tried to get outside—well, I did, anyway. But it's like a wall of green and prickles. It's constantly trying to get in."

Charley looked at the tendrils of ivy worming their way between the wood fibers. "Oh, my," she breathed, her breath misting the new glass. "You can almost see it growing."

Jack joined her, looking at the leaf-plastered pane. "Sadie says the plants are watching us." She was half joking, but Maggie's expression was serious.

"Watching, listening, feeling. That's an acre of garden planted by a witch and tended by generations of us."

Jack felt a shiver down her spine at the tone in Maggie's voice, as if she were whispering to the garden itself. Then Maggie turned to her with a broad smile. "Well, we'll worry about that tomorrow. Is the kettle on?"

Lighting a fire in the cottage seemed strange to Jack given the fate of the last occupant, but the new woodburner lit quickly and the dog flopped down in front of it, making it seem normal.

While Sadie was occupied with the Internet, Jack sat next to Charley. "How's business?"

Charley rolled her eyes. "I don't know how you deal with that old crook, I really don't."

"Pierce? He's OK, and he pays well. Some of the stuff he's looking for is a bit . . . dubious."

Charley glanced at Sadie, then lowered her voice. "Why does he want so many human bones?"

"I have no idea. I think he supplies a voodoo practitioner. I usually get them from Katarzyna Medway, she works with medical waste at the hospital."

Charley spread out her hands. "And it takes how long to deflesh amputated limbs? Yuck. Double yuck. I can't wait for you and Mum to come back and take over."

Jack smiled at her foster sister. "It's not all bones."

"No, it was a ton of nettles last week. I still have the stings to prove it. And owl pellets, which I had to dry off in the oven. The kitchen still stinks."

"Sorry." Jack couldn't help laughing at her expression. "But the money's good. Just don't trust Pierce at all. He'll cheat you in a heartbeat."

"Last time I went to meet him in broad daylight in a shop.

I thought the manager was going to call the police. But he got his goods and I got my money."

"He just handed it over?" Jack couldn't imagine the magic dealer just cooperating, especially with the slight girl.

"Well, I threatened to scream and say he had groped me." Charley grinned. "Who would've believed *him* in the underwear section of a women's clothes shop? He looks like a tramp. He grabbed the money and ran."

Sadie, surrounded by books, her music player, notebooks and colored pens, looked over at them curiously, then went back to tapping on Charley's tablet.

Maggie came in and sat on the end of the sofa beside the teenager. "So, what are you up to, Sadie?"

"I'm writing to Felix."

"Oh." Maggie shot a look at Jack, who looked away, down at the curling flames. "So—have you heard from him?"

"He texts me but he wants a proper e-mail." Sadie swiped her phone then held it out for Maggie to see. "Look at these pictures. He went to America, New Orleans. He's been there two weeks."

Jack stretched out on the new sofa and put her feet up with a sigh. Sadie was still weak, and reluctant to do more than paint a few walls, so fitting the kitchen units and all the odd jobs had fallen to her alone. At least she had new energy to do what needed to be done.

"What do you think of the house, Charley?" Jack looked up at the new ceiling, the duck-egg walls. It had been difficult restraining Sadie's taste for strong colors, but this one they both agreed on.

"It's great. Not exactly my taste, but then I'm going through a purple phase . . ."

"Well, I love it," Maggie said. "It's lovely. I remember staying here as a child, but it was always shabby and cluttered. It belonged to Ellen's mother. I spent a month here every summer, and most Christmases as well."

Sadie closed her notebook. "How long do we have to stay here?"

Maggie looked around the room. "It's not that bad, is it?"

Sadie shrugged. "It's just now I can get out there's nowhere to go."

Jack qualified that. "You can go out for a short period, Sadie, that's all. You need to be inside the circles most of the time."

"I just want some fresh air every day."

The car had circles inscribed into its roof and floor; Jack had scratched them in when the seats were out. It was a mobile haven for them both. "We go out for drives."

"It's not the same." Sadie waved at the front window. "The house is right on the road, but there aren't any pavements or anything. Where could I go for a walk, even for a few minutes?"

Maggie turned to look at Sadie, then back at Jack. "That's why we need to sort the garden out."

"How?" The question popped out of Jack before she could stop it, and was laden with doubt. "The plants grow back within a day. Some of the brambles are coming back through the back windows again. We can't even get scaffolding in to replace the rotten frames."

Maggie settled back against the cushions and stretched her feet toward the fire.

"You know about Thomazine?" She retold the story for Sadie's benefit. "When she was raped she unconsciously cast a protection spell. There's no evidence that she was a witch before. In fact, she was a famous beekeeper and grew herbs and fruit for the castle."

"What do you mean, 'unconsciously'?" It didn't make sense to Jack. The dog stood, shook himself, and trotted over to lay his head in her lap.

Maggie picked up one of Sadie's fallen pens. "Do you know about archetypes?"

Jack shrugged. She stroked the top of Ches's head. "I know the word."

"Think about the first groups of humans. Hunter-gatherers. There must have been people who were good at, say, hunting."

"OK." Jack glanced at Sadie, who was listening.

"Through the generations, hunters who spent most of their time together, produced children who were also hunters. Taller, more muscle mass, faster."

Sadie cocked her head on one side. "They were double hunters? I mean, both parents were hunters?"

"Exactly. Now, there must have been other roles within communities. Like—people who prepared food, people who cared for children, people who were good with animals. Or with magic. Magic was important to people who couldn't understand things like weather, the seasons, nature. It was their only explanation."

Jack smoothed Ches's thick pelt away from his deep-set gray eyes. They were the only thing that suggested the few husky genes rather than the wolf. "What you are saying is, these people tended to breed with each other. Concentrated the genes, that sort of thing."

"Exactly. As modern people, we all have some of those clusters of ancient genes. I believe we all have abilities that we received from our ancestors." Maggie clenched her hands together. "That's where I got my 'witch' genes from. Early shamans or magic users."

Sadie scowled. "I hate that idea, that a few lucky people have superpowers and the rest of us—"

"But that's the whole point, Sadie." Maggie's voice was passionate. "We all have one or two of these superpowers, but we just don't use them in our modern world. Look at Charley."

Charley raised an eyebrow. "Go on, what's my superpower?"

"What's the weather going to be like tomorrow?"

Charley lifted her head as if she were listening to something. "It's going to be drizzly overnight, dry tomorrow, maybe sunny in the afternoon. But I think it's getting colder." Her weather predictions were something of a joke when Jack was growing up, but she rarely planted something outside without checking with Charley first.

"There. What would be more useful for a hunter-gatherer community than someone who knew when a storm was coming, or a drought?"

Sadie ran her fingers through her very short, very red hair, the best they could do to change her appearance. She looked unconvinced, but on some level, it made sense to Jack. She stretched her toes toward the heat. The room was still very bare, just a thick rug covering scrubbed floorboards, a secondhand coffee table, and the two new sofas against the newly plastered walls. The woodburner glowed orange behind its glass door.

"So," Sadie started, "Charley's a weather guru, and you've got your witch genes. What's Jack's superpower?"

"Well, we know she's a fighter, a warrior, for one thing. And she's amazing with animals."

Sadie shrugged herself further into her sweater. "That just leaves me."

Maggie sat next to her. "I think you may have a superpower too."

Sadie started, then smiled. "How do you know that?"

"The garden does. It reacts differently to each of us. It recognizes you."

Jack pulled Ches's ears gently through her fingers, his eyes half closed in pleasure. "Sadie said something about the garden when we first got here."

"Well, it's watching us, isn't it? I mean, it's creeping up the walls, it comes in when we open a window." Sadie closed her notebook. "It sort of—hums."

"That's what I sense, too." Maggie smiled. "Let's try it out. Do you have a coat, Sadie? It's cold out, especially at the end of the afternoon."

Sadie jumped up, and steadied herself on the end of the sofa. "Sorry, my legs are half asleep," she joked, but Jack had seen her wobble more and more recently.

"I'll get your boots," she offered, going out to the car drawn up on the verge outside the house. She looked out, across the wild hedge behind a slumped stone wall, and behind that to the hillside. The afternoon sun touched the landscape with a golden light that touched the bare rock of the fell, raw scars between the close-cropped grass and swaths of heather. She got Sadie's garden boots from the back of the car. The girl's choice had been a floral pattern on a turquoise background. She looked back at the house, at the unmortared stone blocks that made up the front in various shades of dark gray and rust. The windows were lit with a fiery glow from the low sun, echoing the blaze that had taken the old woman. Around both sides of the house loomed elder bushes, threaded with brambles that felt along the front of the house as if going for the windows, like fingers reaching for eyes. For a moment, Jack felt a sting of fear, quickly suppressed. "Chainsaw," she muttered to herself. "Weed-killer." The foliage seemed to shudder, but she ignored it.

Sadie needed to lean on Jack's shoulder to pull on her boots. Maggie drew back the now oiled bolt and the door bounced inward a few inches. She opened it right up and half a dozen vines unfolded onto the floor.

Maggie stood in front of the wall of greenery and faced it, the stems draped across her boots. She gently stroked the larger leaves in front of her. "It doesn't mean to hurt anyone, it's trying to protect the cottage and the people who live here. It just needs to understand there's a new witch in the cottage."

Sadie touched her finger to a larger bramble to stop it falling through the doorway onto her, and flinched back. "Ow!"

"It's OK." Maggie took her hand, and Jack could see blood welling up on Sadie's skin. "It's tasting you. It can't help being covered in spikes. It will recognize you quickly now."

"Enough tree hugging," said Jack. "How do we get rid of all the weeds?"

"The garden needs more space, and the plants all need pruning. In the open, deer and rabbits naturally keep plants trimmed back but the wall keeps them out." Maggie frowned at Jack. "Plants, not weeds," she added. "Ellen had a fantastic collection of rare herbs, and they are all out there somewhere."

"Well, while you make friends with the *plants*, I'm going to take Ches out for a walk up the hill. Keep the fire lit. It's freezing out there."

Jack strode up the footpath toward the hillside. The ground underfoot was littered with stones too big to be gravel, just large enough to turn a boot. Ches bounded ahead of her, enjoying the freedom after weeks confined to walking on a lead with Maggie or Charley.

The grass was short, as if mowed by the wind itself; there were no sheep or rabbit droppings on the ground. She walked briskly, only slowing when the gradient increased enough to bring Ches's tongue out and his flanks heaved with effort.

She felt good. After years of increasing weakness and cold, she was enjoying new energy—in fact, supernatural energy, from one mouthful of blood. She felt as if she could fly up the path and leave Ches behind, if she needed to. The one conundrum she couldn't solve, even with the new clarity and life racing through her, was Felix.

It made her uncomfortable that Sadie was in regular contact with him, and that they often talked about Jack. She wouldn't speak to him. He was safer hundreds of miles away in his city town house, surrounded by his books and students, or on his travels in America. They had shared a connection through Sadie. They had both risked their lives for the girl, there was a bond. Damn it, she had given up what was left of her humanity for the man. Still, part of her had started to long for his arms, his scent, and the look in his eyes when they turned to her. Another part of her still yearned to bite into the smooth skin of the inside of his forearm, and drink his hot, salty blood. She shook the feelings off and turned into the wind.

She increased her pace, the dog trotting beside her, his head constantly swaying to catch the scents of the hillside. Used to the lusher landscapes of Devon, he rarely had the freedom to run so far. He stopped ahead of her, abruptly enough for her to bump into him, and then raised his head. Before she could distract him, or stop him, he filled the evening sky with a full-on wolf howl, the eerie note echoing for miles. He followed up with a second, then a third, then stopped, listening.

Jack had spent the last nine years telling the world Ches was a "Tamaskan sled dog," until she had half forgotten his origins herself. Born to a captive wolf–dog hybrid and a wild wolf, Ches's only concessions to his dog genes were his gray eyes and his partly trained attitude to sheep. He howled again, his initial note dropping four times, falling more than an octave, each phrase echoing differently in the stony valley below. Again, he waited, then trotted on, along the wall beside the path. The light was going fast, a slight mist making the valley and the lake below look disconnected from the sharp lines of the fell. Clouds took on a purple depth as if they were solid, building up across the sky, jostling each other as they scudded east. Even with her new energy, Jack wound her scarf into the gap between her hair and her coat and shoved her hands in her pockets.

When they came out on the peak, the wall ended, and the view was staggering. The red burn in the west cast an orange glow onto some planes, and dropped others into purple shade, as if a giant child had visited with a paint box. The light warmed the gray rocks, and the sky shaded from pinks on one side to violet overhead. Ches, standing on a small pile of rocks that marked the peak, let loose again with a howl, this time letting his eerie notes flow in all directions. Then he sat, panting, the white guard hairs bristling through his gray pelt. He waited, and Jack stood beside him, letting the sights and the wind flow into her.

Far off, another howl answered.

Ches jumped up, threw back his head and called again, this time a rising note.

There was a long pause, maybe several minutes, while Ches waited and Jack grew colder in the wind. Then, with the first stars sparkling on the eastern horizon, the call came back, not one howl but several, twining together into a proper pack call. Jack was suddenly chilled, remembering her first encounters with wolves in Alaska, some ten years before. Ches whimpered, whether from fear or excitement, Jack couldn't be certain.

She called him, but his eyes were fixed on a distant point in the north.

"Ches. Here, boy."

Finally, he dragged his head around to look at her, the reds of the sunset gleaming in his eyes. There was almost no recognition for a moment, then the wolf faded and he thumped his tail, once.

"Come on, stupid dog. I got you a real bone. Come and see Sadie." At the name, he turned and trotted at her side as she retraced her steps back to the car.

Chapter 16

FELIX READ SADIE'S RAMBLING E-MAIL. THE GIRL HAD A lively writing style, and he wondered how she would do in higher education. She was bright enough. The e-mail had a dozen pictures attached.

This is Jack's new room, you can see she hasn't painted it yet . . . Jack, her face serious as she concentrated, fixing skirting to drying walls.

This is Ches in the new front room. We moved out of the one where the old lady was incinerated. Jack's going to make it the dining room. The dog, asleep against a new sofa, half on Jack's feet.

This is the kitchen. Mike and Ari did the plastering, and Jack did all the tiling and put the cupboards in. I helped.

Jack. Jackdaw. The teenager knew how he felt about her. And when he looked at Jack's profile, concentrating on her work, he knew too. His heart lurched in a way Gina could never make him do, even though he was attracted to her. But Jack—Jack was worth waiting for, fighting for.

A simple text from Gina had suggested that they meet for coffee at one of her favorite restaurants.

He put his laptop away and ordered a taxi. When he got to the place a few blocks away, she was sitting at a table in the restaurant garden. She looked up at him.

"So, I suppose you have to go back to England?"

He nodded, and waved to a waiter, ordering a pot of tea. "I have work." It was partly true. "It's been a very informative fortnight. But my students have final year exams coming up."

She picked at a slice of cake with a tiny fork. "Did you learn what you wanted from your visit?"

"It's a difficult area to understand. I'm hoping to follow up a few leads. Julian has kindly arranged an introduction to one of the so-called 'ascended' who is based in Paris. I hope to see her on the way back." He had spent a lot of time with Julian Prud-homme, and his understanding of the magical beliefs of dissem-inated cultures had thrown up more questions than answers.

She pushed a little more cake around her plate. She seemed quietly subdued. "I was hoping to see a bit more of you." She smiled, as if trying to make light of it. "I've really enjoyed our weeks together."

"I—" He looked down at his cup, his thirst suddenly gone.

"She must be very special."

"She?" Felix looked up, staring into her eyes. "She is, but we aren't in a relationship."

Gina pushed her plate away with a sigh. "The thing is, I have a personal reason of my own for knowing more about these people. Which is why I've been doing my research."

"Oh?"

"And when the *orisha* chose me, I knew you could probably help." She looked at the tables around them, and dropped her voice. "I would like—no, I need to understand the process by which one becomes a revenant, what you call a borrowed timer."

"Why?" Even as he said the word, he started to understand. "You are ill."

"I got sick two years ago, leukemia. Chemo, radiotherapy, I had it all. The university doesn't pay well but the medical in-surance is excellent." She sipped her drink, her lashes fanning over her cheeks. "It came back a few weeks ago. I feel fine, but I won't for long."

"And becoming a borrowed timer is the only solution?"

"I wasn't sure until the *bembé*." She turned a ring on her finger around. "I didn't expect anything like that, I was just an observer. But listening to you talking about it—"

"I knew you were interested in the ritual. I just wish you had said something." He didn't know what else to say. "If you've finished your cake, shall we walk? It's a beautiful day."

She finished her coffee and stood, gesturing to the waiter for the bill.

"Oh, I—"

She cut him off, waving a credit card. "My treat."

The streets were more vividly alive than the restaurant. Music eased out of open doorways and windows, the smells of cooking permeated everything, people chatted and looked in windows, stood in groups talking, laughing. Couples seemed to be everywhere, arms around each other, hands clasped, kisses shared.

Gina slipped a hand onto his arm. "Come on, it's not that bad. We're both single; we both had a good time."

Felix felt a crooked smile crease his face. "A very good time. But that wasn't what I was thinking about."

"I've made my peace with whatever happens next, but if there's a chance for a cure—I want that opportunity, Felix."

He stalled for a second, making a man behind him mutter and walk around them. "I understand. But when Jack drank blood, it changed her."

"Changed her, how?" They crossed the road to a small park with tall railings.

"She said she craved more blood. I spoke to an expert on revenants, who said once they drink blood they become driven by it, obsessed. He's part of an organization that works against revenants. It's part of the Inquisition—"

"Works against?" She smiled. "We've heard rumors of extreme views in the Catholic Church but surely they are part of the past.

"The Inquisition is still very active. This is a project they have been working on for centuries." He could remember the look on the face of the four-hundred-year-old revenant, Elizabeth Báthory, as she started to drain the life out of Sadie. The same greedy expression that he had seen, momentarily, on Jack's face she had drunk his blood.

"It's not just the cravings, she's different. She's more aggressive, more assertive. Even more self-centerd. The Jack I knew before would risk her life without thinking to save a child she hardly knew."

She took a deep breath, and he could see her face tighten. "When the *orisha* came into me, I got the impression you'd already made contact with some spirit, as if it were warning me. Something to do with this Jack of yours, I think."

"Do you know what the connection is? Between this entity and the person?"

He could feel her shrug, her shoulder tight against his arm as a group of young men walked around them. "I got the impression that it was saying that one of them was affecting or inhabiting this person. A sort of . . . overshadowing."

They walked on as he tried to think back to the little information the inquisitor McNamara had given him. Jack had taken blood and now craved it like a drug, so much that she didn't want to be around him. But there was something else bothering him.

"Tell me." She looked at him in the yellow light bleeding from a restaurant doorway.

"I didn't know Jack very long before she had to drink blood. My blood." A vivid memory flooded his, of her warm lips against his, her hand clutching his shirt, her body pressed against his. "She changed in so many ways. There were moments when she almost seemed like someone else."

"But you said you didn't know her well, before." She started walking across the grass to a vacant seat and sat down. "I don't see how an infusion of energy could change who a person is fundamentally."

"Maybe that's just part of it." His mind raced, and he almost stumbled over the words. "Maybe taking blood made her more open to being influenced by other beings, your *orisha*, for example."

"Maybe." She slipped her hand down to his, her fingers warm and slim in his. "Perhaps there are risks in taking blood, but what alternatives do I have? I still need to pursue it. Can I come with you, to Paris, to find out more?"

For a long moment he stared down into her dark eyes, seeing the strain there, the fear.

"Of course."

Chapter 17

It was said in Europe that Venice was as far from Roman dominance as Protestant England. It gave courtesy and shelter to all, Catholic, Protestant, Jew and Moslem alike. Yet it also gave a welcome to the Inquisition and its most loyal soldiers.

—EDWARD KELLEY, 1586, Venice

I WAS WOKEN UP ON THE NEXT MORNING WITH THE NEWS that a visitor from Rome awaited me downstairs. I dressed quickly, wondering whether to call Marinello for my protection, but thinking what harm could come to me within his house, surrounded by his servants? I called upon Bartolomeo to wait upon us, and asked that a couple of hall men be on alert to defend me if needed.

I chose my most sober and unornamented suit, being filled with repentance for saving the countess. I also slipped a blade, normally concealed within the binding of one of my books, inside my belt, for one can never be certain of the Inquisition.

I bowed upon entering, and saw Konrad in a plain scarlet robe and simple crucifix. When he offered me his hand I bent to kiss his ring. Indeed, he had some kindness for me from our Transylvanian days, and his very presence, though it brought me closer to the Inquisition, also made me feel closer to God.

I waited until he was seated beside the fire, the mornings

still being cold early in the year, then took a seat upon a stool on the other side of the fireplace.

"You have made an interesting friend in Marinello." Konrad's mouth smiled but seemed short of humor. "A pirate captain, who has sometimes harried ships from Rome and even some from England, for whoever will pay for a quiet passage."

"He has been kind to me." I waited, reluctant to say aught that could condemn me.

After a long silence, Konrad turned to look upon me again. "I find myself in need of an ally in Venice, and had thought that Contarini was a strong choice," he said. "Yet I have doubts about the man, made stronger by finding him associating with a known sorcerer."

"I hoped to find in Contarini an ally," I quipped, "until I found him associating with the Inquisition."

Doubts assailed me immediately, and I regretted my insolence. After a long moment of silence while he stared at me, Konrad suddenly threw back his head and laughed, a great bellow of real amusement that made me smile in company.

"So," he said, still smiling. "What do you want with Contarini, I wonder?"

"I have a commission to fulfill, from a lord back in England," I said. "I attended university with Lord Dannick's son, and he has entrusted me with a task," I found myself explaining. "It is a scholarly request about a piece of art, no more."

He nodded slowly. "I have heard also of a Bohemian captain of guards, seeking a refugee from imprisonment."

I opened my mouth but, like a fish, naught came out. It was true that a lien upon my person and belongings had been issued in the empire, but I had not thought even the Bishop Malaspina angry enough to pursue me as far as Venice. "I merely disagreed with the papal nuncio," I stammered. "My mission is entirely to speak with Lord Contarini and view a carving."

"Papal Nuncio Malaspina is an idiot," Konrad said. His smile faded. "I hear the faintest of dark rumors about Contarini, nevertheless. But we have something more important to consider."

I waited, shaking my head at the servant bringing me a drink upon a tray.

Konrad took a cup, then looked into its depths. "Dee is not with you?"

"He stays in Prague, my lord, with our families."

"And no one has approached you upon that other matter?"

My memory lurched back to the time when we, Dee and I and Konrad, were prisoners in Csejte castle, fighting for our lives and coerced into the most dangerous sorcery: necromancy.

"We have sworn that we will never revisit that time," I said. "We only seek ways to undo that which was done."

"You embodied a soul within a corpse, Edward. That is the pact that you struck, you animated a womb so that the countess could bear a child to the cursed Báthory dynasty."

I bowed my head, in truth in shame, but also to wonder why he had sought me out. I had no intention of revisiting that cruel country with its warlike people.

He sighed, and for a moment we listened to the sound of logs crackling in the fireplace. "But now," he said, "you can put right that unnatural outcome."

"My lord?"

"I am here to gain information about her whereabouts. I have intelligence that she has traveled from Transylvania into France and then toward Venice. Since the Inquisition is following her, she must have left the sanctuary of her own lands with a special objective. I wonder, Edward, if you are not that reason."

"I am not." It was my immediate reaction to deny that I was in mortal danger, but my stomach churned at the thought. "None but I knew that I visited Venice. And when I have completed my task I shall return to Prague as soon as I may. This city has not been kind to me, and I shall be glad to return to Bohemia and then to England."

And receive my handsome reward, I thought, a little excited at the alchemical experiments I intended to set up when I returned to my workshop.

"Then promise me, if you hear anything of her, or even a rumor of her presence, you will send word immediately. I have loyal men ready to undo your sorcery by sword or fire."

"I shall. I promise."

"See that you do, my young friend." Konrad rose then, and murmured a blessing. He smiled down at me. "For with her death may come redemption."

Chapter 18

The garden breathes along the threads that tie it to the fields behind, the copse of trees up on the rise, the hedge running along the road. It stretches its further reaches into the forests beyond, the fells covered with their thin veneer of soil, life trickling into cracks in the rock, oozing into the springs and streams. Underneath, the rumble of all life ripples.

SADIE STARED UP AT THE TOWER, THE STONE WALL REACH-ing up to battlements along the top. "Wow." Looking up made her dizzy.

Jack turned the car into the visitors' car park, avoiding a few tourists. "Well, he did call it a castle."

"Yeah, but—wow." Sadie leaned back in the seat, savoring the warm feeling she always got from being in the car between two circles of sigils. "We won't be long, will we? I don't want to get too cold."

"I'll send you back to the car if it gets too much." Jack parked the car in the mostly empty gravel apron in front of Reception. "You've got your own key."

Sadie wobbled when she got out of the car, breathing deeply to avoid the nausea she still struggled with and had grown to hate. Her "cause of death," barely avoided, would have been to choke to death on an overdose of alcohol and fast food. She had long since decided she would never drink anything alcoholic again. Ever. The cold flowed into her, despite the sunshine.

"Are you OK?" Jack pulled her rucksack out of the boot, looking at Sadie's face.

Sadie made an effort to smile. "I'll have a bit of the disgusting potion, and I'll be fine."

That took the crease between Jack's eyebrows away, and she even managed a small smile. "Keep the bottle in your pocket, just in case."

The hagweed and earthstar potion, which gave Sadie and Jack energy, smelled disgusting, as if a lot of vegetables had gone to die and someone had spooned up whatever seeped out of them. It didn't taste too bad, but Sadie held her breath as she took a sip. She felt warmth creep back into her.

"Come on, then." She led the way to Reception, Jack crunching on the gravel behind her. Inside was a typical gift shop, rows of stuffed animals and books about the castle. While Jack talked to the woman smiling a welcome at the desk, Sadie looked through the toys. The one that had caught her eye was a large toy wolf, the pelt almost as soft as Ches's. "Look, Jack."

She turned to show Jack and became aware of a man, holding her attention.

He was old but dressed in a suit and shiny shoes. When he strode forward, she revised his age. Maybe as old as Felix, maybe a bit more. While she was puzzling over it, Jack turned to Sadie.

"—my daughter, Sasha."

What—oh, yeah. New name.

"Hi." Sadie looked away from the man to see an electric wheelchair beside him, driven by a skinny boy about her own age.

"And this is my grandson, Callum." The boy drew his chair alongside them, staring.

Jack reached out a hand and shook the boy's white fingers. Sadie confined herself to a small smile. There was something about the boy that made her reluctant to get too close.

"Shall we go somewhere private, where we can talk?" The older man led the way up a ramp into a vast hall, echoing with the sounds of footfalls and the chair's whining motor.

Jack and the man drew ahead, leaving Sadie to walk alongside the boy. Cold, that was it. The boy reminded her of the feeling she got when death crept closer.

"Sasha. Nice name." Callum coughed, a dry sound like dead leaves being scrunched.

"I'm trying it out." She looked down at him as he pulled ahead. His hair was the most alive thing about him, thick, long enough to cover his neck, and the color of fudge. "I liked Tara, too. I just wanted to change my name."

"I'm not mad about Callum. It doesn't matter, really, I won't be using it much longer."

He stopped abruptly at a large door that the adults had just gone through.

"What do you mean?" said Sadie.

He coughed again, an effort that left him gasping for a few moments. "I'm—dying. Didn't your mum tell you?"

"Jack? No." She looked more closely at his face, freckles showing against the white skin. He looked bad. "Well, she did say you were ill."

"I need this medicine. Ellen used to make it, but now she's dead—"

"Oh. Right." Sadie didn't know what to say. "I'm sorry." Seeing him was different from talking about him. She could feel the sickness radiating from him.

"It's OK. I've had a long time to get used to the idea."

Sadie followed him into another room, completely paneled, with a dark carpet in the middle and painted boards around the edges.

Jack was waiting at a door in the paneling. "I have to talk to Sir Henry. He suggested Callum might show you around." Her eyes were fixed for a moment on Sadie's, then she nodded. Sadie shrugged one shoulder, and turned back to Callum.

"OK."

Great. Talk with this geeky-looking boy getting colder and colder, when I could be sitting in the car.

"What school do you go to?" Callum had light blue eyes that looked faded against his white skin.

She shrugged again. "I don't go to school." She followed him back through the echoing hall. She stared at paintings that hung on both sides of the huge staircase that wound up each side of the hall and ended at a gallery.

"Grandpa said you've been ill too."

She swung around to look at him. "How does he know that?"

He managed a chuckle before the coughing started again. "Everyone knows—everyone around here. You stayed at Walnut Grove for a whole month, you're in remission from some disease, probably leukemia. The locals think so, anyway, and you have moved into the witch's house." He grinned at her, looking a bit pinker, and reached a paneled door. "Can you open that for me? I'm not supposed to bash it open with my chair. It's about a thousand years old."

Sadie held the heavy door open and he whirred his wheelchair in. "So, what's wrong with you?"

He turned his chair side on to her, and pointed at the wall above their heads. "See him? The man on the horse?"

He was everything Callum was not. Tall, muscular, wearing what she imagined was a doublet and hose. A jacket, and short puffy trousers over tights. His face was hard, with a large, curved nose like an eagle, and the same light hair as Callum's.

The boy coughed again, and fought to get his breath. "That's Lord Robert Dannick, the third viscount."

"I like his horse." The black steed had a mane running down its arched neck almost to its knees.

"He had this." Callum waved his hand over his wasted body. "This type of muscular dystrophy runs in my family."

Sadie turned back to the portrait. "He looks fine to me."

"He had the cure in about 1570, when he was a teenager, like me."

"Wow." She looked across at a smaller portrait over the fireplace. The artist had captured some humor in the eyes, around the mouth, as if he were trying not to smile. He had the same toffee-colored hair. "Who's he?"

"Amyas Ratcliffe. Ellen's ancestor."

Sadie thought back to the story Maggie had told about the first owner of Bee Cottage. "Thomazine's son."

"When he was growing up, his mother noticed he kept falling over. That's how it starts. She confronted Lord Robert, and he told her about the cure. She and her family kept us supplied with it after that, and she refined it, made it work better."

"So that's the cure you want us to find?"

He hesitated and pointed back at the viscount. "That's what they want, yes. I just want to get better."

Sadie turned to glance at him. There was a strange look on his face, as if he didn't know what to feel. "Well, I can tell you, anything beats being dead." The second she said it, she regretted it. "I mean, it's instinct, isn't it? You try to avoid dying."

He looked back at her, his face blank. "The cure comes with a downside."

"Like being sick all the time, or all your hair falling out?"

He looked up at the man on the horse again. "He was really cruel. Once, after the reivers had come down to steal our cattle, he formed a hunt to chase them through the forest."

"What's a 'reiver'?" Sadie's eye had been drawn again to the smaller portrait. It was more realistic than any of the others, almost as if the expression of the man, Amyas, was subtly changing.

"Scottish thieves. The castle was built to defend the area from them. Well, there was a house here before, but the first viscount made it bigger, and built the tower."

Sadie dragged her attention away from the portrait. "So, what's the downside? He must have been pretty fit to do all that."

He stared at her for a long moment. "He killed every last one. For fun."

"Oh. Well, they were bloodthirsty times." Sadie walked around the walls, looking up at the pictures.

"The cure, it makes people very strong, but it makes them more . . . focused. More selfish, aggressive."

Sadie ran her hand along a tabletop that was thick and polished, and almost black, the brown was so deep. "But, that's a choice, surely? Was Amyas like that?"

"No." Callum's head sagged back, as if it were too heavy. "Thomazine changed the cure for him. She didn't want him to be a psychopath like the others. But she didn't tell us how she did that." He jumped as the door creaked, and Sadie turned as it opened. A tall, blond woman walked in, her high heels clicking on the wooden boards.

"Ah, there you are." She spared a small grimace for Sadie, maybe meant to be a smile. "Helen has made your lunch, darling. I expect your friend will want to find her mother."

Sadie realized she was already very cold, and had started to shiver. "I need to get back to the car." She turned back to the boy. "Nice to meet you, Callum. I hope you get your medicine."

He managed a small smile, and waved a hand weakly.

Sadie turned to leave the room, her feet swaying under her.

When she got into the hall, she brought the bottle out of her pocket and drank a mouthful.

Disgusting as it was, she still felt better. On the way through the hall, she saw a picture of another light-haired man, this one barely older than she, dressed in Tudor clothes. Behind him, holding a small pile of books and offering the young man a pen, was another man, slight, with a short, dark beard. She put the cap on the bottle as she studied the picture, wondering what had caught her eye. Under dark varnish were rows of words. "Lord Robert" was prominent, and beside the smaller man the words: "Edwarde Kelly."

Sadie was too excited to rest although she could barely drag the car door open and climb in. Jack was only a few minutes behind.

"Are you OK? You've gone very pale." Jack did her seat belt up and started the car.

"I'm fine." Sadie looked at Jack's profile as she pulled out of the car park. "What did you find out?"

Jack glanced at her. "Go on, you first. You probably had more luck than me."

"Oh, just the Callum illness stuff. But when I was in that big hallway I saw a picture of Robert Dannick and guess who?"

The corner of Jack's mouth lifted. "I don't know. Thomazine?"

"No!" Sadie couldn't stop herself smiling, and she draped her coat over her. "Edward Kelley."

"What? No—our Edward Kelley?"

"Yep. The one who wrote all those papers you sold." Sadie snuggled into her makeshift blanket. "The one who made our borrowed time symbols up."

"You don't know that for sure."

"Well, how many Edward Kelleys were there in the fifteen hundreds who would get painted in a picture?"

"That does make sense," Jack said, slowly. "I mean, this is where the papers and medals came from in the first place, Ellen's loft. And that's what he did, I suppose. Make magical cures and study sorcery."

Jack drove in silence for a few moments, scanning the quiet road ahead. She slowed, then stopped for a man herding cattle across the road.

Sadie thought back over what Callum had said. "But his magical cures came at a price. Callum said there was a change he was worried about. He said the cure can make you really aggressive. But that Thomazine changed the medicine so her son could get better but, you know, stay nice."

"That's not exactly how Sir Henry put it."

A cow stared at them through the windshield, chewing. Sadie smiled. "I've never seen a cow up really close. I'd hardly seen one in a field before I came to live with you." The man whistled, and a dog swept in front of the car as the cow moved on with her sisters. "I don't think I would like to live permanently in a town. But I do miss the shops." Sadie leaned back in the seat. "So, tell me what Sir Henry said."

"He said the family have this inherited condition. Affected boys have this gene. But the boys also have a healthy gene, and this medicine activates it somehow so they get better. Normally they give the medicine much earlier, before the children are too badly affected."

"It might be a bit late for Callum, then?" Sadie felt a twist of anxiety inside her for the pale boy.

"I don't think so. What did he say about this treatment?"

Sadie tried to remember. "He talked about this Lord Robert, I think that was his name. He had this disease where he fell down all the time, and the cure made him better. But then he became really cruel. He hunted down some Scottish thieves and killed them all."

"But this didn't happen to Amyas, who must have been born around the same time?" Jack drove on, across the mucky road and toward the main road.

"Thomazine changed the cure."

"Well, apparently, Thomazine wrote down the formula for the cure and her descendants have kept their own notes. They've treated more than a dozen of the family members." Jack scowled. "He offered me money for Thomazine's book, when we find it. He was insistent. I explained we still haven't found it."

Sadie leaned back in her seat, and closed her eyes as the car turned into the sun. The warmth started to spread through her. "Well, we can't just let Callum die."

Jack didn't answer, and when Sadie opened her eyes, she had turned the car toward the town. "I thought we were going home?"

"We are. I just need to stop for something first."

Sadie stared at Jack's profile. "Are we going to fetch the bird? I've never seen a raven before."

"We are. But I also thought that Maisie might tell us more about Thomazine's book."

Sadie was instantly reassured in Maisie's house. It had a sense of her great-grandmother's home, with every surface covered with knickknacks and the chairs dotted with cushions. She wrinkled her nose at the smell of stale smoke everywhere. Maisie was waiting for them, the front room cleared of cats except for a big tabby, stirred into purring by Sadie's stroking.

"Well, he likes you," Maisie said, putting a tray down on a coffee table. This time she had made a special effort. There was a cracked teapot, stained almost black with tannin, two mugs and a small bottle of a generic cola, presumably for Sadie. "So, you've been up to the castle, eh?"

Jack passed the cola to Sadie. "We have."

Sadie opened the bottle and sipped the drink. It wasn't too bad, and the sugar gave her a little energy. "We met Callum."

"He's a nice boy. He used to go to the local primary school. That was before he had to use the wheelchair, of course, but I knew, even then." Maisie slurped her tea.

Jack was staring at Maisie, her green eyes almost glowing with concentration. "They want Thomazine's book."

"Ah. Well, Ellen always knew that was what they really wanted. That was why they killed her, I told you."

Sadie looked from one face to the other, but they were staring at each other like two cats and didn't notice.

Jack spoke first. "If I had a friend I trusted my animals to, I would probably trust her or him with my most precious belongings."

"I suppose so." Maisie slurped a little more, her eyes down.

Sadie looked at Maisie. "So, do you have the book?"

"I know where it is. You know, where she put it for safekeeping." Maisie put her cup down and looked at Jack. "Drink up."

Sadie smiled as Jack cautiously picked up the tea. She looked as though she were being poisoned, but tasted it, and sipped a little more.

"We can take the bird off your hands now," she said, putting the cup down with a frown.

"About time." The little lady stared at Sadie, so it didn't seem rude to look back.

Maisie Talbot was tiny. Her shins, clad in support tights like Sadie's Nan's, were bowed, as if she had had rickets or something. Her feet had spread out into shapeless tartan slippers.

"And the book?" Jack leaned forward to stroke a thin ginger cat that had wandered in.

Maisie looked back at Sadie, and suddenly shuffled forward

until she was gazing straight at her. One hand reached out, stained orange and smelling of cigarettes, and Sadie jumped as the old woman grasped her chin, turning her face toward the light from the window . . .

"Another witch," she said softly, then her cold, hard fingers released Sadie's chin. "I suppose that Magpie is here, too?"

"Magpie—oh, you mean Maggie?" Sadie shot a look at Jack. "Maggie's staying for a few days. Then we expect another friend, Felix."

"Felix? Who's that, then?" Maisie shrank back into her seat, curled up like a soft, wrinkled fruit.

Sadie answered. "He's my friend. He's our friend. He knows a lot about Dee and sorcery."

Maisie snorted. "What does a man know about witches and magic, blood and bone?" She shunted forward and put her slippers to the ground. "I better meet this Felix, and see Magpie, before I tell you where Thomazine's book is. And you can take that blasted bird with you."

Sadie followed Jack into the kitchen, her trainers sticking to the floor, and the room stinking of dishes piled in the sink, old cat food and the contents of two overflowing litter trays. The blast of cold air from the back door came from a kind of scruffy conservatory, cracked glass and peeling paint suggesting the same kind of decrepitude as the kitchen. The cage gave the huge crow inside maybe room to turn around, but no more. It swiveled its head toward Sadie, and stared with orange-brown eyes. The feathers were black, but gray at their tips where they were splintered and ragged. The feathers under its tail were white with droppings.

"Oh, poor thing." Sadie moved forward without thinking, then stopped beside Jack. "Does it bite?"

"Yes." Jack's voice was cool, and a tightness around her mouth suggested she hated seeing the bird locked up as much as she did.

"Where are we going to keep it?" Sadie watched the bird dip its head a few times, toward Jack.

"I thought we would just give him the back bedroom, until he gets used to us. He remembers me."

Maisie spoke. "You fed it. It's hardly eaten since. I don't like putting my hand in there, even with the glove."

Jack slid her bare hand in the door, and touched the metal bowl inside. The bird, lightning fast, hammered the dish with its long beak with a loud "dink." "I'll just get some food for him." She frowned. "And water."

The old woman was by the kitchen door. "I'll be glad to see the back of it," she grumbled, and went inside.

Sadie stayed, watching the bird, as he inspected her. "Hello, bird." She looked at the mess of torn and fouled newspaper scraps all over the floor. Grimacing, she bent to pick some up, and seeing an old carrier bag, stuffed the rubbish inside it. A wave of weakness swept over her so she leaned against the door to the tiny back garden, overgrown but still dotted with daffodils reaching through the long grass. She caught the bird's gaze, and he suddenly made a deafening knocking noise, then a rumbling squawk. She turned to see Jack carrying two bowls.

"Hold this." Jack handed the bowl to Sadie, opened the door a crack and held the water bowl just inside. After a long moment, when the bird swiveled his head to look at one, then the other, he dipped his beak into the water, then leaned back to let it run down his vibrating throat. He drank a dozen times. Sadie could almost imagine him sighing with relief.

Then he hopped forward, jarring the bowl until it spilled a little and looked over at the food Sadie was holding. Jack removed the water and took the food.

"That's better." Jack smiled at Sadie. "He'll associate you with food as well, that's what will help him adjust."

"Will he be able to go back to the wild?" Sadie watched the bird gulp down beakfuls of food.

"No. He's already imprinted."

"What, like tame?"

"Not exactly, but he isn't scared of humans. I don't know how much he likes them, though." Jack slowly removed the dish, getting a peck from the bird as she did so. "Ow."

Sadie, despite the cold weakness creeping into her muscles, managed to support one end of the cage while Jack carried the other, the bird shuffling about and hitting the bars as she did so. When Jack put the cage down to open the back of the car, Sadie leaned against a door, feeling the sick, choking feeling, and closing her eyes as the sky whirled around above her.

A hand caught her arm, half lifted her away from the side of the car. "Come on, you need to sit down."

Sadie managed to open her eyes enough to see the gutter, and leaned to spit a mouthful of cola-streaked sick into it. She let Jack half carry her around to the passenger door, and help her in.

Although the car was cold, the energy from the two circles of sigils warmed Sadie. Her chest and stomach started to feel warmer, waves of heat slowly creeping outward. She dropped her head back onto the headrest and breathed out with relief. Jack put a bottle of water into her hand, and she drank deep, cleansing the taint from her mouth.

When she opened her eyes, Maisie was watching her, un-blinking like a cat, dressed in a lurid pink checked coat at least a size too big. Sadie wound down her window.

"We really need to know where that book is," Jack said. "If you could just tell us—"

Maisie looked up and down the road as if someone would hear. "Won't help even if you do know."

"Why not?"

Maisie seemed to hesitate, then glanced at Sadie. "You'll need witches to get it. It's hidden in the garden."

"Well, I have a witch in Maggie." Jack sounded frustrated.

"Please. It's important to keep it safe, if nothing else. If it's worth killing for, even dying for . . ."

The old woman gestured for Sadie to open her window more, and leaned in when she did. "They'll listen to *you*," she said, in a hoarse whisper. "They'll let *you* take it. But be careful."

"Where is it?" Sadie whispered back, caught up in the drama.

"It's in the garden, my girl. It's under the bees."

Chapter 19

FELIX SAT IN THE LOBBY OF A HOTEL, SURROUNDED BY flowers and antiques. Gina sat beside him, staring at the décor. Off Montaigne Avenue, the Hausmann-era building dripped late-Victorian prosperity and luxury. The flight to Paris had been long, and he had found it difficult to return to a casual friendliness with Gina after they had shared a bed.

"Monsieur Guichard?" A smiling receptionist called him over to the desk and told him the number of the suite where Julian's contact was staying. "Madame Ivanova will receive you now."

The lift whispered up a few floors, surprisingly modern in the old building, and Gina leaned up against him.

"Is it crazy to be nervous?" she whispered.

He smiled as the doors opened, and he stepped onto deep, patterned carpet that silenced any footsteps. A single sign indicated the Auvergne suite. He tapped on the door, and an older woman opened the door and indicated that they should enter.

"Madame will see you now," she said, in a Russian accent.

"Thank you, Evgeniya." The voice made him turn. A woman, maybe in her fifties, approached him in sensible shoes and a smart wool suit. Her hair, a muted gold, was caught up in a bun on top of her head, and her eyes were the color of caramel.

"Professor Guichard?" She pronounced it in the French way, *Gee-shar.*

"Madame Ivanova." He took her small gloved hand in his. "This is Dr. Gina Larabie from New Orleans."

"Please, join me in my salon." The suite of rooms, each more lavishly decorated than the last, was tastefully resplendent with antique furniture. They passed one man sitting by a fireplace, talking to a much younger woman in an evening dress. In the next room, a small group of older men and women sat around and talked in French. They stopped when they saw Felix and Gina, eyes following them as he crossed the room, and the conversation resumed as they passed. Their hostess didn't introduce them as they walked through. A waiter opened a final set of double doors.

The inner hallway led to a number of rooms, but she led them to the far end and into a smaller area with a corner window.

She offered them drinks, made sure they were comfortable before abruptly opening the conversation.

"I understand you have some knowledge of those some call revenants, professor?"

He nodded slowly. "My knowledge is fairly new. I met someone last year, Elizabeth Bachmeier or Báthory, and she claimed to be one."

She leaned forward and picked up a box of sweets, and offered them, before taking one herself. While her gaze was on unwrapping the chocolate, she said, with studied casualness: "I had heard something of this."

"You knew of her?"

She smiled, then bit into the sweet. He waited while she finished, looking around the room. It was richly decorated with what he was fairly sure was authentic Louis XV furniture. He ran his hand over the smooth carving of the arm of the chair.

"We met each other," she said. "She was a member of an exclusive little gathering of friends." She licked her top lip, claiming a crumb with enjoyment. "We rarely spoke, however. It was better if we were not here at the same time."

"You were not friends?"

"She brought us all into disrepute with her exploits." The woman's accent was some sort of mixed European, as if she had spent a lot of time in Eastern Europe. It sounded a little like Báthory's. "Her extreme tastes brought us all into disrepute."

Felix didn't know how to express the question he wanted to ask. Did this pleasant, rather plain lady drink blood? Gina fidgeted beside him.

Ivanova smiled. "You wonder, I think? At my own involvement?"

He nodded. "I only know what Julian Prudhomme suggested. That there are networks of people who explore that lifestyle."

She waved away the suggestion. "*Ah, non.* The dabblers, the weak, the children who explore. To drink blood is to take life force at its most pure into one's body. For a human, that would be a sexual fetish, an experiment. And blood is not very digestible, *non*?"

"And for a . . . nonhuman? Or rather, more than human?" He watched her mobile face, expressions twisting her mouth, creasing her forehead as she tried to explain in English.

"Ah, you understand. It is *sacré*, you understand? It is the ritual that is special." She took another sweet from the box. "Now these," she said, her pale eyes narrowing with humor, "these are food." The woman's face seemed to change expression so fast she was twitching. Finally it settled into a serene smile.

Gina leaned forward and spoke. "But for you, blood is . . . ?"

She shrugged. "For those that have crossed over from mortal life, blood is energy, joy, warmth." She waved a hand almost like a dancer. "It is immortality."

Gina put a hand briefly on Felix's. "We are interested in that process, of crossing over."

Ivanova glanced at her, then her attention returned to Felix. "You understand that it is given only to a few to cross into the new life." She pursed her lips. "It is not a cure for earthbound illnesses."

Felix leaned forward. "I have heard the Inquisition's definition—"

Again, the expressions shifted from calm to stern, through twitches of something less serene. "Our enemies! You speak of our enemies in my house?" Her voice was quite different, strident, forceful, half an octave lower. Her lips softened into sadness, her voice became almost childlike. "They would kill us, if they could." Her expression changed, then again, as if emotions were running behind the calm façade.

"I'm sorry if we gave offense." Felix looked down, trying to find the right words. "I have a friend who is also a revenant, and in danger of persecution. She is sustained by a magical tradition of symbols."

Ivanova smiled and pointed at the ceiling. "Like these?"

The plaster was ornately patterned, with a molded border and ceiling rose, but between the raised features a painting of a summer sky complete with swallows and clouds hung overhead. It took a little studying to see, woven among trails of cloud and the tails of swallows, a circle of symbols.

"Well, not exactly like those, but I suspect they are used in the same way."

A light tap at the door was followed by the waiter, this time with a decanter and three glasses. She murmured her thanks and the man placed the tray within reach, on a low table.

"A glass of wine, Professor? Madame?"

Felix looked at the decanter. The wine inside was so ruby red it could almost have been opaque. Something in his expression must have betrayed his thoughts, because she laughed.

"I promise, it really is just wine."

"But you do consume blood. May I ask, where from?"

She poured wine into the glasses, and sat back, holding her own by the stem. "There are those who wish to give, and those who wish to receive. This little club, and others around the world, allow that exchange equitably. Some are honored to serve, others hope to be transformed."

Gina leaned forward. "Ascended. That's what a young woman in New Orleans called it."

Madame Ivanova dismissed the idea with a wave of her hand, and sipped her wine. He took a single taste. It was just wine, and very good, but he needed his head clear.

"They have their own *mythologie*, these young people." She glanced at Felix over the glass, her eyes narrowed.

He put the glass down with a clink that echoed in the silence. "A belief that makes them willing donors until they die."

She shrugged. "They choose to die. They are foolish." She shrugged. "I choose to live." She drained her glass with an unladylike vigor and filled it up again.

"And what side effects does this blood have upon the revenants who drink it? People like you?" Felix said.

For a second she looked crushed with sadness, then a cool expression replaced the anguish. "It is not without cost. Yes, life, health, energy. But then—" She drank again, and ran one finger along her lower lip. "Then—it is a whisper at first. A tiny voice that tells you what you want to hear." She stood, and pointed to a portrait over the fireplace. It was of a young, well-dressed woman, head held high, her eyes looking down at the artist from under hooded lids. As he scanned the features he could see it was a younger version of Madame Ivanova. The clothes were in a style of maybe a hundred years ago.

"That was painted two years after the third time I 'died,'" she said, with emphasis on the word. "Living as an immortal, one has to fake one's death from time to time." She adopted the same pose as the picture. "Can you still see the resemblance?"

"I can." The woman in the picture had a kind of arrogant

beauty, lost in the older woman, but there was still something powerful about her.

"I was born in seventeen thirty," she said in a soft voice. "I was from a good family, and I married well. But the typhus that killed my husband and one of my children also had me in its claws. For nine days, I raved and sweated and my servants despaired of my life. But Queen Catherine, who became our empress, sent a doctor to me who specialized in raising curses and curing ills. He made me swallow many potions and laid poultices upon me, many with silver charms inside. I was adorned by these for many months and it was he, referring to a manuscript supposed to be by an English sorcerer, who first drew the circles for me."

"Dee?"

She smiled again, and finished her wine. "Well, that is why I agreed to see you. With the countess dead—and there are few who will mourn her—there is interest in her methods, her magics. She shared none of her secrets—except, perhaps, with you?"

"She didn't explain. But I was there when she died."

A shudder ran through Madame Ivanova's frame, and for a second, her eyes flicked toward the door involuntarily. Then the smile returned as if nothing had changed. "You were not alone. An inquisitor was there?"

"He was." He watched her more closely. Expressions crept across her face like clouds across the moon, so fleeting he could almost have imagined them. Among them was a look of spite, a look of fear, one of childlike amusement. For a long moment, no one was in the ascendant, then she looked down, and when she looked up she was calm. "And two others," he added.

"Ah."

He frowned, looking at her hands, suddenly relaxed in her lap. "Is that important?"

"Was one a revenant? Your friend?"

"Why?"

She breathed out with a little force, as if sighing. "We were wondering. What happened to Saraquel. Báthory's—guardian angel."

Felix remembered the name from Kelley's scribbled journal. "I was under the impression that Saraquel was not a benign presence."

The woman turned her head toward him, her face tense. "It is better that you go now," she said. "I have other guests."

She stood, making Felix and Gina stand as well.

"I am sorry if I have caused offense," he tried, as Ivanova disregarded his hand and turned toward Gina.

"Perhaps you, Dr. Larabie, would like to meet some of my friends? Some seek the same as you."

Gina looked at Felix for a moment, then turned back to the older woman. "I would like that very much."

At the door, Ivanova laid a hand on Felix's arm. In a voice that sounded like a child, she whispered, "It's all in the Book of Enoch, you know that. The angels shared these secrets with us." Then her fingers gripped uncomfortably tight on his arm. "It is best you leave, Professor. For your own . . . safety."

Felix sat hunched over his notes in the airport. Gina had refused to come with him, and stayed with Ivanova over his objections.

He had managed to get through to the Vatican and speak to the inquisitor present at Báthory's death. Stephen McNamara had been reluctant at first to speak.

"I am under investigation for letting Jack and Sadie go free," he finally admitted. "I am suspected of disloyalty, at best, and treason at worse."

"Treason is a strong word," Felix answered. "How much power do they have over you?"

"More than you might imagine, but it is my own conscience that makes me most guilty."

Felix explained about meeting Ivanova.

"We know of Ivanova, of course. We keep a close eye on her activities and her associates, but she has private security that even we haven't been able to infiltrate. I'll pass on the information about her recent whereabouts."

Felix could hear something different in the flat tone in Stephen's voice. "Are you recovered? I mean, you took a hell of a beating from Elizabeth Báthory—"

McNamara interrupted. "Professor, how does Jack seem to you?"

"Fine. I mean, I haven't been much in touch these last few weeks but she has bounced back."

"Does she seem like . . . Jack?"

Felix thought about it. "I didn't know her well before. She seems stronger since, you know. The blood. She's certainly more confident."

McNamara sighed. "Felix, there is so much you don't know. You need to watch Jack. I warned you, she will become dangerous. She may end up like Báthory, feeding on the blood of the weak."

"You don't know her." Felix was indignant. "If you saw how she nursed Sadie back to health—"

"Sadie will never be healthy. It's a miracle she's lasted this long." McNamara sounded tired. "There are people here, influential people, who want Jack and Sadie eliminated."

"But not you."

There was a so long a delay at the end of the phone that Felix wondered if he'd been cut off. Finally, Stephen spoke again. "I cannot be objective. Sadie is a child; Jack saved my life. But look into Ivanova's history: you'll see what Jack will become. I'll send our background file to you. Are you on the same e-mail?"

The file was shocking. Darya Ivanova, a child in the 1730s,

had become Darya Saltykova, a woman who had tortured and killed dozens, if not hundreds, of peasants on her estate. Felix had made cursory inquiries when the inquisitor had mentioned a "Saltychikha," but had never really believed she was still alive. Her gray-haired respectability now hid almost three centuries of unnatural existence.

Saraquel. Felix's knowledge of mythology was broad, but his own beliefs had always been unfocused. A vague belief in God, maybe, but he had nothing so organized as a religion. He had read research on different cultural interpretations of angels, but the Bible offered the widest description. His laptop had several religious books on it, for reference, so he started searching. He found a reference in the Book of Enoch that Ivanova had mentioned, an archaic Jewish text, and settled down to read it in translation.

"And these are the names of the holy angels who watch. Uriel, Raphael, Raguel, Michael, Saraquel—one of the holy angels, who is set over the spirits, who sin in the spirit."

He clicked the icon that gave him the original, but found it an unfamiliar script. A little more research suggested it was written in an Ethiopic script called Ge'ez, from the ninth century BC. He clicked to expand the image of a page of the original Book of Enoch, in Ethiopic. The shapes stopped his breath for a moment.

He sounded out the syllables with the help of the translation to Greek underneath. Sitting back, he removed his glasses and rubbed his eyes, before opening a very familiar file. These letters were very similar to the symbols that kept Jack and Sadie alive, some inscribed in the circles they painted in their rooms, the car, even on their skin. These sigils somehow kept their souls attached to their bodies at the point of death. Most were similar to the original Ethiopic script, which believers considered were the actual ones written by Enoch himself.

"The words of Enoch, where he blesses the chosen and righteous who will live in the day of challenge for the elimination of all sinners and apostates—"

So this, he thought, was what Dee was onto. A book not just of ancient wisdoms and belief from three thousand years ago, but maybe the origins of magic itself.

Chapter 20

*The Báthory family are cursed by God and tainted by
vice and death. Their power is in their ruthlessness,
nothing is more important to them than the Báthory
family, and their castles and lands and wealth. They
know nothing of the duty they owe their people, nor the
reputation of their blood-soaked name. And no name
struck such fear into the peasants of Transylvania as
that of Countess Erzsébet Báthory.*

—EDWARD KELLEY, 1586, Venice

THE NIGHT AT THE BALL, WHERE I WAS TO MEET MY MYS-
terious admirer, was like a dream when one is a child and
knows not the impossible or fantastical. Costumes dazzled at each side, men and women in robes that flew about them
in the dances, revealing the embroideries and silks below. Many
of the women wore their bodices so short I could see their bub-
bies, and men did not refrain from kissing and caressing them.
The wine I was given was rich and sweet, as if it were filled with
honey and sunshine. It intoxicated, as did the music, the stately
pavana giving way to a *gagliarda* until my head spun and I was
dragged in by a lady in white satin. Her breath was scented with
lavender pastilles, which she chewed throughout, her half mask
revealing lips painted scarlet against ivory cheeks. I followed

the steps as best I could, being fond of a caper at home. At the end of the dance she drew me down, and whispered in, I believe, Venetian. I shrugged and spread my hands before her to indicate my lack of understanding, and she brought herself closer. Under the cover of our robes, she squeezed me in the cod, an offer easily understood. I blush to recall it, and bowed in confusion and distaste before she moved on to a more likely mate. I found some security in standing against the walls, and lifted my mask a few times to sip my wine. None came to me, nor spoke. I was free to observe Venice at play.

I could hardly believe that all the flashing stones around me were not glass, so richly did the Venetians ornament both man and woman. Diamond-studded shoes flashed against the pale stone floors, earrings dripped emeralds and rubies onto naked shoulders. Gold glowed everywhere, on vast candelabras, picture frames, jewelry. Men were as ornamented as peacocks, and as immodest as the women. Ah, the women. Dresses with panels that swung away in the dance to reveal underclothes as decorated and embroidered as their kirtles, but as transparent as the finest satins. Skirts were lifted to reveal rounded calves and slender ankles in silken hose.

A woman, perhaps my own height on her scarlet shoes and dressed in black silks that were covered with sparkling stones, left the dance and swayed toward me. When she bowed, I did likewise, not sure of the protocol. Her own mask gave the impression of a silver swan with feathers arching over her hair, which fell around her in a cloak of dark curls. It left her mouth exposed and she spoke to me, soft words that I could not catch. So I leaned closer, cupping my hand behind an ear. She put her lips close to my cheek, and I was intoxicated by her perfume, so rich was it.

"Master Kelley."

I jerked away, not just because my identity was discovered but because I knew that voice. Indeed, I shall never—can never—forget it. It was the creature Dr. Dee and I had created in our efforts to save a dying noblewoman, niece to the king.

"Countess—Countess Báthory," I stammered, stepping away from her along the wall.

"Dear Master Kelley, so cautious?" Her Latin was flawless, her lips framing perfect white teeth.

"I—" My words were dried in my throat as she reached a finger and drew it down my neck.

"I should be very angry with you, Master Kelley." For a moment I could only stare as she licked her lips. "For what you did to me."

"I—did your bidding, my lady," I blustered, walking farther along the wall until I found myself backed into an alcove. "I saved your life, as far as I was able."

Her wide skirts must have hidden me from all but the most astute viewer.

"And yet, I am cursed. Blessed with life, yet haunted by another." She held a fingernail before my eyes, which to my terror had been sharpened to a point, like a nib. She placed the tip on my throat, onto the bounding pulse that fluttered there. "And now, only blood can sustain me, all food is wasted." The pressure on my neck began to sting, to burn. "How might the blood of a sorcerer taste?"

She raised her finger, now stained scarlet, to her lips. Such ecstasy upon her face as I have rarely seen, and a lascivious sucking of her finger, as of a courtesan's vice. I held my hand over my throat, covering the wetness there. She had only nicked the skin, not the vessel beneath, but the blood ran freely.

I managed to stumble out of the alcove and back into the whirling crowd, capering like a fool among the dancers, and out of the ballroom.

A hand caught my arm and in terror I turned, striking at the man who, masked and incognito, held me in such a grip my toes almost left the floor.

"Hold!" he cried, and under his half mask, teeth gleamed within the dark shadow of his beard. I recognized his dress.

"My—my Lord Marinello?" I stammered.

"You found her, then? She is magnificent, is she not?"

"You delivered me to mine enemy!" I was outraged.

"Enemy? What enemy could she be to you, Master Kelley? She offered good gold for an introduction, and will pay more for a consultation on a matter of her health. Where can be the harm in that?"

I leaned closer, to speak soft into his ear. "She is a creature of sorcery and witchcraft, hardly human. What I have seen—"

He turned to bow as a couple walked past us to their waiting boat, no doubt. "She is incomparable. She is much courted here in Venice, where the men who are favored by her grow pale and sickly with love for her."

As the children of her castle at Csejte had, no doubt.

"I know of her and what she can do."

He shrugged. "Rumors follow her. But a woman of such wealth and beauty will always be favored here, even if she is a little inclined toward the . . . cruel. I would not let it weigh with me."

He suddenly swept the lowest of bows, as through the doorway came my lady, her gown sweeping the marble.

"My lords," she said, giving Lord Marinello a hand to kiss.

"My lady." He kept his lips pressed to her white fingers much longer than was usual. He stood up, and met her gaze with his own. "Grant me an audience. One hour in heaven."

She laughed, a soft sound much infused with mockery. "My Lord Marinello, if you bring Master Kelley, you will always be welcome in my *palazzo*." Before my shrinking form, she smiled, then reached to Marinello, touching his lips with one fingertip. Not, I observed, the one with the sharpened nail. "We shall spare Master Kelley's blushes by not discussing it further. Come, yes, come to my house."

Chapter 21

Since the first witch, the garden has watched the house.
Generations have grown, withered and been born again,
always a witch at the center. She, the first, poured her
essence into the ground and fed the elder seedling that
grew there. Blood, seed, tears and rage washed into
the ground, calling upon the trees, the earth, the very
rocks to protect her from her rapist. And the ground
responded, growing the thickest of hedges, bringing up
rocks for the walls, enclosing the witch as she swelled and
grew her child.

THE RAVEN HAD MADE A REFUGE OUT OF THE TORN-UP newspapers and sticks Jack had placed in the back bedroom. He had also left feather dust imprints on the freshly cleaned glass and had drilled dozens of holes into the new plaster under the windowsill. Every time Jack crept into the room he flew at her, or at least leaped into the air, flapping and screeching until she put her arm over her face and put the food down. Every bowl of water was bathed in and turned over, until she brought in a stone block from the garden and glued a metal bowl to it. Now he just dipped his head in it, shaking drops all over the floor and leaving the tiny feathers on his crown stuck up in spikes.

Today, he had perched on the block but flapped off when he saw her and cowered in the corner. Jack had brought the old kitchen chair upstairs, hopefully heavy enough to prevent him from turning it over. She placed it in the corner of the room beside the door, and sat down, holding a bag of peanuts. Her rooks had loved nuts, and even difficult magpies had calmed down when offered them. The bird shuffled from one foot to the other, his tail sweeping the rags of paper with each waddle. As she brought out a peanut, he fluffed himself up and shrugged his wings, stretching his neck into a threat posture and screaming in his broken caw. His mouth was bright pink against the black feathers, and his pointed tongue reached beyond his beak.

"You can shout all you like, but I have peanuts." She rubbed one between her fingers to get the skin off, put the nut on her tongue and chewed it. "Mm, delicious."

She pulled out another one, and threw it near the crouching bird. He cawed again, but with his head tilted so one eye could examine the morsel on the paper three feet from him. She put another nut on her tongue, showing him, then ate it. She ruffled the bag and brought out another one. This fell maybe a foot from him, and he sat silently watching it, watching her, watching it—

He reached out and jackhammered the floor with frustration, bang, bang, until she feared for his beak. When he stopped he stared at her, as if daring her to move, then hopped toward the nut, sweeping it off the floor and then dropping it. He did it several times, as if tasting it. Finally, he swallowed it, and hopped over to the first one.

"You like those, do you? You're a good boy, really, just went feral in that stupid cage." Another nut, this one at his feet, then another, quickly speared and eaten. The next one had fallen halfway between them. He froze.

Jack could feel something inside her, some understanding of

his taut body and hunched wings, as if there were a part of her that could read a part of him.

She relaxed her body, slumped her shoulders a bit, and let her hands rest palms up, as if to say: "I am no danger to you." She had no idea if the bird understood. Something Sir Henry had said came back to her.

Dannick had taken her into a smaller but still grand room in the castle, lifting rope barriers out of doorways. Once inside, he had turned a large key in the lock, making the hairs on Jack's neck and forearms prickle.

"Oh, don't worry." His smile was wide, his eyes intense on hers. "I just don't want to be disturbed." He had walked over to an unlit fireplace and opened a small brass box on the mantel. He brought out a box of matches and lit one, before bending down to the coals in the hearth.

"It's so cold in here," he said over one shoulder. "We do have central heating of a sort, but not in the grander rooms, just in the family quarters." He stood up, brushing his hands together, and tossed the dead match into the tiny blaze. He walked to a chair that looked as if it had come from an exotic throne room somewhere, and sat down.

"Take a seat." He waved at several less grand chairs, but Jack walked instead to the window. Facing the front of the house double doors looked over the long lawn toward a small hill, dotted with a dozen or so oaks. Beyond, the forest started to close in. Jack noted a key in the outside door lock, the thought making her feel slightly safer.

"Your grandson's illness is genetic?" she asked, turning so the lock was within easy reach.

His smile broadened as he looked at her. "My, you are cautious."

"What do you want?" Jack's instincts were to run, and it was an unsettling feeling. No one made her feel like this.

"You are nervous. Please, sit down. I have nothing to gain from harming you."

She shook her head. "I'm fine. This illness you mentioned?"

He relaxed into the chair, stretching out long legs before him. "How old do you think I am?"

"I don't know." She stared at him. He had lines around his eyes, a couple across his forehead, silvering hair at his temples. She stared at his hands, smooth, sinewed, a few raised veins. "Fifty-five, sixty? I mean, you have a grandson." But her thoughts had run back to what Maisie had said.

"I am seventy-eight years old."

She stared at him, but still couldn't see it. "Good genes?"

"Actually, I have fantastic genes. But when I was a boy I started to fall over; I had to hold on to something to walk around the room. Ellen's grandmother made the potion that saved my life."

"With the hair-root." She glanced back at the outside, where a few deer were cropping the grass in the shadow of the trees.

"Exactly." He smiled again. "The potion activates the healthy genes inside us, the hunter heritage."

She walked toward the fire, keeping an eye on the man. "Hunter?"

He sat still, the way she did with wild birds, his hands slack on his knees. "We have always been fighters, explorers. That's my father." The portrait over the mantelpiece was of a man with a shock of white hair but still bolt upright on a chair. The same chair Sir Henry was sitting in, she realized, against a wall of books. "My father was a general in the second Boer war. He was one of the signatories to the Treaty of Vereeniging, the end of the war and the surrender of the Boers, just at the beginning of the twentieth century. That portrait of him was painted when I was already an adult, with children of my own in the sixties. He died at the age of—well, over one hundred."

"And you?"

"I was a child during the Second World War. But I was a major in the British army in Kenya in the Mau Mau uprising. I saw action there, and again in Aden in the midsixties." He smiled again, his eyes narrowing as he watched her. "I was decorated for bravery. Twice."

She studied the books on the shelves, mostly histories, a few old novels. "So, you are from a family of soldiers." She walked back toward the doors. "But you have this genetic problem."

"I suppose, over the generations, people of my class tend to marry people of the same group. Weaknesses, as well as strengths, tend to get amplified."

"Like Queen Victoria and hemophilia?"

He inclined his head with stately grace, almost ceremonially. "Yes. Or the Hapsburgs and their . . . mental problems."

"So, why the program of inbreeding?"

He laughed softly, a deep chuckle. "Inbreeding, no. Selective breeding, possibly. Like creating a more powerful racehorse or a healthier bull. Concentrating the hunter genes, the leader genes."

She had relaxed a little, but her senses were still telling her she was in the presence of something dangerous. "Except for this genetic illness."

"It seems that health and strength are related to this one disadvantage, occasionally seen. You and your knowledge of herbal remedies can overcome that for Callum. Haven't you witches done much the same? You tend to be attracted to more of your kind, increasing the tendency toward witchcraft in your offspring."

Jack didn't correct him. It was probably better that he believed her a witch. There was still something about him that scared her.

And then he had made that offer again. Jack had no doubt he would pay more for the book, and the boy's need was urgent.

A sound dragged her back into the present, like papers rustling, as the raven shook himself then drew a wing feather through his beak.

"There you go. I'm not scary," she said, rustling the bag of nuts, "not like that old bastard Dannick." She slowly reached for a handful, holding her palm out to the bird, showing him. He cocked his head and hopped forward a few inches. Then a few more, until, by straining his head, he could stab the long beak forward. He snatched a few nuts, pinching a piece of skin from her palm, and flapped to the corner of the room. She swore under her breath, and stretched her hand flat, to make the skin harder to grab. He hopped back, this time pecking more gently, taking a few at a time and wolfing them down.

"Oh, you are lovely," she said, smiling at him as he got another few nuts, and sidled closer. She held her breath. He was close enough for her to see the long eyelashes around each golden eye, the little fan of feather strands over his beak. Before she could move, he leaped forward, battering her for a moment with the edge of his wings. She covered her face with her free hand for a second and when she opened them he was back in the corner of the room—with the bag of nuts. He cawed triumphantly, and Jack had to laugh.

Jack could hear Sadie's voice before she got to the bottom of the stairs. Ches was in the hall, waiting for the last walk of the day and putting a few scratches on the freshly painted door. She looked into the living room. Charley and Sadie sat on the sofa, feet on the coffee table, the light from laptops playing on their faces.

Charley looked up. "How did you get on with the crow?"

"Raven," Jack corrected. "Fine. He's bright, and he'll come round."

Charley smiled at her, then her attention was claimed by Sadie pointing something out on her screen, and she chuckled.

Jack reached for a jacket, hanging on the end of the banisters. "I'm just taking Ches out."

Maggie caught her when she was putting her coat on. "Be careful out there."

Jack wrapped a scarf around her neck, and looked across the road to the sign for the local footpath. "I will." It was hard to see what could happen to her with a wolf hybrid at the end of a lead and a knife in her pocket, but she was still spooked by the old man.

The stars were just popping into brightness overhead as the blues darkened, and the air had a chill that made her pull the sleeves of her jumper over the bare skin of her wrists.

"Come on, boy." Sometimes, she thought what a relief it would be to go back to just her and Ches. Whole days with no need to speak to anyone, days without a teenager to look after and entertain. The hillside started to steepen, to catch the breath in the back of her throat with the taste of frost. Ches trotted ahead, sniffing at corners, cocking his leg at gateposts and shrubs that other dogs had marked. He lifted his head and after a moment her eyes made out the low shape of a fox slinking down the side of the hill. She reeled in the slack lead, but Ches wasn't bothered with foxes, he was snuffling the ground, ears pricked forward. Deer, probably, leaving scat on the path to new grazing.

Toward the top of the hill she veered off the path to the outcrop of stones where she had heard the howls, which she had half convinced herself were dogs calling back to Ches. This time, Ches was busy scenting the ground around the boulders, huffing in every crevice, exhaling in a cloud of mist. Rats or voles, she decided. Maybe rabbits. She sat on the boulder, and faced the last red glow of sunset to watch it fade. The stars were multiplying as they emerged from the last of the day, filling in spaces between the biggest glimmers. Working on the house had been a relief after the shock events of saving Sadie from Elizabeth Báthory, or Bachmeier, as she called herself, a woman who had chosen to extend her life by taking others. Here, her mind clear of distractions, she could maybe hear the tiny whispers that she had heard from that encounter. It was as if some little doubt had found a voice. *Don't do it*, it sometimes whispered. Or even, *go on.* They had been at their loudest when she was with Felix, urging her to just stand a little closer, touch his skin, smell his scent. She was still confused by his kiss, her body yearning for something that she hadn't felt before.

Ches had stopped sniffing and stood in front of her, as if she were part of his pack. He scented the air again, just a shadow in the dark. When he lifted his snout and howled she almost felt the urge to howl too. It was such a wild, free thing, announcing to the world that he was a wolf, and male, and healthy. The eerie cry stilled the air around her, until she wondered if the boulders were resonating with it. He howled again and again, the sky echoing with the broken song. Somewhere down the hillside a fox shrieked and a stag bellowed. Then the air settled on her in silence.

There, the first answer. A tentative howl, then a second, stronger. Then voices rolling toward them, exciting Ches to call back. Jack could make out individual calls, maybe six or seven at a time. This time, she had to investigate. Wolves in the Lake District, on fells covered with walkers and tourists?

She started back, Ches hanging back against the lead until she called him and petted him, and she wondered if there was a local zoo with wolves. She had barely gone a hundred yards when another call echoed over the hillside and she froze, this cacophony of voices making her skin prickle as much as

Sir Henry had. It sounded like no animal she knew, calls and shrieks reminiscent of wolf cubs but more . . . aggressive. Hyenas, maybe, or coyotes? Definitely not adult wolves. Another shriek and she was certain. Someone, some humans, were imitating the wolves.

Ches was silenced, shrinking against her side. As she strode away down the hill, she felt shaky, nervous, and angry at herself for being frightened. The little voice in her head whispered a question and it chilled her even further. The animal sound could, she supposed, have come from human throats, but why? Why would humans mimic wolves? Answers crowded into her head and she lengthened her stride, almost slipping on loose stones as she reached the field and hurried toward the lights in the cottage window.

She burst into the house to startle Maggie, who was carrying a tray of hot drinks. "Maggie, where's Charley?"

"With Sadie, in the kitchen. She's got to go back to university in the morning."

Jack threw her coat and scarf onto the stairs and brushed past Maggie into the new living room. "What do you know about people who howl like wolves?" she asked, in a low voice.

"Not much. Just the werewolf legends."

Jack closed the door and folded her arms. "Well, I think that's what I just heard. First wolves, then people."

"Probably just kids, teenagers." When Jack didn't reply, she carried on. "Well, there were animal cults in Europe but I'm no expert. You should tell Felix. Why do you ask?" Jack knelt on the rug and opened the woodburner. She propped a new log on the top of the glowing embers and closed the door, opening a vent to help it catch. The wood smoke smell reassured her, left uneasy by the baying. "I heard wolves howling out there, on the fells, a few days ago. Six or seven."

"Maybe there's a zoo." Maggie sat next to the fire.

"But then tonight I heard humans howling, not just imitat-

ing, really screaming and baying. It was creepy. It scared Ches."
She shivered at the thought.

"Well, there was a spell that led to the legends of werewolves." Maggie put her hands on her knees. "It was supposed
to be invented by the Romans. It's believed to bring out the
beast in the man, or place a bit of wolf spirit in a human, anyway. It makes them super aggressive and powerful."

"And long-lived?"

"Maybe. It's supposed to bring greater strength. Why?"

Jack closed the woodburner door. "Do you know the spell?"

"No. I do know where you could find out more. You could
ask Felix, he's bound to know much more."

Jack stopped, her heart unexpectedly jumping in her chest.
"I'm not talking to Felix. It's too complicated. We don't need
him."

"So you keep saying." There was an acid tone to Maggie's
voice that made Jack even more uncomfortable. "But he still
knows far more about this stuff than either of us."

Chapter 22

If there are greater demons than are found amongst mortal men, I do not know it. For I have met in Venice such fiends with human faces that will haunt me to my dying day. The wicked hide behind smiling faces, the old behind the smooth skin of youth, the penniless starveling behind borrowed silks and paste jewels.

—EDWARD KELLEY, 1586, Venice

MY LORD MARINELLO, IN CELEBRATION OF HIS BAG OF gold from the countess, had gambled and whored his way around Venice with me as his reluctant companion. I was able to observe Venice at leisure, the rich and poor alike disporting themselves incognito. When we found ourselves close to Marinello's house, I pleaded tiredness, endured much jesting about the feebleness of the English, and excused myself.

When I was granted entry into the house, the servant indicated by much waving and gabbled speech that a letter had been brought for me. I thanked the fellow, which probably seemed as much nonsense to him, and retired to my room with a candle to read it.

"My dear Signor Kelley," the letter began. "Upon reflection, I have decided that to allow you to see the tablet, and to show my family your sketches, must be of value to us both. But in private, you understand, not to publish or share abroad. For this reason, I enclose a note inviting you to the palazzo of my good friend as if you visit him, not me. His man will take you to the Padua road. There, my loyal servant Enrico will meet you at an inn called the Seven Soldiers. He will guide you to my own estate. Bring your books and documents, for we may confer and I may benefit from your great learning. Baldassarre Contarini."

I was flattered for a moment, then suspicious. Yes, I do have great learning, but the world supposed that such scholarship was simply reflected from John Dee, I admit, the greater academic because of his many years and experience. I am myself becoming his master in sorcery, however, and my experience is growing. I turned the page to see a few last words.

"For we progress, somewhat, in that matter of ours, and we suspect that you do also."

The matter of ours. Transmutation, chrysopoeia. I was intrigued, and while happy to perform Lord Dannick's commission, the opportunity to further my knowledge of alchemy was seductive. I tucked the letter into one of my books and fell into bed with a feeling of expectation. As was my habit, I balanced a metal cup upon the room handle and performed the simplest of sorceries: a charm for protection.

I awoke in the dead of night as the spell tickled my face and neck, the darkness pressing upon my eyes, the sounds muffled and confusing. There, someone creeping about the hall outside my room. A sound of steps, high heels tapping along the corridor, a man's boots perhaps, the shuffling noise beside them. Then laughter, and I recognized the low voice as Countess Báthory's. I reached under my pillow for my knife, puny defense though it might be. Then Marinello's baritone, rumbling something to her. They stopped outside my room, and a sliver of flickering light shone under my door.

"He is my guest," I heard Marinello say. "I have some fondness for him, I might call him friend."

"He is dangerous. But his knowledge is valuable—" The words were stopped, I judged, by the following sounds, by a kiss or some embrace.

"We shall deal with him on the morrow." The man's voice was thickened, perhaps by wine, perhaps by lust.

They moved on and I lay in the dark, thinking how timely the invitation was to Lord Contarini's house. I had thought to confide my plans to Marinello, thinking it better that someone knew my whereabouts, but now I knew not whom to trust. I slept badly, woken by the first slanting light off the lagoon at dawn, and the sound of the street vendors beginning to cry their fish and goods from the first barges.

Upon waking, I jotted down a brief note informing Konrad of the countess's presence in Venice, lest he did not know, and gathered my belongings. I had decided to travel to the house of Contarini and to get out of this accursed city.

Chapter 23

The garden understands death and birth and death. It does not understand the conundrum of the not-death of the new witch. It scents her footsteps in the grass, her blood on the thorns, and watches her. It sees her weaken, only to recover within the strange symbols scratched upon rocks on the grass. The garden explores the lines and curves, and grows a veil of algae and bacteria over and into them. It fills them with life, and feels the witch grow stronger.

JACK WAS HARDLY ASLEEP WHEN THE KNOCK ON THE FRONT door woke her. She waited to see if Maggie would answer it, but clearly she wasn't up yet. Grumbling, she wrapped herself in her dressing gown and padded down the bare treads to the ground floor. The knock sounded again, insistent.

"I'm coming!" she said, fumbling with the lock for a moment. She pulled the door open.

Felix stood there, no emotion creasing his normally expressive mouth. "Jack."

She pulled the dressing gown around her. "Felix. I—we didn't expect you until this afternoon." She stared at him, seeing some tension around his eyes, lines creasing his forehead.

"Can I come in?" He was coolly polite.

"Yes, of course." She stood back, feeling the heat of a slight flush as she realized she was barefoot, her hair probably standing on end. "Here, let me take your coat."

It was all so ridiculously formal. This was the first man she had kissed, dreamed about, her heart beating raggedly just because he was near. She pushed the door open to the front room, still a little warm from the woodburner embers. He walked in, looking around.

"They did a good job. Is this the room—"

"No. That's next door, but it's nearly as good. It still has a bit of a smell, though." She was babbling, embarrassed. She shook off the feeling. "How did you get on in Paris? Sadie told me you were going there."

"I found some useful leads. How's Sadie?"

"Good. She's been getting out a bit more, much better than I was at her age." A soft footfall on the stairs was followed by the dog nosing the door open. He started to wag, as if pleased to see Felix, and allowed him to stroke his head.

"He's mellowed." Felix's lips twitched into a small smile.

"He has. Now—why are you here?"

Felix pulled off his gloves, and placed them on the mantelpiece. "You. I'm here because of you."

Jack filled up with some emotion that simultaneously filled her with tears and heat. Felix's next words came like a cold slap.

"Because you are stopping me living my life."

Jack sat down, the dog leaning against her, his warm solidness comforting. "How am I doing that?"

He stood in front of the fire and looked down at her. "In New Orleans I met a woman. Intelligent, educated, beautiful, half a dozen years younger than me. But I couldn't be with her because I still want to be with you." He sounded like he was giving a lecture.

"How is that my fault? You know we can't be together, and you know why."

He took a step nearer. "Because, in the emotional fallout of a time when you and Sadie nearly died, when I could have been killed, you decided you couldn't cope with a relationship?"

Jack squeezed her hands together. "You know it was more than that!"

"You drank my blood. I let you. We did that to save Sadie's life. You and me." He abruptly dropped to one knee in front of her, and put one hand over both of hers. "I feel—no, I know—we're stronger and better together. I've done this before, Jack. I've looked into someone's eyes and known that we're meant to be a couple."

"Then Marianne left you."

He shook her hands, clasped in his. "We grew apart. On some level, we still love each other, just not as partners. But you—I'm in love with you, Jack."

Is it as easy as that? Can you just follow your heart, and fall into his arms like a girl in a trashy romance? Jack pulled her hands out of his, and found they were trembling. Staring at his long face, she wondered what she was supposed to do. One part of her just wanted to rest against him, block out the world for a moment. Another part wanted more, an alien, new part of her that craved his skin under her hands, his mouth on hers—she shook her head at the random thought.

"I don't know—" She was stammering again. "I don't know what to say."

"You don't have to say anything." He sounded disappointed, as if he had expected his declaration to open some magic door in Jack.

Something he had said earlier registered. "You mentioned a woman?"

"That's over. I think it was just sex."

It was like a blow to her chest from a sledgehammer. She whispered, more to herself than to him. "You slept with her?" It hurt, it left a massive ache inside her.

"Yes, I did." He was still there, kneeling in front of her as if waiting for something.

When it came, it built up like a storm, first just a prickle in the air, then a wave of pressure and rage inside. "How could you come here and talk to me?" She jumped to her feet, making him stagger back before standing. "How dare you? Did you really think boasting about your other women would make me fall into your arms?"

"No, Jack, listen—"

"I've heard everything I need to know," she said, snapping the words out. Inside she knew this anger was a cloud to hide behind, because her real feelings were much more painful. For a moment she wondered, for the thousandth time, what it would be like to just be a normal woman with a normal man, making choices and decisions that weren't complicated by so much that was unknown.

"Felix!" The shout from the doorway was followed by Sadie, in her absurd penguin pajamas and fluffy slippers. "You came!"

He stepped away from Jack, letting Sadie fly into his arms. Their easy affection was like pouring petrol onto a fire for Jack. Unable to speak for fury, she turned her back on them and stalked out of the room and upstairs.

By the time she had dressed and started back down, Maggie had come down and was talking to Felix in the kitchen. As Jack stood at the top of the stairs, she watched Sadie turn onto the bottom tread, pulling herself painfully up each step with an effort.

"Are you OK?"

"Just really tired." Sadie's voice was weak, a little gasp.

Jack ran down to support her. "Come on, we'll do it together.

Go back to bed for a few minutes, and I'll get you some stinky potion." That made Sadie smile briefly, soon lost in the effort of walking upstairs.

"Are you . . . OK?" Sadie said, clutching at the banister while she caught her breath halfway up. "You look like you've been crying."

"I always cry when I get angry."

Sadie managed a little cough of laughter. "What did he do this time?"

"Slept with someone else."

Sadie clung to Jack's arm and pulled herself up another couple of stairs. Close to the top, she looked at Jack with an expression that made her think she understood. "Well, that must hurt," she said. "Although, it's not like you and him . . . you know. You didn't exactly encourage him. You even sent him away."

Jack helped her into the newly painted front bedroom, the noise causing the bird in the back room to shuffle papers around. Sadie lay on the bed and Jack covered her up with the duvet. "I know, but—"

It didn't feel right burdening Sadie, but somehow she felt as though in sexual and emotional confidence, Sadie was the elder.

"He stares at you all the time," the girl said, her voice sleepy. "When you aren't looking, his eyes follow you around. He even made friends with your dog to get closer to you." She opened her blue eyes, staring at Jack from a paper-white face. "And you jump a mile every time someone says his name. Just say it, get it over with."

"I can't. I'm a borrowed timer, I'm—" The word "wrong" stuck in her throat.

"Because you drank blood. Well, it didn't turn you into a monster, did it?" Her voice faded, as if she were falling asleep.

"I'll get that potion," Jack said, and walked toward the door.

"Boys are tricky," Sadie said, and Jack wondered if she was even awake.

They might well be, but as Jack's sole emotional experience had been a crush on a mechanic at the garage near the cottage in Devon when she was fourteen, she wasn't qualified to comment.

Jack stepped into the kitchen to find Maggie making toast. Jack reached around her to get the decoction for Sadie. When she met Maggie's eye the older woman smiled back, as if in sympathy. Felix stood at the sink, holding a mug, ignoring her.

"Sadie's not too well," Jack announced to them all. "I'm keeping her in bed this morning."

She poured a generous dose into a glass, and turned to the door.

"Jack." The word seemed to have been squeezed out of Felix. "I'm sorry if I upset you. But I do need to talk to you about the blood, the symbols."

"I need to talk to you, too. About Sadie. She's struggling."

"In what way?"

She finished the dose, and debated having a second. She held up the glass. "This way. The potion, the circles, it's not enough. Sometimes she seems better, but today she's really bad. We need to find out more about the magic."

Maggie took the glass out of her hand. "We are. Felix has been working on it."

"Well, we know we can help Sadie with just a few drops of blood." The new energy in her system seemed to hum around her veins. "Why aren't we looking into that?"

Felix answered. "Because there may be serious side effects to taking blood."

She zipped up her coat, left warming by the fire. "Serious. So, have I turned into a bloodsucking serial killer?"

"Of course not. But something turned Elizabeth Báthory into one." He paused, then said: "It's not as if you aren't different. We have to talk about it."

"Not now." She turned to Maggie. "Can you look after Sadie for me this morning? I've got an address for a wolf research place out by the forest. I'm going to check it out."

"Are you taking Ches?"

Jack paused, looking down at the dog lolling at Felix's feet. "Not this time."

The Dannick Environmental Research Project was down a private road, with a barred and locked gate. It led to a lane dug into the hillside, with tire tracks leading into dark forest, overhung with trees and bushes. Mist had saturated the leaves, which showered Jack as she vaulted onto the top of the gate and jumped down. The trail ran downhill into a muddy patch, then up over uneven ground through a stand of pine trees. They were edged by a fence maybe fifteen feet high, with razor wire along the top. Signs warned trespassers of an electric fence, although Jack was fairly sure they were empty threats. She loped along the lane, enjoying the chance to stretch her legs and use up the adrenaline the anger had generated in her system. A man in a baseball cap was standing with his back to her outside a large timber building, cleaning something.

"Hello?" Jack tried to remember to smile, appear friendly. It was made more difficult when she saw he was polishing a large hunting rifle.

"What?" He swung around, scowling for a moment. "This is private property."

"I know, I did ask permission to speak to you from Sir Henry," she lied. "Jackdaw Hammond? Maybe someone forgot to pass on the message?" Jack smiled again, looking the man over. Midthirties, heavy build, blond-haired with a little bit of stubble. Blue eyes, starting to open from the squint that accompanied the scowl. She widened her smile.

"Well, I haven't been told to expect anyone, and this is private property." His eyes were now inspecting her body in a way that she found made her a little uncomfortable. A small part of her almost liked it.

"I'm interested in wolf conservation, and Sir Henry tells me you have a small pack here?" Hours on the Internet and phone with the local council had managed to provide her with that snippet of information, and no more.

"We are a research facility, yes." He put the rifle down, leaning it against the fence. It was just as high as the cabin, it looked designed to keep people out, not the animals in.

"I just had a few questions."

He reached into a pocket to draw out a mobile phone. "No messages from the boss," he said. He shrugged. "But then I don't always get a good signal here."

She watched him collect up handfuls of cable ties, a plastic box, and finally the rifle.

Finally, he looked back at her and smiled slowly. "If I answered any questions to, say, the press, I would get the sack. But you're not press, are you? I'm guessing you're the new witch at Bee Cottage."

"How—" She stepped back involuntarily as he walked past, the blue black steel of the rifle just brushing her coat.

"Well, aren't you?" He laughed, walking up to the wooden building and unlocking the door.

"I'm presently restoring the house for its new owner," she offered, carefully choosing her words.

"And you have a wolf, a male by the howl."

"You can tell that?"

"Sure. And you have a sick kid."

"You can tell all that from a wolf howl?"

"I have spies . . . We shop at the same supermarket, the owner knows everybody . . . Mike Powell, zoologist in charge of the project." He pushed the cable ties into a pocket and held out his hand. She shook it briefly, and his grin widened. "You ever hunt with your wolf?"

She smiled again, this time genuinely. "Too many deer and sheep. Down south I did. He knew where and when he could hunt."

She followed him into the building, which had a desk at one end and a number of filing cabinets and storage at the other. He opened a heavily reinforced cupboard and locked the gun away.

"So, he's a hybrid?" The man turned and stretched an arm past her to shut the cabin door.

She couldn't see there was any danger in telling him details, and then he might volunteer some information of his own. "Yes."

"Dangerous. Dog-wolves can be very unpredictable. And illegal."

"He's great. Friendly to me and mine, anyway. He's a good guard dog." She looked around at pictures on a board, with names underneath. Chulyin, K'eyush, Eska, Pakkak, Shila, Maguyuk and Desna. They varied in color from almost white to dark gray, but were clearly pure wolves, with slightly heavier faces than Ches and the wary look of the truly wild animal faced with a man taking pictures. Something about their posture was odd. Their pelts looked perfect, thick and clean, but their legs were shaven just above the paw, but only on the left. They were all in a defensive position, but most were cowed, as if they were intimidated by the man with the camera.

He paused at a coffeemaker and raised an eyebrow at her. "Coffee?"

"Please," she said, studying the pictures. One heavy, dark animal had the most aggressive posture. "So, I would guess that Desna is the lead male?"

"We gave them traditional Inuit husky names. Desna means leader, so yes. Can you pick out the lead bitch?"

She studied the pictures, but couldn't see many clues. The

other wall had pictures of the wolves interacting, and it was easier to see that one light-haired female was treated with more respect and deference by the others. "That one." She studied the single pictures and read the name. "Chulyin?"

"Good call. You know your wolves." He handed her the drink, no polite inquiries about milk or sugar, so she sipped the searing black coffee. It was as bitter as it was hot.

"So, you have just the seven?"

"At the moment. We did hope we'd get a litter this year, but no luck. We're hoping to double the size of the enclosure, give them more scope for hunting and some privacy. But the cost of fencing an area with steep hillsides and solid rock is so high Sir Henry's trying to find a way to get the price down. Maybe we'll create a new enclosure on flatter land."

"Hmm." She blew the steam off the coffee, looking around. There were various charts around the place. "So, what exactly are you trying to find out about them?"

"I think that's one of those things I'm not supposed to say to a reporter—or the local witch."

"I thought you might, as one wolf lover to another, like to talk about them."

He hesitated, looking into his coffee for a moment. "There's something perfectly . . . savage about wolves. And yet they were the first animal domesticated by humans. We're interested in their primal instincts, the features that made them such good hunters back in prehistory."

"Savage? I thought they were hardly ever in conflict with people unless threatened or ill." She put the coffee down on a clear patch of the disordered desk.

He half smiled, then put his coffee next to hers. He rolled up his sleeve to reveal a purple scar on his left arm. It trailed unevenly from the inside of his wrist, spiraling around to the outside of his elbow. Several round scars suggested puncture wounds.

"Chulyin did this when I inadvertently threatened the pack. I dropped some equipment, went to catch it, she saw it as aggression." He ran a finger down the scar, and grimaced. "Luckily, she missed an artery, but I still bled badly."

"But you got out all right?" Jack watched him pull his sleeve down again. "No problem with the others?"

"I go in armed with last-resort equipment. Tranquilizer darts, pepper spray, cattle prod, that sort of thing. But if I hadn't . . ." He shook his head. "Pure aggression. They would have eaten me alive."

Jack stared at him, trying to understand what made her doubt his account. Maybe his twitched half smile . . .

"Anyway, we do legitimate research, we are registered with all the authorities and are compliant with the dangerous animal legislation."

"So that makes it OK to experiment on captive wild animals?" Jack kept her voice as unemotional as she could, but some of her distaste must have shown on her face, because his eyes narrowed and the smile faded. "There is legislation related to keeping wild animals."

"Legislation that you are not compliant with, I suspect, with your hybrid," he said, folding his arms and leaning against the door frame. "And Sir Henry never gave permission to come up here, did he? What do you really want?"

"I was just curious. I heard them howling."

"I wondered why they were so agitated and howling so often. They probably think your wolf mutt is a threat, with a rival pack."

She tried another smile. "I just share your fascination with them. As you say, they are perfect wild animals, even my 'wolf mutt.'"

He started to cross the ten or twelve feet between them, placing his boots almost silently on the wooden floor as if stalking her. He walked around her, and leaned in as she froze, her heart hammering in her chest. He sniffed her hair, her face, just as Ches would have, then leaned away, smiling.

"What are you, really?" he murmured. "You don't smell like a witch."

She stared at the side of his face, as he inhaled deeply around her neck. There was something about him, some attraction that made no sense. "What do—" she choked, her mouth dry. "What do I smell like?"

"Like someone who is very good at understanding animals." His face was inches away from hers now, his eyes staring at her eyebrows, nose, chin, working his way around to her mouth. His was full-lipped, slightly open. "Someone," he breathed, the coffee scent reaching her, "who speaks wolf." He leaned too close.

She lifted her hands, flat on the front of his fleece, to shove him away. Some impulse stalled her, a flash of imagination of Felix with the other woman. Instead of pushing him, a force inside made her grip handfuls of his jacket, drag him closer and kiss him hard enough to crush her lower lip on one of his teeth. She tasted blood and touched her tongue to the split in her lip. A part of her reveled in the pain and the response from him. He kissed her back, a wave of heat and reaction rolling over her. She gathered her strength, and released the sprung tension in her forearms, pitching him back.

He staggered against the chair. For a second, she thought he would be angry, then she saw he was laughing.

"On your terms, just like Chulyin."

"Can I see the wolves?"

"Maybe." He pushed himself upright from the chair back; this time the smile on his face seemed genuine. "You should come round one evening. I could show you a bit of the real wild." His expression suggested, to Jack's inexperienced eyes anyway, that she had caught his attention. A little bit of the rage she held for Felix made her bold.

"And see the wolves?"

"I'll take you to see the wolves. If you dare."

She stopped at the door, looked over her shoulder at him. "Oh, I dare."

She walked down the track, light rain starting to mist over the trees, and didn't look back despite the hackles on her neck bristling. Part of her had been shocked by what he did, what she did. She had felt his erection pressing into her hip, and wondered why she wasn't surprised at the time. A thirty-one-year-old virgin, she had always thought that her brain had grown up but her body hadn't, just elongated into a gaunt version of the eleven-year-old she had been when the magic was cast to save her life. But now . . . she swung off the narrow path and put her hand on the top of the gate she had vaulted on the way in. She stopped, feeling the wet wood more intensely than before. The thick weave of Powell's fleece had left an imprint in her memory, the warmth of his body creeping through it, the sensation of his lips crawling over hers, his teeth, his breath, the taste of blood between them. Maybe that was what was so exciting, the promise of him. She knew there would be no niceties of emotion with him, just—sex. She was sick of tiptoeing around Felix, even if it was for his own safety.

She sprang easily back over the gate, and landed on the broad track left in the forest for access. The car was still half a mile away, in the Forestry Commission car park, but all her senses were amplified, and the energy charged through her veins. She broke into a run, riding the energy like a wave as she had when Felix had opened a vein for her five months before, when she had suckled on his arm and filled with blood and life and heat. She was breathing harder when she got to the car but every nerve ending was awake. It was almost as if she could feel every organ working, every inch of skin reacting to the pressure of clothing or movement.

As she rested against the car, she heard the first howl, then the next, as if he had got them howling just for her.

Chapter 24

*The Contarini family are, it is claimed, descended from
Roman emperors and comport themselves as such. The
Romans did not just build temples and amphitheatres;
their dabbling in dark magics and transformations are
written into our folklore and legend.*

—EDWARD KELLEY, 1586, Venice

WE ARRIVED AT CONTARINI'S ESTATE NEAR PADUA
late upon the third day: myself and Enrico, two
of Contarini's men, and a page I had been lent to
attend to my person and wardrobe. We were dusty and tired
from the road, little refreshed after staying two nights in way-
side inns. The host of the last had fed me some sort of meaty
sausage, very full of spices which did not entirely disguise the
rankness within. I ate sparingly, but that first bite lay uneasily
within my stomach, and I spent much of the night bloated with
the flux. Dawn saw me unhappily confined to the privy. The
ride, gentle though it was, caused me some discomfort but I was
feeling better by the time we arrived.

Lord Contarini awaited me in a chamber flooded with light,
reflected into the room by a pool before it, the water as still
as glass. The walls were covered with silk hangings and many
portraits hung between them. He greeted me as an old friend,
clasping both my hands and exclaiming at my paleness.

"Have you brought the sketch?" he asked, urgently, as he passed me a glass of wine.

The Dannicks, some centuries before, had gained a sketch of a Roman tablet that resided with the Contarini ancestors. This drawing, and another tablet in the possession of a nobleman in Bohemia, had been my inspiration for what I have to admit was a forgery.

"I have, my lord," said I, as I brought it forth from its leather case as if it were, indeed, a precious artifact. Its trials upon my journey had given it an air of antiquity.

The Bohemian stone, in several dozen pieces, was in the form of a curse. The man in the center of the slab was identified by various signs, and the curse was inscribed around him. The Dannicks' own sketch, centuries old and faded with wear, showed the ritual on which they had based their "cure," taken from an earlier viewing of the Contarini family treasure. What interested me was the closeness of two words. The Dannicks had long believed the word "CRUR" to mean cross, or *crux*, a gallows or tree of execution, or possibly the crucifix. They had interpreted the words into their ritual, which they assured me worked for some. But not it seemed for all, and especially not for their weakest child, the heir.

I had based my image upon the original with elements from the Bohemian tablet, especially in the style of the lettering and the use of the eight-pointed star. The hunchback figure in the original sketch I merely hinted at, to suggest that most of it was lost from what I was calling "the English tablet."

I unrolled the parchment upon a side table, and the count immediately sat down and spread his fingers lightly over the inked marks.

"Wonderful," he said. "So much like our own, and yet different—what is this word?"

I had deliberately left the C-R-U running into a crack, where letters could be assumed missing. "Our scholars are divided," I dissembled. "Perhaps we should compare it with your own carving?"

He glanced my way, and I was still unsure if he meant to let me see it.

I pretended a scholarly interest, and spent a minute describing the squareness of an irrelevant letter—in my forged drawing—then talked enthusiastically about the fineness of the limestone and I bombarded the count with questions on the style of the writing, the quality of the stone and the alignments of the symbols on his own tablet. Eventually, he stood.

"Let us compare them directly." He looked up and Enrico came into the room. Contarini rattled off much in Italian or Venetian, the distinction eludes me. Enrico bowed, and held open the door for us, then raced before us to a high wooden door with an elaborate escutcheon. He produced a key, and scraped it in the lock with some difficulty.

The door opened, leading to a dark corridor lined with paneling, unlike the marble inlaid walls of the villa.

"This is part of the earlier house," the count said. Enrico lit a lamp, its dim light turning the rest of the corridor into a tunnel of darkness. He led the way along the passageway. I was closely followed by the count, who shut and locked the door behind me. After a short walk, a flight of steps led below the ground level of the house. The air became dank, and smelled of the earth pressing in upon the dark walls. Finally, a door so low even I had to duck, and I found myself in a crypt as dark as nightfall and as cold. A flare of light and Enrico cupped his hand around his tinder until a candle spluttered into light. From this Enrico, stepping around me, lit first one branch of candles then another.

The room, lined with slabs of crudely cut pale stone, was no more than a cellar, but it contained only one object. Against one wall, standing upon a block of wood and covered in some sort of linen, was a large irregular shape. Enrico, at the count's command, carefully unshrouded it.

It was far better preserved than I had expected, and I could almost smell the old magic oozing from it. Unlike the Bohemian carving, which had lain in the elements even after it was smashed, the rectangular stone was only cracked in places, not weathered away. It had probably formed part of a pediment in some Roman nobleman's villa, the ornamental panel over a principal doorway perhaps. The central character, the hunched man, was in fact one of two figures, one unaccountably lost in the Dannicks' old sketch. One was leaning forward, and it almost looked as if some creature were emerging from his back, his face elongated into the most tormented scream. His fingers, too, were contorted into claws. This was not the transformation of a man into a superman, as Lord Dannick believed, but the debasing of a man into a beast.

The word "crur" was still there, but a gap between the letters "u" and "r" was filled by a character so small it looked as if it had been added afterward, as if the sculptor had accidentally left out a letter then corrected himself. A tiny circle was set between the letters, showing me the word *cruor* was intended. The Dannicks had believed for hundreds of years that the ritual demanded the use of a crucifix, authenticating it in their minds as a Christian ritual unique to their bloodline. But *cruor* was the Latin word for blood. Whatever this ritual was intended to do there was nothing Christian about it.

I leaned forward to examine the smaller figure, curled upon the ground, the face carved in a few lines suggesting sleep. It was missing a leg, and as I ran my fingers over it, holding a lamp aloft, I realized that it was not a man at all. It was a half-eaten child.

I tried to mask my emotion by bending forward as if examining a word.

"Fascinating. So much is similar," I said, "yet so is much different. This star, for example?" I pointed to my fictional element, knowing my host to be well versed in magics. "This is a design often seen in curses."

He nodded to me, pointing something out in a low voice to Enrico.

I stood back up, smiling at my host. "The tablet is finer even than Lord Dannick's," I said, for a little flattery will often open doors that politeness will not. "And seems related in purpose."

Contarini held my sketch closer to the branch of candles, careful not to drip tallow upon it. "Yet there is a sense that this is a curse?"

I nodded sagely, as if I believed it. "The Dannicks see the ritual—for I need not tell you the tablet describes a powerful magic—as both a boon and a curse." No lie there, what magic did not have both elements within it?

"Well, this sketch will keep our scholars' minds at work for months, Master Kelley, and I thank you for that."

"May I—?" I asked, waving a hand at the tablet.

"Certainly. Enrico will assist." He turned to Enrico and another wave of the fluid language rolled over me.

I pulled out the small leather wallet in which I kept my pens and ink pots, iron oak gall and verdigris. It also held my small pot of invisible ink within a secret compartment in the lid of my bottle. I made much of sharpening my pen, and unrolling my vellum. I knew that to a trained eye one sketch might resemble the other, and decided to draw badly but retain as much detail as possible within my memory. Indeed, the most important message might be within the single word *cruor*.

My lord left and Enrico and I bowed deeply to his departure, then the two of us were left in the dark place. We looked at each other for a long moment, and I hope he was as much pleased by my company as I was by his. A modest man, with a keen interest in the tablet and my interpretation, he asked questions in

precise Latin, and pointed out details and held the light for me.
I asked questions, innocent sounding though I intended them
to be, about the Contarinis. He answered politely, giving little
away save his utter loyalty to his master. He seemed a quiet man,
one whose eyes were keener than mine, and I asked him several
times to examine finer details of the carving. Over time, he grew
more talkative. I learned he was the son of one of the Venetian
traders, an Abyssinian or Ethiopian, as they call themselves.
His father wished him to learn the languages of the Venetians
and the Turks, and Contarini offered the best opportunity. The
boy was brought up as a playmate for Contarini's own children,
and raised with the same tutors and advantages. I contrasted his
early childhood with mine own, the constant stigma of my birth
and poverty upon me, yet we had both been raised by the keen-
ness of our wits and the cultivation of our betters.

I stood back and observed the tablet. "I am still unclear . . ."
I said, in part truthfully. "The purpose of the ritual, you say, is
a healing one?"

"So I understand it." Enrico seemed enlivened by some excitement, some passion within. "The ritual gives health and
long life to the recipient."

Such was true, I thought, of the Dannicks. Though without the ritual, their sons withered like unpicked fruit in winter
winds.

"Lord Contarini is a great man," I ventured, pretending
to study a tiny crack as if it were part of the carving. "A fine
master."

That was sufficient to unlock the careful tongue of the
Moor. He described a man who rode to the hunt all day and
into the night until his grooms swooned in their saddles. Who
had fathered many children upon first one wife then a second,
the first, I imagine, worn unto death. He had a library of hundreds of books, some written in his own hand, and was visited
by scholars from all over Europe.

While he talked, I fumbled with my pen, dropped it, and picked up another. Dipping it in my secret ink within my pot lid, I added a quick note in English of the exact wording upon the tablet. Fussing about the nib, I exchanged it for the first and carried on sketching.

"You are a favored servant," I observed. "I would have thought you a family member."

The man's chest swelled with some peacocking hubris. "I am to be admitted to the circle," he confided, then halted, as though he had said something he ought not.

"Indeed!" I exclaimed, as if I knew what of he spoke. "Then I was right, you are almost family."

Mistaking my words for knowledge, he hesitated, spending a moment pinching out a sputtering wick, and relighting the candle. "I have waited for many full moons, for the auguries to be favorable."

This was familiar ground. Much magic can only succeed at the fullest, or at the death of the moon. "Tonight it is at its brightest."

He could barely control his excitement, hopping from one foot to another. "It is for I, and one other," he said, in a rush, as if he had tried to keep it back. "The grandson of Lord Contarini's brother."

Some tiny bell of question rang in my mind, but, distracted by my task, I could not pursue it.

"Is there a ceremony? I would be honored to attend," I said.

His face fell. "I believe it is just for the circle themselves. I have never attended one, indeed, all the servants are locked within an upper chamber during those nights. The sound of the hunt keeps us all awake."

"The hunt?" I tried to exactly capture the angle of a design I did not recognize.

"The circle celebrates with a hunt around the estate. All

peasants and their animals are commanded to lock themselves within from dusk to dawn."

"They hunt with dogs?" I was not much interested, but allowed the information to flow over me. You never know what will be revealed as useful, or even crucial. Like this single word that I pondered over.

"I think not." The man hesitated, and then his voice dropped to a whisper. "The legend is that the wolves from the mountains come down and hunt with the lords and the ladies, like great hounds, utterly subservient to their masters."

"That would be a sight to see," I said. Rumors, legends, myths. Likely his lordship had some compound where he bred the most savage hounds that might not be released upon the local farmers and their stock. I had known a farmer's children mauled by dogs hunted even by the queen's court.

He stopped, as if he had spoken too much. Instead, he pointed to a tiny dot and asked if it had significance. I copied it with great care, even though I thought it merely a chip on the stone of its great age. His conversation turned to the tablet, and I wondered at his remark that Contarini, surely the eldest son, had a brother who was a grandfather. Contarini was, perhaps, forty years old, perhaps younger, and I speculated that they marry their children young in these parts.

Chapter 25

So much life is born of death, the body seethes with it. Beetles and fly larvae, birds, rats, microbes in great sheets wander under the skin, making it slide away from muscle. The bloated belly has long since burst in a kaleidoscope of greens and purples, rank blood splashed around and supped by plants, greedy for the rich juices.

WHEN JACK PULLED THE CAR ONTO THE VERGE OUTside the house Felix was loading a bag into his car. Her heart started racing. She jumped out of the car. "You're going?"

He started to smile, then his eyes trailed to her mouth, and a frown started gathering on his forehead. "Just getting something for Sadie. I thought you were going to investigate the wolf enclosure."

"Yes, I did, but . . ." She looked up at him, feeling the sting of the split in her lip. Now she knew what she wanted, and intense though the feeling was for the wolf man—lust, probably—it was just an echo of the complex feelings she had for Felix.

Felix closed the boot of his car and paused, hand on the lock. "What have you been doing?"

"Thinking about what you said. About this woman—"

He sighed. "Jack, you told me there was nothing between us—could never be. You sent me away."

She looked at her feet. "Maybe I was wrong. Maybe something is possible with you and me—I just don't know what I feel for you."

He reached a hand for her, and she considered it. Brown, strong fingers, tendons sliding under the skin at his wrist. She knew it so well. Her feet moved without her thinking about it, until she was close enough to feel his breath on her hair. She looked up, suddenly curious. The attraction she felt, so much stronger since she had taken his blood, was irresistible.

She reached for his wool sweater, grasping handfuls of it in an effort to recreate the chemistry with Powell.

"What's happened?" He slid his hands over hers, the warm roughness of his skin catching the breath in the back of her throat. "What's changed?"

"I'm alive, Felix. Finally, I feel like a healthy adult, not a sickly child." She smiled up at him, seeing the dark green and amber flecks in his eyes. "I want to be treated like one." The words rolled in her mind, unfamiliar concepts.

He squeezed her hands tightly, and a smile lifted one side of his mouth. "What happened to 'I'm not ready'?"

Her smile faded as she recalled the confusion he created in her. An approach from him normally sent her running back to the solitary place she had lived in since childhood, to work on rebuilding the walls he'd eroded. "Something happened."

He released her hands and one finger brushed the split part of her lip. "What?"

"Something that made me think of you." She let go of his jumper and stepped back, suddenly shy. "The man who keeps the wolves, Powell, has seven animals up there. He's keeping them for Sir Henry. I think they are doing some sort of experiment there with what he thinks of as their 'savage nature,' but that doesn't make sense."

"You think it's something to do with the werewolf myth?" He rested his hands on her shoulders. "Maggie told me about the howling. There are myths of animal cults all over the world, but there's no evidence at all of werewolves."

"Maggie said there were spells."

He nodded. "The Romans created rituals they believed would change someone into a half wolf at the full moon. Witches were sometimes accused of transforming into animals in medieval Europe as well. They were supposed to use rituals to awaken some inner strength or quality and enhance it."

"He said something about me, as if I had a superpower of some sort. Talking with animals, or something."

He frowned, looking away, his eyes becoming unfocused as if he were trying to remember something. "Sadie and Maggie mentioned the idea of archetypes in relation to the Dannicks. Archetype theory has some proponents."

"I don't understand it."

"Basically, you have hunter-gatherer groups in prehistory. The most efficient use of people is to divide up the tasks by what people are good at. Rather than everyone hunting, some people would be expert in predicting the animals' behavior, reading their body language, understanding their calls, that sort of thing." He sighed, leaning on the car. "Others would be better suited to the running down and killing of the prey."

She nodded. "Maggie explained something similar. Some group members would have intuitions about the weather, others would be healers. Some might even be magicians who worked magic for the group. Others might be skilled at dealing with children, others at creating artifacts like stone knives or skins. Her theory is that these people tended to interbreed, concentrating the genes."

"We know people are attracted to mates with scent and

physical cues which are genetic, unconscious." He stepped away from her.

"Sir Henry said that's what his family did, marrying within their class to produce warriors, soldiers. Hunters." She paused. "Maybe there are characteristics that are stimulated by sorcery. That's how healing spells work. They activate the healthy genes the body has."

He looked down for a moment, his face changing as thoughts chased through his mind.

"What's wrong?" Jack looked up into his face.

"You're different. Sometimes you're the old Jack, like a half-tamed bird, like now. And other times, you are—more assertive, like you were a minute ago"

"Alive. That's what's happened, Felix. I'm starting to feel alive. I can't tell you what borrowed time is like, it's such a struggle to do anything. But now, I feel like my body is waking up, I feel as if I can have a real life. I hardly need the circles and potions some days."

"But other days you still do?"

She frowned. "I have good days and bad days, who doesn't?"

He took a breath, and opened his mouth as if about to say something. Instead, he sighed, and stepped away, his hands falling to his side. "Maggie's in the kitchen, waiting for you. We can talk about it later."

"I'm not part of your research, Felix. This is me, finally with enough energy to *be* me."

"I'm just worried."

She stepped toward the house, filled with unfamiliar emotions. "Afraid for me or scared *of* me?"

He didn't answer, and she opened the door, catching Ches as he flung himself against her.

"Stop it, stupid dog," she said, but Ches stiffened, then pulled back. He sniffed her, almost as Powell had done, then sat, studying her closely. When she looked up, Maggie was observing from the kitchen doorway.

"Come and eat." Her words were impassive, but her eyes were watchful.

Jack felt something odd, uncomfortable, and she shook her head.

"I'll be back in a minute," she said, and kicked her boots into the basket under the stairs before heading up to the bathroom.

It was an unexpected discovery. She supposed this was menstruation, after her first panic that bleeding couldn't be normal. She had never had to worry about it before. Although her body had matured a little in her teens, in some way it had been more like a young teenager's all her life. She had grown used to thinking of herself as naturally having a less feminine body, but as she stripped her outer layers off, she could see the changes in the mirror. Her breasts were more rounded, fuller, her hips filling out. She was still slim, but no one was going to mistake her for a boy anymore.

It was only a few drops. She changed her underwear in the bedroom and went down to dinner.

The kitchen was filled with the aroma of spices, the wave of different tangs almost overwhelming. For many years, her sense of smell had been muted by her semihibernated nature. Now, everything was intense, and her appetite had grown with the new sensations.

"I made something from my new Indian cookery book," Maggie said, putting pans on the table with a plate of warmed naan breads. Sadie sat on a chair with its back to the wall, even more pale than usual.

"Great," the girl said, with no enthusiasm. "But I still feel a bit sick."

"Eat something, you'll be fine. It's all organic." She handed a plate to Jack.

Sadie rolled her head along the wall to Jack to look at her. "What happened to you? You look like someone hit you."

"I went to see the wolf research place out by Grizedale. We got into a bit of an argument, that's all. No one hit anyone. I just bumped my lip." On his mouth. The memory of the kiss made warmth creep up her neck toward her face.

Maggie dished Jack up some fragrant curry. "Watch out for cloves and cardamom pods," she warned. "Did you see the wolves?"

"I saw pictures." The first taste of the food exploded on her tongue, the heat from the chilli, the buttery richness of the sauce. "This is fantastic. I'll have a naan bread too."

"What are the wolves even doing there?" Sadie pushed a little rice around her plate. "Are they going to breed them, or something?"

"They tried to, but the wolves are too stressed." That was it. "Actually, I noticed the wolves were really odd in the pictures. Normally wolves ignore people, they just concentrate on the pack leader. But these were really focused on the one holding the camera. And there was something odd about all of them. They had shaved forepaws."

"Why . . ." Felix leaned forward. "Wolf blood. Are they testing them for something?"

"Wolves don't donate willingly," Jack said. "I'm betting he has to dart or otherwise incapacitate the wolves. They are scared of him because he hurts them."

Sadie put down her fork. "That's disgusting."

"What are they using it for?" Felix took a naan and tore a corner off. Without apparently thinking, he passed it down below table level.

Jack laughed out loud. "You're feeding Ches? Really?"

He grinned back at her. "It's the only way he lets me stay around. He likes being top dog." He pressed his fingers together for a moment. "The Dannicks talk about their 'warrior' tradition."

"And Powell says he's looking into the 'savage nature' of wolves." Jack waved a piece of bread at him. "Which is crap, because there's nothing savage about any animal, there's just survival."

"Maybe the genetic trait he's talking about is countered by some sort of dormant gene that they historically think of as a hunter or warrior gene. That is somehow activated by this . . . potion."

Jack looked at Maggie.

Maggie shook her head, and brushed a white lock out of her eyes. "We use potions to reinforce magic, but it's the ritual that is most important. Like Sadie's symbols."

Felix made a sound somewhere between a laugh and a cough. "Magical beliefs—" he started, but Jack cut him off.

"You don't appreciate our magic, we get that. But you do know that the circles are necessary to our survival because you've seen us—" She glanced at Sadie to include her in the argument, and stopped.

"I'm trying to understand your magic but—" he said, his voice irritated.

Sadie was bone white, her eyes closed, chin sagged on her chest.

"Shit! Maggie—" Jack pushed her chair up and pulled the corner of the table away. She leaped forward to catch Sadie as she slumped from the chair. "Help me!"

Even as she eased the girl toward the floor, she could feel that something—Sadie—was missing. "Help me get her into the circles!"

Felix, finally catching on, swept her aside and grabbed Sadie, half running into the front room with her. Jack pulled the coffee table from the middle of the room and shouted at Felix to put her on the floor, in the center of the circles.

Jack held Sadie's face to breathe life into her, smelling the rankness of the choking sickness that stalked Sadie all the time. Felix felt for a pulse.

"Nothing," he said, his voice wavering. "How did—"

"Out of the way." Maggie swept in, matches and incense sticks in her hand. Jack started chest compressions, trying to remember how long Sadie had been quiet at the table. Breathe, breathe, one-two-three-four-five. She didn't know if she was doing it right, but it had worked before.

Maggie knelt on the other side, pulling Sadie's jacket open, dragging up her T-shirts. Sadie was layered up like a mummy and her skin was cold. Jack remembered that, the cold, always, even on the brightest of summer days. The acrid scent of sulfur hit her as the match was lit, then one of the incense sticks that Maggie made by hand, stinking of burned herbs. Maggie blew the flame out, and Jack glanced up to see it glow.

"Do we really need to—?" she whispered, but Maggie's jaw muscles tensed and the orange tip of the stick sizzled against Sadie's chest.

Jack caught the reek of burned skin as Maggie traced a sigil, then lifted the ember to blow again. She forced herself to ignore Maggie, and resumed the compressions and breaths.

"Come on, Sadie . . ." she entreated as Maggie started searing the teenager's skin again. There, a tiny flinch from the muscles of Sadie's arm, a twitch in a finger. She sat back. "Wait, she's coming back."

But Maggie kept going. She blew again, then started the third sigil. This time Sadie whimpered, and turned her head. By the fourth burn, her eyes flickered open and she took a deeper breath.

"Jack!" she moaned.

Jack reached with one hand and caught Maggie's wrist.

"She needs at least one complete circle done," Maggie hissed back.

"Try the silver solution."

Tears were gathering in Sadie's eyes and slipping down the side of her face. Her hand shook as she raised it to catch Jack's sleeve. "Let her do it," she breathed. "I—I feel like I'm dying."

Jack grasped her hand and tried to warm it with her own energy. "All right, but I'm staying right here." She stared up at Maggie. "Maybe we should try blood."

Felix interrupted immediately. "No blood!" He moderated his tone, his hand gripping the dog's collar. "We don't know enough about the side effects."

Maggie traced the next sigils as lightly as she could, raising red weals rather than the blistering black marks from the first three. Sadie sobbed, her tight fingers trembling in Jack's until the last sigil was done.

"Move the sofa," Jack said to Felix, getting no reaction from him. He looked appalled, disgusted even, frozen by the door. "Felix! Put the sofa in the middle of the room so we can lift Sadie onto it."

He complied as Maggie took Sadie's legs, and Jack gently lifted her body. She smoothed the layers of clothing back as Sadie started shivering. Maggie opened the woodburner, and threw a handful of the same herbs on, closing the damper to drift smoke into the room.

Felix stood back, waving coiling smoke away from his face. "What the hell was that?" He coughed, and sat on the other sofa, watching Maggie and Jack fuss over the white-faced girl, who even now looked barely conscious.

"This is the nature of borrowed time, Felix." Jack tucked a cushion behind Sadie's shoulders and head. "She's barely alive." She turned to Sadie. "Maggie will get you some hot potion, OK?"

Sadie nodded, then stared across the room at Felix. When Jack had first met her she had seemed short for fourteen, but already curvy. Now she was gaunt, her face wasted, her eyes huge in the bony sockets.

"That was a bad one," Sadie managed.

Felix leaned forward. "This has happened before?"

"A couple of times." Sadie choked, putting her hands to her face. "Did I pass right out?"

"In the kitchen."

"I thought I was getting better." Sadie's voice was weak.

"I think you were," said Jack. "I think we all took our eye off the ball. How much potion have you had today?" Jack tucked a throw around her. Sadie had chosen it from a charity shop, its bright colors reflecting some African culture. It made her skin look even more pale.

"You gave me some for breakfast—I can't remember."

"The bottle's more than half full, that's the problem." Maggie handed Jack a mug which stank of hot herbal infusions. "Try and get her to drink the lot."

"You heard, kitten. All of it." Jack looked at Felix and her voice hardened. "This is it, this is our life. Now do you understand why I am so much better? Why I want this for Sadie?"

"You drank human blood." His voice was low, and his face looked twisted with some sort of conflict. "All the traditions I have studied condemn it, they think it's dangerous."

"But since I had one mouthful of your blood I haven't had a single episode like this. I can run, I can go all day away from the circles, I am warm, Felix. Can you imagine what it's like to be always cold? Always exhausted?" Jack choked on her anger. "And you still think we shouldn't give Sadie the same advantage?"

"Let's talk about it outside."

Sadie spluttered on a sip of potion. "Don't you dare!"

"This affects Sadie more than any of us." Jack watched conflicting emotions on Felix's face.

"We don't know what the consequences of taking blood are." Felix's voice was flat. "I spoke to people who do drink blood— there are side effects. They wouldn't tell me everything, but it's already changed you. And the original symbols come from a text—"

"I've changed for the better! I can run, I can—" Jack choked on the words. "You don't understand what it's like to be dying, really dying. It feels like if you just shut your eyes, you will stop breathing. You struggle to stay awake. It's like—"

"Drowning." Sadie held the mug in both hands, looking over at Felix. "It's like you are in cold water, and you feel it taking you under. You know the next breath you take will fill your lungs up and you will die."

"For God's sake—" He put his head in his hands for a long moment. "You haven't been listening to me, either of you. Kelley *knew* there was something dangerous about the ritual he used to create revenants. He created a monster when he gave Elizabeth Báthory human blood."

"You can't compare me to her." Jack took the empty mug hanging from Sadie's fingers. "I'm still me."

"You really believe you're the same old Jack? What did you do with Powell? You came back looking—"

Jack leaned forward. "Is this all because I kissed Powell? Yes, that's how I hurt my lip, I decided to kiss an attractive man. And you know what? I enjoyed it."

"And that's out of character for you." His voice was level but his face looked hurt.

"How do you know—shit, how do *I* know? I've been trapped in some hellish half death since I was eleven years old. Now I'm finally getting to grow up and I'm starting to enjoy it."

"Jack." Maggie's voice was soft. "We're all on the same team."

Jack jumped off the sofa. "No, we're not! You took me because you wanted to save your baby from leukemia. You didn't have a clue what you were going to do with me afterward, did you?"

"I did my best for you. I loved you." Maggie clenched her hands in front of her.

"You didn't expect me to live. You used me, you took my blood to save Charley. And you taught me to do the same to Sadie so I could sell her blood." Overflowing with all the hurtful things she wanted—needed—to say, Jack spun on one heel and crashed out of the room. She grabbed her car keys from her coat pocket and opened the front door.

"Jack, finish what you have to say." Maggie stood in the doorway with tears streaking down her face. "Do you wish I had left you to die?"

"Yes! No—but I can't watch Sadie die, over and over again."

"We'll be more careful," Maggie said, a note of pleading in her voice. "You want what's best for Sadie, I know, but Felix is right. There's something different about you."

"Different, yes." She stepped onto the garden path. "I'm sick of living like a crippled child."

She slammed the door behind her and stalked to the car. Under the rage was a whisper of exhilaration. Damn it, she was going to do something for herself.

Chapter 26

The Contarini are a strong, tall race originating from Padua, where they have a principal estate. They have business concerns within Venice and Florence also, and their sons and cousins are found in many ruling families. The present head of the family is Baldassarre Contarini, a learned alchemist and scholar. He was visited by an Edward Kelly [sic], a sorcerer from England, in the spring of 1586.

—NICCOLÒ D'ALVIANO, *Historica*, 1589

I WAS CALLED INTO CONTARINI'S LIBRARY, A RICHLY DECO-rated room where not just books but scientific instruments were displayed. There I was invited to eat meats and breads with him. We sat together and after a while he dismissed the servants, saying we would attend ourselves. I ate, but my fingers itched to explore the leather covers of the books.

"You like the look of my library?" He laughed at me. "Yet I would wish for a collection such as Dee's."

"It is the finest in England," I boasted, though in truth I wondered if it would still be there when we returned.

"Indeed. I hope to visit it when I travel to London."

I bowed my head politely, chewing the delicate slice of ham I had carved. I offered to pour my host some wine, which was gracefully accepted. He offered me some fruits, which I did not eschew. But the question hung in the air between us.

"So, Master Kelley. How do you like our carving?"

"It is very fine," I said, "and much better preserved than Lord Dannick's."

He sipped his wine. "Lord Dannick must confide in you a great deal to trust you with his family's greatest artifact."

I bowed again.

A breeze, not cold but vigorous, blew around the open window and seeing my slight shudder Lord Contarini stood to close it. "I hoped to compare notes upon the purification of base metals," he continued. "Is this something that Lord Dannick shares with you?"

"Not at all, my lord," I averred. "His interest is solely in the family history surrounding the tablet."

"How did you meet?"

"I met his son at Cambridge, while studying at the university." Not so much a lie, since the younger Lord Robert had gone to the university, and I had been employed to be his tutor and servant. "I had previously been the student of Sir Solomon Seabourne, the alchemist."

"In truth?" The man seemed surprised. "I heard he had some success in making gold from the rotting carcasses of swans."

"I am sworn to secrecy, my lord," I said, but he was not fooled. I had left Seabourne's employ to enter the house of Dr. Dee before Sir Solomon became unexpectedly wealthy. "But I can say it was not putrefaction, but purification that produced the transformation."

"Really?" He pondered the point a long moment. "My own method is more an intervention of the spirits." He swirled the wine around in his goblet. "My great-grandfather attempted the invocation of a demon within this very house."

I was intrigued. Everyone knows that raising demons is almost always fatal.

He must have divined such from my expression, and laughed. "You are right, my young friend. It was a dangerous experiment. He filled a barrel with horse blood, thinking it cleaner than ox blood, called the demon into the circle and constrained it with spells. He must have got one wrong, at least, for the thing demanded human blood and when he would not oblige, it took the life of every last human in the castle."

This is the kind of story I have heard several times. Raising demons is Satan's work, though I thought it polite not to say so.

His eyes narrowed as he examined me, as if trying to divine my thoughts. "You question the legend?"

"If all humans died," I asked, "how may the line of Contarini succeed to this day? Or the story be told?"

He smiled, showing his long, sharp-looking teeth. "It is said that in the distant past, the family was cursed by a witch, whose only son was slain by his overlord, for the crime of poaching. She cursed that no Contarini would father a son, into the third generation."

As one who has lived in a world of queens, I knew the origins of such a myth. I supped a little on the bread, dipped in a bowl of a kind of soup or sauce. "What did your ancient ancestor do, my lord?"

"He set his three daughters to beget sons, as best they could. One daughter became so pious, she attracted the attention of one of the *nephilim*, a creature born of humans and angels. She bore twin sons, but they were disgusted by their human grandfather's pride and sin, and flew away to heaven. The next daughter called upon Satan, debasing herself in his filthy cult, and was ravished by one of his demons. She bore a son, but he was appalled by the kindliness and virtues within his grandfather, and he was swallowed up by the ground and taken down to hell."

"And then?"

"The youngest daughter went into the world and searched for an answer among the peasants to lift the curse. She worked as a swineherd and a dairymaid and a weaver, and she met all kinds of people. They were neither all good, nor all bad, she reasoned, and she would marry none of them. One day, walking in the woods collecting truffles, she was attacked by a pack of wolves. In her eyes, the leader seemed to shift, one minute a black-haired youth, the next, a dark wolf. In her terror, she swooned, falling upon the grass.

"She awoke, astonished to find she was still alive and had not been eaten, but her clothes had been disordered and she realized she had been ravished by the wolf. She gathered her torn clothes about her and returned to her family. There, months later, she gave birth to the first Baldassarre Contarini, my ancestor. Like the wolf, he was neither all virtue nor all sin."

"So when the demon killed every human . . . ?"

"He spared those of the wolf line. My father, his brothers, and myself, a baby in my mother's dead arms."

Chapter 27

It is the season of mating and growing, of pollen drifting and flowers opening to it. Everywhere life is expanding, thrusting into the soil, unfurling into the sky.

MINDFUL OF THE RAGE THAT WAS SIMMERING INSIDE her, Jack drove with exaggerated care and turned toward Grizedale Forest. Farmers had been working on the fields, shedding arcs of sculpted soil onto the roads. Jack could feel her heart banging in her chest. She felt completely alive and energized. She wound the window down, smelled the scents of the night, so vivid since she had been transformed by Felix's blood. She could still remember the way it tasted, the way it roiled into her throat, thick and salty, and so hot. Paradoxically, she could also remember the way he kissed her, the scent of him, the feel of his hair sliding through her fingers. Her body was tingling, she wanted—Felix. She yanked the steering wheel around, driving the car onto the verge by the gate to the wolf research cabin. For a moment, she struggled to catch her breath. She leaned her head back and took a few moments to stop feeling and start thinking. It was time to resolve things with the professor because, she realized on a wave of warmth, it was Felix she wanted. But her body still opened the car door.

She stood by the vehicle, and fought the impulse to get back in and drive back. A sound made her lift her head.

It was a howl, but not a normal one, more like a yelp. Maybe the wolves were playing, maybe one had got a bit rough. The next yelp was definitely not playing, and she could hear something else—a man's voice. The next sound made her vault over the gate and stride up the long path. The wolves started howling, more barking, she realized, than just trying to communicate. They sounded like they felt threatened.

The cold air seemed to prickle against her skin, she felt as if each step were bouncing against the packed earth, as if she had almost enough energy to fly. She started to run, the dark occasionally sending a branch or a puddle her way, but she seemed to know where they were, could brush them aside or leap over them. It felt like she was more alive than she had ever been, racing to protect the wolves, Sadie, everything.

He was standing where he had been earlier as if he'd been waiting there all the time. He had a bag of equipment in one hand, and a long pole in the other. She hit him at a full run, banging him against the wooden cladding of the building.

"What are you doing to those animals?" she snarled, both hands high on his chest, his arms splayed out as they hit the building. He dropped the equipment.

"You came back." He grinned at her, the pale light from the windows gleaming off his teeth, his eyes.

She could feel her muscles soften, her mind become confused. He smelled like wood smoke and cold air and damp wool. And man. It was as if a switch had been thrown in her mind, the one that put Jack and her fears aside and instead gave her body control over her muscles.

Her body's demands drew her up on tiptoes, reaching for that kiss to check it had really been that good.

It was. She had never liked being touched before, but now she just wanted to tear her clothes off, his clothes—it was new, and intoxicating. He seemed to know all the right things to do, how to kiss her, how to hold her. Her brain switched off and her body took over in a haze of sensation: the feel of his hair, the skin on his neck, the scent of him. At the same time, part of her retreated in confusion, revulsion at his stale smell, the rough way he handled her. The reality that he wasn't Felix.

The spell was broken when he dragged her away from the cabin. "Come with me." His breathing was as ragged as hers, but he stepped away and bent to pick something up. The long pole.

"What? Where?" She was still dazed when he took her hand in his and led her along the high fence. "No."

"The enclosure." He let go of her hand to fumble for keys in his pocket, and unlocked the narrow gate. "You wanted to see the wolves."

"But—" She allowed him to drag her in, lock the gate behind them. Reason started to creep back into her thoughts now he was a few feet away.

"It's safe," he said, as if answering the question forming in her mind. "They are scared of me. And this." He waved the pole. "Cattle prod."

That was like a bucket of cold water poured down her neck. She wiped her lips and noticed her hand was shaking. "Why are they scared of you?"

"I'm in charge, I collect all the samples."

"You are bleeding the wolves for the Dannicks." Jack could feel eyes watching her, making the hairs on her back prickle. "For some crazy ritual they believe will make them like wolves."

"Skinwalkers, they call it." He grinned, his hand finding her arm in the dark. "You should see them, it's amazing."

"You've seen them change?"

"There's this ritual. They do something with the blood,

smear themselves in it I think, and go into this animal state. Then they hunt."

"Here?"

"No, this is too close to public land. They do it in their own forest, around the castle. They hunt, naked, like wild animals. Whatever they catch, they tear to pieces. They locked me in the basement of the castle last time, but I could see them going out, and when they came back—they were mad with it."

Jack could feel the spell of his touch, his scent, starting to draw her back in, and wrenched herself out of his grasp. "I thought they just wanted to help the boy."

"The hunt keeps them young, helps them be healthy. Maybe it would help the kid, though he seems pretty far gone to me." This time he grabbed her hard enough to hurt her. "Never mind them, now it's my turn."

A small part of Jack started to panic, waves of fear creeping through the confidence that pushed him back with her own strength. "Let me out."

"No chance. You came. I know what you want."

This time she put some weight behind the push, shoving him away hard enough to fall onto one knee. He staggered to his feet, his breath whistling faster now. She started to move toward the gate.

The next moment something hit her in the face, a bang echoing inside her head and something smashing into her cheekbone. She spun as she fell and dropped face first onto long grass and mud.

It took a few seconds to realize he was sitting on her legs, tearing at her clothes. She tried to roll over but he was stronger and heavier. "No—stop," she panted, struggling under him, feeling her waistband give way under his crawling fingers, the cold air creeping into the gap between her jeans and her jumper. She struggled, thinking feverishly for spells, wrestling moves, anything that might save her. He dragged her jeans down, and she struggled to push back onto all fours, to get away, anything.

This time, the blow was to the back of her head, and the world lit up with jagged flashes of light. She was stunned for a moment, coming around to realize her face was pressed into the mud. She was held by a hand on the back of her neck. She could barely turn her head an inch to breathe. The need to survive became more important than what he was doing. Fumbling with his belt, by the sound of it, grabbing her legs to pull them apart. She stopped fighting, and the grip on her neck relaxed for a moment. She pulled her head up, looking into the dark knowing *they* were there in the shadows, their eyes fixed not on her but on him. She whined, a tiny whimper of distress, the sound Ches would make if he was scared. It was answered by the deepest rumble of a growl from the darkness. She tried to kick the man off, but he was pinning her down, too excited to notice the sound building up around them.

She tried another whine, this time, short bursts of cries as she hyperventilated in her panic. Her senses, reaching into the dark, could feel the lead wolf, Desna, could smell his musk, his breath. He must be just a few feet away. For a moment she saw the flash of his teeth. It came as, despite her kicking, Powell managed to pin her legs apart.

As she braced herself to be raped, the wolf hit the man, the silent attack carrying Powell away from her. She rolled into a ball, sobbing with relief. She screamed, scrabbling around for a weapon, for her clothes. Jack struggled to all fours as the snap of a cattle prod was answered by a yelp, and the wolf fell back.

Powell staggered to his feet, waving the prod around him. "You bastards!" he shouted. Jack could see him holding his arm across his chest. "Try it if you dare, you useless mongrels!"

Jack grabbed at the jeans, still around one ankle, and pulled them up. She managed to stand although the pain in her face was lighting the dark with sparks when she moved.

She felt her way toward the fence, pressing her back into it. "Just let me go."

"They won't hurt me. They wouldn't dare." His voice started the growling again from all around. Jack could just make out the wolves in the starlight, the gleam of a canine tooth here, the flash of a tail there. They were circling to attack.

It came to her, even as fear started to inch her closer to the man and his flimsy defense. He had said it himself, she talked wolf. She started to creep back away from him, attracting the wolves herself.

"Don't move. They'll kill you," he warned, but she ignored him, focusing on the lead animals. The male Desna was back, just behind the shoulder of the lead female.

She yipped, finding the sound under her tongue, the greeting of a wolf to its pack. The wolves froze, their sounds falling away. As she distanced herself from the man, she could see their focus return to him.

She started the growling, turning toward him and crouching forward, her whole body pointing at Powell. One by one, the animals joined her, the growling developing into the first excited yelps from the animal nearest to her.

When they attacked, the wolves hit him low, only the lead wolves snapping at his neck and face, but Jack dove for the lighter-colored cattle prod. Ripping it away from him, she staggered back to the fence as the yowling increased.

"Jack—" he screamed. "Help me!"

A part of her, even as it shivered in terror, wanted to help. Another thought, cool and logical, made her step toward the gate. The animals were in a frenzy, yapping and snarling, a dark shape of moving wolves where the man had stood. Another scream was cut off by a cracking, as if a bone had been shattered. She crept along the fence, feeling behind her as she kept an eye on the animals.

Shit, the keys. She looked at the cattle prod in her hands, and in a moment of disgust, threw it away, the sound of bushes swishing where it hit. The snarling stopped, and at least one of the shapes stood away from the silent body.

She stood, trying to project a calm she didn't feel, the cold mud seeping into her clothes. One by one, the animals joined the first. She could see the lightest fur, just hints in the shadows, so the dark gap in the middle must be the big male. She couldn't guess what they were thinking, her only experience was with a tame wolf hybrid. With a moment of clarity, she realized her best chance was to become one of the pack. She threw back her head, and as best she could, barked three times then launched into the howl. At first her voice cracked, she knew she had nothing like the animals' volume, but took a deep breath, and started again. This time, one of the wolves joined in, then another started barking. Finally, she paused for breath and a deeper howl came from the dark shadow she assumed was one of the dominant wolves.

She assumed a less aggressive posture and started a greeting whimper, allowing the wolves to approach, the lead animals at first sniffing at her from a few feet away. She must be covered with Powell's scent, she knew, as well as Ches's. At least he had been neutered, so there was no testosterone to set off the pack leader. She sniffed back, getting the metallic scent of blood. Was Powell dead? A fleeting instinct made her breathe the intoxicating scent in again.

She started sidling back toward him, back to the keys. One wolf growled, but the others just watched, probably confused, she thought, at attacking their food supply as well as their tormentor.

He was still alive, his breath coming in tiny gasps, but he didn't seem able to respond to her. She reached her hand into his right jacket pocket, and her hand slid through the ripped cotton and into—some hot cavity inside the man's abdomen. Fighting an alien urge to stop and lick her fingers, she retracted her hand, finding the keys tangled in the pocket lining.

She shook off the strange feeling and retreated along the fence, still watched closely by the wolves. She could see the forward ones now, they had stepped closer to the fence, boxing her in by the gate.

"Thank you" she said, unable to guess whether the tone of the words would help but hoping the change in body posture would reassure them.

Desna stepped forward, with the lead bitch—Chulyin—at his shoulder. Acting on impulse, Jack held out the back of her unbloodied hand for them to smell, and she was rewarded when Desna sniffed, then pulled back a little. She fumbled the key into the lock, the metal slipping in her gory hand. Sliding through the open gate, she clicked it quietly behind her and locked it, feeling sudden grief that she couldn't let them out of their enclosure. Rational thought reminded her that seven wolves roaming free in the Lake District National Park wouldn't last a week.

She staggered in the dark, slipping on mud, the adrenaline making her shake. She polished the keys on her sleeve to remove any trace of her own fingerprints, then tossed them over the fence by the gate. Perhaps people would think Powell had dropped them on the way in.

She stumbled down the footpath to the car, shivering, spooked at the sound of a branch snapping in the dense scrub beside the track. She scrambled over the gate, catching her knee on the top, starting to feel the bruises. The car was a welcome refuge, and she took a long moment to catch her breath and lock the door. She sat under the tiny glow of the interior light then picked up her phone, left on the front seat, but still no signal. Starting the car was reassuring, just the rumble of the engine and the flare of bright lights. She reversed onto the road and drove to the public car park and looked again at her phone. The number for the castle was easy to find.

"Hello, Knowle Castle, Mrs. Ellison speaking."

"I thought—" Jack cleared her throat again. "I thought you should know, there was a lot of howling up past Grizedale, in the wolf compound. I thought I heard someone shouting."

"I'm sorry, could I have your name? I'm sure there's nothing to worry about—"

Jack grimaced. They had her number now anyway. "My name is Jack Hammond, I heard someone shouting for help. Please get someone to check that everything is OK."

She rang off, feeling in the dark for the painful cheekbone where Powell had hit her. The flesh seemed spongy but the bone was sound. An exploration of her teeth with her tongue suggested she'd chipped at least one tooth. As she drove the car toward Bee Cottage her hands started to shake. She gripped the wheel more firmly and took the turning for the village.

Despite her natural tendency for seclusion, she had become known at the small supermarket, at least by sight, and the local bank, where she drew money from Maggie's account every week with a card. Not having any formal identity sometimes had its limitations, but cash still worked for most things. The locals had shown a lot of interest in both Jack and Sadie, the girl chatting to the shopkeepers with her story. She—Sasha or Rhia or Tara depending on her mood—was recovering from being ill, and was off school being home-educated until she got better. Jack tried to laugh off some of the more outrageous fabrications, but there was something about Sadie that made older women cluck around her.

She turned onto the road to the cottage, and contemplated arriving covered in mud and blood. Felix, Maggie—she reviewed what she had said. She had never lost her temper like that before, she didn't even feel so angry normally. Maybe it was the new hormones.

Felix's car wasn't parked on the verge, and paradoxically she was immediately angry again. Tomorrow he was off to do some more research, and this was one conversation she needed to finish. She drove past the house, turning around in the next farm lane, and set off for the town.

Chapter 28

I seized my opportunity and persuaded a guest in our house, a brave soldier, to come with me to the cemetery to find the tomb. So we went off before cockcrow, the moon shone like high noon. Among the monuments we came: he to search among the graves and I to sing. Then I looked at my companion, and he stripped himself and all his clothes by the roadside. My heart was in my mouth, I stood like a dead man. But he stood unclothed and forthwith he transformed into a wolf. I would not make a joke of it, I would not tell an untruth, upon the grave of my father. After he had turned into a wolf, he fled into the woods and began to howl.

— PETRONIUS (27–66) *Satyricon* CHAPTER 62,
 believed to be around AD 61

E NRICO CAME TO FETCH ME FOR THE FORMAL RECEPTION upon the following afternoon, dressed in a fine suit of blue. I had within my bags a burgundy doublet of French design, much embroidered, and with new hose from a tailor in Prague I felt myself peacocked enough for even Contarini's guests. Enrico indicated that the company was assembled upon the *terrazza* so I followed him outside.

The terrace ran the whole length of the front of the mansion. Broad steps of limestone led to a formal garden within a mosaic of paths. There were clipped hedges and shaped trees, and ordered lines of flowers created into patterns. They were attended by three or four gardeners, snipping, watering and training. Within the center of flower beds in the shapes of crescents, ovals and diamonds, all created with low hedges, was a pool, many yards across. It featured a fountain dropping a spray that played over the shivering surface of the water.

"Master Kelley!" It was my host, stepping toward me as graceful as a dancer. He offered me his arm and I took it, aware of his great height towering above me. "I hope your investigations were satisfactory?" he said, with a smile.

He had a very long jaw, I recall, and a thin nose. I still could not judge his age. We walked to the end of the terrace where a framework of wood covered an area with shading vines, the brown stems gnarled and as thick as my wrist, as yet unleafed. There several benches and wooden chairs were covered with cushions with finely dressed ladies and gentlemen upon them, or standing and talking to each other in their native language. A table with a snowy cloth, covered with decanters and platters of sweetmeats, stood to one side. Servitors discreetly shuttled back and forth with glasses or plates.

"Observe!" called out my Lord Contarini. "We have amongst us a great thinker from England, colleague to Dr. Dee himself, friend of the emperor and a sage amongst men."

I was flattered, a little, but most of what he said was true. The emperor, while oftentimes friendly, did presently have a warrant for my arrest within the empire and an attainder upon my belongings, but would no doubt forgive as he has always forgiven. Meantimes, he was a good host to my wife and stepchildren. I bowed low to the company, and some did bend their heads to me, also.

A lady, taller than most, and with hair the color of ripe barley flowing about her in a way that we would think of as immodest in England, stepped forward. "Master Kelley?"

I bowed, and Lord Contarini spoke. "My wife, Lady Lucia Contarini. And these young men are my sons." Three young men, one as fair as his mother, stepped closer. They looked about five-and-twenty years old, and yet they introduced me to their children, some of whom were already youths and maids of marriageable age. Truly, I thought, there is something ageless and powerful about these people.

As we progressed slowly around the group I was dazzled by their beauty and strength. None looked much above thirty, yet there was maturity in the questions they asked. They were interested in Lord Dannick, the task he had set me, and asked questions about the "English tablet." I felt small among the company, as they sometimes spoke above my head in Venetian or Italian, and laughed, and made merry. Servants offered me wine, and held little trays of sweetmeats, which I declined lest they return the flux.

One of the men, with a trace of gray in his beard yet as young looking as the others, asked me a question in his own tongue. Contarini spoke to him, and he repeated the question is slow Latin.

"It is said that Dr. Dee knows great sorceries."

I bowed and replied. "Indeed, he is my mentor. He is an adept at the art of magic."

"And speaks to demons." A little flutter upon the listeners, who turned their heads toward me.

"Dr. Dee and I have had conferences with angels." My own voice was uncertain. I had doubts now about the nature of the beings that had spoken through me, and refused steadfastly since to allow another to do so. Instead, I heard only whispers into the back of my mind. But they were always there and I could not prevent them. "I know not of demons, and doubt that any Christian man would have business with them."

There was a ripple of nodding and a seated woman crossed herself. It was she who spoke next.

"What know you of people who are possessed?"

Contarini waved at a cushioned chair, and I sat upon it.

"I know little but what the church teaches, and what is said in holy verses," I said in answer. I looked at the woman again, seeing upon her face what I did not see in the others. She was beautiful but the skin on her face was softened by lines, the skin loose under her chin. Even her hair, mostly confined under an embroidered hood, had not escaped a few silvery strands.

Her voice softened. "We have stories here, of people possessed by the spirits of beasts until they kill their own children. They run through the streets biting and clawing the people they meet."

"That sounds like a madness, my lady," I said.

She looked at me, her eyes gleaming with tears. "It is a terrible fate."

Contarini handed me a goblet filled with wine. "It would be. But such people, close confined, may recover."

I agreed, sipping the strong, sweet golden wine. "I have known that to happen. But madness is not possession."

Contarini lay back in his chair. "The legend I believe Lady Ziani speaks of is that of a man—or woman—filled with the spirit of some noble animal. A lion, perhaps, or a wolf."

I had no sense of nobility from my few encounters from wolves. I would rather be locked in a room with a madman than a wolf. I thought back to the tablet. "I do not understand."

"She speaks of people who live for a few hours free of the restrictions of society, who encourage an animal nature to fill those hours with the wild hunt."

I recalled Lord Dannick speaking in similar terms of a hunt, a time of freedom and closeness to nature. I felt a coldness shiver down my back. "Do you speak of—*daemonium lupum*?" I looked around. There was a coldness about these people, the way a wild animal who is not hungry looks at you, with indifference.

"Demon wolf?" Contarini said, smiling, holding his hands out to the company as if to invite them to mock me. "What is this, Master Kelley?"

"A man who is enchanted to take on the form of a wolf," I stammered, only Lady Ziani looking upon me kindly. "By sorcery. I have heard such legends in Poland and England, and in France they call such monsters *loup-garou*."

A little laughter spread among the listeners, and the shaking of a few heads. I noticed Enrico listening to his betters, looking from me to the others, then to the other dissenter.

"How can that be?" asked Lady Ziani, clasping her hands to her body. "Such is surely the devil's work."

"It is, my lady," I answered, at least sure of my authority here. "Such would be condemned by the church, by all churches."

"I disagree," said a darkly visaged man, dressed in a peacock blue jacket, and smiling at his friends. "There have always been a class of people born to lead and hunt, as there is a class of peasants who are destined to follow. Perhaps it is not enchantment, but simply revealing the man's nature to lead the hunt, not to be hunted nor to watch. Such as we, the nobility, who lead troops into battle. We lead our peasants into productive work, make laws and punish the lawbreakers. It is our place. Is this not true?"

The tablet's images came back to me, and with a lurch within my belly, I suddenly knew what they and the Dannicks were looking for. "I could never help a man take on the nature of a wolf," I stuttered. "It is not possible, and if it were, it would be insane. No man could constrain the wolf's basest instincts to hunt and kill."

"Oh, I agree." Contarini smiled. "There can be no transformation. Such would be contrary to nature." He waved away a servant with a decanter of the scarlet wine. "But to take on the strength and agility of the beast, that is possible."

I thought for a moment, seeing the Lady Ziani staring at the fingers in her lap. "Any such would still require sorcery."

He shrugged, and turned, raising his glass to his fellows. "Our ancestors have called it sorcery, but our children will call it science."

Others toasted the sentiment, but I was left filled with doubts.

"My lord Contarini." I bowed. "What you propose might create a stronger person, perhaps, but what would transform him back? Would he not be left, not only with the power of the beast, but also with his ruthlessness, his single-minded pursuit of his base needs?"

"My concerns, precisely," said Lady Ziani, lifting her chin, I thought, as if to defy those around her. "I would rather be as a lamb, than a wolf. The church—"

"The church, madam," said Contarini, with one of those smiles that revealed his white teeth, "deals in myths and lies."

I was silenced, and my lady was also quieted by the words, and the conversation turned to the weather, and the scenery. The villa, which was more like a palace in my eyes, was set high upon a rise, its back to a forest. The trees here grew not close together, but studded into a green sward, and a few deer could be seen by sharp eyes cropping the grass at the edge of the trees. Paths led through the garden, which was set out before us like an embroidered apron, with double gates leading to the forest itself. Beside the house, I judged, were some walled kitchen gardens and orchards, where servants came and went carrying tools and armfuls of greenery.

But my thoughts ran on apace. The house of Marinello, even with its proximity to the countess and the watchful Inquisition, seemed strangely secure now. I watched the group, their lithe limbs, their strange youthfulness, and wondered what sorceries had wrought them. I could not imagine that nature had preserved all from the touch of the red pox, the passing of years, the burden of age and disease that mark us all. I resolved to get my notes and the drawing away from all of these unnatural people and back to Dee.

Chapter 29

Many seasons ago, the old witch Thomazine had grown weak, and her child sent his own daughter to care for the garden. She planted more trees, some of them new to the area, like the cherries and plums. She brought pigs to grunt and snuffle over pens in the plot, tearing up the roots and ripping at the established trees. They were only forgiven for the richness of their dung, in which new seeds sprang to life.

THE HOTEL CAR PARK WAS FULL SO JACK PARKED ON THE street, walking to the lobby, each step building her rage. In a small corner of her mind, she knew the anger was at Powell, at Maggie, but Felix was closest and somehow the key to her new feelings. Under it all, she was shaking with reaction to the terror. She shrugged off the memory of the man's strength, his weight, his rough hands digging into her skin—

She rang the bell as the front door was locked, and a woman opened it, peering out.

"Yes? Did you forget your key?" She looked again. "Oh. Can I help you?"

Jack pushed past her. "I need to see Professor Felix Guichard. Now."

"It's late. You can't just barge in—I'll call him, but if he doesn't want to be disturbed you will have to leave."

Jack was pacing up and down the dimly lit lobby when Felix came down the stairs. He ignored Jack and turned instead to the flustered woman.

"Thank you. Can we talk in the dining room? I would hate to disturb anyone else."

He didn't wait for her answer, or even look at Jack, but pushed through a door and disappeared inside, the lights flickering on as she followed him into the room.

"Now, what—" He looked at Jack as the lights came up. "What the hell happened to you?"

All the things she wanted to say collided in her throat. She stood glaring at him, tears of frustration and reaction gathering in her eyes. She rubbed her arm across her face, wincing at the pain radiating from her cheekbone.

"I went to see Powell, I wanted to see the wolves. And he, at least, was clear about what he wanted." The words were snapped out.

Felix came closer, staring at her bruises, at the mud still dried on her face and matted into her hair. Then his gaze met her eyes, and a look of blazing anger seemed to light his green eyes. Jack took a half step back.

"You tell me it's too soon, you don't want to rush—then you throw yourself at Powell. Did you get what you wanted, Jack?" His tone was bitter.

The shaky feeling inside became cold.

"He attacked me." She wiped her shaking hand over her forehead. "The wolves defended me. I think they killed him."

"What?" He frowned, reaching as if to touch the bruised cheekbone, then pulled his hand away. "What happened?"

"He tried to rape me."

Felix froze, staring at her, the muscles of his face bunching up around his mouth.

Jack stammered on. "I managed to fight him off, then the wolves—" The memory of the crunching sound as the animals attacked him came back to her with a wave of nausea. "Can we go upstairs? I need to sit down."

"As long as you are quiet." His voice was clinical and clipped. "I don't want the hotel to call the police."

She followed him up the stairs, one hip tender now the emotions were fading from rage into something darker, more painful. She began to feel aches all over, from being thrown to the ground, pinned to the mud, grabbed by strong hands. He led her through the bedroom straight to the bathroom and switched on the light. He leaned forward to start the shower running over the bath.

"Take your boots off." His voice was soft. He turned back to her, looking at her under the harsh light.

She sat on the toilet lid to start undoing her laces, but the wet fabric had felted them together and her cold fingers were stinging and shaking. He knelt on the bathroom floor to tug at them, leaving her looking down at him, the silver hairs scattered in the dark curls, the whorl on the top of his head, the tense shoulders. He muttered something under his breath, pulled one boot off and started work on the other.

Jack felt dreamy as the room steamed up and the feelings softened inside her. She reached out a hand, then saw the blood on it and hesitated. Felix pushed himself up on the side of the bath and looked down at her.

"Get the mud off, and we'll talk. My dressing gown is on the back of the door."

She could only stare up at him, the words jumbled in her mind. The encounter with Powell, however vile, somehow made Felix seem less like a benign teacher and more like a man. She was painfully aware that the only physical experiences she had had in her whole life were a few kisses from Felix, and brutality from Powell.

"Can you help me?" She wasn't sure what she was asking. He reached out his hands, the long brown hands she realized she loved, and she put out her own, greasy with mud and blood. "Please."

He pulled off her coat, helped her with the layers underneath until he paused at her T-shirt, the bruises on her arms and wrists revealed. She looked down at herself, and pulled the last layers off her torso. He turned her gently away from him, his fingers warm on her skin, and she could hear his breathing stop. She looked in the mirror over the sink, seeing the ring of purple marks on the side of her neck, another on her shoulder.

"I didn't even feel that," she said, twisting further around to see the start of dark smudges in the small of her back. "I think he knelt on me."

"I can see." He hesitated, and she undid her jeans herself. Her pants were torn and came down with the jeans, but being naked in front of Felix was surprisingly comfortable—she felt more at ease in his presence without clothes on than she'd expected. She eased her socks off with her jeans, wincing with the pain in her ribs as she leaned forward, and gratefully accepted Felix's arm to climb over the side of the bath and under the hot water.

There was shower gel, some coconut-scented concoction that she poured into her hand again and again, covering her hair, her face, every inch of her body. She rubbed and rinsed, even into the torn skin, until it stung. She was vaguely aware Felix had shut the door, but carried on until every part of her was scoured, every molecule of Powell was gone. Flashes of memories, his hands on her body, his knees forcing hers apart— had she even got away? She leaned her forehead against the cool tiles for a moment, straining for gaps in her memory. Yes. But he had got too close. For a moment she couldn't believe how she had behaved with Powell, it was completely out of character. Insane. She groped for the tap and turned the shower off.

When she turned, she realized Felix had never left, was standing there holding a towel with a strange expression on his face, one she had never seen before. She took the towel and wrapped it around herself, favoring a finger that felt like it was broken, suddenly shy. He reached his arms out, and without a word, lifted her over the side of the bath like a child, and set her on a fluffy bath mat. She stared up at him.

"Did he rape you?"

"No."

The exchange was quiet, matter-of-fact. "Do you trust me, Jack?"

Her reply was instant. "Yes."

This time there was a small pause, as if he hadn't expected the answer.

She asked, hugging the towel, "Can I stay?"

"Yes, stay. Get into bed before you freeze. I'll get a T-shirt and pajama bottoms for you."

She patted herself mostly dry, pulled the T-shirt over her head and pulled the trousers on. Holding them up with one hand, she crawled under the duvet. She sighed, some of the tension finally draining away. The shivering returned.

He turned off all the lights except the bedside one, and stripped to his underwear before getting in the other side of the bed. They reached for each other at the same time, her head on his shoulder, his arms around her.

It was strange to feel the warm elasticity of his skin, the warmth melting her shivers away. She carefully rested her injured hand over his chest, feeling the novelty of the texture of his skin under her hand.

"I went there—" she started, cleared her throat and started again. "I went there because—"

"I know why you went there." His voice was a soft rumble in the dark.

"I was angry with you."

He sighed, his chest rising and falling under her hand. "You're always angry at me."

"Because you—make me feel things." She stretched out her legs, touching the roughness of the hair on his shin with her foot. "When I was taken by Maggie—I was so confused, so upset. I cried to go home every night for months, years, really. I don't think Maggie had expected me to live so long. I think I sort of switched my feelings off." She could feel the warmth of his skin creeping in, and the shivering dying away inside her. "How's Sadie?"

He shifted awkwardly, leaning away from her. "She's asleep, but she seemed better when I left. So, you were obviously very distressed by being separated from your parents?"

"I think I just closed down. Maggie was kind, but she was adamant that I could never go back. Then we took Sadie and I met you. Suddenly, I was full of emotion. Anger with Maggie and guilt at putting Sadie through it. And then I saw you. I never understood that idea, 'chemistry,' but I think that's what they mean."

She idly ran her hand across his chest, and he captured it. "Stop."

"What?" For a moment she was confused, then it dawned on her that she was sharing his bed. "Oh."

"I have a grown woman that I'm attracted to in my bed, so . . . I'm a man, Jack. But you've just been beaten and almost raped." His words had a tremor in them. She heard rather than saw his head turn toward her. "If he wasn't already dead . . ."

She settled against him, and felt him relax. "I went there to see the wolves. I didn't ask to be smacked around and have him . . ." The recollection of what Powell had tried to do seemed unrelated to being in Felix's arms. "I just want to wipe out the bad memories with you."

"That's probably a terrible plan, psychologically. You've been traumatized."

"I feel alive," she said, wondering at her own words. "I came close to being raped, and maybe even killed, and now I feel comforted and warm. And really alive."

He was quiet, his slow breathing the only sound for a long time. "You are euphoric now, because you survived. I felt like that after the night in the church."

"I don't remember much about that. I traveled chained up in the boot of the car, remember?" She smiled in the dark.

"That was later. I thought, in the church, that we were all going to die." His voice was warm into her hair.

Jack could conjure up that feeling too, standing facing the revenant Elizabeth Báthory, unable to stop her slashing a knife into Sadie's arms so she could drink her blood. "But we got out, we won."

"Just. I still can't believe Sadie pulled through." His voice was sleepy now. "I was furious with you when you walked out this evening."

She let her thoughts stray into her fingers, sliding them over his chest, draping a leg over his to ease the pain in her hip. "What Powell tried to do, that was nothing to do with . . . us." The unfamiliar word rolled off her tongue awkwardly and she smiled in the darkness.

"Go to sleep." His hand captured hers, and he held it. "Turn over, go to sleep. We'll talk about it in the morning."

Sleep was one thing, dreams were another. She woke up gasping for breath more than once, the sensation of her face pressed into gritty, cold mud overwhelming her, terror making her heart clatter in her chest. Felix, his body curved against her back, didn't wake, but when she moved, his arms tightened around her waist. It was a strange feeling, as if somehow she had her family back. Was this what people did, when they traded parents for partners? She felt as if she were in a bubble of happiness, even though the clouds were gathering around her.

. . .

Dawn broke and with it came confusion, pain and embarrassment. The light bleeding she had noticed the day before had returned, seeping into Felix's pajamas. She slipped out to the bathroom in the early morning, and was confused as to what to do. She screwed them up and put them on the bathroom floor, suddenly shy to step out in just the T-shirt. She sidled out, trying to be quiet as she looked for her clothes. Felix had stuffed them into a plastic bag, where she realized they probably needed to stay.

"Good morning." Felix was looking at her under hair flopped into his eyes and the beginnings of stubble on his face. "How are you feeling?"

The internal audit, so far distracted by embarrassment, switched to the sensation her body was feeding back. "Well, I ache," she offered. "I also don't have anything to wear and—"

"And what?" He stretched out under the bedclothes.

"I might have a period, I think." The last time she had had to talk about periods she was in year six and Talullah Jamieson told all her friends about hers. "I've never had one before."

He frowned but didn't say anything, making her suddenly self-conscious.

"Here, have my dressing gown," he said. "I'll get dressed and see what I can get you from the lobby."

He pulled on a pair of jeans and a shirt and ran his hand through his hair. When the door shut behind him, she reached for her phone, left out by Felix on the bedside table.

"Maggie?" She couldn't believe she hadn't phoned last night, but she was so shocked . . .

"Jack!" Even through the tinny speaker, she could hear Maggie's relief. "I've been so worried."

"I'm sorry I didn't call. I'm at Felix's hotel. I just couldn't come back last night."

"What happened?"

Jack tried to tell the story calmly, without emotion, but the second she mentioned Powell hitting her, tears bubbled up and thickened her voice. There was no mistaking the distress in Maggie's response.

"You must have been terrified. Anyone would be." She sniffed, and said something in an aside. "That's Sadie, she's better today. We're going to have to take it a bit easier with her. Are you coming home?"

"When Felix is ready. I—I'm a bit stressed, that's all. And I have a few bruises. Well, a lot of bruises," she admitted. "I'm really sorry I didn't call last night. I was just so upset—"

"And you turned to Felix. I thought you had." A long silence. "Do you know what you're doing? With him?"

"I have no idea." Jack smiled down at the crumpled oval where he had slept. "But I feel fine. Well, I feel like I've been run over, but I'm OK. We'll be back soon." Her finger twinged and she looked down at it. It wasn't obviously displaced but was swollen into a stiff, black sausage. She ended the call, and was just inspecting the finger when Felix came back in.

He handed her something in a packet that gave explicit instructions. "This would work better if I had underwear," she mused, and he passed her a second package, containing three pairs of new—if rather large—pants and a new toothbrush.

She gathered them up and went into the bathroom to get changed. Felix was six inches taller so she couldn't reasonably wear his clothes, but she tried anyway. "They only have to get me to the car," she said, as he grinned at her.

"You look about twelve," he said. "I told the landlady you'd been knocked over. I couldn't see anything on the news downstairs."

"News?"

"About Powell. You said the wolves got him. Are you sure he was dead?"

"I think so." She sorted through the items in his holdall, pulling out a jumper. "I called the castle to let them know." She felt strange about just leaving him, but a flash of memory of his weight on her helped her shrug it off.

"Jack—how did you feel last night, before he attacked you?"

She thought about it. "I don't know. Reckless, partly, nervous as well."

"I'm just worried. You seem like two people at the moment."

She nearly snapped something defensive at him, then stopped to think about it. "I do feel strange sometimes, like I'm the old Jack one minute then the new Jack the next. I just put it down to the extra energy."

"Maybe that's all it is." He smiled but he didn't look convinced.

Chapter 30

I went from England to find new customs and new knowledge, and indeed, my travels led to more ideas than I can record in my journals. Not all was easy to learn, and now there are some memories that still leave me shaking in my bed at night, so that I sleep on moondark nights with a lantern, and the door locked and barricaded.

—EDWARD KELLEY, 1586, Venice

WORD CAME AT DUSK THAT AFTER AN EARLY DINNER we were to be treated to a night hunt by moonlight. I found this very peculiar but the company, brought inside by the chill of the clear air outside, seemed unsurprised. After a light meal of almond pastries and roasted fowls of all kinds, we ascended to our chambers to prepare for the hunt.

I was dressed in a well-fitting suit of browns and blacks, and given a close cap for my head that also hooded my face. I wondered what chase takes place at night, yet could hear in other chambers and in the halls the excited chatter of the other hunters. I asked a servant about spurs, but he shrugged as if he did not understand. I resolved to ask the groom in the stable, for I knew I could not ride in my soft boots without them. When a chamberlain came in and indicated he should black my face with some concoction, I stood still, thinking we would perhaps stalk some prey in the moonlight. Somewhere, a wit raised his voice in a howl like an animal, and other voices joined, followed by laughter. High spirits, indeed. I glanced at the mirror, to see myself a dark figure, well disguised. I was escorted to the hall by the servant, where I saw the gathered hunters.

There was not another black coat in sight. The hunters were dressed in simple robes of reds and greens.

"Ah, Master Kelley!" Lord Contarini stepped forward, his form clothed entirely in scarlet and holding a glass. "Drink, make merry for a moment with us."

"My lord?" I sipped the cordial, but it was bitter and I could not drink it.

He bent to address me alone. "It goes better if you drink it. It is a blend of certain herbs that help make the pain less and the forest more beautiful."

My lips were numb where they had touched the potion, and I shook my head. "Pain?"

He smiled, and a servant took the glass from my hand. "My dear Kelley. You haven't guessed, have you?"

It was as if a wall came tumbling in my mind, and I realized this was a game I had not foreseen.

"I am the prey?" I asked, swallowing hard, for my mouth was suddenly dry. "You think to hunt me like an animal?"

"It is the finest sport, Master Kelley."

"What sport, sir, with you on horseback and myself on foot?" I stammered, seeing the looks on the faces of the hunters around me.

"No horses, my friend. Just you on your two feet, and us on . . . ours."

The tablet's confusing pictures flashed into my head. "You are—skin-turners." My mouth filled with bile and my chest tightened.

"No, no. Such is myth."

A growling and whining from an antechamber made him

turn, and myself to stumble a few steps away from him, from his insane beliefs. Two servants held a creature—no, a man—though his face was contorted into a mask of teeth and red tongue, as he twisted at the end of sticks that had nooses about them. At first I thought his skin blackened like mine own, but I recognized his features as the moor Enrico, his face suffused with the blood of madness, his lips frothed about and his hands reaching like talons.

"This is the man infused with the beast's nature. Its strength, its power."

Enrico writhed in their captivity, diving at one of his captors then the next. His eyes stared at me without recognition. Here was my scholarly friend, transmuted by some vile alchemy into a mindless fiend.

"This is the ritual your master Lord Dannick seeks," Contarini said, his tone cool. "I shall regret your death, but you know too much. You have divined the ritual, and we cannot help you form a stronger pack in England. Let their puny cubs wither and die."

He turned to the crowd, addressing them in Latin, even as they leaned in to stroke the transformed Enrico, whose entire focus seemed to be upon me.

"Fresh blood!" the count roared, raising his hands. Their voices fell, except the grunts and snarls of the tormented Enrico, fighting his confinement. "This man is the prey," Contarini waved at me, as I backed toward the great doors to the villa. "Let him run, let Enrico hunt and fell him. Do not feed before Enrico, no matter how hungry you may become. I have a few orphan children to hunt later; you shall all have a chance to kill." He turned to me, smiling, showing all his teeth. "You have until the moon is directly overhead. The farther you get, the better the hunt. And the longer you shall have hope of escape."

He may have said more, but I was out of the door like a rabbit before a fox.

Chapter 31

The elders watch the clearing of the strangling ivy and bramble, the fleeing of the rats and beetles. As the raven cries its captivity and the rooks answer. And still the fragrant flesh yields from the bones, the body claimed by the earth.

Felix was clearing the garden under Maggie's instructions. From the caws and croaks coming from the back bedroom, Jack had her hands full with the half-wild bird. He wondered about her reaction to the attack from Powell. She seemed strangely cheerful around Sadie, and brushed off Maggie's attempts to comfort her.

The reek from this part of the garden, going into the densest brambles, was foul. He slashed at the base of some thorns with shears. The blades clinked against something hard, and he pulled away the tangle of branches. He kicked the long grass and hit something solid. Kneeling down in the spring sunshine, he wiped the sweat off his forehead and tugged at the new growth of greenery.

A wave of stench hit him at the same time as his mind processed long sticks, shreds of clothing—and the heavy boots he was seeing. He stumbled to his feet, and managed to shout for Maggie before nausea overwhelmed him.

She stomped through the long grass and the stumps of the brambles. "Oh—is that—oh, God. Jack! Come here!"

The decayed body of what looked like a man lay twisted on the ground, reduced largely to black flesh and brown bones. Maybe a dozen brambles as thick as Felix's thumb had pierced the body, growing like spears through the abdomen, and threading between ribs. One had forced its way under the man's chin to erupt out of his mouth. New growth dipped into the hollows of the skull, and explored the bones and clothing.

Maggie prodded the body with the rake she was carrying. The man's jacket, although frayed, still covered both upper arms and draped away from the chest. "There's something in the pocket," she said.

"Leave it for the police." He gagged again.

"We're not involving the police."

"What do you mean?" He looked back at the house, to see Jack looking from the window. He waved for her to come down.

"Well, they will want to know what we're all doing here. Jack looks like she's been in a fight, then there's the mysterious death at the wolf compound." Maggie leaned on her spade, keen eyes looking at him from under white hair. "I'm surprised they haven't been here already. It's better if we don't draw attention to ourselves. Especially Jack and Sadie."

He opened his mouth to ask for clarification when Jack walked over the new grass, ducking around the circle of elders, still an island of branches and thorns. Ches, dancing around her feet, started whining.

"What's wrong, I heard you—oh." She grabbed the dog by his collar and nodded toward the body. "Do we know who he was?"

"I have my suspicions," Maggie said, and stared at Felix, unblinking.

"You can speak in front of Felix." Jack looked from one to the other. "Maggie, he's family. Ask Sadie."

Maggie reached into her bulging pockets for heavy-duty rubber gloves. Leaning over the body, she matter-of-factly checked each pocket, then threw the slimy, stinking objects onto the recently cut grass. Finally, she lifted the jacket away from a holster.

"There's a gun," she said, looking back over her shoulder.

"I *knew* the cat was shot," Jack said, stepping away from the thing as it fell beside the body. "The Dannicks must have sent him."

"What?" Felix started, as he backed away from the black object.

"When we got here there was a dead cat in the kitchen, a big one. It had a round hole in its forehead."

He thought about the theory Maggie and Jack had started to develop about the death of the old woman. "You think this man was somehow involved in Ellen's death?"

"I'm sure. Why haven't they sent the police round to ask us about Powell? Because this . . . person can be traced back to them. I'm sure he was supposed to intimidate Ellen into giving up the book, and ended up killing her. Not by shooting, though." Jack grimaced and stepped back a little more. "Maybe he used the gun to threaten her."

"So how did he kill her, then?" Felix looked from one to the other.

Maggie looked at Jack as if still unsure whether to speak. "You've seen Jack use sorcery."

He turned to Jack. "I don't know how she did it, but she exerted some magical pressure on Elizabeth Báthory, certainly."

"Well, someone 'exerted some pressure' on Ellen. And we know they were looking for something in the garden, this black hair-root."

"But that was only a few weeks ago and this body is ancient.

It must have been here months." Felix stepped closer to Jack, upwind of the corpse.

"This body is recent." Maggie pulled the boot, until an inch of slimy flesh appeared above the top. "Allowing for the cold, it's only been here a month or two. Roughly the same time as Ellen's death."

Felix pointed at the thorns, impaling the body. "But in these temperatures, it could have been here for longer, at least from the autumn. And the plants don't grow in the winter, so how did the branches end up right through him?"

"The garden killed him." Maggie had an intense look on her face. "The ground reached up and the plants and animals in it dragged him down."

The smile faded on Felix's lips before it was complete. "That's insane. I mean, it's wild out here, but there are limits to plant physiology."

"Less than you would think. Brambles can grow a couple of feet in a week." Maggie stepped closer to Jack's shoulder. "Ask Jack how they can immobilize someone. They can do much more. The ground under the elders is littered with animal bones, mostly pigeon, I suspect, and a few rabbits. I think the brambles hook the animals and hold them down, then grow into them."

"So he got stuck out here, and then the plants speared him?" Jack's voice was a bit shaky. "That must have been agony, surely he would have made a noise."

"Look at the amount of branches around his face," Maggie said, pointing with a stick. "They may even have suffocated him."

"So what was he doing here? Just to get the herb?" Felix stepped back as another wave of stench hit him.

"He was here to compel Ellen to hand over Thomazine's book, I suspect." Maggie dropped the stick. "And when she couldn't or wouldn't, he killed her."

Felix couldn't keep the skepticism out of his voice. "The coroner concluded that she died of natural causes."

Maggie's eyes crossed from him to Jack, and back again. "Ellen was killed with magic."

"Magic. And you're sure it wasn't an accident?"

"Yes, Professor," Maggie bent, grasping a stick from the clear up. "Magic. It leaves a residue, like a smell. This is just a stick, right? And this just grass."

"Maggie, don't—" Jack started to say, but Maggie ignored her. She inscribed a circle around herself.

It wasn't so much the words, he later thought, but the manner in which she seemed to look inside herself, drawing on an intensity he hadn't seen before. Jack stepped back quickly, but the first sign of the fire coiling from the circle around Maggie was a pink tendril of flame exploring his ankle, making him leap back. The flames, probably only six inches high, seemed to radiate more heat than their size would suggest, and burned with a metallic smell that ate into the stink from the body. Maggie's expression reminded him of Julian's when Gina was possessed, as if she were listening to something beyond the normal world.

Maggie looked up, her eyes narrowed with concentration, then stopped chanting. The fire died away, leaving a tiny scorched line in the grass.

"That's magic," she said, a little breathlessly. "If I can do that, and I'm just one witch, think what a whole garden can do."

"But a garden doesn't think like a human, and it's not 'a garden' anyway, it's thousands of disparate organisms of many species. Not to mention it's continuous with the rest of the land beyond the walls." He bent to inspect the ground. Ice had formed inside and outside the line in shards. "How did you do that? Energy seems to have been drawn out of the ground, the air. How does it work?"

Maggie crouched and took off one glove. She pressed it to the ground, murmuring something. Then she stood up, rubbing sweat off her face with her sleeve. "This garden acts like one massive organism. It's not just what you can see, but fungi and bacteria under the ground, plants whose roots intermingle. Even the branches of the trees . . ." She stood and pointed into the knot of elders. He could see branches that had grown into neighboring branches, as if holding hands. "This is an ancient garden, tended by witches. He murdered the witch, and the garden dragged him down and killed him. Simple."

He felt the last reassurance of science slipping away. "How can you be sure she was murdered when we don't know how it was done?"

"I do know how I would do it." Maggie stood up and faced him, jaw clenched, scowling at him. "The same way I made the fox fire. He started a fire inside her that burned her up from the inside."

Jack put a hand on his arm. "This is my world, this is our reality. You have to suspend your doubts for a moment."

He chewed his lower lip for a moment, the scent of scorched grass still in the air. "I'm not arguing with you; that was a very convincing demonstration. But I need to reconcile it with my understanding of science, too, OK?" He glanced back at the line of ice, now melting in the sun. He glanced at Maggie. "If he killed Ellen with this . . . fox fire . . . why did he need to shoot the cat?"

"It must have gone for him when he threatened Ellen," Maggie said. "The cat and the garden, all the living things within it, are protective of the cottage's owner."

"The garden. Is it . . . sentient, then? Do you think you communicate with it in some way?" He wrapped a glove around the stinking gun and examined it. It was a revolver and, on closer inspection, had fired just one bullet.

Maggie shrugged, and picked up her tools and gloves. "Sadie does, too. She hears it whispering to her." She walked back into the house, back straight.

"She's angry. She hates having to explain magic to anyone." Jack pinched her nose. "Put that . . . thing . . . down and come away from the smell."

"Why can't we call the police and let them worry about how it happened?" He placed the gun on the grass and stepped away from the body.

"Sadie and I need to fly under the radar. We don't have any official identity, no passport or ID of any kind. Not to mention that our fingerprints are on file as missing persons." She stood beside the stand of elders, upwind of the smell. "I can't believe we didn't smell that before."

"It's pretty decomposed. I disturbed a pocket of less well-deteriorated flesh."

She squinted up at him, shielding her eyes from the sun. "We have the strangest conversations."

He smiled down at her. The bruise on her cheekbone was now a shiny, purpled bulge under her eye, and she had several deep scratches over the bridge of her narrow nose. Her blond hair was spilled over her collar in wavy threads. For a moment, he thought he should kiss her, but then a wary look developed in her eyes, and she pulled away. Maybe she remembered what had happened the day before.

"Go in," he said. "It's fine."

He started to follow her back to the house. They reached the back door and he could hear Maggie talking, her voice stressed and high, to someone in the hall.

"Felix!" she called.

He turned to Jack. "I'll go. Check on Sadie and keep Ches out of the way." He walked down the hall, seeing a tall man on the doorstep in a long wool coat. Another man in a suit and a flat hat, like a chauffeur, stood beside a large car.

Maggie turned to him, her face relaxing for a moment. "Professor. I was just explaining to Sir Henry that we still haven't identified the herb he was looking for."

The man held out a hand. "Dannick. Professor . . . ?"

"Felix Guichard." He grasped the gloved hand. "As you can appreciate, the grounds of the cottage are very overgrown and it will be some time before Mrs. Slee can look for individual plants. But it is equally likely that rare species have simply been strangled by nettles, ivy and brambles."

The man frowned. "My grandson's health is declining. I was simply inquiring about progress. Also, I wondered if Miss Hammond has spoken to an employee of mine, Mike Powell? He seems to have absconded with some of the money set aside for a research project my family has funded."

Something about his manner suggested he knew very well what had happened to Powell. "I'm sorry. She has been occupied with her daughter, who has also suffered a setback."

"I understand. Nevertheless, it would help me to speak to her. She was looking for a book that might help my family find an alternative source of the herb." Dannick smiled, but looked at the sky. "Could I come in? It is starting to rain."

"I'm afraid that would be a waste of your time." Felix turned to get his wallet off the small table in the hall. "This is my card. Perhaps it would be better if you dealt with me, rather than Jack while—" Damn, he couldn't remember the name Sadie was using. "You understand, Jack is very worried."

"Of course." Sir Henry took the card. "We are also deeply concerned for a child. Professor of social anthropology. Interesting."

"We will call you the second we find anything that might be useful. But it would be helpful if we knew exactly how the herb works—"

"Well, thank you for the card. I'll be in touch." The man turned away, pulling up his coat collar against the first spots of rain. Before he reached the car, he turned. "Please tell Miss Hammond that if she has any knowledge of Mr. Powell's whereabouts, it would help us. She's welcome to talk to the police, if she prefers. We hope that monitoring footage from cameras inside the project will help us determine exactly what happened."

For a moment, the thought of Jack assaulted and beaten clouded Felix's concentration, but he fought it down. "Of course," he said, the words ground out. "Good luck with that."

He shut the door behind Dannick and turned to Maggie. "We need to find out more about the Dannicks." He shrugged his fleece off and hung it on the newel post of the stairs, over Jack's coat. "Tell me again how the magic could have killed Ellen. How does it work?"

Maggie glanced into the living room, and lowered her voice. "He started a fire inside Ellen."

"By somehow transferring the energy from the garden into Ellen, like the ring of flames you conjured in the garden?" He took a step back, staring at her. Her expression and body language at least suggested that she believed it. "I know you produced enough heat to burn someone but kill them?"

"It doesn't have to be an actual flame, just a point of heat that is too high for life. I've never had to do it, but I saw someone bring down a bull that was charging, many years ago." She sighed, and leaned on the banister. "You saw the fox fire. There are dozens of spells that manipulate heat."

"And you think you could do it?" Felix's mind leaped back to something he had read, years ago. "Dee believed it was possible, but he created a corporeal fire that he somehow used to transfer energy to an inanimate object."

"Dee's methods are all complicated by ritual, but at their heart they're about focusing intent. I don't know if I could kill someone. It would use so much energy it could even harm me to try."

Felix sat on the stairs. "We have a body in the garden, Dannick is threatening to call the police and Sadie is very weak." He pushed his hair off his forehead. "Well, we can at least move the body."

Jack opened the door from the kitchen. "Move the body? Ugh."

"We won't need to." Maggie turned to Jack. "You can see the body is already half embedded in the ground."

"So someone dug a shallow grave." Felix looked from Maggie to Jack, and saw some unspoken message pass between them. Maggie retreated back into the kitchen. "Although how anyone could get out there—"

"The garden is burying it." Jack was disturbingly close. "We're just going to encourage it to finish the job."

He looked down into her green eyes, the color of new leaves. "How are you feeling?"

She shrugged, and touched the swelling on her face. "Shattered, but I'll live. What did Dannick say about Powell?"

"Dannick said he's run off. He says he has CCTV footage of parts of the research center."

She managed a lopsided smile. "There might be a camera in the woods but what are they going to see? It was dark, he attacked me, I escaped and called for help. That's it. The wolves did what wolves do, defended themselves."

"And you're sure he didn't get out?"

Jack seemed to hesitate for a heartbeat and looked down. "He must be dead." She remembered the warm horror of his opened abdomen. "I'm sure." She walked into the living room and knelt by the woodburner. "If she's up to it, I'm going to ask Sadie to talk to the garden. She seems better out there, and she seems to . . . I don't know how to describe it, but the garden lets her in. She's never tangled up out there. It just seems to welcome her. Maggie says it's her superpower."

"And yours is talking to animals?"

She pushed a log into the firebox. "I called the wolves to me last night. I remembered what Maggie said, and just drew on what I knew about Ches. I acted like an injured pack wolf and they came to my defense."

He sat down, feeling old. Jack and Sadie seemed to live in a world he could barely touch. One minute she was concrete, in his arms, pressed against his body in her sleep, the next minute she was back in the world of magic and myth, where he didn't belong.

"All I know is you were attacked and nearly raped, and you came to me for help."

She sat next to him. "I did." When he met her eyes they were staring at him, with some emotion stirring her expressions. "Because I love you, and I trust you. God, that feels weird!"

"Loving me?"

"No, idiot! Saying it." She laughed, a soft low sound, just for him. "I'm thirty-one years old and the last time I had a crush on someone I was about fourteen."

"Well, I was in love with Marianne for more than half my life. But now . . . I don't know what to do with you." He stretched his fingers out, seeing the wrinkles, the signs of nearly fifty years of sun damage and scars. "I'm years too old for you."

She smiled. "Yes. And I'm *way* too dead for you."

He hesitated, then turned to study her again. "I want to go to London, to ask more questions. It's about this blood thing."

"I'm fine, I told you."

"The more we know about the effects of taking blood, the more we can use the information to help keep you—and Sadie—safe. And healthy."

Remembering the close call they had just had with Sadie was sobering for them both. "Anything that stops Sadie collapsing again is fine with me. So, what's in London?"

"Ivanova—the woman I met in Paris—has come over with Gina to a club where people drink blood."

"You're kidding. What sort of people? Are they like me or are they normal?"

He smiled. "I'm not sure we can call people who enjoy

drinking other people's blood 'normal,' but there may be some who are revenants."

"Borrowed timers?"

He reached for her hand and looked down at the pale fingers curved in his palm. "I'm not sure if they are; they may be something completely different. They allow themselves to become very close to death then take blood to give them enhanced energy and, they say, longevity. I'm not sure it's exactly the same, but, yes, I suppose they are living on borrowed time too."

"Why would anyone want to become half dead?" She pulled her hand away, and he let her go.

"They refer to it as 'ascended.' They believe they are a superior kind of being."

She snorted. "Superior? That's ridiculous."

"But by drinking the blood they get extra energy and, they believe, immortality." He hesitated for a moment. "The woman I met in New Orleans is researching it."

He could feel her withdrawal. "Like Elizabeth Báthory. They are trying to be like her?"

"Well, maybe they have found a way to avoid becoming a predator."

She sat still for a moment. "They must become addicted to it, and then what would they do to get more? I can understand how people become hooked on that feeling, Felix, I really can. I felt like I could do anything."

"Let me do more research. Let me find out what Gina has discovered."

"Yes." She drew a deep breath. "Find out more. But when you do, I'm coming with you."

Chapter 32

*In the sovereign Court of Parliament at Dole in the
territories of Espagny, Salvange, Courchapon and the
neighboring villages, has often been seen a were-wolf,
who, it is said, has already seized and carried off several
little children. The said Court, desiring to prevent any
greater danger, has permitted those who are abiding
or dwelling in the said places, to assemble with pikes,
halberts, arquebuses, and sticks, to chase and to pursue
the said were-wolf in every place where they may find or
seize him; to tie and to kill, without incurring any pains
or penalties. . . . Given at the meeting of the Court on
the thirteenth day of the month of September, 1573.*

— COURT OF PARLIAMENT AT DOLE,
 Franche Comte, 1573

THE GREAT STONE STEPS THAT I HAD SO ADMIRED UPON
my arrival were difficult to traverse by moonlight, and
I stumbled down them and raced across the grass. Dew
was disturbed as I did so, and I cursed it as it left a trail to be
followed in the pale light. I scared rabbits under the hedges of
the maze, startling myself into veering onto one of the gravel
paths. Ahead, the safety of the forest beckoned. All the time, I
was deafened by the toc-toc of my heart, my mouth filled with

the metallic taste of my own blood where I must have bitten my tongue or lips while they were numbed. I turned onto the forest path, then forced myself to wait there and think like a man.

I was to be hunted by people who had thrown off humanity for animal bloodlust. How could I use that to my advantage? I felt within my shirt for the pitiful supplies I had thought helpful for a hunt. Wary of meeting a wolf, as I had once had an encounter with a pack in Poland, I carried a small pouch of magical powders in a pocket, some of which might aid me. I had the talisman of earth with me, and—rubbing my fingers across its inscription—one of fire. I was carrying a small sheathed dagger in my waistband and my sketches and loose notes were slid within my shirt and secured by a linen band.

My knowledge of sorcery was still young and not as developed as my mentor's, Dr. Dee. But I knew some tricks that gentleman did not. I spat into my hand, rubbed the bloody spittle into the forest entrance gatepost, then reached in for my sulfur mix and dusted my shoes with it. Thus might I be granted invisibility from dogs, if they used them. Perhaps they would be fooled into going into the forest. I slipped then, not into the woods at all, but along the boundary of the lawn and beyond, into the pleasure gardens.

Here short hedges offered me no shadows, but I hoped the company would not be looking out of windows on that side of the house. With many candles lit within, perhaps they would not see me crossing the formal acres, and into the kitchen garden beyond.

Within one corner was a heap of manure I had smelled on my tour about the grounds not a day ago. Here was something to mix with the powders I held, to confuse scenting by dogs or the brute that Enrico had become. I winced at the stink, but rubbed some of the freshest manure into my palm with the asafetida powder and wiped it upon my hands and boots. These traces would confuse and intoxicate a follower. I have seen it repel dogs with their sensitive noses, and escaped the stocks several times in my youth by the subterfuge.

There was no sound of pursuit, but I looked at the rising moon and cursed it for its silver light, clear through the sky.

Finally I crept along the wall to the corner, stepped upon a water barrel there, clambered up the drain pipe that fed it, and pulled myself onto the top. I have no head for heights and could see little upon the other side but forest, but lowered myself by my hands until I hung in the darkness, then dropped.

Chapter 33

The witches are away and life creeps over the cleared areas, exploiting the fresh ground, the patches of light, the damp soil where rain has been able to get in. Mice and voles scurry after fallen seeds, watched by a kestrel hanging in the wind overhead.

SADIE TURNED OVER ANOTHER PAPERBACK IN THE BOOK-shop, and read the blurb. She couldn't concentrate, her recent collapse had left her with a tickly cough and the local shopkeepers were all fussing over her. Everywhere Maggie went—she must remember to call Maggie Grandma—people asked about Sadie in whispers like she was five. She put the book back and lifted another one. *Tales of the Supernatural Lake District.* She smiled as she read the first few sentences. God, if only they knew.

Not for the first time, she wondered what she actually was. Revenant sounded like she was an animated corpse, but she knew that wasn't right. A revenant wouldn't walk past the chocolate and have her stomach rumble, she was sure of that. She picked a bar of chocolate with raisins and nuts in it. Maggie would frown and put it back, and pick the organic stuff, but it was worth it just to wind her up.

She stepped aside as she heard a whirring sound behind her and turned to see Callum in his electric wheelchair. He looked as pale and sickly as she felt.

"Sasha? Or is it Tara?"

Oh, right, the name's Sasha again. Sadie smiled. "Hi, Callum."

"You look terrible. Are you OK?"

"Relapse." She shrugged, it was the best she could think of and anyway, it was sort of true. "How about you?"

"Chest infection." He smiled weakly. "What have you got there?"

She handed him the book. "I just thought it would be funny to compare, you know, legends with what really goes on."

"Funny." He twisted his mouth into something like a smile. "Only true."

She took the book back. "I'm sorry we haven't found the cure yet. We are getting closer—we think we know where it is."

"If it's still there." He shrugged. "I don't care. I don't really want the cure if—" He paused. "The thing is, they say it's got to be soon. I don't want to change into—"

She could sympathize. "Look, once you have the cure you can fight the side effects."

"But would I even want to?" He pressed his hands together. "My dad, he says once the Dannicks have the cure, they change. They become more focused, more aggressive. Like my mother."

Sadie stepped aside for an older woman with a shopping basket on wheels, and lowered her voice. "Hasn't your dad had the cure?"

"He's not the Dannick, my mother is." He pressed the joystick and the machine glided over to a stand of magazines. "She never got this dystrophy thing either; she was fine." He waved a hand over his wasted body. "He's a good dad, but my mother—I mean, I love her, but she's different. Focused on the family as if we were royalty or something."

Sadie's mind jumped to her own mother. Always chaotic, she had been hit hard by Sadie's faked death, and was still drinking heavily. Sadie spoke to her every day, and thought maybe Angie was starting to pull herself together, but it was still a worry. She looked around the shop, busy with people, and wondered whether Angie would be better living in such a nice place, instead of a housing association flat in a city. "My mum struggles with my illness."

"She seemed OK," he said.

"Oh. That's not my mum." She couldn't explain. "I mean, I live with Jack and all that, but she's like my foster mother."

"Hello." Maggie stepped over, a carrier bag in hand. "You must be Callum."

"Hi." Callum drove his chair back to look at Maggie.

"I'm Maggie Slee."

When Callum raised his eyebrow, Sadie chuckled at his expression. "Foster mother's foster mother. Just call her Maggie." She reeled under a sudden wave of cold. "I'd better go and sit in the car. Sorry, Callum, some other time."

He nodded and whirred away. Maggie put her arm around Sadie's waist. "Put that chocolate down, I've got you some of the butterscotch organic ice cream."

Sadie registered the words but was concentrating on not throwing up. Maggie walked her to the door. She could see the car, parked a few spaces down the street. Maggie's car had the same symbols painted inside it as Jack's, a haven of energy.

"Oh, my book."

"You really want that?" Maggie took it, then felt in her coat pocket. "Here's the keys. I won't be a minute. Just rest quietly in the car."

Sadie focused on walking without wobbling. One step, two. Someone brushed past her, a woman in a hurry. She put a hand on a lamppost to get her balance, then stepped forward. One, two. Nearly there. She put her hand on her chest, over the symbols there, the burned ones stinging but releasing some of their energy. She stepped more confidently to the car, pressed the key fob, then pulled open the passenger door.

Before she could slide onto the seat a hand reached around her waist, crushing the breath out of her. As she gasped in protest, she was lifted off her feet and carried a few feet, dropping the keys. Pushed into the backseat of a car, she turned her head to see a man she hadn't seen before slam the door and jump into the driver's seat. A click beside her locked the door, and her weak fingers flapped at the missing catch.

Fear seemed to drag in the cold, and she started to panic at the thought of collapsing again. "I need my medicine," she managed to stammer, "please, I need my medicine!"

The man glanced at her in the rearview mirror. "I'm sorry. But my son needs his medicine, too. Maybe this will help your mother cooperate."

"But I'll die—" The words failed in her throat. She started coughing, and couldn't stop for a minute. By the time she could focus, they were already on the main road.

"We have a doctor up at the castle. It's only for a few hours: you'll be fine."

Sadie scrubbed at the symbols on her chest to keep from throwing up. A doctor wouldn't be able to help her now. She folded her arms over the sore marks and looked around the car. The other door had a lock on it; she could reach—but then the prospect of jumping out of a moving car at fifty miles an hour didn't make much more sense. She searched her pockets for the small bottle Jack had pressed on her that morning, and struggled to unscrew the top. Finally it loosened, and she drank about half. It gave her a boost, and she tucked the rest into her pocket. She leaned back on the seat and took a deep breath, letting the nausea fade.

The car was expensive, with leather seats and a purring engine that smoothly ate up the miles to Knowle Castle. She refused to engage with the driver, staring out of the window instead.

She was as angry as scared by the time they turned into the castle drive. She had swallowed back the same mouthful of breakfast a dozen times, and was considering spraying the driver with it next time. She was shaking with cold, the effect of being out of the circles. She waited for the car to stop in sight of tourists, so she could attract attention.

She was disappointed when he turned off onto a track marked "Private" to arrive at a small car park behind the castle, away from the tourist area. He opened her door from outside and half carried her into what appeared to be the Dannicks' family quarters. There was a large, bright kitchen with a middle-aged woman loading a dishwasher who had just opened her mouth to speak when Sadie's stomach cramped again. She splattered the floor and her captor's feet, she noticed with some satisfaction.

"Oh, Mr. Dannick, is she . . ." The words trailed away as Sadie, now a deadweight, was carried by the man through a corridor and up a narrow set of stairs. At the top, he pushed open a door and laid Sadie down on a single bed. She struggled to sit up, but he left the room without comment, and shut the door. A key scraped in a lock.

Sadie closed her eyes while she fought the nausea and took long, slow breaths. Potion. She slid fingers, stiff with cold, into her jacket pocket. The bottle was still there, and she managed to drag it out, and sit up enough to finish it off. With a little warmth spreading through her, she fumbled through her other pockets for her phone. It must have fallen out in the struggle. She looked for more potion. Nothing.

She could have screamed. But she did find a pencil that had come free with some puzzle magazine. The point was a bit blunt, the seven-hour drive from Devon had been punctuated by crosswords. But there was enough to at least draw a bit of a circle.

She had never drawn the sigils before, but she'd lived with them for months. The floor ones were a reflection of the ones drawn—and burned into—her chest, so she started with them. Looking out of the single locked window, she could see the sun in the sky over the forest. She guessed it must be about south.

She started by pulling up a carpet then the underlay, which was stapled to the floor. It came up with a lot of tugging, which left her feeling breathless and wobbly, as if she was drunk. Finally, she had enough of a square of floorboards to draw a small circle, just enough to sit in. She drew the first shape, then the next, pulling up the several layers she was wearing to check the orientation as best she could. On the next one the tip of the pencil broke, and she had to draw with the pencil at an angle. By the time she finished the last few symbols, she was scratching them into the varnish and dirt on the wood, but the effect was immediate. She dragged the duvet off the bed, sat on the pillow and wrapped the bedclothes around herself.

She curled up in a little nest of bedding and let sleep overtake her.

Chapter 34

We were called, Dee and I, to the mystery of a creature abroad in Lithuania that seemed to hunt like a giant wolf or monster. The local people were much afraid and some would not tend to their animals after dark, which was leading to many losses of stock. We were taken to see the mutilated body of a boy of some thirteen summers, half of which was eaten away. Dee examined the remains while I stood at the door—the death had been several days ago and it was summer—but he called me in to look into the wounds. Although the amount of flesh removed and presumably eaten was prodigious, enough for a pack of wolves, the wounds were blunt and rounded. Dee was forced to conclude that the predator, God save us, might be human.

—EDWARD KELLEY'S JOURNAL, 1584,
Vilnius, Lithuania

I LANDED IN SOFT RUBBISH THROWN OVER THE GARDEN wall. I found my feet, and apart from a pain in one ankle and a little discomfort in my back, was ready to run again. Beyond the villa the forests were open and soft grass grew underfoot, grazed short by rabbits or deer.

My mind raced almost as much as my feet. My first need was to create a weapon other than my pitiful dagger, and I cast about me for a sturdy bough, but could find none. I cursed the tidy gardeners. I kept the moon, silvery overhead, always upon my left a little, in the hope that I would at some moment find the road we had ridden in upon. My breath came sobbing in my throat now as I ran, and my ankle seemed to throb with each gasp. There! The sound of shouts and the howl of the tormented man. It was answered by other shrieks and calls, I think from human throats, though I had never heard the like. The legend of man-wolves was stuck in my mind. We had investigated two such in the countries of Lithuania and Normandy, and knew the legends well. At the full moon, such men as had wolflike hearts could enchant themselves into the beasts, and would hunt that ultimate delicacy, human flesh, the legend says. In Lithuania I prayed it was just legend, although I now had no time for such terrors, half vaulting, half falling over a tree that lay in my path. Here was a branch or two in reach of my dagger. I chose a tree limb less thick than my wrist but more than my thumb, and hacked away until I could bend it back upon itself, and it split from its parent with a crack like gunpowder. More howls followed, as if in answer. I used the knife to trim it, and roughly sharpened the already ragged end. It was some four feet long and crooked, but with time I could perhaps sharpen it to a point or even attach my dagger to extend my reach.

I looked around, my mind racing. I was not just trying to escape dogs as in a normal hunt, but humans, their senses awakened by their terrible rituals. I knew now that the impossible transformation hinted at by the panel might be truth. A slight incline led me to run down toward, I hoped, the road below. It led to boggy ground, which would hold the shape of my boot prints, and the sound of trickling water. I leaped as far as I could toward the stream, and my feet crunched upon the gravel with a splash. The light was blocked by trees overhead, and I stumbled in the dark, wading shin-deep in water that flowed around my skin like liquid ice.

There, more howls, and nearer. I turned, fear making my heart thump as if it would break my ribs, and could see a flicker of yellow light between the trees. Torches. The shrieks were such as I could not believe came from a human throat. I waded upstream, the darkness making me stumble on flat stones in the water. Then, uphill onto dry ground. I was stood upon a small island, maybe a few dozen yards across, and in the darkest of shadows beneath trees leaning over the stream from each bank. I sat for a moment, catching the breath that wheezed from me, trying to be silent. A shout from downstream, and crazed laughter, then voices, man and woman alike, raised in howls like animals. Now the first splashing, coming toward me. Fleeing now for my life, careless of the noise, I raced into the stream beyond the island. I fought it until the sound of water rushing became louder, and I realized it was not the blood torrenting through my veins. A waterfall above emptied into frothy waters to the dark river. I looked back, hearing many shouts clearly now, and then what sounded like hoofbeats. Even in my terror, I was angry that they had broken their word and sought me on horseback. I waded ashore, and opened my meager supplies. I had some charcoal and saltpeter in paper packets and mixed them together. My brimstone powder was in a small pouch, and I tipped half into the powders, praying that the proportions were correct although I could barely see them. Finally, I folded the paper into a large twist the size of my hand, leaving a corner of paper wound as a tail or a fuse.

A sound came from above the waterfall, not three yards high, then a gasp, whether from me or him I could not divine. I turned to see, crouched upon the bank above the waterfall, the form of Enrico.

I hardly recognized him, his lips drawn back so far it was as if they had been cut off, his eyes glowing in the silver light. He threw back his head and screamed at the moon, then stepped forward upon the stones above the fall. I held the packet between my knees and struck with my tinderbox, once, twice, to catch a little dry grass I kept within. No spark ensued, perhaps flint or tinder was damp—there, upon the third strike a spark hit the tinder and I blew upon it, almost too much in my panic, so that the tiny flame wavered. Then a yellow curl of heat, and I brought the paper to the flame and caught the end alight.

"Back!" I shouted, waving my branch. The fuse burned slowly, the flame shivering in the air then running like a golden thread up the spiral edge. Enrico did not hear me, or did not understand and howled in return. He crouched upon the top of the waterfall before leaping in a prodigious bound, like a deer off a crag, landing just on the very bank of the water. His shriek of defiance made me stagger back, and, in scant time, I hurled the lit parcel at the deranged moor.

The fuse caught as it flew toward him, the explosion sending us both tumbling and a sheet of flame flaring between us. I saw, when the smoke dissipated, fragments of burning paper falling around us, and Enrico kneeling, his hair on fire. He screamed, the unknowing cry of an injured animal, and fell back into the water.

I bolted, grasping my staff in one hand, stuffing my remaining powders into my waistband within my shirt as I went, trying to recall another spell as Dee had described it. I knew I would need to cast it while standing still and facing the thing that was once a learned and courteous man. I staggered into a glade, and turned to see Enrico, limping and using his hands upon the ground like an ape or monkey, leaping toward me. I set my staff in the ground and let him run on, hoping to impale him, but, alas, he divined my purpose and threw himself upon me instead. He trapped my knife against my body and tore at my shoulder with his teeth like a starving dog. I screamed, finding the words I needed within that cry of agony and fear, and the pink flames arose about my body, engulfing the creature. He sprang back, for what beast does not, before the inferno?

Chanting to continue the flames, I stared at the shadows within the sockets of his skull where I fancied red sparks glowed back. The spell the Contarinis had used had awakened a fiend within him. He stalked around the small circle of flame, growling. I thought frantically, trying to recall some counterspell that would reawaken his humanity. Perhaps prayer—but when I stopped saying the words the fire would wither and he would attack. Conjuration? Exorcism? I realized that neither would work if the creature that snarled and drooled at the thought of rending my limbs asunder was part of the human soul. The spell of negation of magic? It would certainly destroy the flames, but perhaps it could bring Enrico back to his senses by killing the transformation spell they must have worked upon him.

I chanted the fox-fire spell under my breath, as I reached inside my shirt for the remaining powders—pitiful. I had the remaining brimstone, powdered iron, a mixture I carry to deter bed bugs, and dried agrimony to bind the flux should I eat bad meat. And salt, yes, salt can confine a creature that is unnatural—but I had no idea if it could revert Enrico. I scattered the iron and salt together within the circle of fire and hoped there would be enough magnetism within the iron to work. With the end of my stick I traced the symbols of the angels' protection, and said the words.

Nothing happened, except my protective ring of flames died.

"Enrico," I intoned in my best stage voice. "Let man overcome beast!"

The words had no magical power, but he didn't know that. For a moment, some confusion crossed his face, his eyes fell to his contorted hands, which were shaped into talons, and he froze. He stared first at his claws, then at me, some frown upon his features in the bright moonlight. He glanced up, then stared transfixed at the silver orb above us. A grin twisted his face, and he looked at me, his head cocked upon one side like a dog, nay, a wolf. He gathered himself from his haunches like a hound, and, with inhuman strength, bounded the four or five yards between us. I saw the shape, but only his white teeth and the red eyes held my attention as they flew toward me. I stumbled away, crying out, "Jesu, save me!" before his claws gripped my throat and all went black.

Chapter 35

The scent of the old witch is fading. Only on the hives is it strong, where she spat on her hands and smeared the old slats with herself, before hiding that thing that smells of every witch the garden has known.

JACK HAD THE RAVEN SITTING CALMLY ON THE EDGE OF THE chair within a few feet of her when Felix opened the door. The bird flapped over her head, brushing her face with threadbare flight feathers, and screeching as if it were being murdered.

Felix staggered back against the wall. "Bloody hell, it's huge!"

She had forgotten he hadn't seen the bird before. It stretched out its neck and cawed at him again.

"I know, I know, he's an idiot," Jack soothed. "Shush, chick, it's all right." Jack glared at Felix. "You could have knocked."

"I just went to look at the body." He seemed wound up with excitement. "Maggie and Sadie covered it with foliage yesterday and it's almost gone. Sadie sat there talking to it—at least that's what she called it. Somehow, it's just being sucked into the ground by the tons of biomass in the soil."

"Well, Maggie said it would." Jack clicked her tongue softly to the bird, watching him put his head on one side then the other. "Be very quiet and still for a moment."

The bird shuffled its feathers with a sound like dry leaves, then dropped them back into a sleek shell. It glanced at Felix and hissed, then stepped forward, waddling on the paper, and looked up at her. After maybe a minute of Jack holding her breath, she reached out a hand as if she had done it a thousand times before. She could see the bird measuring height and distance, assessing whether it was safe. Just before she dropped her arm under its own weight the bird half unfolded its wings, hopped once, and landed heavily on Jack's forearm. Its talons curved cruelly around her arm, and it struggled to keep its balance, leaving the wings open a little. It swiveled its head to stare at Jack and croaked. She grinned, looking up at Felix, her eyes suddenly blurred with tears.

"He did it!"

Felix, who had his back pressed against the door, didn't seem all that impressed. "Put it down. It could peck you in the eye."

"Oh, you clever, clever boy," she crooned to the bird, reaching with the other hand very slowly. For a moment the huge beak was poised as if he would peck it, then he lost his nerve and launched itself off her arm to the floor.

"Are you going to keep it as a pet?"

"He's a wild bird," Jack said, wiping her hands on a rag she had hung on the chair. "But he's probably too familiar with humans to go back to the wild. Maybe a sanctuary that already has ravens will be able to take him. That's not what I'm worried about. I just wonder why an elderly lady with all sorts of health problems had him in the first place."

"How are you feeling?" His change of tone knocked her off balance.

"Oh. Fine. Bruised."

"You were nearly raped." He looked as if he were struggling

to say the word. "And someone was killed in front of you by a pack of wolves."

She shrugged. "Nearly raped. There's the difference, Felix; I got away. And Powell got what he deserved." She walked to the door, and he moved aside so she could open it. When he put a hand out to her, she jumped back at the approach. Her heart suddenly faltered in her chest and she took a deep breath.

"So you're OK, then?" His voice was low, his mouth tight.

Her heart was hammering uncomfortably under her ribs. "Maybe I'm not, but I'm getting there. A few nightmares, a few intrusive memories, that's all." Powell's hands crushing her into the ground, every fingertip leaving a bruise that told the story over her body. Felix had seen that, he had comforted and cared for her. No wonder he was worried. She leaned a little closer. "Look, after all this is over, I'll sit down and gibber about it for a few weeks. But right now, I'm worried about finding the book, and this potion we're supposed to be making for the boy up at the castle, and the dead man in the garden—"

He opened the door, and followed her onto the landing. "I just want to be able to help you, and you won't go near me. This is the first time I've been alone with you since that night."

Her phone beeped, and vibrated in her pocket. "I'm not avoiding you, but such a lot is going on." She glanced down at her phone. "Oh, shit, Maggie's lost Sadie."

"She's a teenager, she's probably seen something she likes in a shop."

Jack ignored him, phoning Maggie back. "What's happening?"

She listened to Maggie's explanation.

"So she needed to be in the car, anyway, for the circles." Jack looked at Felix, her forehead creased. "She wouldn't just wander off."

He stood beside her to catch Maggie's tinny words. They carried a note of panic.

"I found the keys a bit farther down in the gutter. But I can't see Sadie anywhere, and no one in the shops around here has seen her either."

"Who would—" Jack stared up at Felix. "The Dannicks want to put pressure on us."

"Sadie could already be dead. And we did meet Callum, in one of the shops." Maggie's distant voice sounded frantic. "What do we do?"

Jack looked up at Felix. "The Dannicks may have kidnapped Sadie." She turned back to the phone. "I'll meet you at Maisie's. Sadie's stronger than she looks, and she has a dose of potion with her. She should be OK for a few hours. They'll soon see how ill she is."

"OK. The shops all know her and I've given them my number." Maggie sounded a little calmer. "I'll get there as soon as I can."

Jack ended the call and turned to Felix. "We need Maggie to talk to Maisie. Sadie's so vulnerable out of the circles; you saw her the other night. I should never have let her go out . . ."

He started down the stairs. "We can call the Dannicks. Then we'll go over there and get her. We only have to threaten them with the police—"

"Wait." Jack hesitated, looking down at him. "It's not as if we can storm in there threatening to call the police. Sadie doesn't exist, officially. Neither do I. And we have no proof that they have her."

"Who else would take her?" He stared up at her. "Look, what could they possibly want? The potion they keep talking about, that book. They don't want to harm Sadie: she's their leverage."

"We've cleared, what, a quarter of the garden? We don't know where to look for the beehives. Sadie doesn't have days while we look for the book, and then find all the ingredients and make the potion." She followed him down the stairs, and he bundled her into a warm jacket. "Wait a minute, Felix."

"What?" He followed her into the kitchen. "We need to get there."

She poured a whole pan of cooling decoction into a bottle. "OK. Let's go and talk to the Dannicks. But first we need to meet Maggie at Maisie's house. Then we can get them to find the book so we have something to bargain with."

Maisie would only talk to them in person; it was as if she didn't trust the phone. Jack drove Felix to her house, tapping the wheel at every red light or junction, her heart racing at the need to do something, anything. The memory of Sadie slumped at the table kept intruding on her thoughts.

Maggie had parked down the road. Maisie was at home and ignored Jack and Felix. "Magpie," she said at the door, with acid disapproval. "You want the book."

"Don't Magpie me, you old crone," Maggie snapped back. "Sadie is in danger; we need Thomazine's recipe and we need it *now*."

The sneering smile dropped from Maisie's face. "The child? You let the Dannicks get her?"

Maggie flushed, her neck going red. Jack intervened. "Just tell us, Maisie, we're running out of time."

"I told you, it's hidden at the back of the garden." Maisie straightened herself up, looking at Felix. "This is women's business, what's *he* doing here?"

"He's an expert on magic," Jack snapped, "and he cares about Sadie."

Maisie seemed to wrestle with herself for a moment, then turned to Jack. "It's under the hives, girl, that's where we put it. They are beside the old damson. I can show you where it is, it'll let me in. I planted some of those trees with Ellen, the garden knows me."

Jack turned to Maggie. "Take Maisie to the cottage and start on the garden. We need the book right now."

"Do you have any idea what that potion does?" The old woman's eyes were unblinking, staring straight at Jack. "Ellen didn't refuse for no good reason. That boy is better off dead than saved by that ritual."

Jack winced. "Look, let's just get Sadie back in one piece, shall we? Then we can worry about Callum."

She raced for the car, closely followed by Felix, who muttered something.

"What?" she said, as the older women fastened seat belts in the back of the car.

"How much time does she have?"

"More if we get her the potion." She was forced to wait behind a bus at lights, swearing under her breath.

"But out of the circles?"

The air rushed out of Jack in a moment as she counted the minutes and hours away from the sigils. "Honestly? I don't know."

The unspoken truth hung between them. Sadie could already be dying, or dead.

Jack pulled up in front of the castle in a spray of gravel and was out of the car almost before it stopped. She ran into the reception lobby, and pushed straight through the door marked "Private," where Sir Henry had taken her before.

"Dannick!" she shouted, hearing Felix argue with someone behind him.

She threw open the first door she found, then another. Both rooms were empty.

"Sadie!"

"Can I help you?" It was a cold voice, coming from up the stairs, and Jack turned to see a woman in jodhpurs and riding boots looking down at her. She was tall, maybe six feet, and had her blond hair twisted back in an elaborate bun. "You seem to be lost."

"I'm not lost. Where's Dannick?" Jack put a foot on the bottom tread.

"Well, I'm a Dannick, but I suppose you mean my father, Sir Henry. He's busy." She stepped down another stair. "So you'd better deal with me. What is this nonsense?"

"You have Sadie. Sasha, whatever. The girl."

"Really? I think if that was the case, you would be at home making the potion for Callum." She started to walk down the steps.

"It's not that easy. It will take time, time Sadie doesn't have."

The woman's lips curved into a smile without humor. "Time *Callum* doesn't have. She won't make it if Callum dies."

"She will if you want your fucking potion."

The woman paused in her descent. "You have the book? Excellent. Then I'm sure we can do an equitable exchange."

Jack could feel Felix step up behind her rather than hear him, and his presence calmed her down. "You must understand, the garden is completely overgrown. It's taking time."

"My father will be available to speak to you this evening. Nine o'clock. When you will have the potion, finished and ready for Callum." Jack caught her breath, fighting an impulse to charge past the woman. When she started to move she saw a shift in the woman's expression. "My son, Ms. Hammond, as I'm sure you understand, is dying. Time is important; he may not survive another month. One more chest infection—" A fleeting emotion crossed her face. "He's my only child."

Jack lifted the bottle out of her pocket. "Sadie needs this, every three hours. If you don't look after Sadie, I will make sure Callum doesn't make it." She rummaged in another pocket for a marker pen. "And she needs this. Do *you* understand?"

The woman reached the bottom of the stairs, and took the bottle and pen. "If you aren't here by nine o'clock this evening, it's possible neither of them will make it. Do *you* understand?"

Short of storming past the woman and searching the entire castle, Jack couldn't think of anything else to do. She glanced up the stairs to see two men standing there, both young, both looking capable of stopping her even trying to get past. Jack turned on her heel and stalked past Felix. She could hear his voice behind her, barking orders at the woman.

"I want Sadie to phone this number in the next five minutes or we are not leaving, and yes, I will get the police myself. Do you understand?"

Jack ran through the lobby and out to the car, staring up at the windows of the castle. They stared back, reflecting the gray sky beyond, and the park in front of the house. She could feel her breath catching in her throat with a new rage as Felix joined her. He wrapped his arms around her and for a moment she clung to him, letting her racing heart slow a little.

The ringing of her phone made her jump.

"Jack?" Sadie's voice was a thin croak. "I'm OK. I got the potion. And the pen. I managed to make a circle."

"Good girl. We're going to come and get you, don't worry. It will be fine. Felix and I will work it out."

She could hear Sadie choking for a moment, then gasping. "I need to go back to the room," she said to someone away from the phone.

"Satisfied?" It was the woman, and Jack's fingers tightened on her phone until the casing crackled under the strain. "You have just over eight hours."

Chapter 36

*I am an alchemist, I understand the transformation of
base metals to pure metals. But the degradation of man
made in God's image, to vile beast, I shall never forget.*

—EDWARD KELLEY, 1586, Venice

WHEN I CAME TO MY SENSES, I LAY UPON THE GRASS
under a tree, the sky filled with stars so beautiful
I could have cried. There was no sound, no snarling or movement, and I still breathed. I raised my head cautiously, not knowing if it was broken, or my neck, but all seemed
sound. One gasp, and the agony in my torn shoulder filled my
world with fire. It subsided to a throbbing agony and I looked
about me.

In the clearing, within the circle of the trees, sat a nymph.

I know this seems fanciful, but how else does one name a
creature, nay, a female, dressed in a flowing shirt to her thighs,
whose form is revealed rather than concealed by the clinging
garment? I then realized that she was dressed as a man, her legs
encased in immodest breeches.

She turned toward me, her face in shadow, and she pointed
with one booted foot at the creature that lay between us. My
first thought was to thank God for my deliverance, but then
I saw what had befallen him. His open eyes stared up in the

moonlight, yet it was his back that faced me, his neck entirely twisted about. His mouth, his eyes—he had died a brute.

"My lady . . ." I stammered, then cleared my throat. "There are other hunters."

Then she raised her head, as if basking in the silvery light, and I gasped to see her face. Her mouth, her chin and her neck were all black. I knew without seeing that ruby color that they were bathed in blood. And I knew the arrogant tilt of the head, the thin nose, the gleaming eyes, and I felt a cold shudder of fear.

"We will be gone by the time they find him." The Countess Elizabeth Báthory walked to the stream and cupped water in her hands to wash her face and dab at the bloodied shirt. Then she pulled on, not a gown as I had expected, but a man's jacket. She stood, in the moonlight, and raised her face to it as if in sunshine. "Come, Eduárd."

I crawled forward on hands and knees, and despite the pain, pushed myself onto my feet. There I swayed, looking down at the thing that had once been Enrico. His face was utterly white, the fire gone from his eyes, and his mouth fixed in a scream.

She put out a hand, her long white fingers in the light. "Come." She seemed at once imperious and gentle. "He is gone."

I put my hand within my shirt to find my last papers, the drawing I had made of the tablet. "I cannot—I cannot come with you."

"They are close." She shook her hand. "Come, Eduárd, at least live. Then you may spurn my help."

I could hear the howls now, maybe a few minutes away, the one calling to another in animal cries. I took her hand.

She grasped my shaking fingers and ran with unnatural power, dragging me like a child. I put my feet down yards apart and was pulled along until my arm threatened to leave its socket. Finally, we came to a dark glade where I could see nothing but smelled the sweat and ordure of horses.

A man strode out of deep shadow and knelt before the

countess. She spoke in her native language, which I have never mastered, and the man rose. He grabbed at my form with both hands, careless of my wounds when I cried out, and he threw me up onto a horse. Not a pony or palfrey but a war horse, and I clung to the saddle with my good arm. He swung himself behind me and the animal half reared in protest. Some four or five men rode out of the shade of the trees, one leading a great stallion for their lady. With one arm around my chest, my rider pulled the reins until the beast subsided. He called out some command to his men, then put spurs to the horse's twitching flanks.

Each bound of the steed jarred my wounded shoulder, until I nigh swooned with the pain, the arm around me almost suffocating me. Sometimes we were galloping along clearings lit by the moon, other times we pushed through deep shade at a walk, the grass cropped short, we saw, by groups of small deer that bounded away when we disturbed them. I was determined not to faint, and to keep my seat upon the creature for these men represented my only chance of deliverance.

My rescuer rumbled out some question to my lady, who answered with a command. I took it to mean "onward," as we were thrown again into a canter. I could hear the sounds of pursuit now, the long howls more purposeful, interspersed with yips and barks that I could not believe came from the throats of men and—God protect me—women.

The horse we were sharing stumbled, almost throwing us off, and I clung with my injured hand to the man's arm, and the other to the saddle. For a moment I looked down—and down. We had come to an escarpment many yards high, a ridge that looked upon the road beneath. Before we could back the horse—for there was no room to turn it—another of the men called out a warning. I cast a glance behind us as the beast beneath us shivered and rolled its eyes as if to see the hunters that had chased and chased us.

They were assembling behind us in plain view. The silk and velvet robes had been discarded leaving the creatures, for I could not call them human, naked. They were ranged about us in a half circle like the pack of wolves they sounded like. One of the countess's men, his great sword already unsheathed, shouted a battle cry and swung among them, wielding his weapon in great arcs. One was cut down, another retreated, howling at its half-severed arm, but the others closed about him like hounds upon a wounded hart. It sounded like a battle of wolves, yet when they raised their twisted faces, they were unharmed. The man at their feet had lost his shirt and doublet, and lay bloodied, his neck and chest torn about as if half consumed. As I watched, unable to drag my eyes away, one of the monsters reached between his gleaming ribs and dragged out the heart.

I saw that the savage was Contarini, his face twisted with some animal cruelty. His mane of hair was free, his body sculpted like a Roman gladiator, his skin slick with blood. He raised the organ above his head, and all the others crowded around, some kneeling on all fours at his feet. Again and again they howled and shrieked, the women as crazed as the men. Finally Contarini opened his mouth wide, his lips pulled back revealing his long teeth, and bit into the heart. When he had taken a great bite, he threw it to the fawning women—if they were still women—at his feet. They growled and squabbled over it like dogs.

They turned to us, re-forming their group, the injured as well as the whole. The captain behind me spoke again to the countess, our horse stepping uneasily along the edge of the cliff.

Contarini opened his mouth and howled, then turned to us and spoke.

"Let us have him," he half growled, half said in Latin. "And we will give you a good start, lady."

The countess forced her horse forward a step. "You may

have my men," she spake, at one with the black charger she sat astride. "But the sorcerer is mine."

The growling rose to a scream until I was half deaf, the fiends crouched upon the ground as one, and with blood upon their distorted faces, they sprang toward us.

The man behind me wheeled our great horse about as it whinnied in terror, and forced it to the edge of the precipice. Even with his spurs beating cruelly against its flanks and laying the flat of his sword against it, it trembled upon the top. One of the man-wolves flung itself upon us, making my captor reel in the saddle. It forced its way over his back to me, as I crouched against the pommel. I already had a hand upon my dagger, and stabbed at it blindly, again and again as it fell upon my shoulders trying to force my head down. For a moment, I felt its breath upon the back of my neck and its teeth scraped lightly against my spine, but unlike a real wolf, its teeth were not sharp enough to split the skin. It fell farther, over my shoulders, and I slashed at it wildly as it slid over the horse's withers. It fell to the ground, much wounded, and this time the horse took a tentative step over the edge of the cliff.

It started to slip down with the sound of rocks and earth thrown up about it, and it sat down upon the slope, tossing its head back and shrieking in fear. It slid, fell and started to roll down the cliff, and I was grasped about by the man, who, quick as thought, leaped clear of the falling animal. We two men rolled and bounced another few yards, hit some boulders on the way, then fell down the rest of the cliff in a heap of soil and stones. I thought the horse was dead, for it moved none at first. I found myself mostly uninjured but for my torn shoulder when our steed shuddered and rocked itself to a sitting position. Shaking like a hart at bay, it stumbled to its feet. The man caught the reins, and spoke gentle words to it. I struggled to stand.

The sound of battle floated overhead, followed by a great shout of triumph. I looked up and saw such a thing as I would never see again. A black stallion, leaping in a great curve over the cliff, its head forced back almost to break its neck and hooves flailing in the air. I curled into a ball lest it land upon me, but it flew over my head and hit the ground with such a crack, such a noise. The creature fell, its legs splayed unnaturally, then rolled forward onto its head. The woman, for it was the countess, sprang from the saddle as it touched the earth and leaped away from the mortally injured animal.

She stood, her face turned toward the first pink of dawn, then snapped a command to the man. He led our horse to her but it strained away from her touch at the end of the reins. She controlled the horse with a cut of the whip she still held, and he stood trembling, his eyes rolling to me as if to implore me to help him. She leaped upon his back then beckoned me closer, and the man grasped my arm to drag me to the countess.

"Up. Behind me," she commanded.

I could hear the shouts and howls above us had subsided, and looking back I saw a terrible sight.

Many faces, man indistinguishable from woman, masks of snarling hate covered with blood, stared down at us. One started to feel for the edge of the cliff, reaching over.

Despite my wounded shoulder and many sprains and bruises, I put my foot upon the captain's hand and scrambled up onto the horse. It needed no touch of spur nor cut of crop. The second I was perched on the back of the saddle it sprang forward, almost unseating me. I clung to the woman before me, who urged the creature on. I looked back at the captain, to see him holding several of the man-wolves at bay with his sword, and more crawling down the cliff toward him. Then we were around a bend in the dirt road, and away.

Chapter 37

The bees ready themselves. Advance scouts have seen the clearing of the undergrowth, the elders holding together in a circle, brambles shrieking the scent of cut stalks and rotting stems, leaves barely born. Flies and wasps are stirring and the hive is on alert. Bee maggots squirm for food and the workers can barely keep up.

"YOU CAN HEAR THE BEES FROM HERE." MAGGIE WAS standing in the garden, listening. "They're incredibly upset."

Jack shivered in the gray afternoon. Late March or not, there was a nip in the air as the sky started to clear.

"I hate getting stung," she grumbled, shoveling more bags of manure under the remaining shrubs and trees, she supposed in some gesture of gratitude for allowing them to hack back the brambles. She watched Felix drag another half-strangled branch away to the bonfire, trailing yards of ivy. "I hated the hives we had in Devon."

Maggie peered into a tangle of vines and thorns, then carefully inserted one arm up to the shoulder. "There! It feels like a hive, and it's humming. There aren't many around at this time of year and normally they are sleepy with the cold. These are humming like they are going to take off."

Felix stamped the long grass and bramble stumps down to reach her.

Jack stepped closer, looking into the shadow of the bushes. "Can you feel underneath? Maisie said it was wrapped in plastic and tied under the hive itself."

"So she says." Maggie looked at the two of them with her eyebrows raised. "If the old bat isn't completely senile."

"I heard that." Maisie stood by the back door in Sadie's boots, which were several sizes too big. "I put it there myself, Magpie, and I'll thank you to remember I'm old, not stupid."

Maggie opened her mouth to protest, but shut it again when Jack caught her eye. Maisie had been able to direct their efforts straight to the hives, which was the only way they had a chance to make the potion in time.

Maggie stretched in again. "I can't reach. You're going to have to bring the loppers over here and cut these big branches down, but—" She hesitated. "They're elder. I'm not sure they will allow me to. There might be . . . consequences."

Jack checked her watch. "We have less than four hours. We have to read the book, find the herb, make the potion and get to the castle. Just do it."

Maggie took the loppers and murmured something to the tree. The blades snapped together and a branch fell, and Felix dragged it out of the way. Another, then another, and Jack felt as much as heard the humming of the bees, rising in tone as well as volume.

"Maggie, the bees—" she started to say, but Maggie fell back.

"Run!" she screamed, starting away from the hive, staggering over the loose cuttings on the ground.

Jack turned toward the house as Felix, with Maggie's hand in his, shot past her. She could see Maisie's face, slowly morphing into alarm, turning awkwardly in the doorway, getting swept up by Felix out of the way. The world tipped as she staggered, and then the swarm hit.

By a beekeeper's standard she knew it wasn't a big swarm. It was early in the year, when most hives were busy rearing young, but it still smacked into the back of her head and clung to her shoulders. Unlike a normal colony, which would be quite peaceful, this hive had launched a massive attack on what it perceived to be a threat, and in the tiny moment as it hit, Jack sidestepped her first instinct to scream, run, swat the bees, whatever, and stopped dead. Calm. Peace. She tried to find it in herself, even as her heart tripped in her chest, and her skin squirmed at the feel of thousands of tiny feet clinging to the skin of her head, her scalp, pulling on her hair. She found herself mumbling to them.

"Don't, don't—it's OK, it's just that we need to get the book. We're not trying to hurt you." She shut her mouth as the bees flowed from her forehead down onto her face. They tickled her nostrils, and she tried not to panic at the thought of bees going up her nose, and she clamped her eyes and mouth shut at the prickling on her eyelids, her lips. She carried on speaking in her head, hoping it would translate into body language or pheromones or whatever bees understood. The message was simple. "Please don't sting me. We're not trying to hurt the hive."

Under the humming, now almost deafening as they explored her ears, she could hear Maggie and Maisie. They were chanting something, coming closer. The bees increased their sound for a while, and she froze. Then they seemed to settle down, and the tone of their humming grew lighter and softer.

The weight seemed to slide down and settle on her shoulders, and she sneaked a look through her eyelashes.

"Don't move," Felix warned, his voice higher than usual with anxiety. "Just stand completely still."

There was a sensation of stroking, a gentle sweeping of her

hair and face, her shoulders. A burning sensation stabbed her neck, and she tried not to move. Another one. The chanting was constant, the sweeping taking the weight away, the humming more urgent but now from individual bees, not the whole lot.

"You can move in a minute," said Maggie. "Let me take your jacket off first."

Jack could feel the zip being tugged on, then the whole thing slid down and away, taking the weight of the swarm. "They stung me."

"They must have got stuck inside the collar," said Maisie, her voice hoarse. "I haven't seen bees do that in many years. Attack someone, I mean."

Jack still had hundreds of bees wandering over her, a few across her face, others tangled in her hair. Paradoxically, panic started to rise in her at the sight of the remaining insects. "Get them off."

She looked around, to see Maggie carrying a sheet, presumably carrying the bulk of the swarm, trailing a smoke screen of flying bees back to the area of the hive. "We're going to have to clear some more," she said, tipping the insects carefully onto the base of the elder tree that had been lopped. She backed away as the bees started to peel off the main pile, and buzz back through the foliage to the hidden hive. Bees started to lift off from Jack's skin and clothes.

Felix walked up to Jack, and gently knocked a few more off. She walked into his arms, and buried her face against his chest, smelling the warm wool of his jumper, the fresh sweat of the work, the indefinable Felix scent of him.

After a long moment, possibly more than they could spare, she took a deep breath, shrugged off the panic and turned back to the wall of greenery between them and the hive.

"We've got to get that book."

Felix strode over to Maggie. "Let me try. I've got long arms."

It took two more goes, several stings and a thorn deep in Felix's hand, before he could reach the twine tying the bundle under the hives. Maggie passed him a knife, and he hacked away at the cord before it sagged onto a pile of leaves beneath it. He stretched his arm in, Jack peering through from ground level calling out directions. Finally he snagged the plastic-wrapped parcel and pulled it through.

It was a relief to get back into the house, to shut the door against the sound of the still restless bees.

Jack took Maggie's knife, and slid it under the bindings, releasing the book. They fell back as it was revealed.

Almost black with wear and damp and grease, the cover was leather, stitched crudely along the spine. There was no inscription, and it was not much bigger than a paperback. Felix stepped forward as if to open it, but Maggie stopped him.

"It's a spell book. Let me, just in case . . ." As cautiously as if it were booby-trapped, Maggie lifted the cover a few inches. It fell open at a page toward the middle.

Felix bent over the words. "*That cure or remedie for the grate falling sickness of the Dannick*—is that 'lions'?"

"That's it. That's what they're looking for." Maggie reached across the table for a pen and an envelope. "Read out the ingredients. Let's hope they aren't in some sort of riddle."

"*One hand of mouse-ear, rankle-weed and hare-wyrt, digested in a seething pot with one cup of well water.*" He pulled his glasses out of their case and put them on. "It's not hair-root, it's hare-wort."

"Mouse-ear we have, out the front of the house, it's a common weed. I have no idea what rankle-weed is. And hair-root or hare-wort, leaves us no closer. I've never heard of either." Maggie turned to Jack. "I need my books."

Felix was already booting up his laptop. "What book would you normally consult?"

"William Turner's herbal."

Within two minutes an online version of the book was ready to search.

"Look for rankle-weed." Maggie was jumping with impatience.

Felix tapped the keyboard. "Nothing for rankle. Another word for it then, irritate, aggravate?"

Jack tried to remember the book. Herbs were Maggie's interest but as Jack's livelihood was selling magical ingredients, she had read the book a few times. "Try chafe."

"Chafe-weed, there it is. *Galium aparine*, cleavers, goose-grass."

"That's everywhere." Jack jumped up. "Is there any information on the hair-root or hare-wort in the recipe?"

"Well . . ." Felix turned back to Thomazine's book. "Look here."

The page was so grayed and dirty it was hard to read, even without the spidery writing that didn't look English. Jack leaned closer. "I still can't read it."

"No, right along the edges. Do you recognize the plants?"

Under layers of dirt, a thin brown line wound its way around shapes, leaf shapes, Jack realized. "That's mouse-ear. The spear-shaped rosette there. That viney thing with the spikes, I suppose that's the cleavers. That other thing, with the round leaves, must be hair-wort."

Maggie leaned in to look. "Maisie, do you recognize this?"

The old woman waddled forward on her bowed legs, and followed Maggie's finger. "I don't know what you would call it, but it grows along Thomazine's wall."

It did. The new plant clung in tiny clusters sparsely inside the garden wall. It took twenty minutes to gather a handful. Felix had been muttering over the manuscript trying to decipher Thomazine's letters, and finally had a list of twenty or so items. Jack stirred the pot they were cooking the decoction in; then Felix called her over.

"This is an additional list," he said. "Amyas's mixture, she called it."

Jack scanned the list. "Amyas wasn't affected in the same way the rest of the Dannicks were. I think we should give that version to Callum, and give him a chance of not becoming like the rest of them."

"I don't know where we are going to get all these items from. Sapphire, for example. Horsehair, the blood of a corbie, ground spider tangle . . ."

Jack tapped the word on his list. "That's why she kept the raven. Corbie, it's an old word for crow or raven. She needed it for the potion. I suspect everything we need is right here, and if we don't have all the ingredients, we'll still be able to make a potion. You rarely need everything."

"Where are we going to get a sapphire in time?"

Jack called through to the living room, where Maisie was dozing on a sofa. She didn't have a sapphire, but a cluster of gems on a brooch included a minuscule ruby, which Felix explained was the same mineral.

Within twenty minutes Jack had pried out the gem, found horsehair in the old plaster of the back wall, picked up dozens of spiderwebs from the garden and dropped them all into the decoction. The raven put up a fight, but with Jack catching and holding him, Maggie was able to clip one of his overgrown claws down to the quick, and several scarlet drops were added to the potion. She passed the stewed liquid through a strainer and left it in a jug to cool.

Maggie touched her arm. "It's almost eight, Jack."

She looked at the clock. "We need a plan."

Felix folded his arms. "They are never going to let you and Sadie out of that house with their secret."

"They might. If they know we have the recipe and they don't know where it is." Jack rubbed one of the raised welts on the back of her neck. "If they need it regularly."

"Have you ever heard of reverse engineering?" He closed his laptop. "With the potion we give them, a good biochemist can almost certainly work out most of the ingredients by analyzing the residue in the bottle."

Jack fished in the sieve for the ruby, carefully wrapping it in a piece of paper to restore to Maisie's brooch later.

"Maybe. But I don't see I have an alternative." She turned to Felix. "Now, you listen to me. This is a battle only I can win. I know what they are going to do, I understand what they think they need."

"What do you mean?"

"This is my fight, Felix. This is my world, magic and spells and potions. And Sadie is my responsibility."

Felix grasped her shoulders and shook her gently. "I'm not going to sit back and let—"

"No, you're not." She stared up at him, acutely aware that she might not survive the battle that was coming. "But Sadie is my responsibility. Just like Maggie has looked after me since she took me." Tears tingled behind her eyelids and she blinked, hard. "She's always been there for me. She couldn't do more for me if I had been her own daughter. Sadie deserves the same loyalty."

"So while you are risking your life, and possibly Sadie's, I'm supposed to sit here and do nothing?"

"Of course not." She touched her lips to his for a moment, softly. He didn't move, just stared down, anger creasing his forehead. "You are going to carry on reading that book and find a way to break the spell of the 'wild hunt' or whatever they call it. And I will need you to get us out of there once I've got Sadie."

She opened a kitchen drawer, looking for the hill-walking map she used to explore footpaths with Ches. "Here. This is the forest behind the castle, by the wolf enclosure. It's private land as far as the road. You can turn here, then drive along the ride almost up to the house. It's a rough path but it's designed for forestry vehicles."

"And you and Sadie will meet me there?"

"Bring Maggie too. I may need a bit of witchery. I don't know how they will react if they don't get their own way, but I'm hoping to get Callum out as well."

Jack was as ready as she could be. Remembering the wolf attack, she was carrying a few charms and spell ingredients. She wasn't a witch, but she knew the kind of sorcery most people could do, and added a bottle of silver solution to help Sadie. She tucked a hunting knife into the back of her jeans, knowing they would probably take it off her, and a thin stiletto into the side of her boot. She hadn't forgotten the "wild hunt," and had done a bit of research of her own. Telling Felix would only complicate things. She winced as she pulled a fleece on, her muscles still aching from the fight with Powell.

"Are you ready?" Felix said when she opened the door.

"I am. Hopefully they will listen to reason. We have the recipe and can continue to supply them."

"But should we? If it forces people like Callum to become . . . something else."

She zipped up the fleece. "It's what I do, remember? I supply ingredients for sorcery, magic, witchcraft, whatever. No questions asked."

"And you aren't worried that they sent a man to force Ellen to give up the recipe, who ended up killing her?" He frowned. "What are you going to do if they attack you with magic, like they did Ellen?"

"Maybe the coroner was right," she said, soothing him. "It was shock and pain from the fire. She was old and sick."

"Even I don't believe that anymore." He barred her way from the room when she tried to leave.

"I know something about fighting with magic, Felix. And defending myself." She let him hold one of her hands.

"There's still something you're not telling me."

"I am worried about a few things."

He took a deep breath, and sighed it out. "What about?"

"About the fact that my getaway driver is a middle-aged university professor, my backup sorcerer is an elderly witch who mostly enchants plants, and Sadie may already be dead." She put a hand on his chest and pushed him back. "I have some residual energy from the blood you gave me but there are a few of them, and they are supposed to be supernaturally strong. I'm outgunned."

"Then don't go. Call the police."

She shrugged. "That's your human solution, Professor. They'll rush Sadie to hospital and she'll die. Not to mention the fact that she was kidnapped and we faked her death."

"To save her life—" He stopped, hung his head for a moment. "OK. You're right. How can I help, really?"

"Be there. Be there in the forest and be ready to drive like a teenage car thief." She smiled at him, and he put his arms around her.

After the kiss, he murmured in her ear. "You'd better come back."

She smiled up at him, a nugget of optimism warming her. "I'll come back. Or die trying."

He half smiled, but his voice was low. "That's what I'm afraid of."

Chapter 38

My gracious lord, I write in sorrow and with concern about my great and noble ruling lady, Countess Erzsébet Báthory, whose requests to bury children within the graveyard have raised many questions. This last child, the daughter of one János Barbel, being shrouded within a winding sheet, was unwrapped by myself and my sexton, and many strange wounds were laid upon the body. Please, my lord, advise me most cautiously for I have many such caskets within my graveyard and I fear what is happening even as I fear my Lord Nádasdy and his royal wife.

—LETTER FROM THE PASTOR OF CSEJTE VILLAGE, to his superior in Trenčín, 1592

WE RODE IN SILENCE, ME CLINGING TO THE COUNTESS around her waist with one hand, and locked to the back of the saddle with the other. Whatever was not bruised in the battle was certainly damaged by that ride. The road stretched before us in the moonlight, a ribbon of pale against the dark grass, and we rode as if all hell chased us. Finally, she pulled the winded beast up and looked around.

"They will not venture far out of Contarini's land," she said to me, over her shoulder, as if we were friends, not sworn enemies.

I released my cramped arm from her body, and half slid into the road, crumpling onto the ground, my chest heaving for breath. I was not sure that the creature—Enrico—had not cracked some of my ribs. I lurched to my feet and stood swaying before the spent horse, whose head had dropped almost to his knees.

"I cannot—I cannot travel with you. I will not," I wheezed, and rested my hands upon my thighs until the breath came easier, my injured shoulder burning as it took my weight.

"Well, the road goes back to the beasts or forward with me," she said, with a laugh. She guided the horse around to start walking down the road away from the villa.

I looked either side but in truth I was sure I would be lost in the low woods in minutes. I started to follow the horse, feeling within my pockets for my belongings. My knife was gone, the powders gone, only the cursed tablet drawing remained. I thanked God that my most precious books were safe at Marinello's house. The countess paused a few times, listening to distant howls perhaps that I, with my breath laboring and my heart thudding, could not hear. Gradually, she drew ahead, until she stopped at a sign and waited for me.

"We find ourselves at a farmhouse, dear Eduárd. You shall lend me the protection of the illusion of decency, at least." I glared at her, but she simply held out her reins. "You shall play the loyal servant who fought off . . . robbers, I think."

Mumbling to myself, for I took no pleasure in the deception, I took the reins and led the horse within what looked like an enclosure.

The building lay three sides around the courtyard, the main part two stories high. No lights showed at any window, but the faint stamping of a horse told me one of the low wings was stables. The moonlight, growing low in the sky, gleamed off a trough and I led the exhausted beast there. The house, to one side, lay in darkness, and I felt my way to the door.

"Ho!" I shouted, and thudded my hand upon the door. "Help for my lady!"

A light flickered within, through the slats of the shutters in a room upstairs. A man's head was silhouetted against its light. He spoke in gruff Italian, but before I could attempt a little Latin, the lady answered.

After some parley, she turned to me. "Lift me down, like a gentleman."

Thus reproved, I followed the noise of bridle and spurs back to the horse, and placed my hands upon the lady's waist, lifting her down, which stabbed fire in my side and shoulder and reminded me of my hurts. The man emerged from the door to take the spent steed, and a woman, much wrapped about in a cloak, beckoned us into the house.

There my lady was much exclaimed over and taken up narrow stairs to be attended by the landlady, and I was shown to a narrow settle barely padded with a horse blanket for my own repose. I had little time to bemoan it, as I fell into sleep so fast I recall nothing until the countess threw open the shutters in the morning.

"Wake," she cried, adding a term I suspect equated to "slug-a-bed" in her own language. "Go, feed and water the horse."

I moved and my whole body protested. I was stiff with pain, my shoulder screeched when I tried to move it, and I shook with fever. I knew not what infection I had suffered in the bite of Enrico's madness, and could only pray that it would not be passed to me as country people in France believe. I rolled off the low bench, onto one hand and my knees. I could do nothing but groan in pain for a moment, while she stamped about the room, opening a cupboard here, a shutter there.

"Good wine, and some bread," she said, as if to herself. "Here, dried plums and grapes. We have a feast. Get up, weakling, and stop complaining. I have saved your life, and you can at least thank the horse for your deliverance."

I staggered to my feet, spots racing toward me in my vision and the room spinning about me. I clung to the rudely crafted table, and waited until the world was still. "I am injured," I managed to say. She looked as fresh as if she had not fought a battle for my life and ridden off a cliff to save her own. "Where is the farmer? He can serve you."

"Gone away." She said the word with such certainty that for perhaps a minute I believed it as I shuffled toward the door. The morning light stunned my eyes and made my head ache, and my mind thought upon her words.

"Gone where?" I said, as I turned to face her. She looked like a young girl, her hair around her body, her form immodestly revealed by her man's attire.

"Gone," she repeated. "Feed the horse, and I will make food for us."

I struggled to the stable, where the man had at least unsaddled the poor beast the previous night and rubbed him down. I gave him an armful of hay and refilled the water trough. I added a handful of grain for his gallantry and courage last night and spoke gently to the creature. His body had survived but his spirit seemed broken, for he shivered in fear, rolling his eyes even as I fed him. The farmer's other two horses were tethered at the back of the stable, and were grateful for hay and water. I wondered how the man and his wife had gone when their horses remained. I could not shake off my unease at their absence.

I returned to the house, holding on to the doorway, feeling as ill as if I had an ague. She had lit a fire and water was warming in a pot hung over the bright flame.

"Now, Master Kelley, we will attend to your wounds. Take off your jacket."

I was reluctant to do so in the presence of a woman not my wife, but also because she had laid upon the table some torn strips of cloth, some sort of herbal ointment, and, at the end, a knife that looked as sharp as a razor. I undid the laces on my jacket, and squinted inside to see the damage.

My chest, under the torn shirt, was purple with bruises. The edges of a ragged wound were scarlet and swollen and stuck to the shreds of the linen with black blood. I felt unwell just to see it. She reached impatiently toward me, and helped drag the jacket from my torso.

"Sit, sit," she said, all the time peeling back pieces of the shirt. "You are lucky," she mused. "The doublet took more damage than you did."

There were two half-crescent-shaped bites that had torn into the skin and revealed the meat underneath. Nauseated, I looked away, as she bathed away blood and scabs alike. She turned to the pot upon the fire, and pulled out of it a small glass jar or bottle, suspended within the water by means of a string. I looked around the room, seeing signs of modest prosperity, a few shirts hung to dry in the adjoining room, one that of a child.

"Where did you say the farmer went?" The answer struck me almost as fast as I spoke the words. "Are they gone or are they . . . dead?"

"They are the vassals of Contarini," she answered, stirring the contents of the bottle with the knife. "They would tell of our presence, and the direction of our travel. This will be hot but will draw out any bad humors," she said, as she smeared the contents onto the wounds.

The pain was enough to take my breath, take my words, take even my thoughts about the farmer's fate, but slowly the fire became an intense throbbing, glowing from my shoulder, which was swiftly bandaged by the countess.

"I have often bound the wounds of my husband and his troops," she said, tying up the ends. She pulled down one of the farmer's fresh shirts, and held it for me to ease my shoulder into. I winced at the sharp pain in my ribs, and allowed her to dress me. Then she helped me into the torn jacket, which was at least warm. "Get horses. We need to be away. Contarini will find us here. I will pack food for us to eat upon the journey."

I stepped into the stable, struggling to lift down the saddle but finally throwing it over the shaking animal's back. For myself, I saddled the farmer's cob, a hearty-looking gelding with a placid eye.

I went around the stable, looking for a bridle for the cob, and that is when I found her in an empty stall.

She lay in the rough straw like an angel. Her arms were raised, her nightgown spread about her, her bare legs white as the linens and her hair tumbled about her. Her face gazed unseeing, her eyes a little a-cock, as if one eye gazed at the stable and one at the heavens above, which had surely embraced such a tiny creature. Around her throat, the ruby flesh was torn, the wounds ringed about like a parody of a necklace. I staggered out of the stall, and emptied my stomach upon the stable floor, fighting for my feet in the memory of that gaze, those brown eyes already milked in death. I shed tears of pity, then, that I had brought such a cruel fate upon an innocent family. It took me some moments to wipe my face with my sleeve and do the countess's bidding.

I set my eyes upon a rack of bridles, and took the largest one as it looked the most used. I took it out to the big cob, who placidly turned to me, and I held out the bit for his mouth. His great black eyes, so trusting, made me stand with my face against his flank and pray for the child's soul, for my forgiveness, and for God's grace in defeating my enemy. I resolved to bring the unholy creature to her grave.

Chapter 39

The castle grounds had been watered with blood for a thousand years, since the first of that savage race had built the first fortress. Here the deer shuddered every moon at the creatures that hunted them, chasing them up to the cruel fence, rending their bodies, killing the calves. But sometimes, the pack turned upon their own kind.

"YOU HAVE YOUR POTION, WE KEPT OUR SIDE OF THE BARgain. Now let her go."

Jack stared at the circle of Dannicks. They were a tall breed, even the boy would be lanky for seventeen if he could get to his feet. Only Callum's father had a more relaxed posture than the upright grace of the Dannicks, a little softness to his features. His hand rested on the shoulder of the boy, slumped in his wheelchair beside Sadie. She was kneeling beside him on the floor, swaying, her face white and her lower lip caught between her teeth.

"Is it potent?" Sir Henry was as calm as if it were a social question.

"We have, as far as we can tell, made the mixture to Thomazine's recipe." She didn't mention it was Amyas's mixture, not the "Dannick Lion" brew. She held out the bottle.

He nodded to an associate, a stocky dark-haired woman, who snatched it away and opened the top to smell it.

Jack stepped forward to the teenager and no one stopped her. "Sadie." She crouched beside her.

"Go away. They're planning—" Sadie choked, and Jack dragged the earthstar and hagweed potion from her pocket. "They'll kill us both," Sadie managed to whisper before she sipped a little of the liquid.

Jack looked down at the boy, seeing his blue lips and shaking fingers. "Callum, we need to get Sadie out of here."

He looked dull, maybe exhausted himself from fighting his whole family, and slumped sideways in his chair. "They won't let you go. They want to complete the ritual tonight, while the moon is up. They are going to force me to drink."

Jack looked around the room. Most of the adults were in a circle, discussing the potion she had delivered. The dark-haired woman put the bottle to her lips, and threw back her head, moaning as if in pain. Or pleasure, Jack decided, by the way the woman licked her lips and carefully stoppered the bottle again.

"Powerful," she said, turning her stare on Jack. "Perfect." She poured a dose into a glass.

"I don't want it!" Callum waved a hand weakly at his approaching father. "Dad, I don't want it; you said you understood." Tears made his eyes glisten.

"I do understand." He crouched beside the boy, ignoring Jack as she dragged Sadie to her feet, and backed away. "But I won't let you die, Callum."

Two men moved between Jack and the door.

Sir Henry detached from the group and walked over to Jack. "We can't let you leave."

"They're—" Sadie choked again, and slumped in Jack's arms. She let the teenager fold slowly back onto the floor.

"Because you need to complete the ritual. Is that what you

think?" Jack stood straight. "Let me take Sadie somewhere safe, and you can have your hunt."

"Ah. The hunt." He smiled, without warmth or humor. "Normally, we take game, but for this ritual, we need—"

"Human prey. That's it, isn't it?" She turned to stare at Callum's father. "You believe you need your child to chase and kill another human being. Were you going to throw Sadie to the boy like a hamstrung rabbit?"

"The girl is almost dead. I don't understand what she is— she smells dead already. You are the quarry." His nostrils flared as he towered over Sadie. "You can leave her here, and I will promise her a quick and painless death. Or you can take her with you and we will hunt you both. She will slow you down. It wouldn't be a chase, it would be an execution."

"I'll take the chance." Jack could see some expression on some of the people's faces, a look of anticipation, mouths open, a few panting. A quick count numbered eight of the predators, including the boy. He was right: she didn't stand a chance, maybe even without Sadie slowing her down. "Just give us a reasonable head start."

"First, I want to show you something. Bring the boy here, Michael."

Callum's father wheeled the barely conscious boy over.

Sir Henry crouched down, looking into the boy's face. "Soon you will be free of this disease, Callum, do you understand? Healthy, strong, a Dannick Lion like your mother, like me."

The boy's head flopped against the wheelchair cushions. "Let me die, Grandfather, please. I don't want to be—like you, like them."

Sir Henry held out a hand for the potion. "Hold him," he snapped to the boy's father and, with some wrestling, forced some of the liquid down the boy's throat. Even with spitting and spluttering, Callum couldn't get rid of it all, and choked some down.

The change was almost instant. He screamed as if in agony, then thrashed his head against the wheelchair headrest. "Dad!" he sobbed, and his father bent down to comfort him, but Callum found enough strength to push him away. "Don't! Don't let them—"

The glass was lowered again, Callum's head forced back, and the remaining potion tipped down his throat.

Sir Henry stood, an impatient flap of his hand the answer. "Now, the ritual. Annis, Georgina, Thomas, you will prepare the circle. Jonas, you will lead the pack."

He turned to Jack and waved at her. "Let her go, but into the woods. They won't get far." He looked at Jack and a smile spread over his face. "And make sure Callum is in at the kill."

Jack scooped Sadie up in her arms. She weighed so little she was like a bundle of sticks. Callum's father opened the door and led her around to the back of the house. He pointed at a long fence, which terminated at the gate into the forest.

"Your best chance is to head into the woods toward the quarry. If you throw them the girl, you might get away."

"So you're OK with murder?"

"He's my child." He shrugged his shoulders. "What alternative do I have?" He turned to go, looking back over his shoulder. "They lock the rest of us up, for our own safety, but it will be bad out there. Don't put up a fight, it'll go quicker."

Jack put Sadie onto her feet on the gravel when she struggled. "Do you need more potion?" she asked, feeling her wobble.

"I've had most of it already. Jack, can't you hide me somewhere—" She stopped, put her head on one side as if she could hear something.

"They would find you. What is it?"

"I don't know." Sadie staggered onto the path toward the forest. "It's calling me—the garden."

"The garden?" Jack put one arm around the girl, leading her over the pavers, half holding her up.

"Yes." Sadie choked and spat. Jack had to take most of her weight by the time they reached the gate, but once in the shade, Sadie found new strength and pulled away.

Jack whispered quickly. "We need to get going, find water, anything to cover our scent and tracks."

"No—wait." Sadie lifted her head, as if she could hear something. "Follow me." She led the way into the darkest thickets, toward a tree looming over a group of smaller ones. "In here."

The sound of someone screaming stalled Jack, who stopped to hear the eerie cry echoed by more voices, yowling, wailing, screeching—the hunt.

"We have to go." It seemed hopeless, they were barely five hundred yards from the house.

"You go. I'll be safe." Sadie drew herself upright. "Trust me: I'm the green witch, remember? But you, you are the animal one. So go, run, use what you have."

Jack hugged Sadie, felt her arms hug back. "I'll try to lead them away. Just hide, OK? Maybe they won't come through here." Her eyes filled with tears. It was hopeless to try to take Sadie with her, and death if she left her in the weak state she was in. Jack's hope was that they would follow her instead. She let go, and bounded into the woods away from Sadie. From some feral instinct, a long-buried exhilaration born of survival, she let rip with a howl of her own. Many shrieks answered.

Chapter 40

*The fate of that child rested uneasily upon my soul;
perhaps it will always fill me with guilt that I, who
knew what the countess was and what she was capable
of, did not warn the farmer and his wife. But, in truth,
I had not yet understood fully what she was capable of
until that night.*

—EDWARD KELLEY, 1586, Venice

I LED THE BRIDLED AND SADDLED HORSES BACK INTO THE
yard, and inspected the countess's horse for injury. One of
his shoes was loose, so I hammered it back on, my ribs pro-
testing as I lifted his foreleg. The hoof had split a little above,
small wonder after such a fall, and I could only hope that a few
extra nails would help hold the poor creature's foot together.
The countess appeared, a bag slung with stolen goods over an
arm, a dagger secured in her belt.

As I stood there, the farmer's fate—and that of his child—
weighed heavily upon me. The countess paused for a moment,
then shouted at me in Latin. "Quickly, we must go. They are
coming!"

With my injuries I could not mount the cob by myself, so
led him beside an upturned barrel and climbed upon his back
with as much haste as the memory of the monsters howling and
snarling could give me. The countess, astride her charger in

a moment, slapped my horse's rump and set it trotting, then grasped my reins. And so we fled.

I wondered that she did not leave me to our pursuers, so slow was the cob. With a gait between a trot and a canter that rattled my teeth and juddered my ribs, we struggled to keep up. Soon we passed approaching parties of travelers who gave us strange sidelong looks, from the hunched servant to the wild-haired mistress astride her great charger. All fire had gone from him, he obeyed her, but his head was low and his gait uneven. As we reached the main road the spires and roofs of Venice set in the sapphire lagoon gleamed ahead. Finally, the countess allowed the horses to rest and crop fresh grass. The road ran over a small bridge crossing a stream. I led the horses off the road and down the bank to drink, and took a cool draft myself. My shoulder felt better, the fever seemed gone, and I was suddenly grateful that I was still alive. In the company of my greatest enemy, yes, but still breathing, and the early sunshine seemed to shine into my very soul.

As we remounted, the sun was already overhead, a force of heat, and she indicated that we would stop to eat at a large inn. It was beset with urchins selling fruit, begging to take our horses, or to carry my lady's cloak. Each approach by a child to the lady caught my breath in my throat, and I drove them away. She laughed at my efforts and indicated that I should attend her myself. To the landlord, a stout fellow full of his own importance, she spun a tale in mingled Latin and Italian much of which eluded me. But I did gather that we had been attacked upon the road by a great band of ruffians, and it was only with my courage and ingenuity that we survived.

I eschewed the many congratulations, and made the countess's quarters as livable as I could, acting as the great lady's *maiordomo*. I found fault with the bedding, demanded to taste the wine and otherwise suggested my lady's great status. Finally, with a few golden crowns bestowed upon me by my new mistress, I managed to find some simple raiment more suited to a lady than a boy. Ordering great ewers of hot water and the attention of a maidservant, my lady vanished into her quarters to emerge radiantly restored an hour later. Meanwhile, I had sat at the table in the inn's kitchen and been regaled with cutlets of hare, fresh breads and a flagon of well-cooled wine.

While I was there, horses galloped up to the inn, creating a commotion of shouting. It drew me to one of the room's open windows. Men, who were in some sort of uniform, bellowed orders and questioned the landlord.

The cook, whose origins were in Frankish Metz, translated some into German for me. "There is a foul murder upon the highway," he said, bustling about the room, with a placid expression. "Terrible."

"Murder?" I rapidly reviewed my story. "Perhaps of my companions, who were attacked upon the road, and followed the villains into the forest?"

"No," he said, pouring wine and water into a large flagon, ahead of the soldiers' needs, I guessed. "The farmer and his wife, of a small farm some leagues west of here. They were stabbed, it seems, but the soldiers also found a slaughtered child, much mutilated."

My mind conjured a memory of the child, her throat rent and torn, the eyes staring.

"How dreadful," I answered, in the same placid tone as the man, but my stomach lurched at the thought of the countess's work. The image would not be banished, like looking away after seeing the sun.

"Poor child," he said, a frown wrinkling his broad forehead, as he listened to the outcry outside the window. "They say she was attacked by a wild animal, her throat torn out."

I stilled my shaking hands by clasping them in my lap. I

muttered a quiet prayer in English, for mercy upon her soul and upon mine. The maidservant entered the kitchen and addressed me in her own language, which the cook, turning slabs of meat upon a hot griddle, translated.

"Your lady asks for your attendance."

My heart was like a stone in my chest as I trod the stairs to her chamber.

"Ah, Master Kelley," she greeted me when I was called into her presence. "I have ordered fresh horses to take us back to the city in the morning." She sat on a padded bench before a polished metal mirror.

I spoke, my gaze downturned. "There are soldiers here who seek the killer of the landlord and his family."

"Ah." She gazed at me from the mirror, her face slightly distorted.

"Did you have to kill the child?" My sickness made me bold.

"The question should be, did I have to kill the farmer and his wife." She turned back to her grooming, drawing a brush through the lustrous strands of hair.

"But the child—" My words were strangled in my throat by my horror.

"Sustains my life. Look at me, Master Kelley, look at the pink in my cheeks, the light in my eyes. I would be weak unto death without the sacrifice of one peasant child. Now, sit, take a drink of wine, and we will plan our return to Venice."

"I do not understand," I muttered, still surly at being forced to accept the charity of my enemy.

"And it occurred to me that now is a good time to have that conversation that I wished to have in Venice." She turned to me, eyes sparkling like a girl's. "How you saved my life."

I shrugged. "I do not know what I can tell you. I assisted Dr. Dee, certainly, but his is the wisdom and knowledge. And none would have been done without your own Zsófia's help."

"Witch magic. By itself, it could not save me." She smoothed her hair, as lustrous and curly as a head of snakes, from her broad forehead. "My spies tell me that you are becoming renowned for your interest and knowledge in sorcery."

"In its ability to transmute metals, certainly, in the science of alchemy. Not in the transformation of people."

She laughed softly. I was reminded of the first time I had spoken to her, a weary and frail but very human lady, whose plight had touched my heart. "I am still the same Báthory Erzsébet, Edward."

"The lady I knew could not have—" I choked at the memory of her lovely face smeared in the blood of the witch Zsófia, and the dead child laid in the stable.

"I was ensorcelled, and by you, Edward. Such was the flush of strength into me that I craved life." Her eyes were intense upon me, making me blush. "You enchanted me with your incantations. But with life, came the curse."

"Curse, lady?" I was intrigued against my will, looking at the woman I had seen exultant at the kill, now so soft and womanly.

"You saved me with blood, Edward. And my life can only be sustained with blood."

I bowed my head. "Blood was no part of the cure we designed, my lady."

"You knew." An expression, at once more seductive and cruel, fluttered over her features and was gone. "You knew that Zsófia was sustaining me with herbs and blood."

And, in truth, I did. In my heart I knew that the ritual we subjected her to—at swordpoint, in fear of our lives—was ordained not by heaven but by the machinations of a creature whose nature was unknown to me. A creature I had believed to be an angel had haunted me, and spoken to me with the countess's own lips.

"I did what you asked. I did not make you a monster that would kill a child."

She lifted a goblet, and touched it to her lips. "You see, today, I can be refreshed with good wine, fine meats, because I am freshly restored by the blood of that child."

I shrank from the thought.

"But tomorrow, or the next day, I shall be repelled by the sourness of wine, and meat shall taste of ashes and dung." She turned to me, her expression twisted perhaps by sadness. "You have given me life, Eduárd, but I live the life of what the Venetians call a revenant, a creature caught between life and death."

"Yet you live, and can cradle your own child."

"I can," she breathed, so softly I almost did not hear her. "And yet, the voice in my heart craves that babe's blood the most."

"Voice, my lady?" At the word, I felt a shock of cold through my veins, as I recalled the words she had spoken to me on the hunt back in Transylvania, the hunt for two Englishmen and their allies.

"You know him, you carried him to me."

"I spoke only to angels, my lady," I said, with less certainty than ever.

"You created a revenant, a vessel, for a creature that squats inside it. Saraquel haunts my thoughts, demands that I feed him and our mutual body. He commands I feed on fresh human blood."

I was stunned that she spoke thus to me, the possibilities terrifying. Had I invited a demon to possess the countess? Had I helped create a monstrous parasite that haunted her?

"Saraquel." My mind ran feverishly upon my knowledge—extensive, from my studies—of cases of demonic possession and exorcism. But Saraquel had spoken in my mind and to Dee, and had never seemed anything but angelic. But then, my mind argued, he led you straight to the countess, the bottle for the wine that was the creature, be it good or evil. And, contained within a base, mortal body, what other instincts might it release? I longed for Dee's knowledge, for his magnificent library and his clarity.

"I need your help." Her voice was rich and soft, no longer that of a countess, but a supplicant. "I need to know the nature of this spirit within me."

"You take life for the most selfish of reasons." I was suddenly aware of her long fingers, stretched over the carved arm of her chair, as they clenched briefly, whitening the knuckles. I knew of her tremendous strength, and moderated my words. "Like a wild animal, you take the lives of children. That is the nature of a demon."

She shrugged. "I have learned to harvest the blood of my people, also. My servants know that to keep me alive, and to keep the monster inside me asleep, it is better to feed me small amounts of blood. Even, on occasions of great hardship, the blood of animals."

I stood before her. "If you will pledge to take no more lives, I will do all I can to help you."

She smiled, not a pleasant smile, but with the contempt of princes. "You, to offer me terms like a merchant? I could snap your neck between my fingers, or drain you to a husk."

I bowed, my stomach churning, my legs shaky beneath me. "You could. But I am well placed to study this—'sleeping monster'—and perhaps find a way to release you from his governance."

She touched her hand to her throat, where hung a pendant, the head of a dragon, the mark of the Báthory clan. "We shall return to Venice, and you will consult the most learned men. Then you will find a cure, an exorcism to remove this thing, this demon."

I bowed deeper, my mind racing on the words while my memory brought forward the picture of a slaughtered child, all the slaughtered children.

Chapter 41

The garden reaches out for the witch and finds her, miles away. With one web of threaded fungi entangled with the next the distance is nothing, the knowledge carried without emotion or judgment. Here is the witch. Here we draw upon her energy, and she upon ours.

SADIE LEANED AGAINST THE TREE, FEELING LESS TIRED, less exhausted. She tried to calm down, relax as Maggie had suggested, let the tree's energy flow into her. Her heart felt like it was looping in her chest, and she felt chilled, as if she were immersed in cold water. Plant cold, she realized, letting her senses reach out for impressions from the forest, a strange shivery feeling. It was silent; in fact, it was so quiet it reminded her of someone trying to hold his or her breath.

Then it started. A slow tendril of an idea seemed to reach into her mind. She looked up at the smooth bark of the tree, no features standing out in the low light. Some speckles of moonlight fell onto the ground below, but the trunk stood over her like a statue. She reached her hands onto the bark, feeling the roughness, feeling the energy flowing powerfully through the tree, like a stream of cool air. Her fingers tingled with it, then found a shallow hole just above her head. She put her hand in it and pulled herself up. Her feet scrabbled against the tree, but the toe of one trainer caught a tiny bump. Her other hand found the stump of an old branch. She heaved at it, fighting to stay up, her feet shuffling their way a few inches at a time. A ridge, a rough bit of bark, and, finally, she was able to reach the first big branch. She hung there a moment, exhausted, but the tree itself seemed to be pouring energy into her, pulling her onto a fork in the tree. She curled against the trunk, one hand steadying her on the limb above, and looked up.

There was no more light here, yet somehow her hands knew where the branches were, allowing her to weave her way up three more levels. She clung to the trunk of the tree in a hug, the wind swishing through the branches. She could feel some tension in her fingertips, not hers, she thought, but the tree's pressure, as the buds swelled before leaf break or whatever they called it.

"Thank you," she whispered, and had the strangest sensation that the canopy of the tree bent down to listen.

She concentrated her gaze on the bare grass below, spotted with light from the rising moon. She could see it shimmering in her mind, as if it formed a barrier beneath her. A scent quickly developed, almost like a moldy, mushroom smell.

She closed her eyes and waited. She could hear them shouting in weird cries, like animal noises mixed in with words. "Hunt! Kill! Meat!" She thought about her mother back in Exeter, who had somehow adapted to Sadie's magical survival. She was still fragile, drinking too much, sleeping badly. Sadie knew how she would struggle with her death. She wished she'd been able to phone today, maybe say good-bye. She shook herself, and let her sadness flow into the tenuous connection she had with the tree, and in turn with the forest.

A crunching over the gravel warned her they were advancing faster than she had expected. She could no longer hear Jack moving away. They smashed through the bushes on either side of the gate, as if they couldn't wait to file in singly. She could hear them snuffling, like dogs trying to pick up a scent, then they howled, the noise making her ears ache, as she realized they were almost directly under the tree. They moved, as if searching around the trunk.

The first smell was like the moldy newspapers back at the house, then some metallic fungi odor, then the stink of rotten rubbish, rising through the branches of the tree. The creatures—when she moved a few inches and slitted her eyes she could see them loping about on all fours beneath the tree— were naked, milling around beneath the tree as if confused. It seemed the stink of the fungi was putting them off. Then one of them lifted its head, and sniffed the trunk of the tree where she had scrambled up.

He threw back his head and screamed. Sadie almost screamed too, the sound was so shocking, so loud. She looked through the branches, and it seemed he was looking straight back. *Help me*, she thought with as much concentration as she could summon with the thing snuffling its way up the trunk. It swung its weight effortlessly as he clambered to the first branch. She felt the tree shudder. What did Maggie say? Intent, gather intent. She concentrated.

The forest shifted, or rippled, or something. Maybe it didn't move physically, Sadie couldn't tell, but something huge shifted in her brain. The whole forest flooded her senses with growing and swaying and pulling water and scuttling in the dark. It was in the soil and flying in the dark air. First she fluttered in her mind because her hands gripped the trunk more tightly, but she imagined flapping so intensely she could almost feel the air moving between her fingers. The sound of wings beating made her sneak another look at the creature just two branches below her. It was enveloped in insects, moths, bees, anything that was awake in the spring as if it were food for all of them. It swatted, and Sadie felt needle pricks of death as it crushed tiny winged bugs. Owls swept in like ghosts, small birds appeared in a cloud, even a dozen rooks flew in. They flapped in the face of the man, cawing and hooting and piping even in the dark. He leaped along the branch, waving and now howling his distress, the others yelling in answer. As he inched farther along the branch toward the next one, Sadie could almost feel the fibers stretching under his weight, as if a miniature wolf-man were perched upon her own clenched fingers. His shoulders and head were covered with the rooks, just a bundle of black movement in the dark. She lifted the hand, feeling it vibrate as he moved upon it, still flailing at his tormentors. She opened her fingers, splaying them out and then curling them back into a fist. It seemed like the whole forest responded; she was half surprised that her hand didn't snap off.

The bough broke under the creature with a sound like a gunshot, and it hit the ground with a thud and an animal whimper. Sadie could see him hunched on the ground, speckled with more light now, and see the slow movement around it. The others were crawling around him, sniffing and whining, and closing in. For a moment Sadie thought they meant to help their fallen pack member, but when the injured one reacted by snarling defiance she realized they were growling back. A tall blond naked creature, one of the women, Sadie thought, uttered the first shriek, and fell upon the fallen one. He fought back, several fell away yelping, but his cries seemed to turn from defiance to agony, and, with a horrible crunch, his last yowl was cut short.

Sadie looked down in fascinated horror, and a face turned up to the sky, and howled. It was Callum, his voice lighter than the others, his body thin and tall. Sadie closed her eyes and clung to the tree, praying to God, the forest, anyone who would listen, that Jack could find help before another of the monsters decided to climb the tree.

Chapter 42

JACK FLEW OVER THE GROUND WHERE THE LIGHT WAS GOOD, using her senses to navigate the wooded edges, trying to orient herself. The Dannick land ran along the edge of Grizedale forest, and at the back was the wolf enclosure. She wasn't sure they were still there, she hadn't heard them howling, and she had no idea how they would react if she turned up. She suspected they would have been spooked by attacking Powell as they were probably fed slaughterhouse meat rather than living prey.

She vaulted over a fallen tree and hit one of the main rides, wide paths through the forest. The other side of the woodland was more dense, less cleared, and she could hear the movement of large animals ahead. She stopped in the shadows, her heart suddenly racing. Could the Dannicks have got ahead of her already? How fast were they? Three deer raced across the ride, the relief making her knees sag.

She heard the first human howl. They screeched as if they had caught something. She sank onto her haunches and covered her face for a moment. *God, Sadie, please let it not be Sadie.* The scream sounded male—she staggered back to her feet, starting away from the sound, fighting the instinct to go back. Make it quick—there, a scream cut off. Was it Sadie? Grief filled her up for a moment, freezing her. But it was Felix's face that came into her mind, and the promise of that relationship that made her stagger on, rub tears off her face with the sleeve of her jacket, and run across the ride into the undergrowth. She could see the silhouettes of more deer, this time farther off, stamping nervously in reaction to the howling. Finally she found the fence. She started to feel her way along the wire over the cleared ground, probably trampled and kept short by the animals whose scut scented the air.

The six-foot-high stock fence was probably to keep the deer in for hunting. They had said they hunted animal prey. She speeded up as she heard them howl again, this time closer, as if one had picked up her scent. She pounded along, breathing in short gasps, and the incline caught her by surprise, her feet sliding from under her. She skidded down the grass onto a gravel track, the breath knocked out of her by the impact. It was the footpath to the wolf project.

She limped up the path toward the hut, which sat in darkness, but the security light was activated by her stumbling forward. She didn't hesitate, but looked around for a tool, a spade, and crashed it through the main window.

They heard that, the screeches behind her closer. She switched the inside light on and looked for the keys. None, but a large pair of bolt cutters. Close enough, she thought, looking around for the gun cabinet. She quickly hacked through the lock. No tranquilizer gun, which was fine because Jack wasn't sure how to use it, but the Taser was there. She snatched it up, and as an afterthought grabbed a length of chain.

She could hear the breaking twigs and footfalls from the hunters as she raced along the muddy path, slipping on the grass, catching herself on the heavy-duty chain-link fence. She felt along the edge of the gate to the padlock and set the teeth of the bolt cutters on it. It took all the strength in her wrists and shoulders to hack through it. All the time, the panting and baying of the pack was getting closer and closer. They would be able to see her soon.

She slipped inside the compound, listening out for the wolves, and shut the gate behind her. Reaching through the bolt space in the gate, she was able to secure it from the inside and hang the mutilated lock on it, enough for a cursory glance in the dark to see it was still locked. Maybe it would buy her time. Nightmare visions of half men, half wolves from her reading crossed her mind. Maybe they had transformed in some way, maybe they wouldn't be able to manipulate the bolt.

The first pale shadow slinking along the fence, sniffing loudly, dispelled the illusion. It was a man, naked, and clearly still capable of managing a lock. She slid into the shadows of the bushes, hoping her dark clothing would reduce her visibility, and shaded her face with her coat. Every sound seemed amplified in the cold air. Creeping back through the undergrowth made her more aware of the wolves loose in the compound. They had several acres, but in reality that was only the size of a field. The wolves must know someone was in the enclosure and they had had painful experiences of people intruding into their territory. She squashed her instinct to flee from the snuffling, whining humans now gathering at the gate, and hunkered down, calling to the wolves. Half thought, half puppy whine, she hoped the wolves understood it.

A shriek, almost a scream of triumph, and a clang as the gate swung open. The hunters paused to howl, a cacophony of cries that left the night air vibrating when it stopped.

Help me, I'm under attack, I'm one of you— Jack concentrated on projecting her connection with the pack, the few nonverbal cues that had protected her before. She stuffed the Taser in her pocket, and crouched in the grasses at the base of a scrubby tree.

Help me. Nothing. She ran through all the spells she knew, wondering where she could cast a bolt from. She needed to draw the sigils, or at least scratch them in the soil—but the ground was grassy.

A hunter attacked, the weight of his body knocking Jack to the ground. The air was forced out of her with a grunt, and she rolled the smooth hunter off in one movement, scrambling back to her feet. It held out hands, as if in supplication.

"Wait!"

She recognized the voice despite a rasping growl in the back of the words. "Callum?" she hissed, stepping back. "You gave in to them?"

"I had to." His voice was strained, as if he were battling the animal the ritual had invoked. "They forced me to take the potion, then it just happened. It wasn't until I realized they had Sadie's scent that I could even start to think clearly. I keep losing it—" He growled to himself, as if in pain. "I think I helped kill someone." His voice was anguished.

"Not Sadie. Tell me—"

"No! I just realized it could have been her, I wouldn't have been able to stop. It's like—insane, I couldn't stop it."

Jack could remember the heady blast of energy from drinking blood, and knew a little of what he was going through.

"Stay with me, Callum. Remember who you are. We gave you Amyas's potion, not the Dannick one. You can fight this."

A howl from a few yards away made her spin around, back to the tree. The group of hunters gathered around a tall woman—Callum's mother—her hair whitened by the moonlight and her body smeared with what Jack recognized as blood—a lot of blood by the metallic stink of it.

For a moment there was a standoff, the boy cowering between them. Jack recognized the rumble building up around her. It wasn't coming from the now silent hunters, but from the wolves. Jack joined the growl, putting a foot forward to tip the wolves off that she was growling at the human hunters, not the canine ones. Callum squatted at her feet, his face turned toward his mother, his features distorted as he joined the general snarling.

The bushes beside them gave way to an arc of wolves, placed so close to Jack she could bury her fingers in the coats of the lead animals each side, trying to communicate the situation to them. She let the sting of the cold air in her nostrils, the monochrome edges of the hunters before her feed her body language. She started the yipping and the wolves joined in, the heavyset darker male leading the howl. When the first human attacked, the wolves moved as one unit and blocked the strike.

The hunters fell back, yelping and crying out as the wolves snapped and snarled, making leaps toward the humans, then falling back. Callum staggered to his feet and stood in front of Jack.

"Leave her alone! Hunt something else; this isn't going to work."

Jack could feel the energy of the wolf pack coiling around her, drawing her in to join the pack. It sharpened her senses, made her more aware of every muscle as it flexed and tensed. She reached down for the Taser.

She grabbed Callum, and dragged him behind her, hoping the wolves would continue to ignore him. Then she felt something inside her shift, as if some inhibition shrugged and let go. She aimed at the tall blonde, lashing out with her fist, and simultaneously fired the Taser at the heavyset man on her right. The man shrieked and fell to the ground. The woman staggered back and the wolves hit the human pack in a ragged V, taking down three of the men in a block. Jack grabbed the boy and pulled him behind the tree.

"Run, you hear me?" she snapped, into his ear. "Run and get help. Dial 999, anything, say there's a fire at the house. There might be a phone at the cabin."

"I can't," he panted, his voice rough. He was taller than she had expected standing up. "That's my mother—" He leaped at a dark-haired woman, trying to reach him around the tree, and knocked her back. "And I can't stop it, the ritual is too strong." He bared his teeth and howled as if he were in pain.

Jack peered across the mêlée, trying to see what was going on in the low light. At least one of the wolves lay motionless on the ground, and one of the men was howling in agony, blood cascading down from parallel slashes on his chest.

She grabbed Callum by the shoulders and shook him. "The hunt isn't important," she said, urgently. "We gave you the mixture Thomazine created for Amyas. The potion has healed you. It's the ritual that turns you into one of them, not the potion. You have to fight the instinct to hunt."

Another scream, cut off, as a wolf was injured, and she closed her eyes for a second in grief. But the message seemed to have reached Callum and he stepped closer. "I don't want to be like them."

"Then go." She launched herself from the shelter of the trees and cannoned into the biggest of them, whom she recognized by his height as Sir Henry. His face, a mask of blood and teeth, was more animal than human. The Taser had discharged but it still had a hefty stun left, and direct contact with his naked chest sent him yelping away. She called to the wolves in her mind and, with a long howl, raced after Callum over the scrub and fallen bodies near the gate. She wrenched open the bolt, the big female wolf scratching at the wire before she flung it open. For a moment she felt exhilaration as two of the wolves raced free, followed by a third, limping on three legs. They disappeared into the forest on one side of the path, and Jack passed the chain through the opening, bodged a knot in it and tugged on it with all her weight. One of the wolf-men smashed into the gate, reaching for Jack as she pulled away. She loped along the forest ride at the back of the woods.

She could hear something running to meet her and the

adrenaline made her run even faster. As she reached the road, she could feel her energy starting to flag, and turned to confront her attacker. The follower staggered to a breathless halt. It was Callum, still wild-eyed but more conscious of his nakedness, covering his genitals with cupped hands.

"I couldn't make the phone work at the cabin. I'll go back to the house—they won't hurt me."

"No. Get over the fence and follow this path toward Grizedale. Tell the guy in the car there to meet me at the front of the castle."

"Are you going back for Sadie?"

A pain like a spear arced through Jack as she remembered. "Sadie is probably—"

"We couldn't get her. But she was weak, she may have fallen by now. She was in a tree—" But his words were already fading as Jack hit the road and started running toward Knowle Castle.

Chapter 43

*Once a Disease has entered the Bodie, all parts which
are healthy must fight it: not one alone, but all. Because
a Disease might mean thyre common Death. Nature
knows this; and Nature attacks the Disease with
whatever aid she can gather.*

— PARACELSUS (1536), *Grosse Wundartzney*, annotated
translation by John Dee, held in private collection on
loan to the British Library

IT WAS OUR GOOD FORTUNE TO RIDE BUT HALF A DAY BEFORE
we heard a party of men upon the road, and recognized
them as wearing the scarlet and blue sash of Marinello. He
was there also, upon a horse of such temperament that it needed
his great strength to keep its hooves upon the road.

"Master Kelley, well met!" he cried, his eyes all on my companion, as he swept his hat off his head and bowed. "My lady!"

I was swaying in the saddle, sick with fever and pain, and was
soon escorted to a new inn, this a large prosperous place where
the countess's own agent waited. He was soon closeted with his
lady, and I was half carried into a chamber and left to the mercies of a doctor. In vain did I mention the name of Paracelsus.
The doctor scraped my wound with a hot knife, poulticed it
with pungent herbs and bound it so tight I fair swooned with
the pain. Then he forced me to drink some vile brew mixed

in wine, and I fell into a stupor upon a mattress set up within Marinello's chamber.

No one awoke me during the night and in the morning I found myself alone save his servant, who snored on another pallet at the foot of Marinello's bed. I examined the wound, to my relief much drier and eased somewhat in pain, and relieved my swollen bladder in the piss-bucket. Then I pulled on my boots, checked the sketch was still within my clothes, and stepped into the airy hallway. Servants were everywhere carrying buckets and wood, the smell of browning fish and meat drawing me by my nose into the kitchens, in a separate building behind the inn.

There the servants bowed low, chivvied me onto a seat in a pleasant herb garden, and brought me food. I found I was hungry and ate heartily, somewhat comforted to be in the company of a friend. Even though I feared Lord Marinello was under the spell of the countess, I knew she wished me alive, and he: well, he liked me.

When I returned to my lord's chamber I found him naked, washing in a pail scented with rosemary. His servant dashed about him offering herbs, towels and fresh clothes, while my lord threw the scented water about his person.

"Ah, Master Kelley." He grinned and tipped some of the water over his hair, shaking it like a rough dog, all over the floor. His man scurried about mopping it up. "I hear you saved my lady."

T'was she who saved me, I thought, but I bowed low. Then I turned my back upon his nakedness and took a tray from the hands of a serving woman at the door. Better to make myself useful.

I turned and he half smiled again at me.

He was a beautiful creature, if one can see a man as a sculpture. His great tallness ran not to fat but muscles, ropes of sinew moving under skin the color of cream. By contrast, his face and hands were burnished like oak. A scar, like a white rope, traversed his body from one shoulder to the other hip, much puckered at the lowest point. It was as if someone had tried to hack him in two. His smile turned into a frown and I looked away in haste, lest I had offended him.

"I was in Cyprus when the sultan's forces attacked." He spoke as if it were nothing. "At Nicosia with my mother. They landed and attacked the town. For two months we resisted them, but eventually they took the citadel."

I knew of it. I also knew that the invaders killed every man, sparing the women and children only as slaves. I turned to stare at him.

He touched the scar. "I tried to defend my mother. I was ten years old, fortunately not well grown. Her women healed me, and I survived as a slave. As I grew stronger and taller, I was placed in the house of a seafaring pasha. My father's fleet captured his ship, and I was restored to him." He started to dress, sitting on the side of the bed to draw on his stockings.

"Your father was also a sea captain?" I said, placing the tray upon a table.

"An admiral. He led the rescue of the refugees from Famugusta, before it fell to the Turks."

To think of such a fate for a boy. A slave within the Ottoman world was the death of most.

"I was one of the lucky ones," he continued, waving a shirt away and pointing to another. "I was not castrated, a fate which fell to many of my fellows. The pasha hoped to get a ransom for me."

He said something in his own tongue to the servant, who bowed, shot me a look of dislike, and closed the door behind himself. I waited for him to speak.

"The countess," he said, fumbling with his laces. I stepped to him, and tutted at the knot he was working. Pushing his fingers away, I untangled the threads while he continued. "She says you and she are old friends?"

"But since last year, my lord. I worked for the countess. My friend and I were taken to her castle when she was deathly ill, to try to save her." Better that I gave no details. I laced up the shirt quickly, being used to doing my own.

He slid the sleeve up to his elbow, and turned it to my eye. A bandage, reddened with blood, covered the vein. He unwrapped it to show me a slash, a clean wound still oozing, the edges dark. "This," he mused. "This was done to me."

"She put her mouth on you?" I shook my head. "No rapture is worth it, my lord. She is death." I clamped my mouth shut, sorry I had spoken such words to her infatuated lover.

"What do you mean?" He did not seem angry, but curious.

"Do you know of the priest, Father Konrad, of the Inquisition?" He let me rebandage the wound, though it looked unclean. "He has spoken of such a wound, from such a woman."

"I have met him, yes." He tucked the sleeve over the bandage. "He asked many questions of your travels, and when I said you had gone to the palazzo of the Contarinis, was angry. He said you were in danger, so I came here to find you. I discover you have rescued yourself and are alone in the company of that beautiful creature." He tapped my shoulder with his good hand. "Beware my jealousy, my little scholar."

"No need for jealousy, my lord." My answer was a little prim; I was not flattered to be thought of as a man of loose morals. "I am a married man."

"Well, my friend, so am I, but it does not stop me mounting a few mistresses." He walked across to the tray, and selected a morsel. Speaking around it, he said, "Although, this woman intoxicates me."

I clutched at his arm. "My lord," I said, with urgency. "Do not trust her sorceries. She can make one think she is gentle and sweet . . . but she is not a mortal woman, she is evil, contrary to God's design."

I had gone too far. He shook me off, and I stepped back immediately. "I shall overlook your rudeness, and put such lies down to your fever. I shall forgive it, because you saved my lady's life yesterday." He stepped into his plain hose in a somber brown, ideal for riding. "But today, I think it best that you come back to Venice and heal your wounds." He put on his doublet, also plain but of wonderfully woven cloth. I began to lace it, and he spoke soft that only I should hear it. "And I shall worry about my wounds. The greater of which will be to my heart if she come to any harm."

Chapter 44

*Blood drains into the ground, the living energy in it
dissipating as it transfers to the land below. It doesn't
care but it knows, as it suckles the rubied soil for the
blood of the witch.*

JACK FOUND THE REMAINS OF A BODY BENEATH THE TREE
where she'd left Sadie. For a long moment, she couldn't look,
couldn't see if it was Sadie. She leaned forward, braced her
hands on her knees to try to get her breath back. God, no. Callum had to be right.

"Sadie?" It came out more wobbly than she had intended,
and shot into the silence, making her jump. "Sadie, where are
you?"

At first, nothing, then she let her senses explore the silence.
Only it wasn't completely quiet. The trees whispered in the
light breeze, the grass sighed and lambs called, far away.

"Jack?" The voice sounded sleepy, weak, as if Sadie were a
long way away.

Jack scanned the tree, looking up. The beginning of a glow
in the east showed a thickened area of trunk that slowly morphed
as her eyes adjusted. Sadie, clinging to the trunk maybe fifteen
feet up, surrounded by a network of branches.

"Sadie, thank God. Are you OK? They didn't hurt you?"

"I'm cold—I'm so cold." The slurred voice reached Jack but the girl sounded semiconscious.

Jack stood under the tree. "Try to climb down. If you fall, I'll catch you."

"I'm too high," Sadie said, her voice fading. "I'll hurt you."

"If you fall from there you'll probably hurt us both, but if you can come down a bit—"

Sadie didn't answer, just leaned her head into the tree. "I can't." She started sobbing. "I'm so tired."

"Please, Sadie. I can't . . ." *Lose you now.* She cleared her throat. "I'll come up."

"No!" Sadie looked down at Jack, her face pale in what remained of the moonlight. Jack realized she must be frozen, the grass was tipped with frost. "Wait a minute."

There was a sound of rustling some way off, as if the hunters were returning through the forest. A single deer broke from the trees across the lawn, and zigzagged across, its eyes rimmed with white.

"Sadie—"

The ground under Jack's feet shuddered, and she fell back a step. The earth felt spongy, and soft, and she stepped back again in case it dragged her down like it had the body in the garden.

The sound of Sadie's movements brushing the twigs around her made Jack look up.

The girl stood in the dawn light, balanced with only a hand on the trunk, shaking. As Jack watched, heart suddenly jerking in her chest, the girl slid a foot farther along the branch. A tiny snapping sound started all over the tree, and as Jack watched dozens of buds broke, tiny leaves unfurling.

"Get out of the way," the girl said, her voice dreamy. She took another small step along the bough, just her fingertips brushing a limb above for balance.

Jack stepped away, her attention claimed by the sound of sticks snapping somewhere behind them.

Sadie let go of the overhead branch, and crouched to grip the one she was standing on. As Jack watched, aware of the approach of something coming fast, Sadie sat on the limb, wobbled a bit, then inched forward to drop the last twelve feet.

The thud was unexpectedly dull, and quiet, and when Jack reached Sadie she realized the girl was half embedded in soft, damp soil.

"Ow." Sadie reached up a hand, and Jack heaved to get her out of the depression between tree roots. Sadie was shaking, her arms wrapped around herself. "Cold."

Jack shucked off her jacket and wrapped it around Sadie, even as she looked around. In the new light she saw the first naked shape emerge from the forest.

The sound of a car and a crash some way away down the gravel carriage drive suggested someone hadn't worried about the main gate not being open.

"It's Felix," breathed Jack, lifting Sadie up. "He's coming. Hang on."

She dragged the stiletto out of her boot and roughly carved a circle around them in the grass, cutting into the soil. She dribbled the silver solution along the line.

"Are you drawing the sigils?" Sadie slumped onto the grass and hugged her knees.

"No, I'm trying to keep *them* out."

The circle was a long shot, but she hoped all the legends about silver and werewolves had some truth in it. She drew a symbol in the middle of the circle and placed her hand on it, charging it up, trying to find a focus. After a moment, Sadie's hand wavered to cover her fingers.

"How can I help?"

The approaching creatures must have seen them, a cacophony of calls around, whoops, yells, screams, more human now but just as aggressive.

"Just think about focusing power on the symbol, drawing it into the middle. I'll try to direct it at them." The energy bolt needed contact, and she didn't know if the circle would hold them back for more than a few moments. She just hoped she got Sir Henry. Her anger made her fingers start to tingle.

Sadie started to murmur something and for a second Jack thought she was praying. Then she heard Sadie pleading with someone, something. "Do it again, look after us—"

The force Jack had been building started to leach into the soil. Too slow, the silhouettes were maybe two hundred yards away, sprinting. She focused, trying to hold the symbol in her head, trying to trace them in her imagination on the circle on the ground. There—the smallest twist of a breeze flattening a few grass blades as she stood up.

The first two figures didn't even pause. They hit the circle at full speed, the momentum diverted back onto them. The energy they were generating fed the spell, immobilizing every muscle in the attackers instantaneously. The energy rolled both toward the rest, who managed to abort their charge. Jack winced at the sight of the lead man's wrists, both broken by the look of it. The other, a shorter woman, had landed full on her face, the fresh blood bright and red against the dried blood that covered her body.

The next attack carried the remaining pack, five of them, over the edges of the circle, one the tall blonde Jack realized must have been Callum's mother, although her features seemed barely human. Jack held out one hand in a defensive posture and the woman ran straight onto it. The other hand on the symbol, Jack could feel the energy flowing around her, over her skin, concentrating down onto the fingers and discharging into the woman. She screamed, arched her back as if she had been

Tasered and fell onto the grass, shuddering. The others fell back for a second.

Jack reached for her knife and crouched over the almost depleted circle. "Come on, you bastards," she shouted. "What are you waiting for?" She could feel her rage start to charge the symbol again slowly, and hoped her bravado would frighten them off.

Sadie slowly placed her cold fingers over Jack's and something happened. It was as if Sadie realigned Jack in some way, because fresh energy poured into her, not the heat she expected but some cold, wordless rumble.

This time Jack could let go of the symbol and bury her hands in the turf, charging up the circle again until she could see it glowing faintly around them. The group fell back, dragging its wounded members and setting them on their feet.

Sir Henry Dannick, naked, covered with mud and blood, stepped forward. "You cannot stop us." His voice was thick, as if words were difficult. "I could go to the house and get a shotgun and it's all over."

Finally, she could see Felix's car bouncing over the perfect lawn, cutting parallel lines in it and spraying mud behind. The car stopped and Felix wrenched open the door.

He marched forward, then brought up his hand—with the dead man's gun gleaming in it, she realized. "Leave them alone."

The four creatures who still posed a threat turned to Felix, the growl starting as if by instinct.

"Stay back," Jack warned. She could see Callum in the backseat. She wondered when Felix had cleaned the gun.

Maggie got out of the car, a strange look in her eyes. "Don't try to touch them until the circle is discharged," she called to Felix, and walked forward.

"Maggie!" Jack didn't know what she was doing, but the pack regrouped, their focus on the older woman.

"Sir Henry Dannick," Maggie said, her voice rich with derision. "I have a message from Thomazine Ratcliffe, my ancestress. You have caused enough damage to this community, and to my family. This is for Ellen, who never harmed anyone."

She reached out her hand, barely three feet from the man's chest. He just watched her, his lips drawn back from his teeth, his chest heaving. Jack just had time to wonder if those teeth were abnormally long and sharp when his expression changed. He made a whimpering noise that the others recoiled from. Even as he stumbled back, Maggie stepped forward, muttering familiar words. The fox fire—

The man shrieked, fell to his knees and clutched his chest. His face changed color to a deep, purple-red, his hands clawed at his trunk, drawing blood, as if he would open his own rib cage. Finally he fell back, his face almost black, motionless on the frosted grass.

Maggie shook herself like a dog. "Oh, God," she said, putting her hands to her face. "Did I really do that?"

Felix stepped beside Maggie, leveling the gun. "Go home, now," he ordered, with quiet authority. "All of you."

Jack turned to look at the woman who stepped impassively over her father's body to assume the role of leader. "Give my son back."

Felix answered, his voice strong. "Callum isn't one of you. He doesn't need the wild hunt. None of you need to kill. You've just grown to like it."

The woman's face seemed to change in the early light, a strange twist of grief on her face as she looked at the body at her feet. "He's my son," she said, her voice rasping.

"We'll keep him safe," Jack said, wondering that herself. "We'll get him help. You need to control your pack and deal with your dead. Not to mention your wolves are roaming the countryside."

The pack looked to their new leader, and one by one they

turned and limped or hobbled toward the house. Jack counted them. Of the original seven, Sir Henry was dead, a pile of bloodied rags was all that remained of another, and one must still be at the wolf enclosure.

Callum's mother remained, staring at Jack. "We need this. This is who we are." The woman looked over at the boy in the car. "Callum, look at you." Her voice softened. "You are healed; you will be well now, and strong. You will be a Dannick Lion."

The door opened and Callum, dressed in Felix's jacket, stepped out. "I don't want that." His face was still twisted with horror at what he had seen. "I don't want to take a human life just to become like you. You exploit people every day, you only think about making money and winning the big deals at the bank. I'm not like that."

"You will weaken. You will need the hunt."

Felix stepped forward, waving the herbal. "Thomazine Ratcliffe knew that wasn't necessary in the fifteen hundreds, and she told your ancestors they needn't be monsters. Amyas—"

"Amyas was a weakling, a bastard. Callum is a purebred Dannick, from a long line of leaders and rulers."

"They ruled through aggression and violence," Felix said. "Amyas was strong, he went from a shepherd's son to the administrator of all the Dannick wealth. He was bright; he was given an education—that's the real power. That's the advantage Callum needs."

Jack stepped over to the shaking boy, his face washed with tears. "If you love the boy, you will let him go. Change the way the Dannicks operate so he'll have a family to come home to."

The woman looked more human with each passing moment. She stared at Callum. "No. If you go, you can't come back."

Callum looked at Sadie, who was still folded in a heap in the circle. "I can't stay with people who could kill—I can't be like you."

The woman turned and walked away, as dignified as if she

weren't naked but for a layer of grass and dirt and blood. Callum started crying, great hacking sobs. Jack patted him on the arm.

"We'll help you, of course we will." She looked at Felix. "Won't we?"

He half smiled back. "Of course."

Chapter 45

Venice seethes with secrets. Plots, lies, deceptions, abductions. It does not pretend to be else, with its masks and whores.

—EDWARD KELLEY, 1586, Venice

WE APPROACHED THE PORT AT MESTRE AT NIGHTfall, and were welcomed into a travelers' inn. The place was overcrowded, and as we approached I realized that the countess's retinue was waiting for her. I saw many uniforms, many costumes. There was a Turkish party and there were soldiers from all over the continent. There was even a party of wealthy Jews in their caps and robes.

I was billeted in a loft above the stables, along with Marinello, the commander gaining a mattress stuffed with straw. I suspected he would not need it. The countess was ushered into a proper chamber, and much fussed over by her dark-faced women, three of them hissing and spitting in their native tongue. By dark, Marinello had gone to join her, and two of his officers had claimed the mattress, little attention being paid to me.

I was surprised, then, when a boy carried a note to me, written upon a piece of good paper in a fair hand in Latin. I held up a lantern that I could read it.

"Pray meet me outside, that you may learn something to your advantage."

Curiosity above all others is my sin and frequently my downfall, and yet I went. Ah, fool! That note led to a scuffle outside the barn, and I was dragged away from the inn by two soldiers.

"Gently," I heard a deep voice intone, and my terror was complete. It was the voice of the inquisitor, the representative of the Holy Inquisition, which had declared a war upon the Protestants everywhere. "Take him alive."

"My lord," I stammered. "Let me know your business with me."

"You have fallen into the service of the succubus," he said. "My business was in the nature of a rescue, if not for your body, for your immortal soul."

"She lies within—"

Konrad stepped into the dim lights of the stable. "She is guarded by her soldiers. Now, come with us, or face a quick death."

This silenced my words, and I was roughly lifted onto a horse behind one of the soldiers and we rode in sedate style from the inn yard. Beyond, my captor put a spur to the horse, and I found myself riding knee to knee with the Inquisition, Konrad himself leading our journey. When we rode many hours later into the ports, all I knew was exhaustion, and was happy to see a pile of hay, and to gulp down a tankard of wine and a handful of bread.

I awoke, my senses reeling and my stomach heaving. I managed to turn my head before spewing the sour wine and bread of my last meal away from myself. I was rolled in a blanket and sickened but was otherwise unharmed. I was laid on the wet planks of a small boat, maybe fifteen paces long, and mostly open to the dawn sky. It was very blue, I recall, and the motion of the boat very great. The sound of the sea slapping the bows and the shuddering of each wave along its keel told me we were underway upon the lagoon.

Standing in the prow, holding a figurehead lightly for balance, stood an apparition. A man in black clothes embroidered with gold thread, his boots in dark leather extending above his knees and bearing cruel-looking spurs. On his chest, a sash of scarlet; upon his head, a hat of velvet. His coat was ornamented in brocade, and bore heavy sleeves and cuffs. His hand, resting upon the hilt of a sword, was adorned with gold rings. The sword itself was a *schiavona*, the hilt defended by a basket of gilded guards, enclosing the quillons. The blade, judging by the black-and-gold scabbard, was broad—a soldier's sword. It was also long, stretching from the man's waist almost to the ground, and he was a tall man, broad in the shoulder.

He leaned into the movement of the boat, not staggering or falling as it breached the odd wave. The wind scudded into two large sails, one so great it dipped into the water from time to time, I judged, as it sprinkled salt spray over me. I struggled to sit up in the bottom of the boat.

As I did so, the soldier turned, and I saw it was the inquisitor Konrad, though dressed as a knight. He wore no emblem of the Pope, but looked as he was truly, a Reichsritter of the Holy Roman Empire. He looked at me, no animosity on his face, but perhaps he saw some fear in mine for he stepped down onto the deck. There were four pairs of oarsmen I had not noticed, so entranced I had been by Konrad, and he stepped between them.

"Up, young Kelley," he said, reaching his hand down to grasp me by my clothes, and pulled me up to sit upon a crude seat. I could see, then, the prow of the boat cutting through the waves toward the gleaming towers and domes of Venice. "Are you well?"

I opened my mouth, but resisted a litany of all that was unwell with me. A sore head, for a start, and a cramp behind my injured shoulder from lying cup-shot on the boards. "I would deem it a great kindness, my lord, to learn where we are going,"

I said with whatever dignity remained from my straw, mud- and vomit-stained person.

He reached within his doublet and brought out a paper, waving it about upon the rise and fall of the vessel. I closed my eyes as the movement made my stomach turn, then I felt the paper pressed into my hands. He laughed aloud at my shuddering.

"How—how did you find me?" I said, touching my healing shoulder. The bandage remained, and my little finger just touched the sketch within my shirt.

"I paid a man I think you know, one rogue called Bezio. He told me Marinello was looking for you, and I simply followed him."

I opened the paper, scribbled upon it some rude scratching that might be Venetian. The name Contarini was legible. That varlet Bezio, I thought, my rage lending me some courage. "So you had me beaten, threatened and abducted from my friend."

"My poor Kelley, you have been vilely used," he laughed, and sat upon a seat opposite, leaning his sword before him. I rubbed my poor hands, which burned as the blood flew back into them. His expression cooled. "Though, as a heretic, I suppose you deserve a little discomfort. You have led me a merry dance, and, worse, have rendered aid to my enemy. That she-demon."

"She aided me," I had to admit. "Lady Báthory saved me from a group of monsters."

"Indeed?" He stretched out his great boot, jingling the spurs. "What monsters can compare with a woman who suckles the life out of children, a complete reversal of the natural order?"

I choked upon my next words, as I recalled the child at the farmhouse. "She is as monstrous as that and more," I answered. "If I could help you stop her, I would. But the Contarinis—they are a race tainted by the devil and his hellhounds. They would have slain me, but for her."

He leaned forward. "What does she want of you, Master

Kelley? You have transformed her, shackled her soul to that corpse she wears, and given back her life."

I thought back to her story. "It is that—she suffers a spirit that speaks to her. A voice within, she says, that gives her a great appetite for blood."

He looked at the growing city rearing out of the lagoon as we approached. "Interesting. And what were these monsters that she rescued you from?"

I explained my working at the Contarinis' house—save the sketch of the tablet, of course. I explained the transformation from man to raving man-beast, and he nodded slowly, without interrupting.

"I have heard of such," he said when I had finished. "They call them *volkodlak* in Slovenia. My mother told me tales of them as a boy. It means wolf-skin. Such monsters are as men in the sunlight, but the moonlight transforms them into beasts." He sat forward, and signaled to someone behind me. "I have lodgings with Cardinal Malipiero. He provided the ship and the escort. I have but a few soldiers with me." He smiled at me, his lips tight with something that was not humor. "He, my little heretic, would have you chained and delivered to Rome."

A flame of hope flared within my breast. "But you, my lord?"

"I have a bigger prey in my sight." His face turned stony, as I had seen it before, and he clasped both hands around the hilt of his sword. "If I have to sacrifice you or me or the emperor himself to destroy her, I will."

Chapter 46

Something has changed in the garden within a single night. The triumph of another in the line of witches brings more confidence. Plants thrust out more buds, open more flowers. The bees raise more queens for future swarms; the slow, cold snakes birth new serpents to hunt the creeping pestilence of voles and mice. Badgers turn striped snouts into the wind to scent the change.

NO ONE SPOKE IN THE CAR. FELIX HUGGED SADIE TO TRY and infuse some warmth into her, and Callum leaned against the window with his eyes shut. Maggie seemed shocked by her own actions, staring at her hands. It seemed to Jack that none of them would get over the events of the night in a hurry. She pulled up outside the cottage, to hear Ches throwing himself at the door.

Felix lifted Sadie from the car, her head dangling over his arm, and Jack unlocked the door, pushing the frantic animal back. Callum followed, self-consciously pulling Felix's jacket down.

"Maggie, why don't you run Callum a bath and find him some clothes?"

Maggie shook off the inertia that was holding her in the car and nodded. "Come on, Callum."

Jack followed Felix and Sadie into the living room. While he laid the girl on the sofa, she concentrated on building up the fire from the embers left in the woodburner.

"Jack?" The girl's voice was weak but coherent. "We did it, didn't we? We survived and we saved Callum as well."

"We did." She smiled and patted Sadie on the shoulder. "You made it. I don't know how but you did."

Sadie shifted uncomfortably under the blanket. "I don't know either. I ache all over, though."

Jack laughed out loud, grinning up at Felix. "I think we all do." The smile faded as she saw Felix's expression. "What is it?"

"You can't live like this." He sat down heavily on the other sofa, head down, hands dangling between his knees. "You're so vulnerable, all of you."

"Before this, we'd had a couple of decades with hardly any dramas," Jack said, staring at the top of his head. "Just a few minor run-ins with people like Pierce."

"Anyone else could have called the police when they were threatened. Ellen didn't, you couldn't."

She shrugged. "Well, obviously." She watched him lift his head and stare at her. "This is the price of life for us, Felix, you know that."

He sighed, and looked at the teenager. "This isn't good enough, not for you and not for Sadie."

Jack tried to speak calmly, knowing a logical appeal might work better. "So help us. You were finding out about blood—"

He chopped the air with his hand. "Blood isn't the answer. What I saw in Paris . . . whoever, whatever that woman was, she wasn't healthy. She looked like a walking colony of competing thoughts and feelings. She reminded me of someone with dissociative identity disorder." When Jack looked blank, he added, "Multiple personalities."

Jack's doubts flew to the surface and something stirred rebelliously in the very back of her mind. It was like a memory, but a memory that hadn't happened yet, a feeling that didn't belong.

"I—I've been wondering." She paused, trying to reach the feeling. It was somewhere between euphoria, power and rage. "I've had some very strange impulses lately."

He rubbed his hands over his hair. "I know." He sounded angry.

Jack tried to unravel the expression on his face. "If this is too hard for you—"

"Damn it!" His shout made both Sadie and Jack jump. "Do you think I would be here for a second if . . . you aren't part of my research, you are part of my life!"

"I know, I just—" Jack stood up to meet him as he pulled her into his arms.

For a moment he just held her, shaking with some emotion, maybe relief, maybe anger. Then he looked into her eyes and she knew what the emotion was. She smiled back before he kissed her.

"Gross." The word from Sadie was faint but just enough to break them apart.

Felix exhaled. "I'll check on Callum."

"Is it really over?" Sadie pulled the blanket around her shoulders, Ches leaning against her. "Do you think they will come and try to get Callum?"

"I don't know. I expect they will try one day but for now they have at least two dead family members and a lot of injuries to explain." Jack sat on the sofa beside her, and touched her hand to the teenager's cheek. "You're not too bad, are you? I didn't think you could survive outside of the circles that long."

Sadie shrugged, and stroked the dog. She looked as if she were going to say something, then stopped herself.

"Go on." Jack patted the dog's flank, making him lean his head back, tongue lolling.

"Did you know Maggie could do that? She killed him with magic."

Jack's smile faded as she remembered the look on Maggie's face. "If I had known, I wouldn't have been so cheeky as a kid," she admitted.

"Me neither." Sadie managed a nervous chuckle. "I know we talk about the magic all the time, but actually feeling it, seeing it . . ."

"Like you and that tree." Jack shook her head. "I still don't know what you did, but it caught you."

Sadie looked at her hands for a moment. "I just touched the bark and it was like I was touching everything, you know? Like the garden. It just looked after me."

Felix came back in and sat on the other sofa, leaning his head against the cushions. "He'll survive, but he's been through hell. He's just a seventeen-year-old, for God's sake, and he's lived a very sheltered life."

"But he's out of the wheelchair," Sadie said, her eyes shining. "So we managed to help him get the cure without the curse. Like Jack."

"No, it's not the same." Felix bit his lip, then looked up at Jack. "That trip to London, I think we need to make it."

Jack met his eyes, willing him to stop talking in front of Sadie.

In the silence that followed, Sadie started to fidget. "Well, what happened to Callum isn't the same," she burst out. "Amyas, Thomazine's son, he was good, wasn't he?"

Felix turned to smile at her. "Yes, what happened to Callum is different. But remember, he took the potion *and* he joined the hunt. I don't know if it's the hunt or the kill that activates the 'hunter' gene they told Jack they have."

Jack thought back to the time in the house, before they set Jack and Sadie up for the chase. "The potion got him out of that chair by itself. I think they wanted Callum to kill something to be part of the pack. You saw him this evening, Sadie. He was mad, wild, like a feral animal."

Sadie leaned forward, her eyes bright even as her teeth chattered. "But he didn't kill anyone, did he? Not by himself, anyway. And he came with us. Please, Jack—"

"Oh, don't worry, I'm not going to do anything to harm him. I'm just not sure exactly what we can do with him to keep him away from the Dannicks. He's just a kid."

"He's seventeen," Felix interrupted. "He can decide for himself."

"Like me." Sadie's voice was unexpectedly strong. "I can decide for myself, too. I need to do something. I can't expect someone to be here all the time. Maybe blood would be good for me, too."

Jack turned to Felix, her mind conflicted. "It made such a difference to me, just one mouthful—think what it could do for Sadie."

Felix shook his head. "We don't know enough yet."

"There has to be a better way for Sadie to live." Jack took a deep breath. "Maybe if we found out more about the effects of taking blood by talking to people who do we can work out how to safely improve Sadie's health."

Felix sighed. "There's someone I need to meet first in London. I suspect being a borrowed timer makes you less connected to your body. Think what Dee said, or rather Kelley. A soul trapped in its dying body. You put blood into that body, and it might attract other—influences."

"You're talking in riddles." Angry though Jack's voice came out, there was something compelling about Felix's expression.

"That's because I don't have all the information. Take Elizabeth Báthory."

"Sadistic serial killer."

"One of several women with no real history of sadism or

murder in their early lives. Then at some point they became revenants, yes? And then cruelty and lust get out of control."

"Which hasn't happened to me." Jack fidgeted, doubt creeping in.

"You have been behaving out of character. With Powell. With me, even. You have been more reckless, more aggressive."

"I've got more energy, that's why!" Jack's answer burst out of her even as part of her mind recalled some of the impulses she *hadn't* given in to. "I have lived like an invalid a lot of my life, and now I'm feeling better. Can you really blame me for wanting to try new things?"

"And your body is maturing, I understand that. But it's more than that." He took a deep breath, looking at his hands. "I think Báthory was influenced by another entity. There are hints in the folklore of revenants that say they are corpses, animated by demons and spirits."

Jack stared at Sadie, watching her eyes widen.

The girl managed a nervous laugh. "Well, that's crap. Isn't it?"

Jack let the dog slather her hand with his tongue. "Let's go to London and meet this contact of yours. Then I can prove to you that I'm not haunted by evil spirits."

Chapter 47

It has been said of me that I am a loyal friend. I am grieved that this is not so, for it has been given to me to betray not only my friends, my wife and my mentor but even the Lord. I can only pray that God will understand the dangers I have faced and will look upon me with forgiveness.

—Letter from Edward Kelley to Eliza Jane Weston, Prague, 1596, from Constantinople

His Highness Cardinal Prince Malipiero did not like me, nor appreciate that I should be kept in a chamber as if a guest. A closely confined guest, to be sure, and observed at all times by two of Konrad's Inquisition troops, but not chained in some storeroom as he seemed to think more appropriate. My bruised head was bathed and my shoulder rebandaged. I was lent fresh clothes by some nameless servant, and my own were cleaned. I spent one day and night gathering my strength in my captivity, wondering how I could get word to Marinello. The sketch, a little creased and blood-stained from my adventures, was tucked within the edge of the linen bandage I let none but myself touch, and I was soon restored, though bored by my confinement. Konrad came to me the next morning and sat beside me on my bench.

"Now, my friend, we must talk about the countess."

I spread my hands out. "She has sought me out, my lord, and I have avoided her. There can be no profit in getting close to her." I shuddered. "If you knew what she did."

He brushed my horror aside. "I have seen with my own eyes what she can do. And she will keep torturing and killing children if we do not stop her."

"If I can help—" I could think of little I could do.

"Tell me everything that has happened in Venice since you first set foot upon the pier."

I told him in brief, but he interrupted many times, and made me go over it in more detail. Bezio's robbery, Marinello's kindness, the countess meeting me at a dance. I left out Marinello's relationship with the countess, out of the gratitude and friendship I had for the man, but Konrad's questions grew more searching. I told him of the Contarinis, and their strange rituals.

"It makes a strange tale." He was sitting beside me on a kind of rough settle, which I had found uncomfortable to the hindquarters of a man who has ridden many miles in just a few days. "But I need to know what she will do next. She resides at the palace of the doge as his special guest. I cannot act within the palace; relations between the Pope and the council are already poor." He rested one hand on his sword hilt. "I am here as a soldier more than a priest, Master Kelley. As a soldier I need information that will tell me where she will go, and with whom."

I held my tongue.

"You must tell me, Edward; you must tell the truth. Or we shall be enemies and to Rome you shall go as a sinner and a heretic."

I stammered in my distress. "It seems you know what I shall say already," I said.

"Well? Friend or foe, my little Englishman?"

There was a part of me that would sell my friend for mine own safety, but another part that could not betray him. They fought. "I cannot say, my lord."

I looked down at my feet, at the stained boots that had traveled me so many leagues and seemed like to see my end.

His voice was soft. "I applaud your courage, my friend, and your loyalty."

I shivered like a hart before the hunt at the tales I had heard of the tortures, of the executions. I sat miserably, my hands clenched before me.

"Would you like to confess?" I did not expect the offer, and looked up in confusion. I had not worshipped as a Catholic since I was a boy. He half smiled. "Come, Edward, we both know you to have been baptized a Catholic. It will give you comfort. I can send for a priest, or I can hear your confession and bless you myself."

There was the priest I knew, the stately soldier of Rome. I almost broke into tears, such was the kindness of the offer, but I shook my head. Sixteen years a Protestant had left me neither one nor the other, like a cat suckled by a hound.

"Then tell me. Where will the creature be tonight? For I know she sleeps not in her own bed."

I shut my eyes, remembering all I had heard of the Inquisition. I could not deny my own needs, nor did I want to save the countess. I decided to place my fate in the hands of the soldier-priest. "I can tell you where she will be but, I beg you, spare her paramour. He is a good man and innocent in all this. He does not know—"

He leaned his sword tip against the spur on one of his boots with a tiny clink. "Your friend Marinello. Of course. I should have known it."

I clutched his arm. "Wait! I tell you he is innocent in this."

"Then you must help trap her at his house. And if he defends his lady, then you will reason with him."

I let go of his arm, and resolved to do what I could to save my benefactor. "But what can you do with her? She is under the protection of the doge and brings her own guards—"

"What any Christian man should do," he said sternly, standing up before me. "Smite off the monster's head."

Chapter 48

The garden buzzes with life. Flowers flirt with bees and flies, nests are fought over and renewed and filled with eggs. The light greens the cleared areas as the witches restore and prune and water. The season has advanced, the moon turning almost full circle. Everywhere, life.

J ACK GRIMACED AS A DROP OF PAINT SPLATTERED THE NEW window glass. Callum was playing with some electronic device in the garden; since he would be easily recognized in the village, Jack was keeping him out of sight. She had no idea what to do with him despite three weeks of research.

Sadie was putting herb plants into pots and Maggie had been cleaning out the hives. Charley was helping, completely obscured by a beekeeper's suit. Maggie had just gone for a hat and veil and gloves, but so far the bees were quiet. Jack had thought Felix back in Exeter, so it was a shock when he walked out of the kitchen door onto the grass.

Sadie saw him and raced with new energy—courtesy of giant circles in the grass—to hug him. He said something, then put her aside gently and looked up at the scaffolding to where Jack was sitting.

"Are you coming down?"

Jack was seething inside with things she wanted and needed to say, but a part of her was so pleased to see his familiar face she couldn't say anything. The cool expression wasn't so familiar.

He called across the garden. "Maggie, Callum, this affects you as well. I have been to see Mrs. Dannick, Callum's mother."

"You had no right—" Maggie started to say but Felix held up a hand.

"I had every right, as much as any of you. Callum, I've found a family in Italy who have the same tradition as the Dannicks but have given up the 'wild hunt,' as they called it." He handed the boy a rucksack. "Your mother has given you money, tickets and passport, and I have arranged for this new family to look after you there until the scandal dies down here."

The news that several members of the Dannick family had been killed in a freak car accident had kept the locals speculating for weeks. Gossip had added the rumor that Callum was going away for a special treatment for his illness.

"But I don't know anybody there—"

Felix laid a hand on the boy's shoulder. "I know it will be tough, but they understand the hunt better than anyone. The head of the family says there are three other kids around your age in the family, all with this hunter gene. They work on keeping the aggression under control. Her name is Laura Contarini; she's a kind woman. She can even get you into an English-speaking school out there if you want."

Callum's smile was lopsided. "And maybe come back home one day?"

"Let's hope so."

Sadie leaned against Felix. "Have you found a magic cure for me, yet?"

This time sadness was written all over his face, and he kissed the top of her head. "Not yet. But I'm working on it. Because I'm not giving up."

Jack climbed down the ladder to the grass, jumping the last few steps. As she knew he would be, he was there to steady her.

"How did you get on with this other borrowed timer? The old one?"

He grimaced. "We—well, you, really—have an invitation tomorrow to meet her in London. I'm not sure it's a good idea— there's something strange there. Gina is with her—they seem to have bonded."

The sound of the other woman's name sent a chill through Jack, like a wisp of a breeze. "Oh."

He looked into her eyes for a moment. "Gina told me she was seriously ill. Maybe she believes she would be able to become a borrowed timer and save her life."

Jack nodded slowly. "Maggie?"

Maggie pulled her gardening gloves off. "Very few people can be saved—that's all I know. We consulted a seer to find likely candidates to save when Charley was a baby, but even then . . ." Her words tailed off, and she swallowed. "They died before they could help Charley, one in a matter of minutes. We managed to get her back to her family before they knew she had been taken. But the second one—she lived for a few hours." She looked away, at the fell behind the garden. "Jack was the rare exception, like Sadie. This Gina has almost no chance. I could ask the seer to look into it, if you like."

Felix nodded. "Thank you. I want to make sure she's not just being exploited for her blood." He smiled at Sadie. "Maybe this Ivanova will point us in the direction of something that will help."

Something changed in Jack, some strange numbing. It made the words around her muffled and far away, the world around her become fuzzy and unclear. Jack took a breath, feeling it rather than hearing it surge into her lungs. She wondered if she was about to faint—the world went black.

She floated back up from the darkness to find herself standing, not collapsed on the ground. Felix was laughing, the way he laughed when they were alone. She shook her head to clear it, and the garden came into focus. "Sorry, I'm a bit wobbly . . ." She looked around. "Where's Maggie?"

The smile on Felix's face faded into a look of concern. "Are you feeling all right?"

"I felt a bit dizzy, that's all." But, inside, she knew there was something very strange going on. "I thought . . ." She looked up at him. "What were you saying?"

"I was just agreeing with you."

Jack turned away, suddenly frightened. How much time had passed? Something felt very wrong.

Chapter 49

My daughter, that I write to from exile, blessings upon you and your brother and for your patient mother. I cannot explain all that has befallen me but only that I miss you all and hope to find my way back into our beloved benefactor's house. Now I am under the shadow of so many threats I dare not return home, lest I lead them back to you, my beloved child.

—LETTER FROM EDWARD KELLEY TO ELIZA JANE WESTON, 1586

W E SET OUT AT DUSK, A TIME OF SERVANTS AND MER-chants, as the rich were preparing for a night of debauchery or family duty ahead. We were all, even myself, dressed in dark clothing and wore black masks. Another party had departed before us in fine dress and bright disguises, the better to distract spies and informants, of which Venice was filled. The cardinal had left with his retinue, and when none appeared to be looking at the darkened windows of his palace, we left by the servants' door into two boats. There was myself and Konrad, and two of his guards in our boat, and four more in the boat behind. Each man but I carried a sword and a dagger.

The shape of my betrayal had been taught to me. I was to gain access to Marinello's house leaving the door unlatched, if necessary by killing the servant. My heart grieved for that servant, for he had no part in this. Then Konrad's men would search the house, take Marinello alive, if possible, and take the countess, dead. Konrad was specific. The countess was to be cut into pieces to avoid identification, the parts taken far out into the lagoon and spread over the waters.

The plan went easily at first. I knocked upon the door, and a serving man I did not recognize let me in. Before he could bar the door, two of Konrad's men overpowered him with a knock to the head. They tied him up, as I had begged, and gagged his unconscious mouth. But when we allowed the rest of Konrad's men and their captain in, servants set up a cry and guards poured from the hall and raised their weapons. We had expected a couple of the countess's own bodyguards but underestimated their ferocity and their numbers. The dark room, lit only by two branches of candles upon the walls, became a heaving mass of men, each fighting for his life. I ducked low, crouching by the restrained servant, and prayed for deliverance. The men grunted and shouted out in pain, their shadows grotesquely huge and distorted in the flickering light. The stink of fear and sweat, butchered bowels and spilled blood filled the cavernous hall. The cries became louder until the sound of boots clattering on the marble stairs caused some, at least, to pause and look up at the master. Marinello.

I could not but admire him, his great legs in his sea boots, his chest covered in but a loose shirt, a curved sword in his hand. He looked like a corsair, and behind him stood several of his servants, two with crossbows. Finally, the woman we sought, wrapped about in a robe. Her hair rippled down her back to her waist and she smiled, not afraid at all, sure of her lover.

The battle surged to the steps and the countess's remaining men, much savaged, gained the higher ground. Konrad's soldiers staggered back, out of range of the long swords, slipping in the blood. Five men lay butchered or mortally injured upon the marble floor.

"What! Master Kelley? You betray me?" Marinello's voice was more sorrowful than angry, and, with a sound like a whip crack, a crossbow bolt hit one of Konrad's soldiers. One of Marinello's servants knelt to reload as the other took aim at me.

Marinello knocked up his hand. "We have the advantage, my lord," he called over the heads of the men to Konrad. "Be gone, and we will spare your last soldiers."

"We will take the woman." Konrad stood, his face polite, set hard against the misfortunes of the attack. "By decree of His Holiness, and by warrant of Cardinal Malipiero. For she is possessed by a demon that feeds on the blood of innocents."

Marinello frowned in the face of such certainty. "What proof?" he scoffed, but I noticed he glanced over his shoulder at the countess.

Konrad turned to look at me. I staggered forward, lurching over the slain man at my feet.

"My lord, upon the road we did rest at a farmhouse, where a man and woman gave us shelter from the Contarinis. But in the morning, I found them slaughtered."

Marinello shrugged. The fate of peasants meant little to him.

"And their child, a girl of six or seven years, was taken by the countess. She cut that innocent's throat that she might drink of her blood. Or perhaps tore it open with her teeth. But she drained the child like bleeding a pig."

This did shake Marinello. He touched his arm, where I knew the bandage covered his hurts. He glanced down at the woman who had stepped back to the top of the stairs and was looking at us all as if she were royalty, and we were the peasants. Her face changed as I looked, as if two voices within her struggled for ascendancy, then an expression of great amusement curved her lips.

"The countess, yes, she feeds of necessity," she said, as if of another. "And she enjoys it, and mixes pain with lust. But the taking of life is mine. You know me, Edward Kelley. You and I have spoken many times."

I noticed Marinello fall back a pace.

"Saraquel?" I managed to stammer. I covered my eyes for a moment with shaking hands.

"Yes, I am Saraquel." The body of the woman seemed to glow, and I could see the aura of light around her grow until it almost blinded me. The voice seemed to ring in my head, like a hundred men and women together, so I clamped my hands to my head, and closed my eyes against it. "And you know, Edward, of my power. Shall I take the lives of every mortal in this room, sparing none? And leave just my lovely, carnal countess?"

I cried out, the pain in my head as if it were splitting. "No! Spare them!" I screamed the words in English, and could feel strong hands under my arms, supporting me.

"Then you shall save the countess, and I shall leave your fellow men."

The light faded, and I squinted up to see the concerned look of Konrad, and, above him, the angry face of my friend. I stepped forward, and raised my hands to Marinello.

"Let me take the countess," I cried, seeing her quaking as if Saraquel had shaken her as much as me. "For else we shall all die."

"I am prepared to die," said Konrad, hefting his sword up over his head.

"And I!" shouted Marinello.

"No!" Something of my utter conviction must have caused them a moment's doubt, for I was able to take a few steps up the stairs, pushing past the guards.

The sword of Marinello swept forward, toward my face, and a wet thud told me it had found its mark—not my neck but one of Konrad's men who had followed me onto the stairs. I sprinted up the stairs to the countess. Behind me, the battle had resumed, and the dozen or so remaining men fought for their lives. I slid toward the countess, and an unarmed servant screeched and ran into a room behind her. The countess smiled at me as if we were standing in a ballroom, or a garden.

"My lady, stop this," I said, in some delusion that if she could give herself up to Konrad, Marinello at least would be spared. "I beg of you. You can only cry mercy."

"There is no mercy for me," she scoffed, "since your sorcery. It is time for you and me to depart," she said, grasping my hand and dragging me to a door that stood a little open. There I found a trio of terrified women huddled into an alcove praying for their lives. Their light voices added a strange counterpoint to the mêlée beyond the heavy door, which I bolted. She turned away from the women and held out a kirtle. "You shall assist me," she said, stepping into the skirt, and turning that I might lace up the back. She snatched up a net of some golden thread, and twisted her hair into it. My hands were shaking, but I did a fair job of pulling and tying the laces, though the sounds of battle made me fumble. She tucked a dagger, a narrow stiletto, down the front of her bodice to sit under her arm but easily reached from the neck of her gown, then slid on long boots. I knelt to lace them at a gesture from her, knotting them hastily. I leaped to my feet as a banging upon the door began.

"But, how do we—" I started to say, but she pressed a finger to my lips, and then beckoned me to follow. A tapestry hung upon the wall was turned back, and a tiny door, so low I would almost have to crawl into it, was revealed. The lady turned the key in the lock, took it, and pushed open the door.

"Franco Marinello showed me this. Hurry!" she snapped, and I squeezed into it, almost falling headlong down a flight of stone steps as steep as a ladder. I managed to stand, though the top of my head brushed the roof. The light from the door disappeared as she shut it, and grated the key in the lock.

I placed one foot carefully on the next stair down, reaching around for some support. I grasped a rope banister but it almost as soon crumbled into dust. I found another step below, then another. The woman behind me grasped my shoulder and half pushed me along.

"Wait," I said, my breath hardly a whisper in that dark place lest we be heard. "I cannot see."

Another few paces, then something of a landing, and a stumble onto another stair, then another. And so we proceeded, in a counterclockwise spiral, my feet barely finding each deep step and the countess following behind, one hand upon my shoulder.

"Stop." I squinted into the darkness, and thought I saw a gray among the blackness. There! A strip of low light that my eyes sought, as if running down a door. I mistook my step and staggered down the last few stairs, thumping into a wooden panel. I fumbled down the edge—a hinge. The other side led to a latch, which I lifted, wincing at the creaking. The door opened into a cupboard in what I judged must be a kitchen by the smell of it. Something—cold skin—brushed my face and I almost screamed before I realized some slaughtered pig was hung within a meat closet. I pressed upon the door and it sprang open.

The kitchen was deserted; perhaps its occupants had fled for another door. One led to a few steps down to the side alley beside the back of the building. I chanced a quick look out to find it guarded by but two soldiers in Konrad's livery, both facing the main door and the sound of carnage. I reached for a fire iron, a poker or some such, and it found the back of one soldier's head. As the second turned, the countess's dagger found his belly and it was twisted cruelly. He gave a strangled shriek, and I did not wait to see if it was heard. I bolted, my fear giving my feet wings, along the street, down another alley, toward the canal itself. I ran along the narrow stone front before the great houses like a dock rat, as much to escape the countess as the Inquisition.

A great shout from above made me stop, and I turned to see my friend and kind rescuer, Marinello, standing on the window ledge of his house facing the water.

He glanced down at me for a second, his grinning face lit by the lamps shining within, then disappeared back inside for a moment. I feared his death, but before I could look away, he let out a great cry of triumph and threw himself from the window, swinging along the front of the building on a curtain. He let go at the top of his swing, flying past the jetty below. With a great splash he hit the water of the canal, narrowly missing two boats and the quayside.

I ran, terrified of Konrad and his tortures, afraid of the countess and her demands, and I prayed for deliverance. I sprinted along the docks, seeking a hiding place, when I saw before me a ship flying a familiar flag. One of the emperor's many merchants, no doubt, moored against a ship of the ensign of a ship from Rome. I leaped without thought, landing amidships on the Roman ship, and before the sailors could do more than shout in alarm and lift their arms to stop me, I scrambled over the side and onto the emperor's ship.

"Sanctuary!" I shouted again and again, in German, Latin, perhaps in English, certainly in broken Bohemian.

A stout captain came forward and steadied me with one arm. "Name yourself, sirrah!" he said, in stern German. "Why do you need sanctuary?"

"I am Protestant," I said, while shivering, "and persecuted by the Inquisition. I am an Englishman and a visitor of Emperor Rudolf. My name is Edward Kelley."

From the circle of sailors gathering around us, I heard one voice above the others.

"Then I arrest you, Master Edward Kelley, on behalf of the Holy Roman Empire. For all captains are tasked with capturing you for investigation into fraud against the citizens of the Emperor Rudolf for a handsome reward."

My trembling knees gave way, and I sat abruptly upon the boards. I had never been so happy to be arrested.

Chapter 50

"TELL ME ABOUT THIS WOMAN." JACK WAS TAKING A TURN at driving, following the motorway toward the capital. They had stopped only to eat, now were back on the road. Felix was quiet, but Jack was excited. Finally, something she could do herself, rather than rely on Felix or Maggie. "Gina."

"Why do you want to know?"

"I don't know." She overtook a lorry, concentrating in the fading light. "It's something I don't have any experience of." She settled in a lane. "You know. Sex, relationships."

He sighed, and she could see him stretch his feet into the footwell. "I'm not going to discuss Gina with you, Jack."

Miles slid under the wheels and for a long time she thought he had dozed off again. At the point where dusk was giving way to darkness, Jack pulled into a slip road and a service station.

"Do you want me to drive?" He stretched, and undid his seat belt.

"If you like. I just need a coffee." She stepped out of the car into thin drizzle, and turned her collar up.

He opened his door. "I could do with a sandwich."

In the end, they had a burger each and some fries, and large coffees.

Jack mumbled around a large bite of greasy burger. "So what exactly are we doing tonight?"

Felix looked at his watch. "At ten o'clock, I'm supposed to present myself at the Illustrian Club. I'm allowed to escort you there, but Julian Prudhomme says we won't be allowed to see around the club itself, but we will be granted a private audience with Madame Ivanova. That's all I know."

A woman at the table beside them shushed a crying toddler. Jack finished her burger.

"Has any of your research ever spoken about revenants having children?"

He thought about it. "Well, we know Elizabeth Báthory had several."

"Were they normal?" She finished her fries and started on Felix's. "I'm starving."

He smiled at her. He looked older in the artificial light, rumpled. Maybe he was right, maybe he was too old. She felt like she had the energy of a horse.

"I could look into the Báthory children."

"I'm relieved there's another borrowed timer that's not a serial killer. Ivanova, I mean. She wasn't, was she?"

"Not in the last couple of centuries, no, I can't find any evidence of killing or torture. But she did terrorize her Russian estate for decades before that."

"And she wants to meet me." Jack drained her coffee with enjoyment. As a borrowed timer she had reacted violently to chemicals in food, but since the ingestion of blood she could eat anything. She smiled. She was finally getting a childhood. She waved at the toddler. "Kids are cute, aren't they?"

He looked over his shoulder at the child and its mother. "Oh, you mean—"

"Well, it was never an issue before, but if I'm having periods, maybe it's something that could happen one day."

His face creased into something like panic, before he masked his expression and bent over the remains of his coffee. "I think Sadie is enough children for the moment."

She laughed out loud. "I'm kidding! But your face is a picture." Now the idea was out there, she let it run through her head in the silence between them. Children. She loved animals, would a baby be like that? She smiled at the thought.

"Marianne and I did discuss it." His voice was strained. "It was something we both considered, at different times. Never at the same time, so we never—"

She put her hand over Felix's. "Seriously, it's OK. I'm not thinking about it. It's just, now, I'm changing. I mean, maybe we're more than friends, but it's not like we're a proper couple." She thought about it. "Yet."

"Aren't we?" His eyes locked onto hers, and she couldn't look away.

She started to feel uncomfortable. "I mean, it's right at the beginning of things, isn't it? We hardly know each other, but there are all these feelings."

The woman and child had left; there was no one within earshot. "I have trusted you with my life, with Sadie's," he said. "I have lied to the police, defied the Inquisition, even helped kill another human being because you persuaded me to."

"Elizabeth Báthory was hardly human, and Maggie killed Dannick." The light mood vanished. "Why are you so angry?"

"I'm not angry. I'm just thinking how huge the implications might be for the future, that's all. You drank my blood, Jack, and it changed you."

"For the better."

He stared at her. "Sometimes you seem different. Sometimes you are the old Jack, cautious, wary, loyal. Sometimes you are impulsive, aggressive, even."

She thought over the last few months, the mood swings and the behavior with Powell. "Maybe I'm just growing up. All those years on borrowed time I was just half alive. I feel so much better, it's different." But the suspicion of the growing blanknesses was haunting her.

"It's more than that. It's like . . ." He paused, then he bit his lip for a moment. "Never mind."

She drained the last of her lukewarm coffee, and pulled a face. "We don't have time to worry about it now. Come on, or we'll be late."

He leaned over the table and caught her wrist for a moment. "I know you are stronger and I want that for Sadie too. But there may be side effects to drinking blood that we can't see yet."

She stared back at him for a long moment, reading his sincerity, and, under it, anxiety for her. It made her voice gentle. "Then we'd better find out more about it, because we can't go back and undo it now."

It seemed strange to step into new shoes, new clothes, fabrics silky and cool against Jack's skin. Maggie had helped her pick out a few smartish clothes in Ambleside but Jack had a feeling the people at the exclusive club would be much better dressed than her. Felix, in a dark suit, looked somehow less approachable in the hotel room. She hadn't questioned the one room, the big bed, but now she felt awkward and shy.

He squeezed her hand reassuringly as they entered the club, then let go. The warm imprint of his fingers lingered while he spoke to someone at reception. She was acutely aware of the deep carpet, the scent of leather and discreet perfumes. When she raised her eyes it was to a sparkling globe of crystals, some glowing, that made a centerpiece of the ceiling.

"Ms. Hammond," Felix said, his voice very soft. "Could you please come this way? Madame Ivanova is expecting you."

Ah yes, that was the imposture, that Felix had brokered a meeting between two revenants.

The woman in front of Jack was middle-aged—or maybe older. Something about her soft curls suggested artful coloring; her smooth skin looked as unnatural as a doll's. Her eyes were pale, the color of fudge. Felix had suggested that while most things would repair themselves, eyes would become increasingly bleached by sunlight. Elizabeth Báthory had had strangely light eyes too. Jack wondered briefly about her own if she survived longer than expected.

"Ah." Ivanova's face creased into a broad smile. "We meet . . . at last."

Jack had the strangest idea that the woman had almost said "again."

The older woman nodded to Felix, then waved a hand at the sofa, its silky patterned fabrics and gilded legs making it look like it came out of a museum. Jack sat, aware of Felix standing beside her, in her peripheral vision.

Jack took a deep breath. "I was hoping you could tell me about blood."

The woman's expression tensed, then relaxed into a small smile.

"Blood, my friend, is life." She looked away from Jack, to the fire. "Do you not feel the warmth as you drink it?"

Jack allowed her head to drop forward in a small nod, just once.

"And do we not have the right to live?" the older woman said, her voice as calm as the mask of her face would suggest. "Blood, received as a willing gift, brings such energy, such youth. It is a blessing."

Jack shut her eyes for a moment, trying to find the old Jack behind all the new feelings and questions. She looked at Ivanova. "And, there are no consequences for the drinker?"

Again, the expression changed from tense to calm, through twitches of something less serene. Jack turned to Felix. "I wonder if you would leave me and Madame Ivanova alone for a minute, Felix?" She stared into his eyes, trying to convince him.

"We agreed—" He closed his mouth. "I'll be right outside. Remember what I said."

That Ivanova might be as powerful and dangerous as Elizabeth Báthory? She tried to make her smile as reassuring as possible, but he still hesitated before leaving the room. She waited to hear the faint click of the door closing before she turned back to the woman.

"The voice," Jack said. "I keep hearing a voice. Just a few words when I wake up, like the end of a thought."

Ivanova looked down, a quick flicker of her eyelids, then someone else looked back. The skin creased in a smile. "His voice?"

"His?" Jack tensed her muscles, ready for a leap for the door. The room's temperature seemed to rise, as if the fire was lit. "Who is he? The voice, the feeling of—danger."

This time her expression settled into one smile, the eyes staring straight at Jack. "You mean Lord Saraquel. You have been blessed, indeed. Few of us are so lucky. He touches us."

Jack's pulse was racing, but something about the name made it lurch in her neck. "Saraquel?"

"You feed him." She smiled. "You have ascended indeed, to be the vehicle of a great being."

Jack searched inside her for the strange feelings she had been struggling with. Something in the back of her mind was laughing.

"A being that craves blood?"

The face twitched again, and a younger, softer voice crept out, almost like a child. "He craves experience, craves food. Greetings, Lord."

Jack ignored a part of her that tensed her tongue into a response. "Blood." She forced her mouth to speak her words. "It feeds on blood?"

The face twisted again, the voice deeper, louder this time. "We all do. You are just a vessel."

"Can I speak to the real Madame Ivanova?"

This time, the entity inside the woman laughed aloud. "She

is too mad to respond, even if you could get her attention." The face twisted into a parody of regret. "She did not have the resilience of the countess. She barely lasted a century." The woman leaned forward, her expression flickering between the entities animating her. "I think it was being tempted to drain the blood of her own grandchildren that started to turn her."

Jack jumped back, landing on her feet, but the creature was faster and stronger. Its hot fingers grasped her throat and forced her against a sideboard, the edge cutting into her spine. Long teeth were inches from her throat, forcing Jack to put her chin down to avoid exposing it. She could hardly breathe, the drum of her heartbeat thumping in her ears. She brought her arms up hard, trying to evade the face inches from her own. The woman didn't let go, but she did stagger back a little, giving Jack a moment to break the chokehold and spring toward the door.

"Wait!"

Jack paused, her hand on the doorknob. "Stay back, whatever you are."

"I am what you are. You are blessed. You have been fortunate." The creature weaved from foot to foot, as her expression changed dozens of times. "He will win in the end. Do you think Báthory did not fight back to save herself? She even consulted with the sorcerer, followed him his whole life to undo what cannot be undone."

Jack wrenched open the door, almost falling into Felix's arms. She slammed the door behind her. "Let's go."

"What? What did she say?"

Finally, the voice inside her got the upper hand for a moment and she found herself unable to speak, simply stare mutely into Felix's eyes. The memory of his slashed skin against her lips, the gush of blood into her was somehow mixed up with the memory of his kisses, his hands holding her, his body against hers in the bed at the hotel. This was what it, Saraquel, wanted.

Blood would give it the advantage. She pulled away from Felix with so much force he staggered.

"She said—" Again, Saraquel stalled the words. She forced herself to walk away, jogging toward the entrance hall. She could hear his steps following. All the occasions she had craved sensual experiences like food, danger, blood—sex—they didn't just come from her. They came from some creature squatting inside her, the same monster that created Báthory . . . She brushed past the security at the door and into the street.

"Jack!" His voice was strident with anxiety, and she pressed her hands over her eyes for a moment.

"Not Jack—" The voice was ground out past some resistance in her jaw, as if her own body were trying to hold back the words. She wasn't sure he had heard her.

This time, although the sounds muted and the world lost its focus, she could feel the thing expanding inside her, filling her up as if it were stretching her skin. She could no longer speak, and shut her eyes to focus. Her body was responding to the thing—Saraquel—expanding inside her. The need for Felix's body, his blood, was like starvation or desperate thirst.

She could hear her words, her shaky laugh higher pitched than usual. "Sorry, I think it's relief. It's OK, it's all OK as long as I don't—" Not-Jack paused for a moment, and Jack realized she was nestling against Felix, feeling his response, his arms tightening, his body pressing against her. She responded to his kiss, her body knowing what to do, her lips inviting him in. "Let's go back to the hotel." Not-Jack's laugh was light, alien to Jack's ears. The most movement Jack could muster was a trembling in her hands, as she tried not to wrap them around Felix's neck, tried not to pull him down into another kiss.

His breathing was ragged, and for a moment Jack thought he was convinced. But he reached up and took her wrists, not too gently, and unwound them from his neck. Jack opened her eyes, but could see nothing but darkness. Gathering all her energy, she tried to shriek a scream out, but only managed a mew of distress.

Not-Jack smiled. "I'm ready now, Felix. I'm tired of being a weakly child. I'm a woman—you made me a woman with your blood. Together we can be happy."

Felix rested his hands on her shoulders, Jack could feel the warmth seeping into her. A sob built up inside her but was burned away before she could express it.

"But you aren't Jack, are you?"

His hands were tight, squeezing her, holding her body away from his.

Saraquel, if that's who not-Jack was, laughed, this time with a husky humor that shot scarlet lightning through the dark Jack was locked in. "We're both here. We both want you. What does it matter?" Before Felix could answer, Saraquel answered itself. "You've only really known me. You've only ever wanted me."

Tears sprang into Jack's eyes at the lie. She wrestled with the immobility.

"I don't believe that." But there was doubt in his voice. "Let her go."

The thing inside her laughed at him and his hands pushed her away. Jack/Saraquel staggered, and Jack found herself pushing forward, starting to see the dark shape ahead of her as Felix, taking a deep breath of her own.

"Felix," she managed to whisper, then forced Saraquel back. It retreated, a mocking laugh sounding in the back of her head. She opened her eyes fully, and his concerned face came into view.

"Jack—" He advanced but she put a hand out to keep him away.

"No! Don't touch me, I can't stay me—I can't stay me if you touch me. It helps Saraquel, the thing inside."

For a long moment they stood, not touching, staring at each other.

"We can work on this," Felix finally said. "This is possession."

"*We* can't do anything." Jack took a step back. "This is what drove Báthory to kill. I'm a danger to you all."

"Jack—" His voice was choked with emotion. He reached out a hand, but she stepped back, turned and started running, sure he couldn't catch her.

She kept going, knowing she was right, that someday Saraquel would seduce him, feed on him, even destroy him. She ran along the Embankment, along the river, past late dog walkers, a few drunks, a homeless man muttering over a restaurant bin.

She could feel Saraquel writhe within her, teasing her with the remembered taste of blood, of the power. She lurched away, staggering onto a bridge, and leaned on the edge.

The water gleamed back like ink, twinkling with the streetlights dancing over its surface. She climbed over the barrier, dropping onto the substructure, balanced over the water. For a long moment she let the memory of the ones she loved wash through her: Maggie's kindness, Sadie's courage, Charley's warmth, Ches's loyalty, and, stabbing through her, Felix. Felix.

This was the only power she had to protect the ones she loved. It was an easy decision, and a short drop to the Thames below.

Historical Note

Writing a story rooted in the past is always a balancing act between being as grounded in the evidence as possible, and telling an engaging and believable fiction. Edward Kelley was an extraordinary thinker and traveler, and was in Europe in the spring of 1586. I don't know if he went to Venice, but he could have done. I like to think so, anyway.

Marinello and Konrad are invented. I can't believe they didn't exist somewhere, because there are some amazing characters from this period of history. Research is a swamp into which a writer can just get lost, following pirates, explorers, rogues and heroes through history.

With all this uncertainty about such interesting and sometimes infamous characters, I have stretched history to suit story. If this causes any offense, I apologize.

Acknowledgments

I have a lot of people to thank.

Firstly, Michael Rowley for editing and nursing my muddled draft into a proper book. His endless enthusiasm for fantasy is infectious. It's a pleasure to write under his leadership at Del Rey UK with such a diverse and talented group of writers.

Charlotte Robertson, my agent, for agreeing the ending was dodgy and encouraging me to rewrite it. All while making me feel better about my writing and inspiring me to write more, and better. It's great to know she can guide me through the world of publishing, which is bigger and more complicated than I imagined.

My patient beta readers Bethany Coombs and Downith Monaghan, fine writers themselves, and I look forward to seeing their books on the shelves one day.

My friend Ruth Downie, author of a series of books set in Roman Britain and published by Bloomsbury USA. It has been great to learn from someone who's been in publishing much longer than me, and is kind enough to answer my dafter questions.

My noisy family, who have cajoled, read, argued and encouraged, especially my eldest son, Carey. He is my first editor, and he's usually right.

My husband, Russell, who was happy to drive all day from Devon to the Lake District, just so I could explore Hawkshead for the book. We talk about the characters as if they live somewhere in our creaky old house. I'm looking forward to finishing the next book with them all.

And finally, for those who have read my books, I just hope you enjoyed reading them, because I loved writing them.

Thank you all.